A Crash Sounded From The Back Of The Warehouse...

Vanessa saw that nothing was disturbed in the studio area. Her painting still stood in the corner where she'd left it. She raced to the door that led to the back storage area, where several hundred thousand dollars' worth of art awaited transfer.

"Fiona?" she called, surprised to find the lights in the back were off.

She was starting to back away when a shaft of light flashed through the darkness, hitting a mirror that bounced the beam around the room. Then the light went out completely, leaving her in the dark with whoever had wielded the flashlight. A scream lodged in Vanessa's throat. She turned to run, but a sharp pain flooded her senses as something thudded against her skull.

Blackness erupted as she fell to the floor, but she stayed conscious long enough to see his silhouette as he turned the flashlight on again. He leaned over Vanessa, and a deep voice hissed in her ear.

"I told you, you shouldn't be here alone...."

ANNE MARIE BECKER

An award-winning author of romantic suspense, Anne Marie Becker has always been fascinated with people and how they "work"—inside and out—which led to degrees in biology, psychology and counseling. Now, her roles as wife, mother, writer and domestic goddess satisfy her curiosity. She explores the dark side of criminal behavior and the saving powers of love and hope through her Mindhunters series. Book one in the series, *Only Fear*, won the 2009 Golden Heart Award for Best Romantic Suspense. For more about Anne Marie, please visit her at www.annemariebecker.com.

AVENGING ANGEL

ANNE MARIE BECKER

CARINA
PRESS™

For Mom, for everything.

Recycling programs
for this product may
not exist in your area.

ISBN-13: 978-0-373-06285-0

AVENGING ANGEL

Copyright © 2012 by Anne Marie Becker

www.CarinaPress.com

Printed in U.S.A.

AVENGING ANGEL

Acknowledgments

This book wouldn't be the same without the enthusiasm and thoughtful advice of the team at Carina Press, especially my amazing editor, Deborah Nemeth. Your help is much appreciated.

A huge thank-you to my beta-readers, especially Timothy Becker, Andrea Edwards and Daniel Warniment, for their reviews of early editions of this manuscript. And to my sisters at The Ruby-Slippered Sisterhood, thank you for your support.

I extend my gratitude to Addison Fox and Anna Taylor Sweringen for their willingness to assist me with descriptions of New York City, particularly their extensive attention to detail when it came to the Chelsea area. Your information helped me bring the art community there to life. I'm also grateful to Scott and Deborah Farris for their descriptions of Puerto Rican culture in New York City. Any errors in these depictions are completely my own.

Finally, thank you to the Brainstormers group at Northern Arizona Romance Writers of America (NARWA). Your enthusiasm for the kernel of an idea that grew into this novel helped motivate me to give Noah and Vanessa their happily-ever-after.

PROLOGUE

March

GRAINS OF SAND glistened white in the moonlight, bright against the midnight-black backdrop of her wet hair. With the back of his gloved hand, he brushed a few stray strands off her cheek and to the side, so that it fanned out around her with the rest. He smiled in satisfaction. More sand from the beach sparkled against the pale skin of her face and arms. Blue lips were parted slightly, as if she could take in that last breath she'd been gasping for so recently. Blank indigo eyes stared up at him. He gently closed them. In its wetness, her white sundress clung to every curve, a hint of dark nipples showing through.

She was, in a word, perfection. He'd do her justice.

Taking her limp wrist gingerly in his hand, he lifted it, positioning her arm outward and upward. He repeated the action with her other arm, then tilted her chin up toward the sky.

Sitting back on his haunches, he took in his creation. *Even better than I'd imagined.* Young. Pure. Ready to embrace what was to come. And she had. She'd done exactly as he'd asked, and he would honor her sacrifice.

He stood and stepped out of the protected cove, the soft sand giving way under his feet. He'd brush away all traces of his footsteps. Nobody would ever know he'd been here.

The tang of salty air hit his nose and cooled his perspiring skin, causing a light dusting of sand to encrust his bare arms and legs. He looked up and down the deserted stretch of beach. Nobody would see them here, hidden in the cove—not that anyone was around at this early hour of the morning. He'd chosen the setting carefully, as always.

He turned back to his victim. She had once been known as Lisa, but with his help, she'd emerged from the frothy waves of the ocean as one of his angels. The Angel of Water. Now she would rise to her eternal reward. Pulling his equipment from the bag he'd stashed behind the rocks earlier, he began his process with a thrill of anticipation for the result. The full moon would begin its descent soon, and his light would be gone. He had to work fast.

ONE

July

Noah slid the key into the slot. Blood pumped harder through his system as the lock gave way with a satisfying click. He pushed open his friend's apartment door. The stench of forgotten food hit him squarely in the gut, causing his empty stomach to clench. Thank God he hadn't had time to grab breakfast. After jumping on the first flight from Chicago to New York City, he'd opted to get here as soon as possible instead.

"Diego?" Noah called. The hum of the air conditioning unit in the window was his only answer.

He shut the door and walked into the darkened apartment. Despite the morning sunshine, with the blinds closed and the window unit cranked to Igloo, the place was like a tomb. He winced. Poor choice of words, given recent events. And his friend had every right to hide out for a few days if he wanted to. But damn, it took real dedication to ignore what had to be over two dozen calls from the extensive Sandoval family.

Noah grimaced, one finger lifting the lid of an old pizza carton lying on the kitchen counter. An almost-empty milk jug sat next to it, the obvious cause of most of the unpleasant odor, although the greasy Chinese food containers were probably equally responsible.

Noah's heart twisted. His friend had obviously hit the wall. Though Diego was an NYPD homicide detective, finding his niece's murdered and partially torched body in an abandoned warehouse had driven him into a cave. Still, the Sandoval family was so close. Always had been. Diego should have been able to lean on them.

When they'd called him with this latest news, Noah had immediately taken some personal leave. Besides, as a homicide detective himself, murder investigation was just as much his area of expertise as Diego's.

Turning away from the cluttered kitchen, he kicked a pile of laundry—dirty or clean, he didn't know—out of his way and excavated a path to the bedroom. His knock on the closed door received no answer, so he opened it. Another subchamber of the dark, cold cave lay before him, but the dim light from the cracks in the blinds revealed that this one had an occupant.

"Diego?"

The body sprawled on the bed didn't respond. A pillow lay over his head, an arm on top locking it in place. He wasn't dead, though. He might want to be, but his chest rose and fell in a regular rhythm under the thin white sheet.

Sitting down on the side of the bed, Noah flipped on the bedside light and nudged him, adding a light punch to the man's biceps. "Diego."

The pillow shifted and dark eyes slid open. Diego tugged the earbuds from his ears, hard rock blaring from them as he tossed them to the nightstand next to his iPod. He rubbed his hands over his haggard face. Despite holing up in his apartment for days, he appeared not to have slept. "What do you want?"

"Nice to see you, too," Noah said, surprised at the degree of relief that coursed through him upon finding his friend alive and responsive. He'd been more worried than he'd admitted to himself. "I came to check on you. You couldn't call your family and let them know you were still alive, after all they've been through this week?"

"Didn't want to talk to them. To *anyone.*"

"What the hell? The Diego I know wouldn't sit around and wait for…death."

Diego scowled at him and pulled himself into an upright position against his headboard. "I'm not waiting for death."

"So, what then? You're moping?"

Diego swung his feet to the floor and sat beside Noah with his head cradled in his hands, his elbows on his knees. "No, I'm reviewing the information in my head—over and over and over again—until I figure out what the fuck I'm missing."

"You can't do that at the police station?"

The bed shifted as Diego rose. He paced back and forth in his plain white T-shirt and gray jogging shorts. "I was told I couldn't look into it. Hypocrites. Like they wouldn't want to be in on an investigation that involved any of their family members. They're afraid that, in my emotional state, I might contaminate more evidence." The hard edge to his voice showed just what he thought about his colleagues labeling him *emotional.* He slammed the side of his fist against the wall. "Fuck."

"*More* evidence?"

Diego's jaw clenched, but he didn't meet Noah's gaze. From the bits and pieces he'd gotten from the Sandovals, Noah knew something had happened at the scene when Diego had found Natalee. Apparently, something *emotional,* whatever that meant. But, hell, how was he supposed to have reacted?

Whatever had happened, Noah would get to the bottom of it. "So you took a leave of absence, too, huh? Guess that means I've got a partner in this investigation."

Diego stopped and stared. His dark, bad-boy, Antonio Banderas good looks transformed as a slow smile spread across his features. "Partner?"

Noah held his arms out at his sides. "I'm at your disposal for two whole weeks."

VANESSA SURREPTITIOUSLY glanced at the clock on the wall behind her employer's head. It was nearly five, and her fellow sales associates squirmed and fidgeted. They were all eager to go home. Willowy, fiery-haired Fiona caught her glance and rolled her eyes before looking back to their boss, Lance Atherton. Beside her, tall, broad-shouldered Jesse smothered a knowing grin.

"It's vital that we're all on the same page here," Lance was saying. "Atherton's is just starting to make a name for itself as the premier art gallery of New York City." And Lance was obviously worried that his name was about to be tarnished by a lowly intern's murder. "While we'll all miss Natasha—"

"Natalee," Vanessa corrected through gritted teeth for the third time that week. Her fists clenched. After what had been done to Natalee, her frustration had been steadily building, especially when Lance didn't seem to care about anything except the bottom line.

He cleared his throat. "Yes, of course. *Natalee*. She seems to have been well liked, for an intern."

"She was an intelligent, talented girl with a bright future. And she was dedicated to this gallery." The thought of the young woman being brutally murdered sent a shiver down her spine.

Lance pursed his lips, and his pale cheeks thinned, emphasizing his hawkish nose. "All the more reason to keep our mouths shut. The less we get involved, the less the gallery is in the news—in a bad way, that is. *Natalee* wouldn't want her death to tarnish our reputation."

Jesse spoke, his perfect white teeth flashing against mocha-latte skin. "This kind of publicity could actually help the gallery. Everyone loves a good murder mystery." A mop of short, dark dreads moved as he shook his head. "People are drawn to the morbid."

Lance put his hands on his hips, or where his hips would have been if he had any. "Absolutely not. Nobody breathes a word to anyone about this murder or you'll be looking for a paycheck elsewhere. Especially with the charity auction tomorrow night. The exposure from that is much more likely to yield fruit."

"And by fruit, he means money," Fiona muttered under her breath. "That kind of fruit doesn't grow on trees."

"As your employer, I'm telling you to avoid the media and police. Keep this matter private. Let the police investigate in their own way."

"And if the police ask us questions directly?"

"Answer, if you must. But—" Lance held up a finger, "—keep your answers to a minimum. We want them to wrap up this case as quickly, but as quietly, as possible."

"And to find Natalee's killer, of course," Vanessa added.

"Of course." He frowned at her. "I don't intend to hinder an official investigation. I just don't want my name tied to it, if possible—especially when the media gets hold of this story. We don't want the gallery to seem unsafe."

"She was taken from the alley just out back, at five o'clock in the afternoon, on her way to the subway." And when Vanessa had left an hour later, she'd been the one to find Natalee's purse on the ground. She'd been the one to call the cops. Confusion had turned to fear for her protégé, and guilt. If it hadn't been for her, Natalee would never have had the job, never been at the gallery, and she'd still be alive today. "Still, there's no reason for them to assume it was linked to Atherton's."

"But the media would have a field day speculating. You know how it works. They'll start insinuating this area of town is unsafe. Chelsea is the center of the New York City art world, which means it's the heart of modern culture in this country. Think about what would happen to our livelihood if people stopped visiting here because of an isolated incident."

"Maybe it *is* unsafe," Jesse said.

She couldn't disagree. From what Vanessa had heard through bits of information released to the media, what Natalee had endured was nothing short of horrific.

"We are not going to perpetuate that myth." Lance's gaze moved over them. "I trust I'm clear on this."

Ready to return to their preparations for the charity auction—the gallery's first black-tie gala event—so they could escape for the evening, the three of them quickly nodded, then scattered when he waved a hand at them in dismissal.

Vanessa scooped her chestnut hair behind her ears, trying to control her shaking. Turning toward the small office she shared with Fiona and Jesse in the corner of the gallery, she stopped when Lance placed a hand on her shoulder.

"I hope you understand my position."

She swung to face him but avoided eye contact. "I understand where you're coming from."

"And why."

She was silent a moment, unable to rein in her temper. She looked up at Lance. For the thousandth time, she wished she were taller than her five-foot-four frame. "I'll never understand *why*. Finding justice for Natalee is worth our full cooperation."

Lance closed his eyes and pinched the bridge of his nose as if praying for patience. "I'm not suggesting we don't cooperate."

"No. You're saying don't offer up anything the police don't specifically ask about."

"You have to understand the pressure I'm under to make this gallery a success. Landing this auction was quite a coup. It's been mentioned in the society pages for months. If this event overshadows it…"

"Event?" Vanessa's cheeks heated. "Natalee was kidnapped and *murdered*. It wasn't an *event*."

"The police will handle it. Natalee's murderer will be caught."

Vanessa blew out a breath. Arguing would be a waste of her time and energy. She comforted herself with the thought that she'd already done what she could to help the investigation. Earlier in the week, well before Lance's decree, she'd given the detectives what information she had. She hadn't been able to tell them much other than the time Natalee had left and where she'd been headed, but it was something. And if they asked for more now, she would give them more, Lance Atherton be damned. Because someone out there had killed a vibrant young woman for no apparent reason. "I have work to do—if you want this auction to go ahead on schedule, that is."

Lance smiled and patted her shoulder, obviously relieved at her capitulation. "Of course. Don't let me keep you. Oh, and I almost forgot. Kenneth called earlier." A speculative gleam lit his hazel eyes. "He mentioned they're planning to redecorate their offices at the firm. He will be coming to the auction, won't he?"

Lance wanted to use her relationship—or ex-relationship—with Kenneth Barnes to create more business for the gallery. Biting the inside of her cheek, she turned away. "Maybe. Thank you for the message." She waited until Lance disappeared into his office across the hall before going into her own and dialing Kenneth's number.

"Hey, baby."

Kenneth's surprising good cheer hit her like a blast of icy air. He'd been MIA for weeks since their last argument. Her hurt pride had been too large a chunk to swallow, so she hadn't called him. Here he was, sounding as if nothing had ever happened, when she thought they were over.

"Lance says you're thinking of redecorating." Could that be the only reason he was looking for her now?

"I didn't mention it? Huh. Guess I've had a lot on my mind with my current caseload." That was an understatement. "Look, baby, I'm sorry I haven't called. They've piled the work on me and I want to make partner and all…"

Vanessa rubbed at the pounding beginning at her temples. As a high-profile criminal defense attorney, Kenneth was always busy. She waited for him to say something more, *anything* about his disappearing act. The silence stretched on, finally broken by a sigh from Kenneth.

"I have a lot to make up for, I know." His tone was contrite, but then, he was good at sounding sincere. It was part of what made him a good lawyer. "I was wrong. There, I said it. Now will you talk to me?"

She checked her slender wristwatch. She had things to do before she could leave for the night. She doubted she'd have the energy for personal issues of this magnitude until the auction was over. "Now's not really the time."

"I know you're busy too. You've got that charity thing tomorrow night. I'm still invited, right?"

She didn't need the tension, but he was a charming, well-liked individual. Perhaps he could help work the crowd of rich and powerful patrons while she made sure the auction ran smoothly. And it would make her boss happy. "If you can make it."

"Excellent. I'd like to get together for a drink tonight, if you'll be up." Which meant he planned to come to her apartment around midnight, as per his usual pattern. Probably wanted to talk her into letting him spend the night at her place.

But whether that was because he missed her or because it would be convenient to his place of work, she didn't know.

Vanessa winced. Was she just a warm body? A place to sleep, with the occasional intimate encounter? That was what their relationship had been downgraded to in recent months. She'd become some kind of comfortable, permanent booty call. At thirty-three, Vanessa wanted more. But they did need to talk. She'd had a lot of time to think while they'd been apart, and it was time to bring the gavel down on their relationship.

She sighed. "Sure. Midnight should be fine." She doubted she'd sleep much tonight anyway, with all the auction preparations running through her head.

"I gotta go, baby. Got a client on the other line. See you tonight."

"Bye," she said, but the hum on the line told her he'd already hung up.

Shoving aside her misgivings along with her irritation, she gathered her things and let the prospect of going to the warehouse cheer her. It was a large building, and the portion that faced the main street had been walled off to form a separate space with tall windows that let in an abundance of natural light by day. Several of the gallery patrons had indicated an interest in learning to draw and paint, and when she'd pointed out to Lance that providing classes would only increase their loyalty to the gallery without much overhead cost to him, he'd agreed to make part of the warehouse into an art studio. She taught an oil painting class one night a week there, but mainly it was a refuge, a place to escape and create when she had the time.

The moist summer air chased away the chill of her air-conditioned skin as she stepped out onto the sidewalk. The scent of roasting lamb from the Greek restaurant down the block tickled her salivary glands, but dinner would have to wait. The evening was pleasant, and the neighborhood unusually quiet. She turned onto a street where the shadows lengthened in the setting sun, and troubles came back to haunt her.

Natalee's body had been found in an abandoned building less than two miles from here. Vanessa had a hard time believing anyone would have a grudge against the sweet, earnest girl. Certainly not enough to take her life, or to do the things that had been done to her.

Vanessa rubbed her arms against a sudden shiver. She could return to the gallery and ask someone to walk with her, but when she'd left, Fiona had been busy double- and triple-checking the arrangements for the auction, and Jesse had been on the phone with a client. Besides, if Lance caught her standing around, he'd be angry that she was wasting time. The man had the sensitivity of a wild boar.

Her three-inch heels clicked along the sidewalk at a brisk pace. The hairs on the back of her neck rose and she glanced over her shoulder. A man had stopped several yards behind her and appeared to be studying a pottery display in a storefront window. Was he following her? She couldn't be sure. Medium height and build, with brown hair, he seemed average in every way. She supposed he was what the police would call nondescript. Except for the little hook in his nose that made it slightly skewed. Those were the kind of details her artist's eye noticed, and that would be helpful in describing him to the police.

One hand came up to tug on his ear. Was he concentrating or trying to hide his profile?

She hurried to the next intersection and chanced another look as she crossed at the light. The man was gone. In fact, the street was now empty. Eerily so. Her heart thumped wildly. She felt the dampness of perspiration at her forehead.

Once within the safety of the warehouse building, she locked the door with trembling fingers and slumped against the wall, exhaling a breath of relief and inhaling the reassuring aroma of oil paints, charcoal pencils and turpentine.

Your imagination's just running overtime. But her body didn't believe it. It was several minutes before her muscles stopped quaking and she could push herself away from the wall to begin her night's work.

TWO

NOAH LIFTED A CLEAN, neatly folded white towel from the stack by the locker room door and wiped the sweat from his forehead. "Next time, I'll beat you."

Diego sent a smirk over his shoulder as he led the way to a group of lockers. "Yeah, right. I'm just better than you."

"In my defense, it's been years since I've played any hoops."

Diego arched a dark eyebrow. "Maybe you're getting old."

"That goes for you, too, then, buddy. We still have a few years until the big four-oh." And he could still remember all the birthdays they'd spent together until now. There had been a lot of them. "Are we still planning on Vegas for number forty?"

"I'm game if you are. Better than the roller rink fiasco of '89."

Noah groaned. "Don't remind me." That birthday had been awkward for many reasons. Simply turning fourteen was one of them, but not knowing how to skate…Noah had spent more time on the floor than he had on his feet. In front of the girls of their eighth-grade class. That was a memory he'd rather forget. "Nothing better than spending your birthday with a sore butt."

Diego laughed and Noah was relieved to see some flicker of his old friend. After scrounging together enough items to make them a late lunch of peanut butter and jelly sandwiches, Noah had hoped some physical exertion at the YMCA would help. Time was short in a murder investigation, and it had already been almost a week, but first he'd had to get Diego out of his apartment and away from his dark thoughts so he could discuss the case objectively. As objectively as possible, anyway.

Noah peered around the row of tall lockers and saw that the room was empty. "Now that we're alone and exhausted, do you want to fill me in about Natalee's murder?"

The light in Diego's brown eyes dimmed as he sat down hard on the bench and slumped back against the lockers. "No."

Noah waited patiently.

"I know I have to. But I'm still trying to process it myself."

"Process? Have you been talking to the police shrink?"

Diego shifted. "I might have met with him once."

Noah nodded. "Good. 'Cause I've got to say I've never seen you like this." He sank down on the bench next to him, gazing at the newly painted lockers across from them.

The gym had put some effort into sprucing itself up since he'd moved to Chicago ten years ago. Though he occasionally returned for short visits, he hadn't realized how much had changed since he'd left. One thing had stayed the same—the visceral reaction he experienced whenever he came back to New York. It was like being gut-punched by memories, both good and bad.

His friend had changed too. Diego was more guarded than his usual easygoing self. Whether that was a product of age, experience on the force, or grief was anybody's guess. A combination of all three was the likely answer.

When Diego remained silent, Noah continued, following a hunch. "If they're not letting you near the case at the NYPD, I'm guessing it has something to do with you discovering Natalee's body. Am I right?"

He went still. "Some detective work there, Sherlock."

"Well, you're certainly not giving me anything to work with. I took two weeks of vacation that I'd been saving—"

"—that you were probably never going to use, knowing you—"

"—to come out here and help you. And you don't even want to talk about it. I'm planning on camping out in your living room for the next two weeks. You're going to have to give me some details if I'm going to help. You said something about contaminated evidence?"

Diego's shoulders stiffened, and Noah almost wished he wouldn't share what he was about to say. A sheen of moisture made his friend's coffee-brown eyes almost black. "I touched her body."

The silence that followed was thick with meaning.

"Shit." Not only did Diego have to deal with his niece's horrific death, but he had to deal with the guilt of possibly having ruined any chance of bringing her killer to justice. "What happened?"

"When I saw her, saw that she was…" Diego stopped and swallowed before continuing. "I rushed forward. My first thought wasn't to protect the fucking scene."

"You reacted as most people would."

Diego snorted. "Doesn't excuse it. We're not most people. We have experience with crime scenes, know how important it is to preserve the evidence." He shoved a hand through his hair. "I hadn't slept in days, searching for her. And then to find her, like that…"

"We'll find other evidence. We'll get this guy."

"She was only seventeen. She was going to start community college next month."

Noah hadn't seen Natalee since she was in elementary school but had a vivid image of a smiling young girl in dark braids, with a gap where her two front teeth should have been. "How's your sister?"

"She's a wreck. Natalee was Olivia's whole world."

Noah shook his head. "How did this happen? Why her?"

Diego stood and yanked open his locker, pulling jeans and a polo shirt from within. "Questions I've been asking myself over and over again for the past week. How are any of the victims we ID every day chosen? Why do these murders we're supposed to solve happen?" He paused and sucked in a deep breath. "Look, it's all really close to the surface, you know?"

Noah nodded. "Why don't we go grab a beer?" Maybe Diego would continue to open up with some liquid courage.

"After a shower. You stink."

Noah shook his head, relieved that his friend still had his sense of humor under all his new defenses. "That stink, my friend, is you."

"Yeah? Then it's the smell of victory, old man." Diego grinned before turning serious again. He clasped Noah on the shoulder. "I'm glad you came."

Noah swallowed a sudden lump in his throat. Since he'd left the Sandovals behind along with the rest of his past, he'd convinced himself he didn't need a family. But at least part of him—a part long ago buried—missed it.

TWENTY MINUTES LATER, showered, dressed, and with his hair still damp, Noah sat across from Diego in the corner booth of a bar they'd visited frequently while attending the police academy. It too had changed. Someone had spiffed it up for the classy crowd of Thursday afternoon happy-hour drinkers, dressed in their suits and skirts. And someone had replaced the cheap bottled beer with fancy, locally brewed drafts.

The East Harlem neighborhood, where Diego's family had settled after leaving Puerto Rico, and where Noah and Diego had grown up, was familiar but different. Sure, there was more crime than before, but someone killing an innocent young woman for apparently no reason? "Did Natalee disappear near here?"

"You'd think so. It's where she lived, where she hung out with her friends, where she went to school. But no."

"Where then?"

"Work, of all places. In Chelsea."

Noah sat back in surprise. "I didn't realize Natalee had a job."

"Yeah, well, you haven't exactly been around much." He shook his head. "Sorry. Low blow."

Noah took a gulp of beer, letting the coolness of it quell his defensive flare of temper. "You know I had to get away."

"Hell, no. I never understood that. Still, we all thought you'd come back, I guess." Thankfully, instead of pursuing the topic, Diego sat back, slinging one arm over the black leather back of the booth. "But I'm avoiding your questions again."

"Noticed that."

"Nothing much gets by you." Diego finally met his gaze. "Which is why it's good you're here. I'm too close to this. Natalee was sweet and kind and…" His throat worked as he swallowed whatever else he'd been about to say.

"I'm here to help, but all I know is what Marcos could tell me."

Diego's older brother had called Noah the moment Natalee's body had been found, and then again when

Diego shut himself away from the world. Marcos's concern had been palpable, increased by the frustration of having no idea what was going on with his niece's case. The police weren't revealing any details, and Diego had gone incommunicado.

"Tell me more about Natalee."

Diego ran a hand down his face, seemed to pull on his detective demeanor like a suit of armor, and dove in. "Natalee loves—loved—art. She was always a creative person. Drawing. Painting. Sewing. Knitting. You name it, she tried it, and she was good at it, too. At her school's career day a few months back, she met a woman named Vanessa Knight who works at an art gallery in Chelsea. Practically runs it, to hear Natalee talk about her. Well, this woman took Natalee under her wing and let her intern at her gallery a few hours a week after school and on the weekends. Natalee loved it there." Diego paused, seemingly entranced by the bubbles rising in his nearly untouched glass.

"I take it that's where she was abducted?" Noah prompted after a moment.

Diego nodded. "She didn't come home that night. That was last Friday." Almost a week ago. The trail could already be ice-cold. "Sunday night, a cruiser responded to a call about some suspicious activity in a warehouse that's under construction down by the Chelsea docks. The officer knows me, knew my connection to Natalee, and called me right away when he realized what he'd found. I was the second person on the scene."

Knowing that had to stir up painful images, Noah steered his friend away from emotional territory, for now. "Could the murderer have been someone she knew? A boyfriend maybe?"

"No," he said immediately. "She didn't date."

Noah gave him a disbelieving look.

Diego swore. "Look, I know it may be hard to believe, but she wasn't the typical seventeen-year-old. She wasn't into boys yet."

"A late bloomer?"

"Something like that. Growing up with an absentee asshole as a father might have had something to do with it. Olivia tried to shelter her as long as possible."

So maybe she was innocent around men, too innocent to see the potential dangers. Noah hesitated to ask the next question, but it was important to the case. "Any sign of sexual assault?"

"The medical examiner is still forming his report, but I was able to get a little bit of information out of him—" his jaw hardened, "—before my LT demanded I stay out of the case. But no, it doesn't look like Natalee was sexually assaulted. Thank God for small favors," he muttered.

"And you're certain she was abducted?" Noah returned Diego's hard look with a shrug. "Teenage girls have been known to run off on occasion—whether to meet boyfriends, friends or strangers—and so I have to ask why you're so certain."

"They found her purse in the alley behind the gallery. Besides, Friday was Mama's birthday. We had a big family party planned that night. Natalee never showed."

Noah had spent many afternoons at Estella's house after school, scarfing down homemade cookies. She was a gentle, loving woman who had watched over him like a second mother—or a first. "Estella must be taking that pretty hard."

"Mama would have been torn apart no matter what. I haven't called my sister since I was suspended. I don't have a clue what to say. I just wish I knew what to do to help them."

"Like finding the killer on your own."

"The department won't let me do anything official, so fuck them. I'll go rogue if I have to." Diego took a chug of his drink before pinning Noah with his gaze. "You in?"

"I'm still here, aren't I? Keep talking."

"THE NERVE OF HIM," Fiona muttered. With careful fingers, she wiped a cloth over a sculpture on one of the warehouse shelves.

Vanessa kept her eyes on the painting she was inspecting. "Lance's just trying to protect his interests, and those of the gallery."

Fiona cast her an incredulous look. "So you agree with him?"

"Not in the least." Vanessa frowned. "But I don't want you or Jesse getting into trouble. There's been enough pain."

Fiona's look softened. "I'm sorry. I know losing Natalee hit you harder than anyone."

"Her grandmother was by twice this week, leaving flowers in the alley where she was abducted. I didn't know what to say to her, and yet she included me in her ceremony. Natalee has a loving family."

Fiona placed a hand on her shoulder. "Compared to yours, you mean?"

"Compared to anybody's. Kenneth called today," Vanessa said, both to change the subject and out of curiosity for Fiona's frank opinion. Fiona had a way of understanding people—men, in particular—that was eerily accurate.

"Ah."

"That's it?"

Fiona sighed and her long red hair shifted against her shoulders. "Well, it's about time. He's left you hanging for weeks. What excuse did he give this time?"

"How do you know it was an excuse? Maybe he finally proposed."

She rolled her eyes. "With the mood you're in tonight? Come on."

Sinking down into a foldout metal chair, Vanessa gave in. "He's been busy."

"Again."

"Again. But he wants to come by later tonight."

"Again."

Vanessa nodded. "Seems like he's ready to fall back into our familiar pattern."

"Are *you*?"

That was the big question. "You think I'd be crazy to stay with him."

Fiona pulled another metal chair from where it leaned against the wall, unfolded it and sat beside her. "I didn't say that. But if you're planning your future around a man who can't seem to make time for you in the present, I'm worried what kind of life you're setting yourself up for."

Me, too.

"What you need is a fling." Fiona's eyes sparked with mischief. "A good, old-fashioned one-night stand, or one-week affair. Get out of your head, away from the pressures you've put on yourself, and decide if Kenneth is really what you want."

"A fling in today's world? Are you nuts?"

Fiona rolled her eyes. "I'm not saying you go out and sleep with the first man you meet. You don't even have to sleep with anyone. Heck, even a little flirting would be good. Just have some fun. The important thing is to get outside the box you've put yourself in. You've been focused on art and Kenneth for so long, you don't know what your options are."

Was Fiona right? She'd always prided herself in being

a creative thinker, a flexible person. After all, most artists were able to view the world in unique ways, were open to new experiences. "I just don't think I could."

Fiona cast her a pitying glance. "Then you'll be stuck with what you get. Take control, honey. Besides, I have to wonder if you're truly dating Kenneth anymore, and why you've seemed so much happier without him."

"I've already been thinking that things are over between me and him."

"I'm relieved to hear you're at least thinking about it." She gave her a hug. "It's tough to give up what you have and gamble with the unknown, but if you're not happy... I'm sorry I have to leave. I'll cancel if you need me."

Vanessa waved her off. "No, no. Go have fun. Your brother's only in town for a couple of nights. I can handle things here. And I can always call Jesse if I need help."

"You work too hard."

"I promise I'll take a dinner break. Okay?"

"I'm going to hold you to that. I want to see the receipt tomorrow morning. I have to run back by the gallery to finish up some paperwork first, then I'm off to party. You're welcome to join us when you're done here."

Vanessa shook her head. "Thanks for the offer, but I've got plenty to keep me busy."

"All work and no play...you need some frivolous fun in your life."

Frivolous fun. The thought of it sounded deliciously appealing and decadent, like champagne and strawberries. Something to indulge in that would lead to trouble only if taken to the extreme.

After Fiona left, Vanessa tried to focus on inventorying and preparing the items scheduled to go up for auction the next evening. Her fingers ran over the pure lines of a marble sculpture, and she found comfort in the cold solidity of it. Of something that had been formed from a simple rock, shaped and polished to reveal the beauty within. She felt a kind of kinship with it.

A ringing disturbed the quiet of the warehouse and she moved into the dark front area—the studio she used as a classroom—to get to the phone. It rarely rang here, but perhaps it was Lance checking in on her.

"Hello?"

Silence greeted her.

"Hello?" she asked again.

"You shouldn't be there alone." The raspy male voice was followed by a click of disconnection and the hum of a dead line.

Dropping the phone back onto its cradle, Vanessa rubbed her arms against the sudden goose bumps that had erupted there. "Pranks," she muttered to make herself feel better. But the image of the crooked-nosed man on the sidewalk looking into the window display came to mind. "You're being paranoid, Vanessa." Still, she checked the locks on both the front and back doors and switched on more lights.

She tried to return to her inventory but her head wasn't in it. Instead, the blank canvas resting upon an easel in the corner of the studio called to her. Grabbing her paints and brushes, she set up, adjusting the lighting until it suited her. The familiar smell of turpentine and the vivid colors she squeezed from tubes onto her palette both soothed and energized her as she prepared to take her fear and anger out on the white vastness before her.

Noah and Diego took a cab to the Chelsea district. The sun was setting as the pair examined the galleries on the neat, tree-lined street.

A sign pronounced one storefront Atherton's Art in a

way that somehow managed to be both understated and pretentious. A black-on-white ink sketch against a red silk backdrop was the only thing in one large window. In the other, a black marble sculpture of a couple entwined in an eternal embrace drew the eye.

Diego tugged on the chrome bar that ran the height of the glass door at the entrance, but it didn't budge. "Locked." Rapping his knuckles against the glass produced a hollow sound. The dim interior didn't give them much hope.

Noah read the numbers etched on the window. "It is after hours." Finding anyone here at this time of evening was a gamble, but neither of them was willing to go home empty-handed. Besides, every moment that went by, Natalee's body got colder, as did the killer's trail.

But a moment later, a slender redhead came at a brisk walk from somewhere in the back of the gallery, stopping on the other side of the door. "We're closed." Her words were muffled by the thick glass. She pointed to the sign that listed the hours.

Diego took his badge from a pocket and held it up to the glass. The woman's eyes widened and she moved quickly to unlock the door, then stood back to let them in.

A quick survey of the interior showed paintings hung well apart, not crowding each other, each given their own space to shine. Sculptures and overpriced bric-a-brac stood on pedestals, their individual spotlights turned off for the night.

The woman bit down on a plump bottom lip. "Are you here about Natalee?"

"That's right." Diego handed her his business card. "What can you tell us?"

She cleared her throat and glanced behind her toward

a hallway that disappeared into the back. "Not much, unfortunately." Her words were almost a whisper.

"Who is it, Fiona?" A tall man in an expensive suit emerged from the hallway. Everything about the man was thin—his silver hair, his face, his body. He looked as if he were made of dough and had been stretched on a rack. Seeing Noah and Diego, he quickened his pace. "I thought I heard voices out here."

"The police are here." Fiona shifted her weight nervously.

"I'll take it from here. You were about to leave anyway, weren't you?" He watched her hustle away until she disappeared, then he turned back, looking his visitors over from head to toe. "You don't look like detectives."

Noah gave a self-deprecating smile as he gestured to his attire. He was wearing a plain T-shirt and blue jeans instead of his usual suit and tie. But then, he hadn't expected to question anyone that evening other than Diego, at least not until they'd returned home from their basketball game. His friend looked slightly more respectable in khakis and a lightweight polo shirt. He sensed that the man—presumably the gallery owner—enjoyed feeling superior, whether mentally or wardrobe-wise, so he encouraged the illusion of inequality. "We're coming off a plainclothes assignment." Thank God the guy seemed to take his statement for granted and didn't ask for identification, or he might find it unusual that one of them was from Chicago. Carrying oneself with confidence went a long way to reassuring people you were who you said you were. Even if you weren't. "A colleague asked us to check on something for Natalee Ortega's case since we were in your area. Are you Lance Atherton?"

Hearing that they weren't the primary detectives on the case caused one of the many furrows on Atherton's forehead to disappear. Still, the man was wound tight enough to shit diamonds. "I am. What do you need?"

"Information about Natalee."

"Such as?"

"What she did around here. Her hours. If any customers took a particular interest in her."

Atherton bristled at the last comment. "I assure you, Detective, our customers have more to concern themselves with than an intern at our gallery. They are important people with important positions, doing important things for our community. Did you see the list of sponsors for tomorrow's charity auction?"

"I'm sure they're *important*," Diego said, his voice hard.

Noah exchanged a warning look with Diego before turning back to Atherton. "Actually, no, we didn't see the list. Do you have it handy?"

Atherton looked as if he might argue, then snapped his mouth shut and marched to the back. Diego and Noah took the opportunity to look around the gallery, taking note of the paintings and artists' names that they could read in the dim lighting before Atherton returned, a crisp pamphlet in his outstretched hand.

"I trust this will help allay any suspicions about our clients."

Noah took the paper and glanced over it. "This is just an ad with some of the featured auction items. What about the rest of the artists? The collectors, the people who intend to bid?"

"The coordinator, Vanessa Knight, has the list of artists and donations. As for the collectors, they don't officially register until they check in at the auction tomorrow."

"Then we'll be back."

"But—"

"In the meantime, we'd like to speak to Miss Knight."

Atherton drew himself up to his full height. "She's unavailable."

Annoyed with the man's evasive manner and lack of cooperation, which he apparently had tried to press upon his staff if Fiona's hesitance was any indication, Noah took a step forward. "Unavailable as in 'not here' or 'not going to talk to us'? If it's the latter, I'm going to have to ask why."

Atherton's lily-white skin flushed pink and sweat popped out on his upper lip. "She's not here."

"Where can we find her?"

"She's gone for the day."

"That's not exactly what we asked, now, is it?" Noah turned to Diego. "I'm getting an uncooperative vibe here."

"Yeah, me too," Diego said. "It's enough to make me suspicious."

Atherton didn't rise to their bait. "Vanessa left for the day. I'll let her know you were here and that you'll be in touch soon." He moved to the door and held it open. "Good evening."

Diego handed Atherton his card on his way past. "Just in case you think of something that could actually help us." The man took it without looking at it.

Standing on the sidewalk seconds later as Atherton locked the door behind them, Noah spoke under his breath. "He acted like he has something to hide."

Diego stared hard through the glass as Atherton retreated to the back hallway again. "Maybe he does."

"But he doesn't seem like a killer."

"More like a self-absorbed prick."

They'd taken a few steps down the street, intending to find the nearest cab or subway station, when Diego reached into his pocket and removed his vibrating cell phone. "Detective Sandoval." He stopped suddenly, holding out a hand for Noah to do the same. "I'm listening." He gestured to Noah, who retrieved a small notebook and pen from the back pocket of his jeans.

Diego scribbled down an address. Satisfaction was evident in his slow smile and the laugh that followed. "Thanks, Fiona. You don't know how much I appreciate this." He put his phone away, tore off the piece of paper and shoved it at Noah.

"What?"

"This is where Vanessa Knight is at this very moment. Some warehouse a couple blocks away. She's working with the auction merchandise there. *Alone.*"

Noah's eyes widened. "Fiona was suddenly full of helpful information, was she?"

"Yeah, despite her boss. And that's why *you're* going to visit Ms. Knight."

"I'm not following."

"Fiona also said that Vanessa has been warned by Atherton not to talk to the police and that she's loyal to the gallery. She said Vanessa hasn't eaten dinner yet. And she thought she might be particularly vulnerable to your—" Diego coughed to hide a chuckle, "—charms."

"What about you?"

Diego's smirk faded. "I still have a friend or two on the force who might fill me in about any developments in the investigation. I'm off to do some charming of my own."

THREE

A KNOCK at the studio's front door jerked Vanessa out of the creative fog she'd happily sunk into. From her perch in the back corner, the canvas shielded the door from view.

Maybe Fiona had left something behind. But she would eventually dig out her key and let herself in. Despite the work she had yet to do for the auction, Vanessa had finally had a breakthrough on the piece she'd been trying to start for weeks. She just needed a little more time to get the color just right.

A harder, louder knock brought on a flutter of nerves. She debated whether she could simply play possum, but the studio lights were clearly evident from the street. She forced herself to leave her stool and move to the door.

"Miss Knight?" a male voice called through the door. "Someone at the gallery told me I could find you here."

Not a complete stranger, then. At least he knew who she was. And he seemed polite. Killers weren't polite, were they? Still, she was hesitant to unlock the door. "Just a minute." She ran to the back, grabbed her phone and texted Fiona. *Did Lance send a guy over?*

It only took a minute for Fiona's reply. *No, I did. You're welcome.*

More curious than scared now, she unlocked the door. Vanessa's breath caught at the sight of the owner of the male voice—and the decidedly male body it belonged to.

"I thought maybe you'd snuck out the back." In an endearing boyish manner, the man tucked his fingers into the front pockets of his jeans and rocked back on his heels, a half grin on his face. Though his dark blond hair was short and well-groomed, a shock of it fell across his forehead.

But it was his eyes that drew her. As an artist, Vanessa had always found eyes so expressive. The window to the soul, some people said. The light blue ones focused on her now held a certain uncommon crystalline intensity. The shade of sky she'd been working on in her painting a moment ago suddenly seemed drab and gray. This man's eyes...now *there* was a blue sky. The edges crinkled. "Are you okay? Fiona said it would be okay to come over..."

"Yes, of course." She'd been staring. "I'd forgotten I'd placed that ad. It's been weeks and nobody responded. Please, come in."

She closed the door behind him. He came to a stop in the middle of the studio and she eyed the specimen. He had definite potential. She walked in a slow circle around him, her eyes taking in the hint of a chiseled chest beneath his gray T-shirt, the lines of a fine gluteus beneath his faded but nice-fitting jeans. His biceps rippled and forearms contracted as he crossed his arms.

"Like what you see?" Amusement laced his husky words. Still, he let her finish her circuit.

"I have to make sure you'll be a good fit." The double meaning of her words came rushing at her and she nearly tripped.

His eyebrows lifted. "For?"

"The position, of course." She cocked her head, her hair brushing a bare shoulder and making her skin turn to gooseflesh as if he'd touched her. She tugged off her paint-smeared apron. "You're here about the ad I placed for a nude model, aren't you?"

His nostrils flared, and Vanessa was reminded of the

magnificent, proud stallions from the days in her youth when her mother had pushed her into riding lessons. The pleasant smell of hay and warm, fresh-cut grass suddenly came to her, along with a remembered sense of freedom.

She cleared her throat and stepped away. "You're just in time. I'd given up on getting a response before my class focuses on anatomical sketches next week."

"Anatomical sketches?"

"Would you mind taking your shirt off?"

The smile that took a slow trip across his lips had her heartbeat stuttering. "Part of checking out the merchandise? I assure you everything's there."

"So I can see what kind of muscle groups I can lecture the class about," she said with some annoyance. She hoped he wasn't one of those smug, egotistical men who thought their bodies were sculpted by the gods. That would be a disappointment, though she didn't analyze why.

As he pulled his shirt over his head, she had to remind herself to breathe.

In. Out.

His abs were cut, his chest chiseled, and his shoulders rounded but sleek with muscle. She suspected next fall's class would be full of females, young and old, with a sudden passion for drawing, if word got around about the model she'd found for the summer class.

He watched her as she completed another lap around him. A couple of interesting scars near his shoulder blade and down by his trim waist, just above the waistband of his jeans, caught her eye. Some people would be put off by such markings, but she appreciated them—as an artist, she reminded herself, despite the sudden urge she had to run her fingertips along the white skin.

"So, do I get the job?" Was that impatience she detected under his amusement?

"Is Tuesday evening a problem?"

"Not at all."

She extended a hand. "Then I'd like to offer you the job, Mr…"

"Crandall. You can call me Noah." His hand was warm and calloused and…intriguing.

She pulled her hand away, trying to resist the image of those rough hands on her skin. It must be Fiona's advice that had put her in this state of mind. She shouldn't be thinking these thoughts. But it had been so long since she'd felt such a spark of desire. Kenneth certainly hadn't nurtured the flame of passion. Not in months. She'd begun to think there was something wrong with her.

She shoved Kenneth into a tiny corner of her mind. She planned to break up with him tonight, so a little harmless flirting didn't count as cheating.

Get real, Vanessa. Nothing was harmless with this dangerously good-looking man.

"The class meets here at seven. You'll be paid a hundred dollars for two hours of sitting."

"Nude."

She stifled a grin as he seemed to squirm. "Fully." Sometimes she loved her job. "Have you ever done anything like this before?"

"Posing in the nude? Not for a group of people, and not for money." His smile slipped and he put his shirt back on. "What if I get nervous? Or cold?"

"You'll do fine. It's tastefully done. I'll pose you." She turned away, using the cleaning and packing of her paint supplies as an excuse to hide her hot cheeks. She'd never been shy about art before, but something about this man, some intangible pull, made her feel vulnerable. "You'll be so focused on relaxing enough to maintain the pose that, after a few minutes, you won't even know anyone's there."

He followed her to the sink and leaned against the black laboratory-style counter. The soft hairs of the brush she was cleaning slid between her fingertips, slick with the liquid detergent she used to remove the final remnants of vivid oil color from the bristles. The tactile sensation sent a shiver down her spine.

"I would feel much better if I knew exactly what I was in for," he said. "Do you think you could join me for a drink and we can talk about it?"

She avoided his gaze. "I have work to do."

"It wouldn't take long. It's just down the street. I'm supposed to meet a friend at the Bamboo Hut for dinner, but you could keep me company in the bar while I wait."

Vanessa washed her hands as she thought up an excuse. Fiona's words fought to be heard over the roar of blood in her ears. *Frivolous fun.* Maybe having drinks with Noah would be harmless. It would be a step toward opening her mind to the possibilities, wouldn't it?

"Okay." She shocked herself with her response. Noah looked surprised at her acceptance too. "Just a quick drink, though," she hastily amended. "I've got plans later, too."

His grin widened. "I'll take what I can get."

THE BAMBOO HUT was packed, even at nine o'clock on a Thursday. The smell of citrus blended with tangy Asian spices had Noah's mouth watering, as did the morsel of woman at his side.

His hand moved to rest at the small of Vanessa's back as they wove through the crowd toward the bar that filled half the establishment. Decorated in ebony and cherry-red, with a glossy black bar top that reflected the flickering tea lights placed throughout the room, the atmosphere was dark and intimate.

Spying an empty table for two in the corner, he steered Vanessa toward it. A waitress quickly appeared to take their drink order, then disappeared into the background.

"I thought you said you were meeting someone." Her lips pursed in lovely reprimand.

Noah shrugged. "It's early yet."

"And when she arrives, she won't mind finding you tucked away in a candlelit corner, having a drink with me?"

He bit back a smile at her attempt to dig for information. "*He* won't mind at all."

"Oh." Suddenly, her eyes widened.

His laugh rumbled in his chest. "And before you go there, no, the *he* I'm expecting is not a lover. Just a friend."

He watched her relax, the tight little body he'd been studying sinking against the red velvet back of her chair. *Studying* as a good detective would. It was part of the investigation, purely innocent.

Yeah, right.

As assignments went, so far he was enjoying this one. Not only was Miss Knight exceedingly easy on the eyes, she had an open quality to her expressions that hinted at a reservoir of passion under the surface. The nude modeling angle had been a surprise, but as he'd been looking for a cover that would get her to relax around him enough to ignore her boss's orders, it was a welcome suggestion.

The waitress arrived with their drinks and left.

His gaze immediately went to Vanessa's bow-shaped mouth when she smiled. Her lips were lush and utterly kissable. "Please don't worry. The students in my class are local art students or patrons of the arts. They know what to expect, and are professional in their demeanor. For a lot of them, you aren't the first nude model they've worked with. You're nothing but an object of art to them."

"Like a bowl of fruit on a table?" He gave an exaggerated wince. "That hurts."

She laughed, the throaty sound rippling through him. She wrapped her lips around an olive from her martini, tugging it from the plastic toothpick. "Somehow I think your ego can take it."

Her sleek hair—all gleaming walnut and smelling of some rich spice—shifted as she angled her head. Her expression sobered, but the alcohol was doing its job quickly—especially on her petite body. Her movements took on a much more liquid quality. The rosy shade of her cheeks darkened pleasantly, and he wondered what thought had warmed her that way. He didn't have to wait long to find out.

"Okay, I'm just going to lay it out there. Some inexperienced guys worry about, um, becoming aroused during the session."

He nearly choked on his drink. Hell. He hadn't thought of that. "Does that happen?"

"Not usually. But it can."

"So how do I avoid that, uh, circumstance?"

He watched, entranced, as she pulled the second and last olive into her mouth, her pink tongue making a quick appearance. Resisting the urge to call the waitress over with more olives, he assessed her for signs that she was trying to seduce him. But she didn't appear to be aware she had his body tied up in knots. Her silky voice and graceful movements had him thinking of old-time Hollywood actresses who could seduce you with a crook of the finger or a cock of the hips. And her oblivion to her charms made her power all the greater.

"Baseball stats."

Nope. Definitely not trying to seduce him. She'd lost him. "Huh?"

"Or your mother."

He rewound the conversation. "Ah. That'll distract me enough to keep from, uh, getting excited."

She tipped the last of the martini down her throat and his eyes were drawn to the slim lines of her neck. She swallowed and smiled. "Or so I've heard." Velveteen brown eyes warmed with empathy. "Like I said, my class is made up of professional artists or people who are used to admiring art. They'll look the other way if… something…happens."

Noah barked out a laugh as she gestured in the direction of his lap. It was a good thing she couldn't see through the dimness of the bar that *she* was causing something to happen. Despite his personal vow to avoid romantic entanglements, Vanessa Knight was an unusually tempting distraction.

"But in my experience," she continued, "*it* doesn't usually happen. The studio environment's not exactly the ideal circumstance."

What she didn't apparently understand was that just being near her put his system on high alert. If she was going to be in the classroom, which he was pretty sure she was, he was going to have to memorize some baseball statistics.

You won't even be around by Tuesday.

Reality crashed in as he remembered the reason he was here. If he and Diego were lucky, they'd find the leads they needed to arrest Natalee's killer within a few days. Unfortunately, he hadn't found a way to bring up Natalee in a way that Vanessa wouldn't close up like a clam—assuming she was following Lance Atherton's example of avoiding the police. Since she seemed to love everything about her job, he was betting that was a safe assumption.

She dropped the empty toothpick into her glass and

pulled the strap of her purse over her shoulder. He felt a moment of panic when she shifted in her seat. "You're not going yet, are you? Let's have another drink."

"I'm sure your friend will be here soon, and I'm guessing you'll be okay on Tuesday. You might find you like modeling."

He reached out and took her hand. "But the night's still young."

"And you have plans." She didn't pull her hand away. An encouraging sign.

He mustered a sheepish grin. "Okay, you got me. I didn't have plans." He released a breath when she settled again, though her other hand hadn't let go of the purse strap. She looked as if she might still bolt.

"What?"

"I was hoping I could talk you into dinner."

"So the story about being nervous about posing in the nude was bogus?"

"Well, not entirely but…I needed an excuse to get you to go out." He frowned. "Pretty pathetic, huh?"

Rich brown hair swung against her shoulders. Her delicate scent wafted toward him, along with a hint of paint. "Not at all. It's kind of…sweet. Nobody's taken the trouble to, well, *trouble* themselves for a date with me in a while."

"That's criminal."

Her mouth widened into a smile that sucked the air out of his lungs. "I think dinner is a lovely idea."

"I thought *you* had plans."

"Not until later."

He wondered who she was meeting at such a late hour, but quickly stifled his curiosity. It didn't matter anyway. She was all his for the moment. He'd get the answers to his questions about Natalee and move on. But there was no law that said he couldn't enjoy her company in the meantime.

ABOUT HALFWAY through a glass of rich cabernet, Vanessa wondered what the hell she was doing. She was a lightweight—both with alcohol and with flirting. The sweet, citrus-infused sauce in her meal made her mouth water almost as much as Noah did. Frivolous fun, indeed. She was falling under the spell of the handsome man sitting across from her. He leaned forward as if he were actually listening to every word she said.

But sitting across from Noah Crandall, male model, was surreal. And more comfortable than it should be, considering her recent relationship and impending breakup with Kenneth. Her anger at Kenneth had dissipated as the pleasant effect of the martini and wine relaxed her. She wasn't in any rush to get home to an empty apartment and wait for her so-called boyfriend to grace her with his presence. And she certainly wasn't looking forward to the talk she needed to have with him.

Enjoy where you are, and who you're with, while you can. Seize the moment.

She didn't know where the little devilish voice came from—maybe from the bottom of her wineglass—but she decided to obey.

"You can't possibly do all of that on your own." Noah forked a bite of spicy beef and noodles. He promptly returned his piercing blue eyes to her as if she were the center of his world. It was a feeling she hadn't experienced with Kenneth in a long time. Maybe not ever. And she found it highly addictive. That had to be why she was still sitting here, at ten o'clock at night, with a near stranger.

Well, not quite a stranger. You have seen him half-naked, the devil inside her said.

At her giggle, Noah's smile widened. "I think I may have drunk too much," she admitted, setting her glass down with a sigh. "Sometimes I wish I had more meat on my bones. I could drink more." *Great. Now I sound like an alcoholic.*

"I think you look rather...fabulous."

She blushed and tried to focus on another topic. It wouldn't do to get used to this kind of attention. "The auction's a lot of work, but it's for a good cause. And I do have help. Or I did."

"Past tense?" Noah's eyes were intent on hers. "Did your help quit?"

She toyed with her food a moment. Lance had told her not to talk about Natalee, but Noah might be someone safe with whom she could share. Not only was he listening respectfully, but he was a stranger. Someone who had no reason to spread whatever she said any further than this table. "She...died. Or rather, she was killed."

"I'm so sorry." And he really looked it. "Was it an accident?"

"Murder. She was taken from the alley behind the gallery where I work."

"That's horrible. Any ideas who did it?"

Suddenly preferring her wine to the rest of her dinner, Vanessa picked up her glass and rolled the stem between two fingers, watching sparks of light bounce off the rich red wine within. "None. She was a sweet girl. I can't imagine she'd have any enemies. It must have been a random act of violence." She shuddered. It could have happened to anyone. Fiona. Her.

Elbows on the table, Noah leaned forward. "There's more, isn't there?"

"She wasn't just murdered. She was kidnapped. And tortured. The monster partially burned her body." Feeling shaky, she set her wineglass down. Noah immediately reached over and took her hands, stroking his thumbs over her fingers.

"You're trembling."

"God, what she must have gone through."

"Sounds like you cared a lot about her."

"Well, yeah, I wouldn't want to hear about anyone going through something like that, but Natalee...she was such a special person. Sensitive, you know? One of those rare people who gave more than they took. And she had talent, too." She felt the heat of anger flash in her blood. "She had such a bright future. Somebody robbed her of that."

"Did she have any contact with anyone that was unexpected or out of the ordinary in the days before she disappeared?"

Vanessa thought a moment before shaking her head. "Nobody I can think of."

"What was she working on for you?"

"The auction, primarily. Keeping in touch with the artists and patrons who'd promised to donate pieces. Making sure all of the arrangements were going according to schedule. That kind of thing."

"And she never mentioned any strange interactions with customers? Or maybe a boyfriend?"

"Not that I remember."

"Maybe you'll remember something that will be helpful. You never know."

She smiled. "You're sweet to be so concerned."

"You're sweet, period." He lifted one of her hands and brought it to his lips. The warm softness of his mouth brushed her right hand.

A shiver skittered across her skin, raising gooseflesh. "Somehow I don't think this is the first time you've seduced a woman."

"Mmm." He nipped at the soft pad of a fingertip. A full-on shudder ran through her body. She swallowed. He smiled. "Is that right?"

"A regular Casanova." She lacked the willpower to pull her hand away as she should.

And he'd be a heck of a lot of fun.

The little devil on her shoulder sounded suspiciously like Fiona. "Shush," she muttered.

"Pardon?"

"Nothing." Gently, with much regret, she tugged her hand away. "I'd better get going. Thank you for a wonderful dinner, but I have to get back to work."

"You have to go back to the warehouse? This late at night? I'll walk you." He signaled for the check.

"No, really, it's just a few blocks away." But having him there might stave off the fear that kept creeping up on her when she was alone.

"I walked you here, I'll walk you back. Besides, I always pay for a date and walk the woman to her door."

A date. She almost corrected him but stopped herself. What would it hurt to pretend for a few more minutes that she'd been on a date with someone new and exciting? "Okay. But I get to keep the receipt."

He looked up from signing the check, surprised.

"I promised Fiona I'd take a dinner break." She shrugged. "She demanded proof." Just wait until she told Fiona she'd not only taken a break, but she'd gone out with a handsome stranger, even flirted a bit.

Vanessa did feel safer having Noah beside her as they walked the few blocks through the moonless night back to the warehouse. Feeling impulsive, she linked her arm with his. The biceps next to hers was firm, and a dusting of light hair tickled her fingertips where they lay on his forearm. She pulled a tad closer, inhaling the clean soap scent of him.

"Are we near where Natalee disappeared?" Noah's question startled Vanessa out of her reverie.

"She was taken from behind Atherton's."

"In broad daylight?"

Vanessa frowned at the direction his thoughts had taken as they walked down a dark, deserted street. "It was early evening. Still light. Still people around, though not in the alley, I'm sure. It's a private parking area for the gallery and leads toward a more traveled street. She was taking her normal shortcut to the subway station. Many of us do. I found her purse on the ground when I left about an hour later." She burrowed closer to his heat for comfort. They were approaching the warehouse building, and she didn't want to let go of Noah's arm.

"You're safe with me. I promise." With her arm tucked against his chest, his words rumbled against her limb and reverberated through her.

She forced herself to release her grip at the door. She unlocked it and turned with a shy smile, tipping her head back to look up at him standing so close. "Thank you for a lovely dinner. It was nice to have company."

"Maybe we can do it again sometime."

Her breath caught as his gaze fell to her lips. Was he planning to kiss her? Should she allow it? Her mind raced as fast as the blood pumping, hot and heavy, through her body. She hadn't come to a decision when he suddenly took a step back.

He wasn't going to kiss her. The crushing disappointment she felt was answer enough to her questions.

"Good night. I'll see you Tuesday. Maybe we can have drinks after the class is over?"

"I'd like that." She found herself answering before she could overanalyze it. "Good night." She entered the studio, closed the door behind her and leaned against it. The dream of what his lips would have felt like against hers sent a phantom tingling across her mouth.

A crash sounded from the back of the building, from the direction of the warehouse, and her dream shattered. *The auction merchandise.* Had Fiona returned and knocked something over? Or maybe it was Jesse or Lance with some last-minute additions.

Her eyes, already adjusted to the dim light after her walk with Noah, saw that nothing was disturbed in the studio area. Her painting still stood in the corner where she'd left it. Not bothering to flip on the lights, Vanessa raced to the door that led to the back storage area, where several hundred thousand dollars' worth of art awaited transfer to the hotel ballroom.

"Fiona?" she called, surprised to find the lights in the back were off.

She was starting to back away, toward the comfort of the studio, when a shaft of light flashed through the darkness and across the wall in front of her, hitting a mirror that bounced the beam around the room. Then the light went out completely, leaving her in the dark with whoever had wielded the flashlight. A scream lodged in her throat. She turned to run but a sharp pain flooded her senses as something thudded against her skull.

Blackness erupted as she fell to the floor, but she stayed conscious long enough to see his silhouette as he turned the flashlight on again. He leaned over her and a deep voice hissed in her ear.

"I told you, you shouldn't be here alone."

FOUR

"VANESSA?"

A light shake of her shoulders brought her back to consciousness. She knew that voice.

Noah.

With awareness came pain. It slammed through her head with a vengeance as she opened her eyes. She winced and her eyelids slid closed.

"Turn off the damn lights," Noah called to someone, who immediately shuffled around in the background. A moment later, he spoke again. "It's okay now. Let me see those sexy brown eyes." His arms tightened around her in encouragement. The bottom half of her body was cold, but his body heat warmed her torso. She was halfway in his lap, her bare legs still on the hard concrete of the warehouse floor. She opened her eyes. The lights had been dimmed.

"What happened?" she asked.

"I was hoping you could tell us." His voice was low and soothing. "You went inside. I walked away. When I looked back at the building, the lights were still off, so I came back. But the door was locked. I heard a motor starting and someone pealing out of the side alley. I rushed around back. The door was open. I found you on the floor."

"The man?" Keeping her words to a minimum reduced the pounding against her skull to a slow, regular cadence instead of the piercing pain to which she'd opened her eyes.

"Man? Was there only one?"

"I think so. License plate?"

He frowned. "All I could see were the brake lights before he turned out of the other end of the alley. Dark colored van." His eyes narrowed on her. "Any idea who he was?"

She focused on Noah's eyes, a calming blue, rather than the bustle of activity from the policemen she detected in her peripheral vision. Noah must have called them. She suddenly remembered the brief glimpse she'd caught when the flashlight had come back on, before she'd passed out. "No. He wore a black ski mask and black clothing. Even had black gloves."

A police officer approached from deeper within the warehouse. "She give you anything, Detective Crandall?"

She stiffened. *"Detective?"*

NOAH CURSED under his breath as she pulled from his arms.

Shit. He hadn't wanted her to find out this way.

She stood. Hot anger glittered in her eyes, in stark contrast to her pale face.

He got to his feet. Hell, he'd had to show the officers on duty his badge so they'd let him stay with her without asking any questions. And so they'd give him some space. So they'd let him hold Vanessa.

"Look, I—"

"Save it. I just want to see if anything's missing and go home." She rubbed a hand against the back of her head and he wondered how badly it was hurting her. He'd felt the lump himself while she'd been out. She'd taken quite a hit.

"The NYPD will have some questions for you first."

"You're not NYPD?"

He shook his head. "I'm from Chicago. Here on personal business."

Her eyes narrowed on him. "I'm guessing you weren't looking for a job as a nude model. So why were you interested in me? How am I part of your 'personal business'?" Emotions played across her heart-shaped face as she no doubt recalled the conversations they'd shared over the past few hours. Her jaw dropped as understanding dawned. "Natalee."

He nodded. "You could say she's family."

"I could say whatever I wanted, since I obviously have to fill in the blanks myself. You apparently aren't capable of simple honesty." Despite the heat in her tone, she rubbed her arms. He immediately motioned to a paramedic who'd been waiting in the wings to check her out.

"You were unconscious for several minutes and could be in shock," Noah explained when she took a step back. Her lips pressed into a thin white line as he reached for her, and his hand fell away. "This man will examine you and make sure you're okay."

"Don't act like you care," she shot back, but her body shook harder and the words were forced through chattering teeth. She accepted the blanket the paramedic wrapped around her and sank into a chair. It was hard to believe it had only been a couple hours since he'd discovered her here, happily absorbed in her work. Now she was shaken, confused and guarded.

Noah gritted his teeth against mounting frustration. It shouldn't matter what she thought of him, as long as he got whatever pertinent information she possessed. But for some reason, with Vanessa, it did matter.

"I do care. I care about finding Natalee's killer. And I'm starting to wonder if you know more than you're letting on." After all, why would someone target her for attack? It was too convenient to be coincidence. He turned to the paramedic. "When you're done, let me know. I'm sure the police will have questions for her, and I want to be there."

He stepped into the studio area, where he could have privacy and still see Vanessa through the doorway. She looked so small and fragile wrapped in an enormous flannel blanket, with only her head and a small white hand showing through. It pulled at something deep in his core. Whipping out his phone, he jabbed a few keys.

"Learn anything?" was Diego's immediate question on the other end of the line.

"Not much. Working on Vanessa, but she's not in any shape to be grilled. She was just attacked. I think the guy ran when he heard me trying to get in the front door."

Diego sucked in a breath. "Natalee's killer?"

"Who knows? Could have just been a thief. She didn't get a good look at him, but he was dressed head to toe in black. Escaped in a van as I arrived. He forced the lock on the back door. With the auction tomorrow, he could have been looking for a big score. But then again, two attacks in one week? Hard to believe that's coincidence." His gut told him this attack was somehow linked to Natalee's death. "What about you? Did your leads pan out?"

"NYPD is waiting for the crime scene report. They're questioning people who live or work near the warehouse where Natalee's body was found. So far, nothing. However, they should have the results of her autopsy by morning. At the moment, it sounds like you've got a better lead than I do. I'll be right there."

"Let me handle this, Diego." He saw Vanessa wince as the paramedic gently probed the back of her head. "I lied to her. She's pretty touchy about it, and pressuring her for more information about Natalee isn't going to help after what she's been through tonight. I'll learn what I can and report back to you." She scowled when the paramedic shined a penlight in her face. Noah had the impression she'd have shoved the man away from her if she could have. He couldn't resist a smile. "Look, I'd better go."

"I'm counting on you, buddy."

"Yeah, I know." After hanging up, Noah moved to Vanessa's side. "How is she?" he asked the paramedic, ignoring her glare.

The man kept his attention on his watch as he finished taking her pulse, then looked up at him. "Her vitals are normal. Possible concussion. She should come to the hospital for a thorough exam, but she refuses."

"I can take you," Noah offered her.

She pushed up from the chair. "No, thanks. A couple of aspirin and I'll be fine."

SHE WAS TIRED, frustrated, mad as hell, and aching in places other than her head, though she'd never admit it to Detective Deception.

"Let's sit you in the other room. It'll be quieter there." He motioned to an NYPD officer and led her into the studio.

Her warm, inviting space still smelled of turpentine and oil paints and immediately soothed her. The dizziness and roiling in her stomach subsided as he sat her down on a stool and pulled one up beside her.

Though she'd never admit it, she was glad for the supportive arm he'd lent her. And his quiet presence kept her calm and collected as the officer—who looked to be all of twenty years old—asked a steady stream of questions about her attack. But when she mentioned the phone call she'd received earlier, and that the attacker had said the same words to her as she'd lost consciousness, Noah's quiet dissolved.

"What?" His disapproval was clear in both his voice

and the look of disbelief he sent her. "Why didn't you call the police? After what happened to Natalee, you'd think any sane woman would be extra cautious."

She stiffened at his insult, then bit back a wince as pain shot up the side of her body. She'd have some bruises tomorrow on the side she'd fallen on. "It seemed like a harmless prank call."

"What exactly did he say?" The officer leaned forward in youthful eagerness, apparently thinking he'd gained a lead. He seemed oblivious to the glares she and Noah were sending each other over his head as he dutifully took notes.

"Something about how I shouldn't be here alone at night."

"Nothing else?"

"No, that was it. I was busy and quickly forgot all about it."

"It looks like he broke in through the back door. Is anything missing?"

"I was about to check, if you guys are done probing my mind and prodding my body." She felt sick to her stomach. If even one item was missing...

Noah's hand reached out and squeezed her cold one. "It's okay. It can wait until the morning."

"No, I have to do it now."

"You're in no shape—"

She jumped up, gritting her teeth as a wave of dizziness threatened to suck her under. "The auction's tomorrow night. I was supposed to do an inventory tonight anyway. I can't—"

"Okay, okay." He stood and rubbed his hands over her shoulders in a soothing manner. It felt too good to shrug away. Besides, he anchored her when she felt as if her aching head might separate from her body and float away. "I'll stay and help." He scowled as she opened her mouth to argue. "I'm staying. That's it. You're not working here alone, and the task will go quicker if I'm here to help, right?"

She swallowed her pride. Besides, what if the thief came back? What if her head injury was more severe than she suspected and she passed out while alone? And Noah owed her. She could use him to get through the night and then never see him again. Pressing her lips together against any further protest, she jerked out a nod.

Noah turned to the officer. "Is that all for now?"

He rose, closing his notepad. "Let me know if you discover anything missing. We'll finish dusting for fingerprints and be on our way." Vanessa doubted they'd find anything. The man had been wearing gloves. She remembered seeing them just before he'd turned off his flashlight and used it as a club.

THOUGH THEY MADE quick work of the inventory, it was almost one in the morning by the time they'd finished checking every item against her list.

"Everything's here," Vanessa announced, and some of the rigidness went out of her spine.

"It wouldn't have been your fault if something was missing."

"That wouldn't matter to Lance."

Noah frowned. "The guy's a jerk."

"At least he sent a security guard over for the rest of the night," she said, eyeing the man who'd taken up his post near the door.

She swayed and Noah's hand reached out to steady her. "Whoa. I think it's time to get you home. Unless you'll take me up on a side trip to the hospital?"

She pulled away. "Home. I can get there myself."

"Do you have a car at the gallery?"

"In New York City? Are you crazy?"

"Right. I'll walk you then."

"Just to the subway." She'd planned to call a cab, but if Noah was offering his protection, she might as well save a few bucks and take him up on it.

She grabbed her purse and hurried past the spot where she'd been attacked. That was the last thing she wanted to think about before she headed outside in the middle of the night. As it was, she'd have to pass the place where Natalee had been abducted. She locked the building, nodded to the security guard and walked beside Noah in silence.

But when they got to the subway station, Noah still didn't leave her side.

"There are a few other people around. I'll be fine." She knew she sounded petulant but was too exhausted to care. "Surely the thief's long gone. Even if he weren't, he wouldn't go after me in public."

"You are the most stubborn, argumentative..." He blew out a breath and turned away as a train arrived with a squeal of brakes. "I'm walking you to your door. Besides," Noah added as they boarded the train and the doors swept closed behind them, "your attacker may have been Natalee's murderer."

She was thankful for the bench they sank onto as her knees suddenly went weak. "But why would he come back? Why would he be in the warehouse?" And why hadn't he killed her?

"That's what I've been trying to figure out."

"And that's why you're sticking to me like glue. Because of Natalee." She should be grateful for his company, but instead she was angry. Really, was what he'd done so bad? He was, after all, trying to help solve

Natalee's murder. They should be working together. No, it was her pride that was hurting more than anything, and wasn't that selfish considering what Natalee had gone through? "I'm sorry."

Her apology had him whipping his head around to look at her. "You're apologizing to me?"

"You were doing your job. Using me was part of finding Natalee's killer."

He had the good grace to wince. "*Using* you?"

"Isn't that what it was?"

"Well, yes, but saying it out loud… We did have some fun." His charming smile was back in place.

She snorted. "Right. I've been a barrel of laughs tonight."

"Well, maybe not quite a barrel…"

She rose as the train approached her stop, eager to be on her way before he reminded her how much she really had enjoyed his company this evening. Despite the deception, it had been the best time she'd had in a long while.

It was hard to stay mad at a gentleman. He even stepped aside to let her board the escalator up to the ground level first. Despite the late hour, the night was still warm as they walked along the sidewalk.

She sighed. "Look, if you want to know about Natalee, I'm happy to help. All you had to do is ask. I want her killer caught, too."

"Your boss gave us a different impression."

"He can be such an ass," she muttered, surprising a laugh out of Noah.

"I think I like you, Vanessa Knight."

And just like that, the night seemed less dark, her step less heavy.

"What's not to like?" She tossed the comment over

her shoulder and went up the steps of the brownstone where she lived.

Ascending the two flights of the inside stairway to her small apartment, she sensed his solid, reassuring presence behind her. She unlocked her door and led him inside. She stopped short, and Noah bumped into her from behind.

"Where *the hell* have you been?" Kenneth roared.

FIVE

VANESSA GROANED INWARDLY. She'd forgotten all about Kenneth. "Is it midnight already?"

"Well past." Kenneth stalked toward her. His gaze shifted slightly to the man behind her. Noah's large frame filled the doorway. The two men were nearly equal in height, but somehow Noah seemed to take up more space. "And you've brought home a stray, I see."

Vanessa refused to cower under the weight of his judgmental gaze. "Kenneth, this is Noah Crandall. Noah, Kenneth Barnes." Walking into her home and kicking her heels off, she let the two men face each other down. She was too tired to deal with explanations tonight.

Kenneth gave Noah a terse nod then spun on her. "You haven't answered my question."

"Keep your voice down." She pressed her fingertips to her temples to assuage the throbbing pain there. "I have neighbors." It was a fact that never failed to rub him the wrong way—that she lived in a cramped old apartment instead of the luxurious loft or fully outfitted townhouse her parents would have supplied had she chosen a different career path. The path they'd mapped out for her.

Tonight's brush with danger had reinforced that life was too short. She was more determined than ever to follow her own road, even if she needed an all-terrain vehicle to navigate it.

NOAH STEPPED farther into the small apartment, closing the door behind him. Who the hell was this Kenneth guy?

He was handsome and well dressed. Judging by the fact that he'd shown up in business attire after midnight, the man worked long hours. And even if he hadn't obviously possessed his own key, the air of ownership the man exuded led Noah to believe he was someone significant in Vanessa's life.

A brother? *No, too jealous.* A lover, then. She *had* mentioned she had plans later, implying that there was someone special in her life. He'd thought she might be making it up, giving herself an excuse to leave early, but there actually was a *someone.*

A stab of unwanted envy almost had Noah leaving the couple to their impending argument, but he couldn't abandon her. He hadn't meant to immerse himself deeper in her life tonight. But there was an undercurrent of anger in Kenneth, and Noah's well-honed police senses were on high alert, especially since she wasn't being overly warm toward the overbearing jerk. The last thing she needed was to deal with a domestic dispute tonight, and he'd stay until the guy either calmed down or left.

He arched an eyebrow in question at Vanessa's overbright smile. He didn't like the glaze that had settled in her eyes or the stiff set of her shoulders. She was barely holding it together.

"Would you like a cup of tea?" she asked.

"Vanessa." Coming from Kenneth, her name was both a stern command and a warning.

"I'd love one," Noah said, effectively drawing the man's anger to himself, matching the flare of challenge in his eyes. "Why don't you start heating the water while Kenneth and I get to know each other better."

Kenneth's lips curled. "Good idea."

She shot Noah a wary look. He nodded in encouragement, and she turned to go through the doorway just off the living room. The sound of running water soon followed.

Kenneth looked him over as if Noah were some irritating remnant he'd found stuck in his teeth. "Who are you?"

"A friend."

"I know all of Vanessa's friends, especially those who would bring her home at almost two in the morning."

Did he now? "And who are you?"

"Her boyfriend. In fact, we're practically engaged. If you were a friend, you'd know that."

But Kenneth's professed confidence didn't ring true. The woman who'd sat across from him earlier that evening drinking wine, laughing and sizing him up beneath hooded eyes had definitely given off an interested vibe. Though muted and sometimes buried, it had still been there, an invisible connection between them. He would bet a month's salary that Vanessa and Kenneth weren't in happily-ever-after land.

Noah snorted. "*Practically* engaged is quite different from engaged."

A red flush crept up the man's neck. "We've been together for two years."

Two years? Kenneth didn't seem like the type to drag his feet when he wanted something, so he was either a moron to let a woman like Vanessa slip away, or she wasn't really into him. Either scenario perked Noah up considerably. "Still, that's a far cry from married."

"What business is it of yours?"

Good question. He didn't need to be involved in this. With less-than-model parents, he'd always avoided the mere thought of relationships. Vanessa's entanglements were certainly none of his business. And yet he couldn't walk away. He shrugged. "Just making conversation.

Look, she's been through a lot tonight, and she needs a good night's rest. I suggest you give her a break."

"A break? She should have been home hours ago, and she walks in with you in the middle of the night, all chummy? She has a lot of explaining to do."

"And I said you should leave her alone." He enjoyed the flash of anger in Kenneth's eyes. Antagonizing her boyfriend might go beyond what Vanessa would put up with in their newfound, tenuous truce, but he couldn't resist.

She chose that moment to reappear from the kitchen, her face so pale against the dark hair framing it that for a moment Noah regretted involving her in the investigation. If he were at all chivalrous, he would back away. Too bad for her, chivalry was dead. He still needed those answers he'd promised Diego.

"I think you both should leave," she said.

"I thought you were making him tea." Kenneth's voice was sharp, as was the look he shot her. "And you and I haven't talked yet."

"We can talk tomorrow. I'm tired." Her exhaustion was evident, but Kenneth either didn't see it or didn't care. He opened his mouth and she held up a hand to ward off his argument. "No, I've had enough for tonight."

"Vanessa." Kenneth's anger turned to pleading when he saw that his bullying tactics weren't getting anywhere.

"I believe the lady made her wishes clear." Noah stepped between the pair. "This is her home, after all. Let's go, Kenny. You know where you can find her in the morning, don't you?"

His scowl returned. "Of course I do."

Noah stood in front of Vanessa until Kenneth got the message. He wasn't budging until the other man did.

As Kenneth stormed past, Noah couldn't resist bending to Vanessa's ear, giving the impression of intimacy.

"Sleep well, and I'll check on you tomorrow." He slipped his business card into her skirt pocket and let his hand brush the sweet curve of her hip. Her sharp release of breath heated his cheek. "My number's on there if you need anything." He pulled back to look into her startled eyes. "Anything."

DIEGO TRIED to hide his impatience as he braced himself for a torture he'd never imagined having to endure. The medical examiner on duty limped toward him, looking rumpled. Either the old man had napped on his couch again, or he was one of those gentlemen of science who appreciated the Albert Einstein look, bushy mustache and all. With Roland, both possibilities were likely.

"Thank you for agreeing to this. I know it's late."

Roland shuffled toward the door across from Diego and fitted a key into the lock. "Could lose my job." Before turning the knob, he peered at Diego through the lower half of his bifocals. "I've known you awhile now. This must be killing you."

"I couldn't sleep tonight. I had to see her one more time."

"I can let you say goodbye to her, but I can't do anything more if you're not part of the official investigation. Not without approval from higher up, you understand."

"I know."

"You sure you want to do this? It's not pretty."

He gulped down the bile that rose at the image of his niece, partially burned. "I have to. Besides, I already saw her at the scene." And his other contacts at the NYPD didn't seem to be making any headway. He was out of options.

The bushy white head nodded.

"I know it's not her anymore, anyway." He knew all

too well that he'd never see his lovely niece again. Instead, he'd fight to remember how she'd been when she was alive and vibrant.

He steeled his resolve. He'd seen victims of fire on a couple of cases. He'd even seen Natalee's body at the scene, when it had just been him and the initial rookie officer on the scene. Before backup had arrived and forced him away. In his pain, he'd touched her, possibly contaminating evidence. But he hadn't been able to control the sudden muscle weakness that had him sinking to the warehouse floor, the need to brush a finger along the unscarred portion of her face, or the howl of pain that had escaped as more officers had arrived and pulled him away.

Roland nodded and opened the door. He handed him a pair of medical gloves and a mask to tie around his mouth and nose—to help with the odor and further contamination of evidence, but some part of him wanted to reject the impersonal nature of this visit. Her funeral was scheduled for Saturday morning, and this might be the last time he'd see her. Olivia had ordered a closed-casket funeral, and rightly so. Nobody in their family needed to remember Natalee this way.

Her face was still beautiful—on one side. One olive cheek had been lightly burned in a trail that continued down her neck, as if the flames had licked upward from her body but had been quenched before they could touch her dark hair or the majority of her face.

He gritted his teeth so hard they ached. He'd kill the bastard who'd done this to his family. Despite the desertion by her father, despite her almost-poverty-level household, despite all odds, Natalee Ortega had grown into a bright young woman. And now she was dead.

"I'll give you a moment." Roland backed out of the room and closed the door quietly behind him. Through the observation window, Diego saw him head down the hall, away from his office and toward the vending machines. Good old Roland was a stickler for his routine. Diego had dealt with him enough to know he had an insatiable sweet tooth, and that sometime around two in the morning, in the middle of his night shift, he would shuffle off to satisfy his craving before settling back into his work.

That gave Diego about ten minutes. He moved quickly, leaving Natalee on the table as he exited into the hall and crept in the opposite direction of the vending machines, toward the ME's office.

Since Natalee was a recently processed victim, her folder was easy to locate. Her file was in the Out box on the desk, waiting to be forwarded to the appropriate authorities. His contacts had told him they'd receive the file in the morning, but he couldn't count on being provided the information. He'd take matters into his own hands.

Diego grabbed the file and peered into the hall, which was empty. Moving on quiet feet to the assistant's area, he fed the papers into the copy machine and winced as it whirred to life. Thank goodness Roland was a little hard of hearing.

After grabbing the sheath of printed papers as well as the originals, Diego returned quickly to the office and restored the file. He shoved the copies under his shirt and tucked the bundle securely into his waistband before heading back to his niece.

"YOU STOLE AN official document?" Noah stared hard at his friend, who returned his look with a glare. A few hours of sleep hadn't been enough to erase the fatigue that lingered after a long night, and they were both cranky and frustrated. Diego had gotten back late, after Noah had already dug out some clean sheets to make up a bed for himself on the couch. And yeah, it had worried the hell out of him that Diego hadn't been home at two-thirty in the morning. Hadn't even left a note, and hadn't answered when Noah had tried to call his cell phone.

"I couldn't be sure my contacts would just *give* me the information," Diego said. "So I had to take it. We need all of the facts if we're going after this guy."

Noah turned away to pour a cup of coffee and to hide his disapproval of his best friend's tactics. He'd never known Diego to break the rules. Despite his passion for the job, he was a by-the-book cop. In one of their classes at the police academy, he'd even reported a fellow student for cheating. Apparently, those ethics were only in force when Diego wasn't emotionally invested. Everyone had a breaking point, and being shut out of Natalee's murder investigation had been his.

Noah got a second mug down from the kitchen cabinet. It was the last clean one and the sink was overflowing with dirty dishes. He'd make it a point to wash some before they headed out this morning. And to throw away the half-empty cartons of spoiled food that were lying around. Diego didn't seem to notice that his housekeeping had suffered in his grief. Or maybe it had simply ceased to matter.

He set a cup of strong coffee in front of his friend along with the sugar bowl and a spoon, then took the stool next to him at the small breakfast bar. "So what did the report say?"

Diego took a gulp of coffee without so much as a flinch at the scalding it must have given his mouth. "Haven't read it yet. Haven't been able to bring myself to open it."

It couldn't be easy reading the ME's clinical analysis of a family member's death. The cold, scientific presentation of facts, not to mention the detailed descriptions and pictures, would be difficult for even the most seasoned detective. Diego was experienced, but he was human, too.

"Want me to take a look?" Noah offered.

Not meeting his gaze, Diego nodded. "Yeah. Thanks." He jerked his head toward the coffee table. "I left it over there."

"I'll review it after breakfast but I need you to do something for me."

"What?"

"Check in with your family. Let them hear your voice."

"I was going to call Mama today, anyway. The funeral is in the morning."

Feeling the need to lighten the mood, Noah rose and grabbed the box he'd placed on the counter.

Diego finally looked at him with interest as he noted the logo on the side. "Pastries? From Capelli's?"

Noah's early morning errand paid off as his friend sank his teeth into a flaky, chocolate-filled croissant. A grunt of satisfaction soon followed.

Noah tried to hide his relief that Diego was eating something. "I've been craving these since I left for Chicago." He selected a pastry for himself. "We have to keep our strength up. We have a snobby art gallery owner to deal with today. And we've got to find a way to attend the equally haughty auction tonight." He had a hunch part of the solution to the mystery of Natalee's murder lay in how the murderer was linked to the gallery, but they'd have to get around Lance Atherton first.

"What about your connection to a certain staff member there?"

"I don't want to use her anymore." He stiffened himself against the guilt he felt at the term *use*. Vanessa had accused him of using her to get information about Natalee, and she'd been right. The memory of her innocent brown eyes filled with anger—and, worse, hurt—had hit him in the gut hard. Last night he'd fallen asleep with the image in his mind, and it had been the first thing he'd thought about when he'd awoken.

"You're not going to let your sense of chivalry get in the way, are you? This is Natalee we're talking about. She's family."

"And I know you think that means the rules don't apply, but you're wrong. One wrong step, one illegal action, and you could jeopardize finding justice for Natalee."

Diego dropped the remainder of his pastry on the counter and brushed his fingers with a napkin—with more force than was necessary. "I may have already done that by disturbing the scene. I have to make up for that, any way I can. If you disagree with my methods, you can take a hike. Nobody asked for your help anyway."

"Goddamn it, you're too close to this. Your emotions are getting in the way. You're not thinking straight."

Diego stood there, hands clenching and unclenching at his sides, for several moments before speaking. "I'm going to take a shower and get dressed. *I'll* go see Miss Knight this morning, because I'm afraid you're letting *your* emotions get in the way. And I'll find a way into that auction tonight. Natalee's killer could be there."

As could Vanessa's attacker. "No, I'll do it. She doesn't even know you. I'll talk to Vanessa and then we'll both attend the auction." He couldn't trust Diego not to use more illegal means of gaining information. If his actions last night were any indication, he'd become a wild card.

Besides, he wanted to check in on Vanessa and see how she was holding up after last night's events. Though she'd been angry with him upon discovering the truth of who he was, she'd acted more civil toward him by the end of the night. He only hoped that with the clarity of the light of day and after some sleep, she wouldn't curse him for the dog he was and refuse to help them.

No matter what her feelings today, he was determined to attend the auction, both to find the attacker and to protect Vanessa. He owed her that much.

TWO DOZEN RED ROSES sat in a crystal vase on Vanessa's desk at the gallery. For a moment, her mind jumped to the time she'd spent in prospective-nude-model Noah Crandall's company last night, before he'd become Detective Deception. She'd built up a few defenses against the hurt after he and Kenneth had left, but in her sleep, when her walls were down, she'd dreamed of Noah. Her body had reacted instinctively to the remembered feel of his strong arms cradling her, the touch of his long fingers as they'd wrapped around hers. Those memories had balanced out the times she'd woken in a cold sweat, images of a gloved hand wielding a flashlight jolting her right back to that cold warehouse floor.

She reached out to pluck the card from its plastic stem in the middle of the bouquet. *Missed you last night. Love, Kenneth.*

"Secret admirer?" Jesse asked, perching on the corner of Fiona's desk.

Fiona's lips curved in a sly smile. "We can only hope."

Vanessa handed the card to Fiona, who read it and grinned even wider. "What are you smiling about?"

Fiona tapped the card against the desk. "Well, Miss Sour Puss, this is encouraging."

"How so?"

"Kenneth says he missed you last night, which means you chose not to let him stay over. And now he's the one on the ropes. Exhibit A." She gestured to the massive display of flowers.

Vanessa moved them to a side table so that she could see her friends across their desks when she sat down.

"So what happened?" Jesse asked.

"Noah Crandall happened."

Fiona arched a sculpted brow. "The detective?"

Vanessa's jaw dropped. "You knew he was a detective?"

She grinned. "I was hoping he'd *happen* to you."

"You could have given me a heads-up."

Jesse held up his hands. "Whoa, I think I missed something. Back up a minute."

Vanessa explained all that had happened—from the mistaken assumption that Noah was applying for the nude modeling job, which had Jesse and Fiona holding their sides in laughter, to the attack at the warehouse and Noah coming to her rescue, confessing to his real purpose.

Fiona's amusement immediately faded. "You were *attacked?*"

"Are you okay?" Jesse asked.

Okay was such a relative term. Was she *okay* with the fact that a handsome, charming man who had her hormones in an uproar was, in fact, a liar? Was it *okay* that he'd lied to her because he thought it was for the greater good? Was it *okay* that her head throbbed with every step she took and she had to pull herself together before this evening's event or she might lose her job? Or was it *okay* that it was time to break things off with Kenneth for good?

Am I okay? "I will be." She forced a smile. "Especially after this auction is over. And if Lance finally gives me that raise, I'll be on cloud nine, permanently."

Fiona rolled her eyes. "If he doesn't give you a raise and a promotion after what you've put together for tonight, I'm going to have a little chat with Mr. Boss Man."

"No need. I'll just threaten to take my expertise elsewhere."

"Good girl. Now, are you going to use the same threat on good ole Kenny-boy?"

"Kenny?" She laughed. "That's what Noah called him last night."

Fiona's eyes sparkled with delight. "I knew there was something about that guy I liked. So, is he going to be *the one?*"

Vanessa nearly choked. "I just met him."

"I wasn't talking about marriage, sweetie. I was talking about the *other* 'one.'"

"Oh. The experiment."

Jesse coughed. "I think I missed something again."

Fiona grinned. "We had a little chat yesterday about ways to decide if Kenneth is the one for Vanessa. You can probably guess which way I'm betting."

"Add me to that list," Jesse said. "Did you take a test drive?"

Vanessa rolled her eyes. "Not you, too. That's not my style." Though recent events were certainly challenging that belief. Noah's hand brushing her hip before he'd left the night before was one such event. Her skin still burned beneath her clothing. "I believe in love."

Fiona made a clucking sound. "Ah, the artist's soul. Jesse, you're an artist. Do you believe in everlasting, soulful love?"

He smiled absently. "Absolutely. And if you find it, hang on to it. Life's short. But finding it is the trick. It's a rare thing." He flicked a finger against one of the crimson blooms in Vanessa's bouquet. "Red roses, on the other hand, are cliché and common." He fumbled in the desk drawer before holding up a pen. "I told Lance I was coming in here for a pen. Better get out on the floor again before he comes looking for me."

Fiona watched Jesse leave. "Romantics. It's wonderful, really, that someone believes in true love—as long as you're not setting yourself up for something painful."

"Let's change the subject, shall we?" Vanessa sat forward and lifted the receiver of her office line. As she confirmed the hotel arrangements for the catering one last time and put in a call to the trucking company that was due to pick up the merchandise, Fiona drifted away to work the floor of the gallery. Her lilting voice intermingled with Jesse's as they talked with customers. It was busier than usual with the auction generating a buzz. Jesse had been called in to work an extra shift, and even Lance was on the floor.

Vanessa sighed and closed her eyes. The headache she'd had for the past twelve hours was almost gone. She'd pushed it to the back of her mind, intent on her lengthy to-do list for the morning. She took a deep breath to focus herself, but when she opened her eyes, Kenneth stood before her. She was tempted to close her eyes again and see if he'd be gone when she reopened them, but she couldn't avoid him forever.

He aimed the full power of a charming smile on her, but the lines at the sides of his mouth were just a little too white.

"Hello, baby." He draped his coat over a chair and came around the pair of desks to kiss her. He settled for her forehead when she didn't turn her face up to accept his greeting. "Do you like the flowers?"

"They're beautiful. You've always had great taste." Great, expensive taste. Which was one of the things that lurked in the back of her mind. She'd shoved it aside as silly insecurity, but something made her want to take it out now and examine it. Kenneth was a name-dropper. He enjoyed knowing people in power, liked being recognized for what he did, reveled in the power and prominence that went with his career and social position. Was that why he stayed with her? Because her family was wealthy and connected, and had been part of the most affluent of New York City society since the early 1900s?

It didn't really matter anymore. She was going to break up with him.

Kenneth settled one hip on the edge of her desk, forcing her to either lean back to look up at him or appear rude. She pushed back in her chair so that his leg was no longer brushing her arm and looked up, waiting.

"I was hoping you'd call me when you received the flowers. I wanted to talk. In fact," he added, spreading his arms wide, "I'm all yours for the morning. I thought we could go to breakfast and talk things over."

"Today?"

"Well, yes. It isn't easy to clear my calendar for an entire morning."

"You do realize what today is, right?"

His brow furrowed. "Friday."

"Even though I've wanted to sit down and talk for weeks, you want to talk now that *you're* ready to talk." She put a hand to her forehead. Damn. The headache was suddenly a monster clawing at the inside of her skull.

"Baby, you know I've been busy…"

She waved a hand to cut him off. "Apparently you haven't realized that *I've* been busy."

He looked blank for a moment before nodding. "The auction. I still plan to be there, of course, despite this big trial that starts Monday." He grabbed her hand. "I want to support you."

She resisted the urge to pull away. "Look, right now you can support me by giving me some space. I've got a lot to do to make sure everything runs smoothly tonight. I promise we can talk after the auction."

"It's a date then." He bent down to give her a peck on the cheek, and this time she turned her head to give him a full kiss, curious to see if it could rekindle some kind of spark. He accepted the invitation, kissing her a long moment before pulling away. Grinning, he gave her a cocky salute before snatching up his suit jacket. "See you tonight."

Once he was gone, Vanessa was surprised at her reaction. Relief. When his lips had been on hers, she'd experienced none of the passion or fire she'd hoped to feel. But then, they'd lost whatever passion they'd had months ago.

She couldn't help but compare the way she'd felt in Noah's company to the way she felt with Kenneth. The detective—whether a liar or not—had stirred her body and mind like nobody had before. Not even Kenneth during their best of times.

"You okay?" The sound of Jesse's voice brought her attention back to the present.

"Yeah," she said. "What's up?"

"The truck's at the warehouse. Driver just called."

"Thank goodness. At least something's going right today."

From inside the shop across the street, he'd watched her arrive and disappear into the warehouse. Alone. Even after her encounter with him the night before, Vanessa Knight was being so careless, walking by herself. It was a public sidewalk in broad daylight, but he could make things happen and nobody would be the wiser.

A security officer lounged by the doorway, taking a smoke break as he watched two deliverymen struggle with a dolly that carried a particularly large marble statue. They eventually made their way to a truck that waited in the alley, ready to be loaded with auction items. Including *his* piece. There hadn't been time for him to collect it. After he'd knocked Vanessa out, he'd had to make a quick getaway when her friend had come back to pound on the door.

It had all been for nothing.

His painting was still on the auction block, waiting to go to some undeserving person. He couldn't allow that to happen. He had to retrieve his angel. The one that Nigel's moronic son had let slip through the cracks. Donating it to an art auction—the man didn't have a lick of sense when it came to culture. He didn't appreciate true beauty the way his father had.

He quickly shoved all emotion away. Now wasn't the time to think about things that would only upset him. He had to focus. He had to get the painting back before the auction.

And after the auction, after his angel was safe, he'd work on the next piece. He hadn't thought, with all that had happened, that he'd be able to choose another. Until he'd felt the silky strands of her velvet brown hair slip between his fingertips as she lay on that cold warehouse floor. He'd broken his own rule, removing a glove just to satisfy the need to touch her. It had been worth the stolen moment.

Her. She's one of them.

SIX

"You okay?" Noah asked.

Vanessa looked up from the papers on her desk to find him standing in the doorway, his brow crinkled with worry. Despite the maelstrom of complicated feelings he'd stirred up, she was soothed by his concern. It was incredibly sweet.

Unless this was all part of another scheme to get information.

Oh, damn. She didn't know what to think anymore. She could barely think, anyway. Her head had begun pounding again shortly after Kenneth's departure. Supervising the loading of the delivery truck had been a good distraction, but it hadn't been enough.

"Uh, yeah, I'm just…" Tired of pretending, she stopped and sat back in her chair, pressing her fingertips to her temples. "This headache won't go away."

He perched on the desk in front of her, leaning toward her. "Here, let me."

He reached forward, gently pulled her hands away and replaced them with two of his fingertips on each of her temples. The gentle pressure and slow circles brought immediate relief. Her eyes closed as she bit back a groan of pleasure.

"I know you don't trust me," he said, "and probably won't believe anything I say right now, but I'm really sorry about how things went down yesterday. I wish…"

His silence had her opening one eye to look at him. "What?"

"I wish we'd met under different circumstances." The heat in his gaze melted the last of her anger. His thumb lightly brushed her eyelid, encouraging her to close it again.

But with her eyes closed, her other senses were heightened. "Feels good." Her mumbled words ended on a blissful moan as his fingers slipped through the hair at either side of her head, moving to massage her scalp. As she inhaled again, the spicy male scent of him infused her senses, and she realized he must have moved closer to her to reach the back of her head.

"Still a bit of a bump back here."

She heard, rather than saw, the scowl that accompanied his statement as he carefully probed around the injured area.

"I iced it off and on all night."

"So you didn't sleep?" Again she detected concern in the rough timbre of his voice.

"A bit. Not well."

Suddenly his hands left her. She bit back a cry of disappointment.

"The truck is gone then?" Lance asked.

Her eyes shot open at the harsh tone of his voice. Thankfully, Noah had heard him coming and let go of her, but he was still leaning against her desk, so close that she could still feel his body heat. His position was much too intimate for two people who'd just met.

Noah seemed amused by Lance's glare. Judging from the hostility emanating from her boss, she guessed that he already knew Noah was a detective interested in information about Natalee. Which didn't bode well for her, since the object of his hostility had been practically fondling her a moment ago. Lance was sure to think she was fraternizing with the so-called enemy.

She sat up straight, trying to gain a few inches of distance from Noah. "The auction items are all safely loaded. Besides myself, the guard you hired was there to supervise, and he's tailing the truck to the hotel where he'll guard the merchandise during the unloading, and then at the ballroom up until the auction. I double-checked that they all had the correct directions before they left. I'll be heading to the hotel in just a bit to start setting up."

"Good. Thank God nothing was stolen last night, and you look none the worse for wear." Lance had briefly checked on her when he'd arrived this morning, quickly excusing himself to personally check the inventory at the warehouse, making sure the artwork was accounted for. "Lots to do today."

Noah ignored the man's dismissal. "You have that list for me yet, Atherton?"

List? Vanessa watched with covert curiosity as her boss flushed.

"Still working on it," he muttered. "Lots to do," he said again, giving her a pointed look she knew was meant as a warning. *Don't talk to this man about the gallery.*

After Lance walked away, Vanessa rose, scooping up the invoices she'd been poring over. She needed to have a last-minute meeting with the auctioneer about the estimated values of the items. He was experienced in art auctions, but it was just one of the many things she had to check and double-check today. All her stress and fatigue would be worth it. If tonight was a success, it would do wonders for her reputation and career.

She started to step around Noah to get to her briefcase, but he took her arms and gently turned her to face him.

"Wait. Just take a breath, okay?" His hands maintained

their grip when she tried to pull away. "For God's sake, don't these people know what you've been through?" He flicked a disgusted glance toward the roses sitting on the side table. He clearly didn't think much of Kenneth's attempt to mollify her.

The heat of his palms warmed her through her thin sleeves. But it was his legs—not quite trapping her, but on either side of her like an embrace—that felt like flames licking her outer thighs. God help her, she wanted to lean into him and press her entire length against him. Her body stiffened in resistance, making her head throb again. She bit back a wince.

"You've had this headache since last night?"

"It comes and goes. Those magic fingers of yours helped for a bit." She attempted a grin. *Keep it light and move along. Take a step away.* But her body wouldn't obey.

He frowned at her attempt at levity. "You should see a doctor. A crack to the skull can be serious."

"It's just a bump. You felt it yourself. It's already half the size it was."

"Yes, but…"

She forced herself to step away, breaking contact. "It's not that bad. I haven't lost consciousness since it first happened. Besides, I have a lot to do. I really need to get going."

"Have you even eaten today?"

"I'll be fine." Unable to remain immune to his concern any longer—it touched her more than she could allow—she felt a lump in her throat she couldn't explain.

"I'll take that as a no. I'm taking you to lunch."

No way. She was too confused when she was anywhere near him. She jerked open a drawer in her desk, took out one of her private stash and held it up. "A protein bar. It does the body good. I'll be fine," she repeated.

His gaze fell to where she gripped the handle of her briefcase and she forced herself to relax her white knuckles.

"Yes, I can see you'll be fine." He muttered a curse that had her eyebrows lifting.

"Was there something you needed?"

"I wanted to check on you." He seemed to hesitate.

"And?"

He grimaced. "I hesitate to ask, but since Atherton seems reluctant to cooperate, I was hoping you could get me the name of the donors from the auction, as well as the names of people you invited. I promise we'll be discreet. It would give us a place to start searching."

Had he been nice to her because he wanted something again? "I'll talk to Lance on your behalf." She already suspected her boss's answer based on how he'd eyed Noah just now. Judging by Noah's scowl, he knew the answer too. A firm and resounding *no*.

"Thanks, I appreciate that. I'll let you get back to work. But I'll be at the auction tonight to check on you."

"The auction? Why?" Her heart tripped over itself. He was *that* worried about her?

"Diego and I believe Natalee's killer might show up. Or the man who attacked you. And it's very possible they're one and the same."

"WELL?" DIEGO ASKED the moment Noah entered the apartment.

Noah laid the tuxedo he'd rented across the back of a barstool. "I read the ME's report." After seeing Vanessa, he'd taken the file with him to a coffee shop. "How is the family?"

"Mama's holding steady. Olivia's a wreck, but she's surviving." Diego's tired eyes met Noah's. "The funeral's all set for ten tomorrow morning."

His heart twisted. "I'm sorry. Your family didn't deserve this." They were the kind of people to take in lost souls, not to lose them. "Did you find out anything new?"

"Olivia couldn't think of anybody who would hurt Natalee. And she recognized all of the numbers on Natalee's cell phone. No strange calls. I was hoping, since Vanessa received a call the same night she was attacked, that we would find a lead in Natalee's contact list, but no." Diego gestured to the file in Noah's hands. "What did you think?"

Noah avoided his gaze by examining the apartment. A dirty plate sat near the clean dishes he'd left on a rack to drip-dry that morning. Diego wasn't cleaning up after himself yet, but at least there was proof he'd eaten the sandwich Noah had left him for lunch. He'd even moved the plate from the counter to the sink when he was done. Definite progress.

He settled on the couch and set the folder down on the coffee table.

Diego sat in the nearby overstuffed chair. "Look, if you're trying to spare me, don't bother. I've already seen her body. What I have to endure is nothing—*nothing*—compared to what she went through. And what Olivia's going through every day wondering who, what and why this happened to her little girl. Let's just pretend she's a victim like any other case we've had to work."

Noah leaned his elbows on his knees and flipped open the tan folder. "Female, Latina, age seventeen—"

"She would have been eighteen next month."

"—found at an abandoned warehouse near the docks,

a couple miles from the gallery." A picture in the file showed how the medical examiner had found the body.

"She was lying on the floor, her legs straight, ankles together, her arms outstretched at her sides. Kind of like that drawing of the medicine man I've seen in books."

"Da Vinci's *Vitruvian Man*."

"Yeah, that. Except Natalee's arms were raised higher." Diego grimaced. "Before I grabbed her. But I swear, I laid her back down almost exactly how she was when she was found."

"Sounds like he positioned her that way on purpose." Nobody fell into that position naturally. There was no doubt in his mind she'd been posed. "One has to wonder why he bothered."

Diego nodded. "Why risk leaving DNA or some other evidence behind with further contact?"

When a killer took the time to position a body, he had a reason—whether it served his own purpose or he was trying to throw off the cops. If it was the first reason, they might very well have a serial killer on their hands.

Noah's thoughts immediately went to Vanessa. Had her attacker intended to take her, too, but been scared away when Noah had returned to the scene? He couldn't control the flash of raw fear that went through him, imagining her beautiful body laid out like Natalee's, half-burned and left for him to find. "I know some experts at a place called the Society for the Study of the Aberrant Mind— they call it SSAM—back in Chicago."

"Sam?"

"It's an organization that specializes in studying the behavior of violent criminals and tracking them down. Would you mind if I gave my contacts a call and shared some of this information?" He didn't mention that he suspected a serial killer and that hunting them was SSAM's specialty. Diego didn't need any more heartache until Noah's suspicions had a stronger foundation.

"Better yet, fax this to them." Diego jabbed a finger at the photo.

"It's as good as admitting you stole the file."

"And you think I give a flying fuck what happens to me now?" He took a breath and rubbed a hand across his face. When he spoke again, he sounded as tired as he looked. Noah refused to believe it was defeat he heard in his friend's voice. "I just want Natalee's killer found. I don't care about anything else. Give them all the information they need."

Noah nodded. "Done." He looked closer at the picture and compared it to the ME's notes. "She'd been burned up one side of her body and across her abdomen and chest, but the spread of flames was stopped."

"He spared most of her face."

Which Noah found particularly interesting. "You'd think one would burn a corpse in order to render it unidentifiable. That wasn't the case here. I doubt he did it to spare her *life* at that point. He must have had a reason for leaving her face untouched." Noah glanced at the file, remembering the detail that had frozen him to the core. It had reinforced his fears that this could be a very real, very twisted, serial murderer. "There were traces of a fire retardant cream on her face that would have stopped the spread of flames."

But why? The why had always fascinated Noah. Unfortunately, it wasn't always a question that could be answered.

He flipped to the toxicology report that had given him a small measure of relief. "It may help you to know she was drugged."

Diego's head lifted out of his hands. "What?"

"Natalee had a heavy-duty sedative in her system. In fact, the cocktail of drugs found in her blood is likely what killed her."

A sheen of moisture formed in his friend's brown-black eyes. "She didn't feel anything?"

"According to the reconstructed timeline and the report, I don't think she was awake for the final part." The most painful part.

"God." Diego's throat worked as he swallowed several times. "At least that'll be some comfort to my family." A bit more hopeful now, he leaned forward, glancing over Noah's shoulder at the report. "What else?"

"No hair or fiber evidence left by the killer." He flipped to another page. "But this was interesting. Could be nothing, though."

"What?"

"There was a drop of what appeared to be dried blood on the floor a few feet from the body. It was miniscule, but since the rest of the area had been swept meticulously clean—presumably by the killer—the criminalists found it. Tests came back as oil paint. The kind you can buy in an artist's supply store." Noah's thoughts went to Vanessa, who had been painting the night before.

"Natalee worked with artists all the time," Diego said.

"What had she told you about her job?"

"Not much," he admitted with a grimace. "She'd been so busy with high school graduation and her new internship these past few months that I hadn't seen her much, other than at family gatherings."

And Noah recalled how big and boisterous those could be. It was possible to see every family member there, but not always easy to have one-on-one conversations. "Was she taking any courses in art? Painting?"

"I'll ask Olivia. I don't really know. She was always

exploring something artsy, though. Knitting, jewelry-making, pottery. After her father left them years ago, she escaped through creating things. Guess it became a part of her."

"I'll ask Vanessa tonight if she knows anything about Natalee's hobbies. She teaches an art class at the studio that adjoins the warehouse." Maybe she even taught the bastard who did this. He made a mental note to review her old class rosters. "If this drop of paint," he added, tapping a finger against the close-up picture of the dark red stain, "wasn't somehow brought to the scene by Natalee, it could have been dropped by her killer."

"Which means he likely has a connection to the art community," Diego finished.

Which meant Vanessa likely had a connection to *him*.

VANESSA SWALLOWED another aspirin with a gulp of caffeine—in the form of a strong black coffee Jesse had brought her—as the last of the auction items was set up for display. Only after she was alone in the hotel's grand ballroom, with the security guard taking up residence outside the main door, did she let down her defenses. She rolled her head on her shoulders, trying to ease the tension that had taken root and blossomed.

She deserved to relax. Every item had made it safely. Each was set up on its pedestal, easel, or table around the perimeter of the enormous room. Beside each piece, she'd placed the corresponding number and description from the auction catalog that had been sent to their mailing list of art collectors.

Of course the moment she had time to think was the moment Noah's words came back to her. He thought the killer could be here tonight. She shuddered. The only comfort was that there was little a person could do in front of the crowd they were expecting. To distract herself, she admired the art around her.

She paused in front of a painting, her gaze drawn to the subject's face. It was a woman, her head thrown back to the heavens, her arms outstretched in silent supplication. Droplets of water and sand clung everywhere—to her creamy skin, to her dark, wet hair. Even to her eyelashes. Something about the quiet desperation and hint of anguish tugged at her heart. It had caught her eye several times in the past few days. The information card said the artist was anonymous.

The woman was an intriguing contrast of dark and light. A study in opposites. She was wet, clearly having just emerged from the ocean, yet she was reaching toward the sky. Yearning for something different. It echoed the yearning Vanessa had been experiencing lately.

She shook her head, breaking the spell. This was no time to get lost in daydreams. The doors opened in half an hour, and the hotel's staff would be arriving to man the bar at one end of the room and circulate among the guests with trays of food. Silk-draped chairs and tables with white linen cloths and fragrant flower centerpieces already filled the middle of the room. The patrons would be allowed time before the bidding began to mingle, enjoy cocktails and peruse the merchandise that, until now, they'd only seen in the catalog that had been mailed to them weeks ago.

"Miss Knight?"

She jumped as the auctioneer spoke to her from behind. She gave him a warm smile and extended her hand, hoping he wouldn't notice it was shaking. "Mr. Lyle. I'm so glad you could be with us today."

"The Warm Embrace Foundation is near and dear to my heart. I had a young nephew who died from leukemia.

His mother felt so alone and depressed. If only the family had been given access to the kind of support and resources the foundation provides for the families of terminally ill children…" His voice drifted off as emotion overcame him, and Vanessa squeezed the hand that still held hers.

"That's exactly why I picked them as our first charity." She'd had to fight Lance, who'd wanted to choose a larger, well-known organization so they'd have that much more gallery exposure through advertising. But after she'd explained that every news station and newspaper in town would want to feature such a new foundation, and that it was cliché to support what everyone else did, he was on board. "We're glad we can help such a wonderful cause."

Showing Mr. Lyle the merchandise up close, along with explanations of their individual points of value, as well as directing the caterers when they arrived, left her little time to worry further that her assailant might attend the auction. After a last, satisfied look around the room that spanned an entire side of the elegant hotel, she hurried to a nearby ladies' room where she'd stashed a change of clothes.

This was to be a gala event, so glitz was called for. The delicate ebony sequins in the bodice of her clinging black sheath caught the low light. She touched up her makeup and hair, wondering what Noah would think when he saw her in her finest. Would he find her sexy?

Startled by the thought, she bit her lip, instantly regretting that she'd smeared her fresh lipstick. She had no business thinking about Noah tonight. And certainly not in that capacity. He was just background fluff, though she had trouble thinking of a man with all those hard planes and angles as "fluff." Still, he would be at the auction because he was a man on a mission, and she was not the target. She'd probably barely register as a blip on his radar, which was as it should be. He was hunting a killer.

She returned to the ballroom, where guests were starting to arrive. Jesse and Fiona were greeting and checking them in at the door, giving them numbered paddles for bidding. The lights had been dimmed appropriately—with spotlights on the merchandise to show it off, and lowlights on the glamorously dressed women to show them off. An appetizer and dessert buffet had been set up near a bar at the back of the room, along with room to mingle. The aromas that filled the air were heavenly, a blend of rich food and heady wine along with the occasional whiff of expensive perfume. Vanessa made a final pass of the ballroom before moving to the double doors at the entrance to check in with Fiona.

Vanessa's friend took a moment to survey her attire before she spoke. "Wow. I'm glad you went with the shorter dress. Shows off those gorgeous legs."

"The heels make them look longer than they are."

Fiona rolled her green eyes. "Take a compliment, sweetie." Seeming to remember where they were and why, she sobered. "Okay, here's the deal. Lance's guy is in position here at the double doors." She jerked her head toward the security guard standing at parade rest a few yards away. "There are also a couple of men circulating the room. They're in tuxedoes so they blend in. And they're both devastatingly handsome," she added with a wink.

So Noah had made it after all. Vanessa's pulse stuttered at the thought of him in a tailored tuxedo. She forced herself not to turn and scan the room for a glimpse of him. "Both?"

"Diego Sandoval is here, too."

"The guests?"

"More arriving every minute. They're signing in with

Jesse out front and Lance is mingling but he's getting impatient waiting for you to say something to the group. He's about to take charge of it all himself. You'd better get in there and work your mojo."

The next hour was a whirl of faces and names, trays of food, refilling of champagne glasses, and conversations about everything from private schools to the works on display. Her initial adrenaline rush had cooled, but her cheeks were still warm with excitement as she happily chatted about one after another of the nearly one hundred pieces of contemporary art. She'd assembled one of the finest collections of new artists the city had seen on display in years. At least, that was what the journalist from *The New Yorker* had told her.

Being busy helped take her mind off the possibility that her attacker—who might or might not be Natalee's killer—could be nearby. Still high on praise, she was surprised when she turned to seek out a glass of water for her parched throat and ran into someone instead.

No, not just someone. *Noah.*

More specifically, Noah's chest. The same hard chest she'd found so tantalizing not twenty-four hours before, only this time it was even more magnificent clad in the starched white shirt and form-fitting black jacket of his tuxedo. Or maybe it was less magnificent now that it was hidden away.

His arm reached out to steady her as she jerked back in surprise. "I'm glad you came."

His lips curved into a smile. "I promised I would be here."

Someone cleared his throat behind Noah and he moved aside to reveal another man. "This is Diego."

Vanessa took a quick survey of the man, who was handsome in his own right—as dark as Noah was blond. And her portrait-artist's eye noted the resemblance to Natalee right away. "Natalee's uncle? I'm so sorry for your loss." He nodded, looking uncomfortable. She lightly squeezed his forearm through his jacket. "I've told Noah that I'll help in any way I can."

"I, uh, appreciate that." Diego's gaze went to her fingers and she immediately removed them from his arm. "Thanks for putting our names on the guest list so we could get past the front door."

She smiled to cover the awkwardness she sensed between them. "I figured there'd be no stopping you two anyway. You may want to steer clear of Lance Atherton, though. He doesn't want anything to ruin his big night."

"Good advice. I'm going to head to the other side of the room. Spread out a little."

Noah gave a little wave to Diego but kept his eyes on her. "You say Atherton doesn't want his night ruined, but *you* did all of this. This is your night." Under his heated gaze, she resisted the urge to press a cool hand to her flushed cheeks.

He surveyed the room and returned to her with obvious approval. She basked in it, and in the way his breath hitched and pupils dilated as his gaze skimmed her dress.

"You look lovely." His words had taken on a low, husky quality, and she felt an urge to lean closer. Maybe run a hand down his crisp shirt. Nuzzle her face into his freshly shaved neck and breathe deeply of the scent she knew she'd find there. A musky mix of spice and salt that would have her pressing her lips there for a taste…

"I knew you had to be around here somewhere. Sorry I'm late."

Kenneth's voice came from her side and she quickly jumped back from Noah, though she'd never taken the steps toward him she'd pictured in her mind. No, they'd remained several respectable feet apart during their exchange.

"It's okay, Kenny. We didn't even notice you weren't here." Noah's smile was charming but his eyes were hard.

"Noah, wasn't it?" Kenneth slipped a possessive arm around her. She took advantage of their all-too-civilized conversation to compose herself. He grabbed a champagne flute from a passing waiter and toasted into the air. "Nice of you to support Vanessa."

"Noah's a detective. He's here looking for Natalee's killer," Vanessa said. Her nerves fluttered at the thought that the killer could be anyone of the hundreds of people standing around them.

"And the man who attacked Vanessa," Noah said.

Kenneth's arm tightened at her waist. "Attacked?"

"That's what I was trying to tell you earlier." Actually, she hadn't wanted to discuss it, or reflect on it, so she hadn't tried hard at all. She filled him in with a barebones account of the previous evening, leaving out the details of her dinner with Noah.

"Thank God you're okay. Well, that explains a lot. I'm glad to hear someone's working on it."

"She deserves my undivided attention." Noah's eyes sparked with a light meant only for her. Was he thinking of the night before, when they'd shared drinks, and so much more? She'd felt a deep connection to him in those short hours.

"Do you see anyone suspicious?" Vanessa asked Noah.

"Nobody stands out. But I'll keep my eyes open."

"You do that," Kenneth said. "Vanessa deserves to relax and enjoy herself."

As if she could do that.

Noah stiffened suddenly, looking over her shoulder. "Well, I think I'd better move along."

Vanessa heard Lance's booming voice interrupt the conversation of the group behind her. She nodded in understanding, grateful that he was thoughtful enough to avoid added tension tonight. "Thanks for coming."

"I'll be nearby if you need me." His look was so intense that she couldn't fail to grasp his message. If her attacker was here, he would be ready to leap to her defense.

"He's popping up all over the place, isn't he?" Kenneth's gaze followed the other man through the crowd. Hers couldn't help but follow him, too, noting the confident way he carried himself. He maintained his easy charm and conversed with New York City's elite as if he were one of them and always had been.

Lance made his way to her, a satisfied smile curving his lips. "Looks like I underestimated you, Vanessa."

She nearly staggered with the rare compliment. "Well, thank you."

"I'm thinking we could put your newfound talents to good use. Have more of these auctions—not all for charity, of course—assuming this one is a success. We'll know more after the money comes in."

"The bidding will start soon. I'll start seating people in a few minutes."

"Did Vanessa tell you about her excitement last night?" Lance asked Kenneth.

"I just heard about it from—"

Sure that Kenneth was about to mention Noah's name, and that it wouldn't go over well with Lance, Vanessa interrupted. "We've just been talking about the break-in at the warehouse, and how I happened to stumble upon it at the wrong time."

If it hadn't been for Noah's dinner invitation, things could have been a lot different for her. She would have still been in the building, doing inventory or lost in her painting when the intruder broke in. If he'd been desperate enough, if Noah hadn't come back to check on her, would she have been killed? And would it have been as horrible as Natalee's death? She shivered, but Kenneth, his arm still around her, didn't seem to notice. She couldn't help thinking that Detective Noah Crandall would have noticed any little tremor of her body. His intense blue gaze missed nothing.

"Was anything damaged?"

"Only Vanessa's head," Lance said with a chuckle. "Thankfully, nothing was taken. I added a security guard, just in case."

Kenneth's gaze turned to her, but instead of expressing concern, his lips were pressed together in anger. "I can't believe you didn't tell me about it last night. You made me look like an idiot."

"There was nothing you could do. Besides, I'm okay now." And she had an auction to begin in just a few moments. Now wasn't the time. "I have to track down Mr. Lyle."

HE TRIED TO HIDE his disgust. *The crème de la crème, indeed.* A rare few had the refined appreciation for art Nigel had exhibited. And Nigel's son—present tonight, no doubt only to see how much money a certain item of his father's art collection was worth—was among the worst of the pretenders.

His mind only half on the circle of conversation going on around him, he made appropriate generic responses as he sipped his champagne and covertly glanced around the room. Three guards. And his angel sitting right out in the room for all to see. It had once been for Nigel's eyes only.

Though he regretted that his *Angel of Water* was now out in public, he couldn't help but feel some measure of pride that she was displayed so beautifully. Under her very own spotlight, each grain of sand—he'd mixed some into the paint—seemed to sparkle.

But her few minutes of fame were almost over. He *had* to get her back. She was his. If she couldn't be with Nigel, she belonged with him. She certainly didn't deserve to be sold off to the highest bidder as if she were some common whore.

His fingers tightened on the stem of his champagne flute, his smile frozen in place as he tried to focus on the chattering woman so obviously flirting with him. And she was so obviously married, too. She would never be one of his angels. Only the pure would ascend to their rightful place in heaven.

When the earthly elements were honored appropriately through sacrifice, aligning with heavenly demands, all would be well again.

The melodic tones of Vanessa Knight's voice caught his attention. She was looking particularly lovely this evening in her ebony dress, her hair flaring with mahogany highlights when she moved from spotlight to spotlight talking about the art. He wondered if he should paint her this way.

But no. He had other plans. She was Earth. Elemental and stable. Grounded and elegant, despite the shithead boyfriend who'd been milking her success tonight. He knew now that she was one of *them*. Just as he'd known Natalee was one of them. An angel on earth who deserved to be ascended to her rightful place. And he alone had the power to make that happen for her. He alone recognized their true purpose. He alone made the choice. He always followed his gut, and his gut told him she was the final element of his series.

The final angel to break free of her earthly bonds.

Even without Nigel, he had to be true to their vision.

He would paint the *Angel of Earth* as a tribute to his mentor, though it would never be seen by Nigel. He'd never see the *Angel of Fire* either.

Nor would any of the pretentious pricks parading around the ballroom. The *Angels* were his. His and Nigel's.

As pain stabbed at his chest, he excused himself from his overeager conversation partner and moved through the room.

Three guards. He'd find a way. He would not fail.

SEVEN

VANESSA BLESSED the endorphins that had her on a natural high as she sank into a nearby chair, kicked off her three-inch heels and rubbed her aching arches.

"You're glowing," Noah said, leaning over her shoulder. His breath grazed her ear, sending tingles of excitement across her already-heightened senses. He came around and sat in a chair beside her. "And you should be. You did a fabulous job."

"Attend many art auctions in your line of work, Detective?"

"Well, you got me there. But I heard what people were saying, and I can tell by the look of satisfaction on your face that you believe it was a hit. *You* were a big hit."

Around her, the empty tables held discarded paddles and empty glasses that testified that tonight hadn't just been a dream. She'd succeeded. In fact, she'd been congratulated on a fine job more times than she could count. The auction had gone smoothly, and now only a few stragglers remained to admire the pieces that would be delivered to them tomorrow. Several bidders had already taken their pieces with them.

If only her mother could see her now. She wished Sylvia Knight would have abandoned her monthly bridge night to attend. The money raised would help hundreds of families through the Warm Embrace Foundation. The reporter from *The New Yorker* had even promised a full article in their next magazine. Vanessa had made sure he was introduced to the board of the foundation at the auction, so that the focus would be where it belonged—much to Lance's chagrin.

If she smiled any bigger, her cheeks would ache. "You're right. It *was* a hit, wasn't it?"

"Damn right it was," Fiona said, overhearing her question as she came forward to grasp her shoulders and lean down for a quick hug. "Jesse's helping pack the truck with the last of the easels and pedestals that go back to the gallery. I have to run. But I wanted to tell you what a smash this was, and that I never doubted it for a second."

"You and Jesse were a big part of its success."

"That's sweet, but we all know who deserves most of the credit." Fiona hugged her again, her lips near Vanessa's ear. "Go get him, tiger. He's all yours." She smiled a goodbye at Noah and left them alone again.

Vanessa was on the verge of inviting him for a drink at the hotel's bar to celebrate when Kenneth appeared. He'd come and gone from her side all evening, mixing with whichever group seemed most popular at the time.

"You did it, baby." Kenneth pulled her out of her chair and into his arms. "Let's go celebrate. You made me proud."

"I made myself proud," she murmured, ducking away before he could kiss her.

"I've got late reservations for us and a few important guests at that French place nobody can get into. We'll have to hurry or we'll be late."

"Excuse me," Noah said, his expression neutral. "I'll leave you two to your evening."

"Wait." She didn't want the night to end this way. Things were too perfect, mostly because having Noah there had made her feel safe. She'd been able to focus on the auction. "Thank you."

"I'm just glad he didn't show up, but that doesn't mean he won't. Make sure you don't go anywhere alone."

"Did you get the lists you wanted from Lance?"

"No. But I'm not surprised. Now that the auction's over, if you could talk to him…"

"I'll try." She'd send them herself if Lance continued to stonewall them.

"If you could include the rosters of your previous art classes, that could be helpful, too."

One of her students could be a killer?

He read her distress. "I just want to cover all the bases. No reason to suspect anyone in particular yet." His gaze moved to Kenneth. "Make sure she gets home safe."

She tried to hide her disappointment when Noah walked away. "Who did you invite to this late dinner?" she asked, turning to Kenneth.

"My partners at the law firm and their spouses. And a few of my past clients." He bustled her through the lobby of the hotel and out to the curb.

She extricated herself from his hold as he hailed a cab. One immediately drove up. "What if tonight hadn't been a success? What if I hadn't won the blue ribbon for best in show?"

"What?" He frowned in annoyance. "Baby, we can talk about this in the cab."

She allowed him to settle them in the taxi and give the driver directions, but she didn't let the subject drop. "Well?"

"Well, what?"

"What if I hadn't been a hit?"

"I would have spoken to Atherton about keeping you on, of course." He squeezed her knee, then slid his hand up her thigh until it disappeared under the hem of her dress. She stiffened against the contact, but he didn't seem to notice. "Or I would have found you a job elsewhere, if that's what you wanted. But as my wife, you won't ever have to work again."

Her eyes widened. "Pardon?"

"Marry me, Vanessa Knight." Shadows chased light across his face as the cab sped along the dark city streets toward the restaurant.

"You're...you're asking me—" no, really, he was *telling,* a part of her brain corrected, "—to marry you, and it's in a cab?"

She couldn't help it—she burst out laughing. She had half a mind to lean forward and ask the driver to stop and let her out, but who knew if she would be able to find another cab in this area of town on a busy Friday night. Besides, their destination loomed in the distance. She couldn't help but feel alarm. She'd soon be surrounded by Kenneth and his adoring fan club.

"I know it's not moonlight and roses." Kenneth pulled his hand away from her leg and straightened his tuxedo jacket as they pulled up to the curb in front of one of the most posh restaurants in the city. "But we have dinner and champagne waiting inside."

"Along with a dozen or two of *your* closest friends," she muttered.

She followed Kenneth inside, where they were led to a private dining room. She was welcomed by his colleagues with hearty handshakes and a few hugs but quickly forgotten as he regaled them with his latest conquests in court. She forced herself to eat some of the meal, wishing she were anywhere but there, then tried to focus on the conversation around her, stifling the yawns that were starting to hit her in waves. It was close to midnight and she was exhausted. She'd been going almost nonstop for weeks, and her experiences the night before had left her out of

sorts as well as sleep-deprived. And with the adrenaline
rush of the auction gone, her headache was back. She
reached for Kenneth's hand and gave it a squeeze, hoping he'd catch the unspoken request to take her home.
Then, tomorrow, when she was at full strength again,
she'd break up with him.

Kenneth turned and gave her a smile. He cleared his
throat dramatically, catching everyone at the table's attention. Vanessa swallowed a groan. He didn't have to make
their departure a big production.

"Everyone, we're glad you could come this evening to
celebrate Vanessa's success, but also to share in our announcement. We're engaged."

Vanessa's mouth dropped open and her face heated
with anger. She hadn't agreed to marry him. But amid
the congratulations and the bottles of champagne that—
of course—had to follow such an announcement, she resigned herself to another half hour at the restaurant.

"Well, that'll ensure a victory," one of Kenneth's coworkers—his name was John something—said with a
wink.

"That has nothing to do with the case," he said, "though
it certainly won't hurt." A chorus of laughter greeted his
statement.

"What are they talking about?" she hissed into his ear,
pulling on his arm until he looked at her.

He shrugged. "That stolen Van Gogh the police recently recovered? My new client is accused of the crime.
I guess they think my having a fiancée with connections
in the art world will influence the judge in a positive way
or something."

Kenneth had known exactly how things would look.
Hot rage flooded Vanessa and she stood. "I'm leaving."
Something in her tone must have warned him that she

was serious. He immediately rose, too, saying goodbye to the group for them both.

A short cab ride later, Kenneth broke the silence as they walked into her apartment building. "You've been quiet since we left the restaurant. Is this some kind of silent treatment?"

"I'm thinking." In actuality, she was trying to decide the best way to break things off. Just last night, she'd accused Noah of using her. He had nothing on Kenneth. She hadn't wanted to break up tonight and ruin the good mood she was in, but things were getting out of hand.

"Thinking. That sounds ominous." He added a chuckle that echoed along with their footsteps in the stairwell. Once again, he wasn't taking her seriously.

"I never said I'd marry you," she began as she led him inside her apartment, then closed the door to give them the privacy she'd need to deliver her blow. She made the mistake of pausing to take a deep breath before forging ahead. He rushed into the breach.

"That's just a formality," he said.

"We're not right for each other."

He went completely still, then forced a grin. "You're exhausted. I won't stay here tonight. I've got a few things to do in the office before we leave for your parents' house tomorrow anyway."

She smothered a groan. She'd forgotten about their plan to spend Saturday afternoon and Sunday at her parents' place in the Hamptons. This night, which had started on such a high note, was going downhill, fast.

"Get some sleep and it'll all be clearer in the morning."

"I don't need—"

He stopped her protest with a kiss to her forehead. "I'll be by to pick you up tomorrow afternoon. One o'clock?"

"I won't be back from Natalee's funeral and the gathering at the Sandovals' house until at least two."

"Right. Forgot about that." He spun toward the door. "Two it is then."

"But—"

He was gone before she could object. Unspent frustration plucked at her nerves, wound tight as a guitar string. Suddenly she didn't feel the least bit tired. She was wired.

She stalked around her apartment, punching a pillow, clattering a teacup as she made some tea, muttering to herself about her oh-so-sensitive boyfriend.

Ex-boyfriend.

Whether he'd heard her or not, she had broken up with him. She'd make him realize that tomorrow. Before they went to her parents' house. Because visiting her parents, and her brothers, who were lawyers like Kenneth, would be an unmitigated disaster. They would all be on his side. And smooth-talking Kenneth would know how to work that, along with everything else, to his advantage.

There was at least one thing she could do tonight to right some of the wrongs in her life. From her purse, she pulled the flash drive she used to bring work from the gallery home and slipped it into its slot on her computer.

NOAH PEEKED in on a softly snoring Diego before closing the bedroom door and flopping onto the couch in the living room. After scouting the auction without any successful leads, Diego had become increasingly morose. Once home, they'd discussed the case until Noah had pressed Diego to have a drink to relax and he'd finally crashed, several days of stress and lack of sleep having caught up to him.

Noah had felt tempted to indulge too. If nothing else, a bit of alcohol might have loosened his jaw, sore after having had to grit his teeth and bear it every time Kenneth had sidled up to Vanessa. Something about the guy rubbed him the wrong way. That, combined with the lack of a killer's head to bang against the wall, was enough to leave him frustrated on many levels.

At least Vanessa was safe. He'd watched her slide into a cab with Kenny-boy before he'd forced Diego into a cab of their own.

The muffled musical tune of a cell phone had Noah lunging for the pocket of the rented tuxedo jacket draped on a chair before he realized it was Diego's ringtone, not his own. He'd been hoping Damian Manchester from SSAM would call with information, but so far the fax he'd sent hadn't led to anything other than Damian's promise to look into it.

He found the phone under Diego's discarded jacket on the breakfast bar. When the caller ID came up as the NYPD station, he didn't hesitate to answer.

"Hello?"

"Diego, I've got a tip for you on your niece's case," a female voice said.

"Yeah?" Noah kept his voice low, hoping she'd continue to mistake him for his friend. If this woman was willing to help with the case, he couldn't let her hang up.

There was a pause on the other end. Shit. He needed this tip. Diego needed this tip. But Diego was passed out in the other room, finally getting some much-needed rest.

"Who is this?" The female's voice was now laced with suspicion. "Tell me, or I'm hanging up right now."

He switched tactics. "My name is Detective Noah Crandall from the Chicago P.D. I'm a friend, here to help Diego find Natalee's killer. Please, if you know anything that would help—" he glanced toward the closed bedroom door, "—he could really use a lead right now."

There was another period of silence and he thought maybe the woman had in fact hung up. When she spoke it was hurried and low. "A call just came in to 911. A body was found in a townhouse on Park Avenue. The wife says she and her husband came home late from some function. Involved Atherton's Art. Name rang a bell, you know?"

Noah's breath seized in his chest. A lead? A real, solid lead?

"The husband was found dead in his study an hour after they got home, when she went looking for him because he hadn't come to bed. He'd been strangled, and the painting he'd purchased at the auction was gone. Apparently, he'd stayed up to admire it while having a nightcap."

"You've got a lot of information, Officer..." He waited, but she didn't supply him with her name.

"Look, a detective is on the scene now. ME should arrive soon. Just thought Diego should know in case it's connected. If you ask me, he got a bum rap for the way he reacted at the scene. We may bleed blue, but we're human."

"Thanks." The line went dead before the word was out of his mouth.

He quickly fished his own cell phone out of his pocket again and dialed a number from his contact list. Despite the time—nearly one o'clock, and only an hour earlier in Chicago—Damian Manchester answered on the first ring.

"Damian, it's Detective Crandall. I'm sorry about the late hour."

"Noah. What can I do for you?" There was no fatigue in the man's voice, but then, Noah hadn't expected any. Damian Manchester rarely slept. He was too haunted by the monsters of society he hunted. He'd founded the Society for the Study of the Aberrant Mind, better known as SSAM, several years after his teenage daughter—also nicknamed Sam—had died at the hands of a serial killer. The murderer was never caught, and Damian had taken the investigation into his own hands. Though he had yet to find his daughter's killer, he and his elite team of profilers, security experts, criminalists and other specialists were well-known for their success with other cases.

"There may have been a development in that case I sent you."

"Holt's still looking over the fax and checking with his contacts at the FBI for related murders. What news do you have?"

"I just received a very strange call. A tip. There was another murder tonight, and it might be related."

"But you're suspecting it'll be difficult to be invited to the crime scene."

"Exactly. I was hoping…"

"Say no more. I'll put in a call."

Noah felt as if a boulder had been lifted from his shoulders. A call from Damian Manchester could move mountains. "I appreciate it. My friend's in bad shape."

"Understandable." Yeah, if anyone could understand the pain of losing a loved one to violent crime, this man could.

"NYPD is on the scene now. And tomorrow is Natalee's funeral."

"And the killer could show up there." Some serial killers had a morbid fascination with the funerals, graves or the scenes of their crimes. There was a possibility that their man would be there.

"I could really use some backup. I don't want to trouble Diego any more than we have to tomorrow."

"If you can keep an eye on things at the funeral, I can send Becca and Holt to the crime scene," Damian offered immediately. Becca Haney was one of the newly trained security experts on Damian's staff. Noah assumed Holt was a profiler. Two members of SSAM's elite team, and they'd been placed at Noah's disposal without hesitation.

"I can't tell you how much I appreciate this."

"No problem. You've helped us out with a few cases here in Chicago." The recent Fearmonger case had involved someone Damian loved as much as the daughter he'd lost. "Besides, the important thing is catching a killer before he kills again. SSAM worked with the NYPD on a cold case a couple years ago. I know some people there. I'll see if they can keep the processing of the crime scene to a minimum until my people get on site."

After hanging up, Noah used his phone to check his emails. Vanessa's name caught his eye. His lips curved into a smile as he saw what she had sent. The file that contained the list of auction guests and the artists who'd donated. And another file that contained her art class rosters for the past two years. She had to have gone behind Atherton's back to get him these.

He glanced at the time the email was sent, his grin growing. If Vanessa was on the computer at one in the morning, she wasn't doing other things with Kenny-boy.

EIGHT

VANESSA CRACKED one eye open, reluctant to face the day from hell. Natalee's funeral, followed by officially breaking up with Kenneth, then topped off with visiting her family to explain what they would probably see as her throwing away the best thing that ever happened to her. It promised to be a banner day.

All on the heels of her glowing debut in the world of charity art auctions.

What a difference a day makes.

She forced herself to rise and shower, dressing in a sleeveless charcoal-gray dress, slim black belt and heels before trudging to the kitchen to put on a pot of coffee. She opened the morning paper, hoping the review of the auction in the Arts & Culture section would cheer her. Despite the resounding positivity of the review and the emphasis on the Warm Embrace charity, tears pricked at her eyelids. Natalee had worked hard to make this auction a reality, and she should be celebrating its success. Instead, her friends and family were preparing to honor the bright light that had been Natalee Ortega.

A knock at her door startled her. She wasn't expecting anyone, and certainly not at eight in the morning. Through the peephole, she saw Noah and felt her spirits lift. Maybe she wouldn't have to face this day alone after all. She opened the door and took in his well-groomed appearance as well as the tailored cut of his dark suit.

"Hi. I know it's early and we're not invited."

She peered around him and spied Diego Sandoval standing on the stairs, his hesitant, hunched posture indicating his uncertainty about their welcome. Or maybe he was weighed down by the stress of the day. He gave a small nod in greeting, but his face was grim.

"Please, come in. Would you like some coffee?" She led them inside and closed the door.

"That would be great." Noah followed her to the kitchen, with Diego lagging behind. "We thought maybe you'd be going to the funeral this morning, and that you could use some company."

"It was thoughtful of you to include me." She stretched on tiptoe to reach into the cupboards and removed a couple of mugs as they sat down at her table. The presence of two large bodies made her small kitchen seem positively tiny. "I was able to get the day off from the gallery, but Fiona and Jesse weren't so lucky. It would be good to have company."

"And we wanted to thank you for sending that file with the names we've been trying to get from Atherton."

Vanessa shrugged. "He should have given it to you first thing. Just keep my name out of it, please."

"There's another reason we're here." Diego's hard tone surprised Vanessa.

"It can wait," Noah said.

"What? I'm not going to sugarcoat it. We need her help."

She filled three mugs with coffee and set them on the table, then offered sugar and cream, which they declined. "Okay, let's have it," she said, taking a seat. "What else can I do to help?"

"I was going to wait until after the funeral." Noah sent a look toward Diego. "There was another murder last night. Somebody you may have known."

She pressed a hand to her mouth. "Who?" *Dear God, please don't let it be Fiona or Jesse, or anyone else I care about.*

"A man named Arthur Cromby. I checked the list you emailed. He attended the auction."

She remembered speaking with Mr. Cromby and his wife. Again, she was struck by how much difference a day could make. He'd been alive and breathing yesterday. Today, he no longer walked this earth. "What happened to him?"

"He was strangled in his home, late last night."

"You think it was Natalee's killer who was responsible?" She shivered.

"We don't know yet."

Diego grunted, drawing their attention. "But Natalee's murder, the one last night, and your attack…they all have one thing in common."

Vanessa nodded. "The gallery."

"You," Diego corrected.

She looked up sharply, her stomach twisting. She pushed her bitter coffee away.

"Or the gallery," Noah insisted. "You don't have to scare her."

"Maybe she *should* be scared."

She held up a hand. "I'm already scared. After the attack…"

Diego's red-rimmed eyes pinned her. "Did you know Arthur Cromby?"

"Yes. He's been a customer of the gallery for over a year now. He collects the works of up-and-coming artists, particularly painters whose medium of choice is oil. I thought he might like a particular piece when I saw it and I steered him toward it last night." She rubbed her arms against a sudden chill. "That poor man."

"The painting he bought at the auction was stolen, along with a few other valuables that were in his study at the time. But the thief didn't bother to go through the rest of the house, or to find the safe that was hidden in the study."

"So you think the painting was his primary target, and the rest was just covering up the crime."

Diego nodded. "Which is why we need someone experienced in the art world, and who knows this painting in particular, to help us."

"But what can I do?"

Noah took her hand and she was surprised to see it was shaking. He squeezed it. "We need a detailed description of the painting and a list of possible suspects—people who may have had an interest in the piece, the name and address of whoever donated it, and anything you can tell us about the artist. Mrs. Cromby said the painting was unsigned."

"That's right." She remembered searching for a signature herself.

"Your boss will be pissed." Diego's eyes met hers as if challenging her to defy her employer.

She'd already risked her job by sending those files behind his back. She wasn't sure she could go against Lance again. Not when she was so close to having the career she'd always wanted.

Noah spoke into the silence that seemed to drag on. "Think about it before you answer. We want to focus on Natalee this morning, anyway."

"Natalee comes first," Diego agreed, rising from the kitchen table. Vanessa scooped up their empty coffee mugs, intending to rinse them quickly in the sink, but Diego touched her arm as she moved past him. "My niece will continue to come first until we find her killer. If this guy is after you too…"

He left the thought unspoken, but she caught the gist. Despite the fact nothing had happened at the auction, they still felt she was in danger. That she was, perhaps, their only link to the killer. But if the man they sought had been after the painting, now that he had it, wouldn't she cease to be a target?

Not if you can help them.

She had specific knowledge about the art world. If that was enough to help the police find the killer, she was in danger all over again. Would her funeral be next?

THE CHURCH OF ST. PAUL was a majestic stone structure that served as a hub of activity in the neighborhood most of the Sandoval family inhabited. Natalee had spoken so fondly and so often of her family and where she'd grown up that Vanessa felt as if she knew the people filling the pews, waiting to say goodbye. Diego went ahead of them, headed for the front of the church. As she walked the center aisle beside Noah, Vanessa prepared to excuse herself and take a seat near the back, but he grabbed her hand and tugged her along with him.

"There's room up front yet. Come sit with me."

"But that should be reserved for the family," she whispered back. Diego took his seat in the front row, next to Natalee's grandmother, Estella. He bent to whisper something in her ear and give her a kiss on the cheek. Estella turned to observe their arrival, then rose and came forward to Noah, her arms out to embrace him. Though plump, she was pale and looked fragile in his arms. "*Hijo.* It's good to finally have you back."

Hijo? Had Natalee's grandmother—Diego's mom— just called Noah *son?*

"Estella, I'm sorry…" He stopped, his throat working against the backdrop of her white hair as he swallowed.

Mrs. Sandoval nodded and squeezed him once more before releasing him and turning to her. Tears lit her brown eyes as she took Vanessa's hands. The two of them had last seen each other behind Atherton's Art, when Estella had come to see the spot in the alley where her granddaughter had been abducted, leaving candles and a wooden cross as a type of vigil while they'd waited to find her again. At the time, there'd been hope she'd be found alive. But that hope had only lasted a precious, short time.

"It would mean a lot to Natalee that you're here today." Estella smiled. "It means a lot to me too."

Vanessa nodded and sniffed. With effort, she swallowed her tears. "She was a special young woman, and she'll be missed by so many people."

They took their seats in the front as music indicated the start of the service. Noah sat by her during the mass and personal tributes to Natalee. He was there for her when she returned to her seat in tears after delivering her own speech about Natalee's rare talent for art and her gift for dealing with people. Her words seemed so small, such an ineffective way of describing what the young woman had come to mean to her. Noah's arm wrapped around her shoulders, providing a solid, comforting warmth as she dabbed at her eyes.

Diego provided the same support to his sister, whose sobs could be heard throughout the church until the soft notes of the choir and organ in the rear balcony echoed off the tall cream-colored walls. As Vanessa said a silent prayer for the Sandoval and Ortega families, her gaze wandered to the stained-glass windows that sent slivers of light across the pews.

After the ceremony concluded, everyone was invited

for refreshments. Though Noah walked her to Estella's home, Vanessa was surprised when he remained by her side after their arrival.

Natalee had such a caring and close family. It wasn't fair that they'd lost her. The funeral Vanessa had attended for her own grandfather a few months ago had been a stilted, sedate affair followed by a catered buffet. Every clink of a polished silver fork against a bone-china plate could be heard in the absence of conversation. Here, colorful mismatched pots and platters piled with food lined every available counter and table space. The comforting sounds of easy conversation and, yes, even laughter, surrounded her.

Noah handed her a paper plate and spooned some kind of delicious-smelling rice dish onto it. "*Arroz con gandules.* You'll love it. And that's *pernil.*"

"Looks like a pork shoulder."

"It is. Taste it." He placed a slice on her plate before loading his own.

After they'd selected their food, he led her outside to the building's common area, where they claimed a couple of folding lawn chairs placed under a shade tree. She observed her surroundings as she managed a few bites.

Seeing what had drawn her attention, he gave a sad smile. "The neighborhood really pulls together in a crisis."

She balanced her plate on her lap. "Was your family close?" The expression in his eyes was suddenly shuttered. Recognizing she'd struck a painful chord, she rushed on. "My family isn't close either. Not like this."

"They've got something special here, all right." Admiration was clear in his voice. "They always have."

"I'm going to have this someday." At her quiet words, his gaze swung to her. "The family, the closeness." *The unconditional love.*

He studied her a moment before nodding. "I believe you will."

"But you won't?"

He shook his head. "It's not for everyone."

Yeah, right.

A buzzing in his pocket had him reaching for his vibrating cell phone. "Sorry. I've been waiting for this call." He turned his attention to whoever was on the other end of the phone connection. "You're here?…Do you want to head over now?" He set his plate on the ground. "I'll meet you there."

A stab of disappointment hit her. She covered it by taking a sip of her iced tea. "You have to leave?"

"I'm afraid so." He lowered his voice. "The crime scene at Cromby's house has been made available for a limited time to a special investigation team I called in from Chicago. They just got off the plane. I'm meeting them at the estate."

"What about Diego?"

Their gazes found the man slumped at a picnic table yards away, his tie askew, a beer in his hand. People around him were talking, but he appeared disengaged. "He's got enough to deal with today. He'll be better off here, surrounded by family."

"How about me?"

Noah's confused gaze turned to her. "What?"

"I'm available. I wouldn't touch anything, I'd just *be* there. An extra set of eyes, maybe?"

He was shaking his head before she finished her sentence. "It's the scene of a murder. You don't want to see that."

"The body is gone by now, isn't it?" There could still be blood and other stuff she didn't want to think about. Still, something made her want to go with him. He had supported her at the auction and the funeral. She wanted to return the gesture. "Besides, you said you needed my help and I'd rather feel useful."

"Maybe you could work with the mindhunter to help develop a profile of the killer."

She glanced at her watch and winced. She was supposed to meet Kenneth soon. She still had to find a way to break things off with him. "I have to be somewhere at two, but I have a couple hours. I'm at your disposal, Detective Crandall."

Rising, he took her plate and cup and tossed them into a nearby garbage bag. "Let's go offer Estella and Olivia our condolences."

"You should eat something."

Diego looked up from the cooler he'd been reaching into and met the gaze of his older brother Marcos. He huffed out a sad laugh. "Doesn't really matter what I do. Won't bring Natalee back."

Marcos took the bottle of beer from his unresisting fingers.

The contents of the last bottle had been swirling in his knotted stomach, anyway, as he'd listened to the stories about his dearly departed niece. Did nobody else see how futile sitting here, remembering, was? He was ready to chase down some perpetrator and slam him up against a wall, but he couldn't even do that. They'd threatened to take his badge away if he didn't take some time off.

"True," Marcos said. "Nothing will bring her back now. But Natalee would want you to continue life as normal."

"What? I'm not supposed to grieve? That's bullshit."

"Of course you can grieve, but we also honor her by living our life the best way we can, not sulking in a corner."

"Let him sulk," Olivia said. Their older sister came

from the kitchen doorway where she'd been listening, un-observed. "He doesn't have anything better to do."

The beer in his gut threatened to rise up and embar-rass him, so Diego grabbed the bottle back from Marcos and twisted off the top. He took a quick swig to keep ev-erything in place.

"Don't be so hard on him," Marcos said in his defense.

But Diego didn't want defending. Not today, of all days. Maybe not ever. What he'd done might cost Olivia justice for her daughter.

"She's right," Diego said, unable to meet their eyes. "Because of my actions, I'm sitting around here on my ass instead of being able to do a goddamn thing about this shit." He stood suddenly and tossed his bottle into a nearby trashcan, taking some pleasure in the clink of shattering glass as it hit the side of the metal container. It echoed the shattering of hope he'd felt in church earlier as they'd paid tribute to Natalee.

Olivia's dark eyes took his measure. "So what are you going to do about it?"

"Noah and I are working together to find the monster on our own."

She glanced around. "I don't see Noah here. He and Miss Knight said goodbye an hour ago. All I see is *you,* moping around."

He hissed out a breath as he realized she was right. Noah was nowhere to be found, nor was Vanessa. "I prom-ised the family justice, and I meant it."

"And yet you've been thrown off the case. What good is that?"

Diego restrained himself from grabbing his sister's arms and shaking her. Her anger was at the situation, not at him. But, damn it, he had a right to be angry too. Olivia hadn't seen Natalee lying on the ground, cold and dead, her body posed as if it were some doll that could be used up and thrown away. He doubted she'd have been able to keep from running to her, snatching her up and cradling her. He still remembered the way the dead weight of her head had felt against his chest before he'd come to his senses and laid her back down.

"I'm doing all I can," he said, all heat and passion gone from his words. He was tired.

"It's not enough." Olivia turned and left.

Diego barely felt his brother's hand on his shoulder, he was so numb.

No, it wasn't enough.

NOAH FOLLOWED Vanessa through a wrought-iron gate and up a short walk to the Park Avenue townhouse where Cromby had been murdered. The quiet wealth of the neighborhood around them was so different from the Sandovals' tiny apartment home that the change was jarring. The woman beside him didn't seem overly impressed, and he wondered what Vanessa's life had been like growing up. He'd received indications that her family had money, mostly from things Kenneth had said and the way she'd moved with confidence and grace through the ritzy auction crowd. Had her family home been anything like this? He got the feeling he and Vanessa were from different dimensions and it ruffled feathers he never knew he had.

He knocked on the door. "Maybe Lurch will answer."

Vanessa grinned. "It is a little on the imposing side, isn't it?"

"Not your style, Miss Knight?" he asked, turning the knob. Since it was a crime scene and the new widow had reportedly removed herself to a swanky hotel, he hadn't expected anyone to answer if he knocked. Except, maybe, Lurch.

The corners of her mouth turned downward at his flip question. "Not in the least."

"Ah, so you're more the picket-fence-front-porch-swing-dog-in-the-yard type." The type that usually sent him running in the other direction.

She marched past him through the door he held open. They followed the sound of voices through the marble foyer and down a hallway to an open door. Noah heard her suck in a breath. No doubt she'd detected the stench of recent death that still hung in the air. Thank goodness the body had been removed by the medical examiner hours ago, or it would have been punch-to-the-gut overwhelming.

"Vanessa, wait." He stopped her outside the room from which voices of the crime scene team drifted. "You don't have to go in there."

"I want to help." Determination flared in her eyes as she tilted her small point of a chin higher. She'd do anything for Natalee. Hell, she was the kind of woman who would slay dragons for anybody she cared about. The sparks of temper and protectiveness he'd seen over the past few days told him that much.

"Be careful where you walk." He turned on his heel and walked into the study. Four men stood at one end of the large room, surrounded by floor-to-ceiling bookcases and a few tasteful but comfortable armchairs. An empty easel stood near the desk at the opposite end of the room. The men turned as they entered.

"Noah," one of them said, silver eyes warming in greeting.

"Damian." Noah recovered from his surprise and stepped forward, taking the man's hand in a firm handshake. "I didn't expect you to come."

"I think I may be able to personally help this case."

Seeing Noah's arched eyebrows, he continued. "My ex-wife has connections in the New York City art world."

"And she'll help?"

The older man frowned, deep creases bracketing his mouth. "It'll take a little persuading. Perhaps even some begging. But once she understands the situation, she'll help."

Beside him, a man about Noah's age extended his hand. "I'm Dr. Holt Patterson, one of the profilers at SSAM."

Noah returned his handshake. "I appreciate you coming so quickly."

"I'm glad to help. Besides, my son wanted to see the Big Apple. Hard to explain to a seven-year-old that there wasn't really a giant apple." He winked at Vanessa, and Noah drew her forward to meet the team.

"This is Vanessa Knight. She works at Atherton's Art and organized the auction where the stolen painting was sold last night. Natalee was her intern at the art gallery."

The other two men in the room were introduced as an NYPD detective from a different precinct than Diego's and a crime scene analyst who had helped with the initial processing of the scene and was there to supervise SSAM's involvement.

"The room's already been cleared by the principal investigators, but the NYPD wants someone on hand to document anything our group touches or does," Damian explained. They probably wanted to learn from the well-respected SSAM professionals, as well.

A woman joined them, entering from the French doors that opened onto a square of neatly trimmed grass inhabited by several Greek statues. He recognized Becca Haney, a security agent at SSAM, from the case he'd helped with in Chicago. She stepped carefully around the area where the body had been, sticking to the perimeter of the room.

The pixielike blonde gave him a broad smile. "Hey, Noah. I just finished a security sweep."

"And?" Damian's tone was all business.

"No signs of a break-in. Whoever did this either simply walked in the front door or was invited in."

"So Arthur Cromby may have known his killer?" Noah asked.

"Not only is it possible, it's likely. It would explain why there were no alarms set, even though the place is equipped with a security system and he'd just brought home a painting for which he'd paid well over twenty thousand dollars."

Cromby had obviously trusted whoever followed him home from the auction. Noah mentally reviewed the myriad of faces he'd observed the evening before. "Mrs. Cromby didn't hear anything? Didn't know her husband had plans to meet with someone?"

The NYPD detective spoke up. "She says she took a long bubble bath and had music playing. The master suite is upstairs *and* at the opposite end of the house, so it's possible she wouldn't have heard a doorbell or people talking."

"Or a phone call," Holt added. "And the victim was strangled, which in itself implies he knew his killer. Trusted him enough to let him get close."

"You assume it's a *him,* then?" Vanessa asked.

Holt nodded. "Cromby wasn't tall, but he was fit. Would have been difficult for a woman to overpower him. There's no sign of struggle here, other than some claw marks near the victim's throat, which were probably made by Cromby when he tried to get the lanyard off him."

"Surveillance?" Damian directed his question to Becca.

She shook her head, frowning. "The cameras were off. Apparently they're only on when the alarm system is set. But I had our communications guy look into the phone records and he just got back to me. Cromby received a phone call around eleven o'clock last night, an hour before he was discovered by his wife."

Noah mentally crossed his fingers. "Please tell me we have the number."

Becca grinned. "We do. It narrows the field, but not by a lot. It came from the hotel where the auction was held. And more specifically, from the public phone in the lobby."

Vanessa gasped beside him. Noah didn't like the sudden paleness of her face. "So the killer *was* at the auction?"

"That, or observing from close by," Becca said.

The NYPD detective cleared his throat. "I've got someone gathering whatever the hotel's surveillance cameras may have captured in that lobby at that time." He grinned sheepishly. "Wish we had the luxury of moving through unofficial channels, like SSAM." Damian Manchester wasn't above pursuing information by whatever means necessary.

"Which is why we're glad you're here, Vanessa." Holt punctuated his statement with a small smile meant to put her at ease. "There are other leads we can pursue in the meantime. You may be able to fill in some blanks, especially regarding the painting Arthur Cromby had just acquired. It went missing, along with several other items."

"But you don't really think the thief was after the other stuff." Vanessa's guess was met with a nod.

"We think that was to try to throw us off, but it was poorly done. Whoever this is may be familiar with violence, but isn't really a thief," Holt explained.

And didn't that make Noah feel oh-so-much better? Vanessa was in the middle of this mess, had already been attacked, and was putting herself in more danger simply by helping them.

Because he'd asked her to. *Hell*.

NINE

"I UNDERSTAND YOU sent Noah the guest list," Damian Manchester said. "That'll be a good place to start. But if there's anything you can tell us about the guests, it would help guide us." Vanessa frowned. "I know many of those people are rich, famous, or both, not to mention notorious for prosecuting when their privacy is violated, but you never know what small piece of information might lead us to the killer."

This was for Natalee. And Arthur Cromby. And whoever else this guy had hurt or planned to hurt. "I'll help," she said. "But I need your promise you'll be as discreet as possible when talking to these people."

Damian nodded. "Of course."

"There are other notes that might be helpful. They're at the gallery but I only have about an hour."

"It's vital that we get started on that list." Noah's brisk tone had her narrowing her eyes at him. "Kenny-boy will just have to wait."

She felt her hackles rise. "I wasn't suggesting…" What was it with him today? Since leaving the Sandovals' and heading to Cromby's house, it was as if he were deliberately trying to push her buttons. She sucked in a breath to control the hot temper he'd stoked and dug down deep for patience. "I need a ride to the gallery and I have to be home within a couple hours." Kenneth she *might* be able to put off, but her mother? Not a chance.

Noah scowled. "Sorry we're inconveniencing your *personal* plans."

Her mouth dropped open, but she promptly closed it. Confused by Noah's sudden coldness, she turned her shoulder to him, addressing Damian and Holt instead. "I'll get you the notes on our clients, and if it's possible to answer your questions within the next two hours, I'd appreciate it."

Holt was much more accommodating. "Of course. We can talk now, in the other room and then Noah can take you to the gallery."

"I just need to make a quick call first."

After Noah and Holt escorted her to the dining room down the hall where they could sit at a table, they moved to the other side of the long room and bent their heads in quiet conversation, giving her some privacy.

She tried Kenneth's cell phone, but he didn't answer. He was with clients at all hours, it seemed, especially with a trial starting Monday morning, so she left a message. "I won't be able to go with you today to my parents' house. I still intend on going, but I need to do it alone. We can see each other Sunday night and discuss, um…things."

Hanging up, she caught Noah watching her, questions darkening his blue eyes. She waved to the cherry-wood chairs surrounding the table that had been polished to a mirrorlike shine. "Gentlemen, how can I help?" She was suddenly eager to get on the road and put some distance between herself and the city, even if it was to go to her mother's house.

Holt pushed his glasses up farther on the bridge of his nose. "I'd like your help shaping my profile of the killer. The painting is a key piece. We just need to discover why. Noah filled us in about the attack on you at the warehouse two nights ago. If it is related, the guy was likely after the painting then too."

"And if I hadn't interrupted him, he would have had the painting that night and Cromby would still be alive." In her peripheral vision, she saw Noah look away. It was her fault a man was dead. Her fault a woman had lost her husband. Her stomach churned.

"Noah doesn't remember the piece from the auction," Holt said.

"I was too busy observing the crowd." Noah's words were clipped.

"So we need you to recall whatever details you can," Holt continued.

Vanessa forced herself to focus, zoning in on Holt's calm, melodic cadence rather than Noah's frown. "There was something about that piece."

"What?"

"Nothing I could put my finger on, or describe to you. It was just…different. It spoke to me, if that makes sense."

"Had you seen it before?"

She shook her head. "Not before it arrived for the auction about a week ago. Natalee had shown me a picture weeks ago, but it hadn't done the painting justice. She did the paperwork on the donation. It was from the Springfield family. Nigel Springfield had died just a few weeks before, and I got the impression his son Lawrence didn't appreciate the arts like Nigel did."

"Did you know Nigel? Was his death suspicious?"

"I only knew him in passing. Saw him at a couple of functions to support the local arts. His reputation was strong, though, as a true patron. To give you an idea, there's a hall at the New York City Museum of the Arts named after him." She thought back to the article she'd read about his death. "If I recall, he was diagnosed with some type of cancer several months ago. Nothing suspicious. He was in his early sixties."

Holt wrote down some information on his pad of paper, then met her eyes. He was a handsome man. There was a friendly, boy-next-door innocence about him that was attractive. But when she looked closer, his hazel-gold eyes were almost sad. His hair was darker than Noah's, more brown than blond. And his smile didn't light her up inside.

And the fact that she was comparing this man—or any man—to Noah Crandall was alarming. As if he was some kind of benchmark for excellence.

Holt waited expectantly and she realized she'd missed his question. "The painting," he said. "You said there was something about it. What did you mean by that?"

Gooseflesh rose up on her arms. "Shivers. It gave me shivers when I looked at it." They probably didn't understand, but some works spoke to her, as if she were in tune with the feelings of their creators, or their subject matter, on another level. "It was a powerful piece, full of emotion."

"Any idea who the artist was?"

Absently, she rubbed her bare arms. "There was no signature. No stamp of the artist."

"Perhaps the Springfields know," Noah suggested.

She scoffed. "Nigel Springfield may have known, but I doubt his son, Lawrence, did. He's the polar opposite of his father when it comes to art appreciation. Oh, he *appreciates* the millions his father's collection will no doubt bring him when the rest of it goes up for auction next week at Sotheby's, but that's about it."

"Why did he donate this piece to the gallery if he's auctioning the rest elsewhere?" Holt mirrored her posture. He was easy to talk to. She imagined he was good at his job profiling criminals. What had Noah called him?

A mindhunter. Yes, she could believe it. Holt Patterson with his sad hazel eyes could gently probe her brain for the information he sought and she probably wouldn't even realize it.

"Taxes. It was an unsigned, unknown piece. Compared to the rest of Nigel's collection, it was nothing. His son will probably have a lot of estate taxes due. A donation to charity would be one way to offset some of those. You know, if you check the catalog we sent out, there'll be a picture of the painting."

"Catalog? Can you bring us a copy of that too?"

"Sure. There's an extra one at the gallery." As long as Lance wasn't around. He'd flay her hide for helping the SSAM team. They weren't even official police investigators.

"Before you leave, I'd like to get an expert's take on the meaning behind the artist's work."

She pushed back from the table, feeling restless. "Mind if I walk? I think I can picture it—the painting—better if I walk."

Holt waved a hand. "Be my guest." He leaned over his pad, pen poised as if expecting some important details. She'd try her best. She wanted the killer caught as much as the rest of them did.

Walking back and forth behind Noah's chair, she pushed the rest of the world away. "Oil painting. Twenty-four inches wide by thirty-six inches tall. A woman is the main subject, and fills the foreground. Her eyes are closed, but her face is raised toward the moonlit night sky, her arms raised on either side of her head as if begging for something." She'd had the impression the woman was seeking divine intervention. But for what? "Her hair is dark, and seems wet, but is fanned out around her."

"Why do you say *wet?*" Holt asked. "How can you tell?"

She thought for a moment before she realized why she'd had that impression. "It seems to glow. To reflect the light. There are a couple strands positioned across her cheeks, as if stuck there. And sand. There were grains of sand in her hair and on her face, catching the moonlight." She'd sworn she'd felt their grit when she'd given in to temptation and run her fingertips gently across the painting. "Just a few grains, but enough to give the impression of water. And an ocean as endless as the sky she reached for was painted at her feet."

"Were there any landmarks in the background? Anything to tell us where it could have been painted?"

"No. Just water and sky blending together. The focus was definitely the woman. *She* was the artist's message. He wanted her to be saved."

"Saved?" The eyes she'd closed shot open at Noah's question. He studied her intently. "You believe that's the message?"

She nodded, though she hadn't known that was what she'd been thinking until she'd said the words out loud. "It's definitely the impression I get, but then again, interpreting art can be so subjective."

Noah and Holt exchanged a look.

"What?" She felt her old defenses rallying. She could hear her mother's response when she'd tried to explain an abstract painting at a museum they'd visited when she was in high school.

"It's just a bunch of swirls of color. Pretty. But it can't possibly mean all of that."

"You don't believe me?" She pinned Noah with a glare.

"Take a breath." His hands shot out in front of him as he approached her, palms out. "Just the opposite. I'm amazed you got all of that."

She forced herself to draw a deep, calming breath.

Though he was close, he didn't touch her. She wanted him to, she realized. With an intensity that scared her, she wanted him to pull her into his arms and hold her tight. *What's wrong with me?*

"Nothing," Noah said.

She'd spoken her question aloud. Mortification bloomed in her cheeks.

Holt rose and scooped up his notepad. "I think that's enough for now, Miss Knight. If it's okay, I may call you with more questions after I see the catalog you mentioned."

She nodded. "You should be able to reach me on my cell."

Holt stopped at her side, his gaze both intense and full of understanding. "It's okay to feel emotional about art. Sometimes I look at the paintings my son did in school and get all choked up. I wish his mother was around to see them." With that, he left her and Noah alone in the dining room.

"He did that on purpose," she whispered.

"What?" Noah remained two steps away, but he'd dropped his hands.

"Shared a bit of personal information so that I wouldn't feel embarrassed or intimidated."

"Is that how you felt?"

She thought for a moment. "Not for long. He's good at what he does. Who did you say these people are again?"

"They're from an organization based in Chicago. The Society for the Study of the Aberrant Mind."

And now they were dealing with aberrant behavior here, in her world. In her gallery. But she was glad they were here. Noah had made this happen.

"I think they'll be able to help. Thanks for calling

them." She cocked her head. "You're doing the right thing for Diego, you know."

His gaze held hers for a long moment. "No, I don't know. I don't know what the hell I'm doing sometimes, but I want to help. That family has given me so much." Vanessa waited for him to say more on the subject of his mysterious past, but he didn't. She wasn't surprised, but she was disappointed.

"It's been an emotional couple of days." She hesitated, not sure how to put her feelings into words. "And remembering that painting…well, let's just say I got a strange vibe. I'm not sure why."

"Kind of like a detective's gut feeling, maybe." A moment of understanding passed between them before he glanced at his watch. "Let's go. You'll want to get on with your…weekend."

If he'd suggested they do something else—anything else—she probably would have jumped at it.

THE GALLERY was bustling with the normal Saturday tourist crowd, but even busier than usual after the auction.

As she and Noah entered, Jesse paused in conversation with a customer and excused himself. "Are you okay? I'm sorry I couldn't be there today."

"The funeral was a beautiful tribute." Vanessa nodded toward the back. "Is Lance here?"

"No. You know how he likes his weekends off."

She had counted on it. She led Noah to the back, waving a quick hello to Fiona as they passed her with a customer.

Vanessa closed the office door. "Natalee worked here." She showed Noah to a small desk in the corner of the office she shared with Fiona and Jesse. The flowers Kenneth had given her sat on top, reminding her she'd have to deal with him soon. "She started at the gallery in April, working only a few hours a week until she graduated high school. For the past month and a half, she was out on the floor with customers as much as possible. She loved working directly with people."

Noah pulled a chair over to the desk and rummaged through the drawers, finding little besides the typical office supplies. The bottom drawer held a hanging file folder marked *Warm Embrace Charity Auction*. Vanessa read over his shoulder as he glanced through its contents.

"See anything that stands out?" he asked.

"Those are the notes I mentioned. It's a copy of the mailing list of our customers and artists that I emailed you, but she's added to it. It includes pretty much anybody who has been connected with the gallery in the past. She'd done a lot of work calling and asking for donated items, obtaining estimates of value for each work of art, ramping up interest in the auction, that kind of thing. There are a few scribbles where she corrected contact information."

Nigel Springfield's name was on the list with a note that said *Deceased* as well as a date. He'd died in late April. His name had been scratched off the mailing list and replaced with his son's, Lawrence Springfield. Vanessa frowned.

"What?" Noah asked.

"I know she did more than this. There's got to be more somewhere." She nudged him aside, her fingertips flying over folders as she flicked through the drawer. A few minutes later, she sighed. "Nothing."

"At least you tried." Noah squeezed her arm. His mood had swung back to supportive, and it had Vanessa's head spinning. But she would rather have him this way than quiet and surly. "What about the catalog? Damian and Holt will want to see a picture of the painting."

"Of course." But she wanted to keep her copy if possible. "Fiona probably has an extra one." She moved to Fiona's desk and found the catalog in a drawer. A legal pad was stuck in the middle and Vanessa pulled it out, her pulse jumping as she saw that the notations on it were in Natalee's handwriting. She held it up with a triumphant grin. "I forgot that she used Fiona's desk when she had to make calls."

Noah looked them over. "Looks like a kind of phone log."

Vanessa flipped to the catalog page with the painting's picture on it. "And here's the mysterious stolen painting."

He studied it a moment. When his eyes met hers, approval shone in their blue depths. "It's just like I pictured it in my head, thanks to your description. You've got a real talent for details."

She blushed with the compliment, suddenly aware of how close they stood to each other. "Thank you, but it doesn't really help, does it? We still don't know who created it or why it was stolen." She flipped through the phone log to find the Springfield name.

"Hey, it's something. We might not know what yet, but sometimes you have to gather all the pieces of the puzzle before the picture takes shape. I'll get these notes and the catalog to Damian. Maybe the team can make some sense of them and turn it into a lead. In the meantime, I'm certain he'll want to speak with Lawrence Springfield."

"That might be difficult."

"Why?"

"I've met him before and I agree with Natalee's estimation." She pointed to the notes Natalee had made by Lawrence Springfield's name. "He likes his privacy unless it involves furthering his own interests. Judging by the number of entries in the phone log, Natalee had to work really hard to get him to talk to her. The only thing he likes more than fortune is recognition, so he was probably waiting for a personal call from Lance. She'd called a dozen times before he finally made a commitment."

"Natalee was persistent and patient with him. Maybe that'll be enough for us, too."

But they both knew they didn't have that kind of time to wear him down. She pointed to a note in the margin. *In it for the money.* Was that a reference to Springfield? But how had that applied to a charity auction? "I've got an idea."

Ten minutes later, after a lengthy phone call to Lawrence Springfield involving some smooth talking, she'd managed to finagle a meeting with the man at his home the next day. If he was truly in it for the money, she'd just dangled a serious carrot. Because of the painting he'd donated, the rest of his items would then bring in double when he sold them because of the notoriety linked to the murder. "I merely suggested we write an article about how he donated the painting."

"It was great thinking." Noah's easy grin faded as their gazes locked. An electronic tune she recognized as *The Good, the Bad, and the Ugly* theme song played and he jerked his eyes away to glance at his cell phone. "It's Diego."

Regret stabbed at her as the moment of connection was broken. She turned away, straightening the papers she'd deliver to the SSAM team.

"Yeah, well, you didn't need to deal with that today." Noah's voice rang with frustration as he addressed Diego. "You need to be with your family and they need to be with you. Besides, we have it covered. The SSAM team is processing the scene and Vanessa and I are looking over Atherton's auction list now." He glanced at her as he spoke. "In fact, she got us an interview with Lawrence Springfield, the man who donated the painting that was stolen." His face darkened as he listened a moment. "Hell, Diego, you can't do it all yourself. I'll fill you in later." He clicked off the phone, his good mood gone.

"He's not happy we disappeared to investigate without him." Vanessa saw in his face that her guess was correct.

"Not a bit. Let's get you home. I'm sure you're eager to get on the road."

Not a bit.

TEN

"HELLO, PRISCILLA."

Damian Manchester's ex-wife spun to face him when he finally spoke. She'd left a message with the doorman to send him straight up to her penthouse via the express elevator. His unobserved entrance had allowed him the luxury of a quiet moment to observe her as she stood by the floor-to-ceiling windows of her sitting room looking out over the city and a glimpse of Central Park. The afternoon light filtering through the windows backlit her, shining bright off the blond hair pulled into a chignon. There was no hint of gray, though she would be sixty next week. Among her peers, gray was a death knell.

Damian, on the other hand, wore the silver in his hair like a badge of honor. He'd battled through life's horrors and come out alive and kicking on the other side. Priscilla had been through many of those battles with him, but the war had ultimately torn them apart.

"Damian." She acknowledged him with an inclination of her head. No smile. Not that he'd expected one. She waved him to a sofa covered in some delicate flowered pattern. He refused to be made uncomfortable, however, and sat and leaned back, yanking a pillow out from behind him. "Coffee?"

"I'd love some." He waited as she sent someone for coffee and then sat herself on a chair across from him. The upward tilt of her chin and straight set of her spine was familiar, even after all these years. She was in defensive mode. It was up to him to knock her walls down. "Are we ready to dispense with the niceties yet?"

"Niceties are all we have left." Her expression was stiff, set in stone.

Once upon a time, they'd been good together. But all that had changed when a monster came into their lives and sucked the joy away.

Still, there had to be more of their relationship left than *niceties*.

"Bullshit."

One corner of her mouth rose, a crack in the wall. She waved a servant with a loaded tray into the room, then took the time to pour and sweeten the coffee to Damian's taste herself. He accepted the cup and saucer, marveling at how they reflected her—elegant and sturdy, yet capable of shattering if not handled with care.

"It's obvious you need something, or you wouldn't have come here." The hurt in her eyes shocked him, but she quickly looked down, avoiding his gaze as she stirred her own coffee. "I'm not sure what li'l ole me can do to help you, the illustrious crime fighter."

"You were never *li'l ole me,* Priscilla. You were always a force to be reckoned with."

"As were you." Her quick smile faded, and he felt a stab of disappointment. There'd been so few smiles those last years. Their daughter had disappeared when she was thirteen, the victim of a serial killer. Their marriage hadn't survived that kind of pain. For several years afterward they'd tried sticking together, neither certain how to interact anymore. But eventually they'd drifted apart. He hadn't had the energy to put up a fight when she left, or when he'd received divorce papers a couple months later.

Certain Priscilla didn't want to go down memory lane

with him, he recalled his purpose and set down his cup and saucer with a tiny clink. "I'm interested in a couple murders that occurred in New York City in recent weeks."

She arched a thin brow. "Would Arthur Cromby be one of them?"

He shouldn't have been surprised. She had powerful friends, and gossip spread like wildfire in her world. "Yes. And Natalee Ortega."

"I read about her in the paper." She pursed her lips. "So, you think they're connected. How can I help?"

He didn't hide his shock. "Just like that? You'll help me?"

She scowled at him. "I would think you, of all people, would understand why I want to help put a killer behind bars."

Yes, he did. Their daughter's killer had never been brought to justice, but each time he helped another victim's family find peace, he found some small measure of it for himself. "I need your connections."

"Done."

They fell into an uncomfortable silence for several moments, Priscilla twisting one of her rings around a finger as she obviously gathered the courage to say what was on her mind. He had a horrible feeling he knew what it was.

"Any news?" she finally asked, her blue eyes imploring.

Sam. She was asking about their daughter, Samantha, and whether his exhaustive investigation through SSAM's resources had yielded any hope of bringing her killer to justice.

He shook his head, as crushed as she was after almost two decades of dead-ends. "Nothing."

She sniffed and sat up straighter in her chair. "But you keep trying."

"Yes. I keep trying." Until his dying breath, he'd never stop.

No sooner had Noah dropped Vanessa off at her home than her doorbell rang—in an obnoxious, hold-down-your-finger-way-longer-than-necessary kind of way. Then the banging started before she could yank open the door.

Peeking through the peephole first, she couldn't help but remember how she'd done the same thing earlier that morning, and how her body had tingled when she'd spied Noah waiting on the other side.

This time, no tingle. It was Kenneth, and judging by his scowl, he wasn't here to comfort her.

She swung open the door, a hand on her hip. "You don't have to pound. You even have a key." She held out her hand, palm up. "Speaking of which, I'd like it back."

He stalked past and swung to face her as she closed the door, ignoring her outstretched hand. "You leave me a message like the one you left earlier and don't expect me to react? Especially after I see *him* dropping you off two hours after *I* was supposed to pick you up?"

"As I said in the message, I don't intend to go with you to the Hamptons. We'll discuss things when I get back on Sunday evening. Now, I have to get going if I'm going to catch the next train in time. My cab should be waiting." She knew how her mother felt about people who were late, and would like to avoid *that* lecture at all costs. She wiggled her fingers, reminding him she was still waiting for her key.

"Let's get going then." He surprised her by grabbing the overnight bag she'd just left by the door and marching out before she could object.

She stood for a moment, gaping, before grabbing her purse and chasing after him. By the time she caught up to him in the street, he already had the bag in his illegally double-parked car and was holding the passenger door open for her. There wasn't a cab in sight.

"I'm not taking no for an answer," he said when she skidded to a stop in front of him. "I'm an invited guest this weekend too. Besides, I paid your cabbie to take a hike."

Someone in the car behind his honked a horn. She could see by the set of Kenneth's jaw that he was immovable on this. *Fine.* He wanted to face her family with her? The weekend couldn't get any worse anyway. Resigned, she folded herself into the front seat of his luxury coupe and buckled in for the two-hour ride.

Over an hour of silence passed as Kenneth navigated the car through the city. Vanessa was just allowing herself to relax when he spoke. "It's okay to be scared."

Totally lost, she played back their last, brief conversation, back on the street in front of her apartment building, but failed to find the connection. Was he finally talking about her attack? "Scared?"

"About marriage. That's what your recent behavior is about, after all, right?"

Her behavior? She pressed her lips together.

"It's okay," he continued. "I understand what you're going through. I wasn't too hot on the idea of marriage, either. At first. You've brought me around."

She gritted her teeth. The last thing she wanted right now was a full-on argument in the car when they were still a good half hour from her parents' house.

"Frankly, I'm surprised you're not dragging me down to the jewelry store and demanding the biggest rock they have." Kenneth chuckled, oblivious to how deep a hole he was digging for himself. His gaze was on the road so he didn't see her mounting anger. "After all, isn't that what every woman wants?"

"With the right man, maybe."

He reached over and squeezed her knee.

She looked out her window, not sure if she wanted to

laugh or cry. Should she confront him now and show up at her parents' doorstep with an angry Kenneth in tow for the rest of the weekend? Or should she wait until after she made it through what was already sure to be a difficult dinner? She opted for the latter, and would hope Kenneth or one of her brothers would still give her a ride home afterward. Otherwise, she'd have to call a cab to the train station.

They fell back into silence as a summer rain began to fall against the windshield. The gentle, rhythmic sound of the windshield wipers lulled her as she tried to let go of her frustrations, tried to focus on anything but the irritating man beside her. Droplets slid steadily down the window.

Water. Such gentle water. So different from the tone of the painting.

The stolen art had been on her mind all afternoon. The piece didn't even have a name. Maybe Lawrence Springfield knew more about it. Perhaps his father had kept records of his collection. Lawrence hadn't put a title down on the form Natalee had him fill out, but that didn't mean that if Vanessa had a conversation with him and picked his brain he wouldn't remember something that would possibly help the investigation.

"We're here." Kenneth made the announcement as he turned into the drive. Her parents had moved out of the city to live in their summer house fulltime a year ago, after her father's retirement. They kept an apartment in town for when her mother felt the need to be near her friends and social obligations, which turned out to be almost every week. Despite the tension that filled Vanessa at the thought of dealing with her family, the sight of the large home in front of her brought back some warm childhood memories—mostly of exploring the beach alone on the stretch of sand near the house, watching the gulls dive for their food, and sitting in the hammock reading or daydreaming.

Kenneth took their bags from the back of his car and followed her up the steps to the door, which swung open the moment she raised her fist to knock.

"Mother's upset," her brother Julian said in greeting. He softened the message with a quick peck on her cheek as she stepped past him into the wide marble foyer. Droplets of rain fell from her hair onto the marble floor. Four years her senior, he played the older brother well. But it was Peter, six years older than her, who lorded his status as firstborn over both her and Julian.

"Joanna is keeping her occupied." Julian chuckled as he took the bags from Kenneth, nodding a greeting. "Of course, with the hellion twins running around, Mother's disapproval has become a permanent fixture."

So, Winnie and Wayne were here, too. The four-year-olds would provide a much-needed distraction this evening. Suddenly she was feeling much better. Perhaps the dinner would go quickly, they would all head to bed early after the kids wore them out, and she could enjoy some quiet beach time in the morning, right up until it was time to go back to the city and interview Lawrence Springfield.

"So nice of you to grace us with your presence." Sylvia Knight stepped out of a doorway down the hall and came forward for the requisite double-cheek peck. Vanessa obliged, catching a deep whiff of the rose-scented perfume that was as much a part of her mother as her carefully coiffed hair. She had a sudden flash of memory—age eight, practicing piano with Mother beside her, smiling down as she mastered her lesson. She couldn't remember the last time she'd seen that look of pride.

Vanessa tried for a bright smile as she shook off the memory. "Mother. It's good to be here."

But her mother's attention had already turned to Kenneth. "I'm so glad you could come." Her smile genuine, she embraced him. At least there was one advantage to having Kenneth with her.

Martin Knight stepped out of his study and spied them in the foyer. "I thought I heard voices out here." He shook hands with Kenneth and gave Vanessa a kiss on the top of her head.

Julian returned from placing their bags upstairs and she felt a moment of panic. Had he put Kenneth in her bedroom? God, she hoped not.

"Well, you've missed cocktails," her older brother Peter said as he and his wife Joanna came out of a room down the hall. "But I'm sure we can find something wet around here to drink," he added with a wink at Kenneth. Both alumni of Harvard, he and Kenneth had much in common. Peter had brought Kenneth home for dinner one evening, which was how he'd been introduced to Vanessa and inducted into the family fold.

"But you're just in time for dinner," her mother said, taking Kenneth by the arm and letting him lead her to the dining room.

Dinner was surprisingly bearable. The food was wonderful as always, and Kenneth's ability to charm a crowd kept attention off her. But when he tapped his fork against his wineglass, she froze. The delectable lamb she'd just consumed became a lump in her stomach.

No. Oh, no, no, no, no. Not again.

Frantically she tried to gain Kenneth's attention, but it was too late. His face flush with alcohol and a sense of victory, he rose and lifted his glass. The family focused on Kenneth. Even the twins had gone still.

"Vanessa and I have an announcement to make."

NOAH HAD TRIED to put thoughts of Vanessa out of his head all evening, but it was no use. It didn't help that her faint scent had lingered in his car as he drove from a meeting with the SSAM team to Diego's apartment. It also didn't help that he was purposely trying *not* to think about what shit-storm awaited him there.

After stewing all afternoon, Diego would be, in a word, pissed. He'd already left several angry phone messages regarding Noah's disappearance from the Sandoval household in order to chase a lead on his own—the very same thing Noah had warned him not to do. But there was one monumental difference. Diego currently had a blurred sense of right and wrong when it came to pursuing Natalee's killer. Noah at least had some objectivity.

As expected, Diego went on the attack the moment he walked in the door. "What. The. Hell? I thought we were friends. *Best* friends. Brothers, practically."

"Oh, now that it's convenient, you remember." Noah stalked past him and sank into the couch, both to keep the argument from coming to blows and to suck the wind out of Diego's sails. If he was spoiling for a fight, he'd be disappointed. "You didn't miss much. I thought I'd spare you one more crime scene."

Diego shoved a hand through his thick hair. "Don't you think *I* should have been the one to decide that?"

Noah gave him a hard look. "No."

Moving to the kitchen, Diego flipped open Natalee's folder where it lay on the counter. Her stolen ME report. He grabbed a page and tossed it onto the coffee table. A picture of Natalee's body lying on the warehouse floor skidded to a stop in front of Noah. "I have to find the asshole who did this to her. *I* do. It's my responsibility."

"You've placed that upon your own shoulders. Nobody—not even your family—expects you to do this without help. That's why they called me."

"I'm the one who fucked up. My colleagues think I contaminated evidence. So, yeah, *I* have to do this. If you have a lead, I need to know immediately."

Noah sat back against the cushion, deflated. His friend was going through hell and there was little he could do about it. His gaze landed on Natalee's photo. Suddenly, he leaned forward and dug in his pocket for the copy he'd made of the painting's photograph, from the Atherton auction catalog. He'd left the original with Holt and Damian.

"What?" Diego moved to his side.

Noah unfolded the copy and placed the two pictures side by side. "This is the photograph of Natalee from the ME's file. This is the painting that was stolen."

Diego looked at each, then at Noah in disbelief. "*This* is the stolen painting? How could I have missed seeing it at the auction?"

"You weren't looking at the art, you were watching the crowd, as you were supposed to. Besides, we didn't know the painting would be important until it was stolen." Noah lunged for his cell phone. "I have to call Damian. And then I have to find Vanessa. She has to see the similarities. It might help her contribute to Holt's profile."

"You're going to show her the photo of Natalee?" Diego asked, surprised. But a spark of hope flickered in his eyes.

Noah stopped pacing. It was a gruesome picture but he thought she could stomach it if it meant getting one step closer to finding the connection between Natalee's killer and the artist. "She can take it."

VANESSA SNAPPED UP her cell phone when she saw who was calling. "Oh, thank God."

"Now that's what I like to hear when a woman answers the phone," Noah said.

She wished she could see the teasing light in his eyes. "I need to hear a rational voice right now."

"What's wrong?" All hint of humor was gone from Noah's voice.

All hell had broken loose in the dining room after Kenneth's announcement. Fury building inside, she'd stood the moment he was done with his speech and, amidst the cheers and congratulations of her family, calmly denied Kenneth's claim.

"I'm sorry, Kenneth. We're not getting married. I never said yes."

And then she'd used the twins as an excuse to hide out. Part cowardice and part self-preservation, she'd offered to give Winnie a bath while Joanna gave Wayne his. Watching her four-year-old niece sing and splash in the bubbles that filled Sylvia's huge tub, Vanessa felt her anger dissipate. Thinking how small her problems were, and how sweet it was having some time with her niece when Diego was missing his own, humbled her.

But remembering Diego and the investigation made her want to call Noah. In the end, she'd talked herself out of it. He didn't need to be involved in this mess. Then, as if he'd sensed she was at the end of her rope and needed him, *he'd* called *her.*

"Are you okay?" Worry was clear in his voice. "Where are you? Are you in trouble?"

"No, no. Nothing like that. Family problems."

He expelled a breath of relief. "You made it to the Hamptons then?"

"Yeah, but I need to get out of here."

"So, leave."

"Can't. I drove with Kenneth and he's threatening to

send away the taxi I ordered unless I talk to him. I'm holed up in the bathroom with my best girlfriend." She winked at Winnie and dabbed a pile of bubbles at her chin, giving her a pointed white beard.

"Who?"

"My four-year-old niece. She's great company." Winnie giggled and reached out to pat a bubble beard onto Vanessa's chin.

"Do you want me to come get you? I still have the rental car."

Yes. "No. I'll be okay."

Kenneth chose that moment to call through the door. "Vanessa, I'm not leaving until we talk." She sighed. It was time to get Winnie out of the tub and into her pj's anyway. She couldn't avoid her family any longer.

Overhearing Kenneth's mild threat, Noah swore. "He doesn't know much about tact, does he? I'm coming. Tell me where you are."

"It's a bit of a drive. I can call a taxi to take me to the train station or a hotel."

"I had something to talk to you about tonight anyway."

"A new lead?" Hope flared. Had the SSAM team already found something?

"Possibly. Just give me the address."

ELEVEN

AFTER VANESSA tucked Winnie into bed next to her brother and read them a story, she gathered her overnight bag, which now sat waiting in the front hall, and chatted with Julian, who was the only one who seemed to be in an amiable mood. But Noah would be there soon and she had to settle things with Kenneth, who'd apparently decided to give her space after all. Finally, she bit the bullet and went in search of him. She found him in her father's office, a glass of scotch in his hand. His tie was askew.

"I suppose you're done avoiding me." There was a note of hostility in his voice.

"I'll be leaving soon." She glanced at his drink, then at the half-empty bottle that sat next to it. "I hope you're planning to stay tonight."

"Your family has been very welcoming." His eyes gleamed as they pinned her. "Unlike you." He wasn't used to not getting what he wanted. Or what he thought he wanted. She'd thrown a wrench into his plans.

"I've been trying to tell you for days now what I finally realized this past month. We don't belong together."

"That's bullshit. We were meant to be together. Can you imagine the life we would have?"

"Yes." And that was the problem. It wasn't the life that would make her happy.

The doorbell rang and Kenneth's lips curled. "That must be him now." He sat his drink down, stood and straightened his tie. "Guess I should congratulate the victor."

Vanessa eyed him warily.

"I'm here for Vanessa." Noah was speaking to her mother as Vanessa entered the hall. His voice was deep and sure, a balm to her battered spirit.

"Like hell." Behind her, Kenneth's tone was obnoxious. She could smell the alcohol on the exhalation of air that brushed her cheek. "You're here for yourself. You're trying to take advantage of this family."

By now, her father and Julian had also arrived, stopping on the fringe of the action. Their gazes were on Noah, openly curious. Damn. She'd put him in the middle of a three-ring circus. And the ringmaster was pushing past her with a twisted smile.

Kenneth looked to Sylvia. "Vanessa doesn't even know this guy."

"I know enough," Vanessa said. Her gaze went to Noah, whose face was impassive.

"Do you?" The glint in Kenneth's eyes brightened. "Did you know he's the offspring of a coke-addicted whore and an alcoholic? That he had to rely on strangers to care for him because his own parents wouldn't? *That's* how he became an honorary Sandoval. They took him in out of pity."

Noah's impassivity gave way to tightly controlled anger. "Someone's been doing some investigative work of his own. Amazing what money can buy on such short notice."

"He even spent time in juvie. Is *that* the kind of pedigree you're looking for?" Kenneth asked her, ignoring Noah's comment. "An unwanted street rat? He's from a different world than us."

Her gut churned with anger at Kenneth and, God help

her, pity for Noah. She couldn't meet his eyes, regretting that she'd brought him anywhere near her family.

Her mother turned to Noah with an assessing gaze. "Whoever you are, this is a private family matter." She turned to Vanessa. "You and Kenneth should sit down and discuss your future like civilized, rational adults."

"I tried that, Mother." Vanessa pulled herself up to her full height. "He wouldn't listen. We're done. We were done months ago."

Kenneth's mouth dropped open as she moved past him to get her bag from where she'd left it against the wall. "You're not leaving."

Noah took a step forward but was stopped by a hand on his arm. Her father's hand. Tall and still in good shape, Martin Knight was an imposing figure when he chose to assert himself. Now, he stepped past the two men facing off in his front hall.

"Are you sure this is what you want?" her father asked her.

"Yes." She answered without hesitation.

He smiled gently. "Then go. But promise me you'll take care of yourself." His attention turned to Noah briefly before he looked back at her. "And be careful."

She nodded and resettled the strap of her overnight bag on her shoulder. Her mother averted her gaze as Vanessa passed her. Once outside, Vanessa turned her face up to the sprinkles of rain that held the promise of another summer shower and sucked in several breaths of fresh air. She felt the weight of her bag lift as Noah took it from her.

His gaze wouldn't meet hers and she felt a tightness in her chest. She'd brought him into this mess, subjecting him to Kenneth.

"Noah, I'm—"

"Let's just get out of here." He put her bag in the trunk

while she settled herself, then slid into the driver's seat beside her. She watched until the house was a dot in the sideview mirror.

The silence gave her time to focus on relaxing the knot that had sat in her gut all evening.

"Thank you," she finally said when they were well away from the Hamptons.

He turned his head briefly from the road to look at her. "Anytime."

She frowned. "Seriously. Thank you. I'm sorry for what happened in there. Kenneth had no right—"

"He had every right, as your boyfriend."

"—he had no right to drag all of that out in front of everyone. He's a bully. And he's not my boyfriend. Not anymore. He hasn't been for weeks, actually. I couldn't believe the way he acted back there. You didn't deserve that."

Noah wouldn't look at her. He simply drove down the dark, rain-splattered road. She bit her tongue for several miles, keeping the questions she wanted to ask at bay. She sensed he wouldn't want to talk about what Kenneth had said, and she didn't want to push him, but she wondered if there'd been truth to the statements.

"I really am sorry," she tried again.

"Don't be. You're not responsible for what Kenny-boy says."

She examined his profile. Every stiff muscle in his body gave off a don't-go-there vibe, so she let it drop.

WITHIN MINUTES, Vanessa had fallen asleep, her legs curled under her, bare toes peeking out at him from beneath her thigh. Noah let himself relax, now that she couldn't ask the questions he'd sensed in her every time she glanced his way.

His anger at Kenneth for his treatment of her and his

cutting remarks had simmered throughout the drive. But seeing Vanessa at peace now beside him somehow made things better. Somehow, amid the stabbing memories that Kenneth had stirred, he'd come out ahead.

She sighed in her sleep, drawing his attention to her mouth. Her lips were raw. She must have gnawed on them. He reached over to brush back a strand of chestnut hair.

The brick face of her apartment building came into view and he felt a strange sense of loss. After circling several blocks for a space, he parked and gently woke her, watching her hooded eyes focus on him and a soft smile curve her lips. He imagined it was the same expression she'd wear if she woke beside him in bed after a night of loving.

She stretched and looked around. "We're here." Sleep made her voice husky. She slipped her feet back into her sandals, then climbed from the car. Noah retrieved her bag from the trunk and they walked along the quiet streets in silence. Inside the building, he followed her up the stairs to her apartment.

"Would you like to come in?" She unlocked her door and stepped inside, turning to face him as she nibbled her delicious bottom lip.

At least, he supposed it was delicious—a fact he'd like to confirm with a thorough investigation. It was after midnight, she sounded tasty and looked tastier, and hell yeah, he wanted to come in.

"I'd love to," he said before he could analyze all the reasons he shouldn't.

She waved him in. "Mind if I pour some wine? It's been a hell of a day."

Hell was an understatement. The funeral, the murder scene, the argument with her family and encounter with

Kenny-boy—yeah, it all added up to a year's worth of trouble in one day.

Without waiting for his answer, she went into the kitchen and returned a short time later with two glasses of red wine.

She settled next to him on the couch, precariously close. "Thank you for picking me up."

It was hard to think as her arm and leg brushed his. Maybe she was aware of her effect on him. Was she, perhaps, seducing him? More likely, she was too tired to realize how close she sat.

But then she turned toward him. He could smell—could almost *taste*—the wine on her cherry lips. She gazed at him through eyes bright with purpose. Her smile, hesitant at first, bloomed into a wicked grin.

Shit. She *was* seducing him. And here he sat, unarmed against her charms.

Held spellbound, he waited to see how far she'd take this charade. Because it could only be a charade. Kenneth had been right about one thing. They were from different worlds. She leaned forward to place her wineglass on the coffee table. Her breast, whether she was aware of it or not, pressed into his biceps as she shifted.

"Vanessa." Her name was little more than a hiss of breath between his teeth. "I'm no white knight."

"Good. That's not what I want tonight."

Before he could protest, her sweet lips met his. It was a tender kiss, just her softness against his grim smile. One of her hands moved to his thigh, and his body jerked in response. He was so hard it was painful, and images of what would happen if he gave in to her tempting, oh-so-generous offer ravaged his brain, beating down his defenses.

Her other arm came around his shoulder, her hand resting on the sensitive skin at the nape of his neck. A jolt of need shot through him and he groaned, opening his mouth to hers.

A taste. Just one taste.

He fisted his hands against the couch cushion, refusing to obey his body's command to pull her into his lap and crush her against him. Somehow he sensed there would be no turning back if he allowed himself that much leeway. He didn't want just a taste of her, he wanted swallows, gulps, *all* of her. His tongue swept into her mouth. He drank in her flavor, overlaid with the heady spice of ripe red grapes.

With a moan of satisfaction, she pressed closer, angling herself to explore his now-open mouth with abandon. Lost in the pleasurable sensation of her tongue gliding over his, he didn't realize until he felt her heat against his erection that she'd climbed into his lap. She'd hiked her skirt up to her hips and was straddling him as she pulled his head closer.

While her mouth wreaked havoc with his, her hands were bliss in his hair, stroking his scalp, tugging him into position, right where she wanted him. Her pelvis shifted in his lap. With a groan of surrender he wrapped his arms around her, locking her in place, holding her against the hard ache that wouldn't let him out of its grip. Not until it was satisfied.

One taste of this sensual woman could never be enough.

THE TASTE OF Noah Crandall, the delicious feel of him, hard between her legs, even with their clothing on, was even better than Vanessa had imagined. Of course, she'd tried not to imagine them like this at all. But tonight, of all nights, she needed him. Needed him with a fierce ache she'd never felt before. She wanted to soothe his hurts, and because he wouldn't talk about his past, she knew of no other way.

She wriggled and took satisfaction in the growl that rose from deep in his throat. His hands gripped her hips as though he were afraid she'd float away. It was a distinct possibility, given the bubbles of delight tickling her abdomen. She rubbed his tongue with her own, exploring, melting into him, celebrating when he returned her ardor with equal ferociousness.

Her hands moved from around his shoulders in a slow glide down his chest, to his stomach. She shifted away— just an inch—just enough to slip her hands to the belt buckle that impeded her progress.

He jerked his mouth to the side, panting for breath. "Wait."

Not what she wanted to hear. "Why? You want me."

"No denying that." He tilted his head back, chin toward the ceiling, to avoid her lips when she tried to capture them again. It was so much better when they were kissing instead of thinking. Her mouth landed on his jaw instead, so she nipped a trail to his ear, where she nibbled a moment before trailing her tongue down his neck. She felt the shivers she evoked within him, the quick little rise of his chest as he sucked in a breath, but still he kept his face averted.

Finally, she pulled back. "What's wrong?"

He met her gaze, drifting the back of one hand over her cheek. It felt cool against the heat of her face. "*This* is wrong. I'm taking advantage of you when you're vulnerable."

"Don't you think I can make that decision?"

He looked her in the eye. "No."

She scrambled off his lap and to her feet, straightening her skirt. Embarrassment made her turn away. *Stupid.*

"Clearly, I'm not capable of thinking for myself. *Obviously,* I don't know how to make good decisions. Is that what you think? And why not? It's what my whole goddamn family thinks." She kept her back to him as she fought for the breath that was coming in shaky gasps. "I won't need your help again, but thank you for tonight."

"Thank you?" A creak behind her indicated Noah had risen from the couch, just before she felt his heat at her back. His breath warmed her ear as he leaned down. "Is that what this was, princess? A thank-you romp in the sack?" His words were like shards of ice.

She spun to face him. "I think more of myself than that."

"I doubt that."

Her anger rose up, threatening to choke off her air. She felt her cheeks burn. "Excuse me?"

"Look who you've let into your bed up 'til now."

Low blow. "I see now that I didn't really *know* Kenneth."

"And you don't know me either. You probably see me as some poor castoff kid looking for attention."

The fight went out of her and she reached to touch him but he backed away. She let her arm drop.

"Don't," he said.

"You're not that kid anymore. We all have demons in our past."

The lines around his mouth went white as his scowl deepened. "So this—" his hand swept toward the couch where she'd pounced on him and she felt her cheeks flame hotter, "—wasn't a *thank-you* romp so much as a *pity* fuck?" She flinched. "Well, I don't need your pity."

Her chest was so tight she could barely suck in a full breath. "You need something. Something's missing inside."

"I'm doing just fine on my own, sweetheart. Just fine."

His nostrils flared and he spun on his heel. The click of her front door echoed in her ears as he left her standing, uncertain and unsatisfied, in her living room, the warmth of him still evaporating from her skin.

"MAN, YOU LOOK like a train hit you," Diego said the moment his friend walked in. His frustration at waiting the last few hours for news was immediately pushed aside.

"And I'd hoped you'd be in bed already." Fatigue was heavy in Noah's voice.

"I couldn't wait to hear what you found out when you showed Vanessa the photo of Natalee."

"*Shit.*" Noah dragged his hands down his face. "I forgot."

"You…" His bark of laughter was without humor as irritation shot through him. Here he'd been sitting for hours, unable to think of anything but finding Natalee justice, and his friend had forgotten. "You *forgot?* How the hell could you forget to show her a damn photo?" He glared at Noah until understanding dawned. "Ah. The woman. Maybe you're no good to me on this case after all."

Noah jerked open the refrigerator and turned his back on him as he pulled a beer from within and twisted off the cap, tossing it onto the counter. Seeming to rethink the action, he swooped up the cap and threw it into the trash. The hard edge of Diego's anger softened.

For days now, Noah had been trying to take care of him the best way a fellow confirmed-bachelor could. Just because his own life was in shambles and his career was likely in the shitter didn't mean he had to take it out on Noah. But damn, it was like a black cloud hung over him every second of every day. He couldn't shake it.

"Look, I'm sorry I jumped down your throat," Diego offered.

Noah sat down on the barstool next to him. "I deserved it. I lost sight of the goal." He shook his head. "Fuck. Who am I kidding? Every time I'm around her, I seem to lose myself a little. But God, when she kissed me..."

"*She* kissed *you?*" That was a shock. Sure, Vanessa Knight was a warm-blooded woman, but he'd have bet good money that underneath it all, she was a proper, blue-blooded woman too. "I'm guessing it was worth losing yourself, at least for a few minutes."

Noah's smile was grim. "Yeah. Except now..."

"She left you tied in knots, huh? Wouldn't go through with it?"

"I stopped her." Frustration was thick in Noah's words. "And then I accused her of seducing me out of pity..."

Diego stared at his friend for a long time before shaking his head. "Man, I got a thing or two to teach you about women."

He scowled. "She's not your typical woman."

"I guess not. She managed to do the impossible—get under Noah Crandall's titanium shell."

Noah didn't respond immediately, taking a deep drag on his beer bottle instead. "Whatever. I'll talk to her about the picture first thing in the morning. I promise. No distractions this time." He moved to the couch and rifled through the suitcase on the floor nearby, pulling out a pair of clean boxers to sleep in.

"That's *if* she'll speak to you. I'd be happy to talk to her."

The frigid glance Noah shot him made him grin. This woman had definitely gotten to him. Diego couldn't remember a time that had ever happened before. Noah had been with women in the past, sure. But never for long. In college, more than one fraternity brother had joked that he was a robot, able to resist the women who'd attempted to turn his head for more than one night. He was always careful to hold part of himself back. Diego didn't think that had changed in the years since Noah had left New York.

"Don't make promises you can't keep, brother," Diego said, rising and moving toward his bedroom. "We need her help. If you can't get it, I will." He closed the door on a scowling Noah. He had a feeling his friend was making all kinds of empty promises lately. If the man thought he could stay focused on the case when that woman was around, he was mistaken. Unless Noah could keep his hands, and his mouth, off Miss Knight—and Diego had serious doubts about that—he would be little help.

It was time to jump back into the investigation, whether Noah liked it or not. He wasn't able to be entirely objective either, but at least he recognized the fact. He just didn't care. Sometimes objectivity was overrated. In this instance, finding Natalee's killer trumped all sense of reason and rightness.

It's not enough. Olivia's words had rung in his ears all evening.

Fuck no, it hadn't been enough. A killer was still roaming free. Diego had covertly scanned the crowd at the funeral, but nobody had stood out as unusual. Most had been friends or family he easily recognized. The same crowd that had been at her baptism, where he'd stood up as her godfather. Or at her First Communion.

"Will it taste like cardboard, Uncle Diego? Maria says the host will taste like cardboard."

Diego laughed. "And how would she know what cardboard tastes like?"

Pigtails slid to the side as Natalee thought about it. "She is a bit weird."

He ran a hand over her head. "Tell you what. I don't

think it'll remind you of boxes, but if you think so, we'll go for ice cream after the service is over."

Her grin revealed a gap the loss of her front tooth had recently created. "Mint chocolate chip?"

"Of course."

"But you were going to take me for ice cream anyway."

"You got me there, squirt."

The church held many memories for their family. Only this time he was flooded with helplessness instead of hope and joy.

Years ago, he'd sworn to protect Natalee as her godfather. He'd failed.

Today, he'd promised justice for his family. He didn't plan to fail again.

Noah might not be able to keep his promises right now, but Diego would sure as hell keep his.

THE BRUSH WAS a familiar weight in his hand, the soft swishing and scratching noises like a lullaby as he applied paint to canvas. Still, it didn't relieve his frustration, or the feeling that he had to hurry. He hated to be rushed, but he had to finish this one tonight. Time was running out.

His fingertips turned white as they tightened on the slender wood of the handle between his fingers. *They* were rushing him. His piece wouldn't be perfect, but then, Nigel wouldn't be here to see it, anyway.

Damn her. Vanessa Knight was working with those detectives, trying to help them find him. And he'd thought she was one of his angels.

He smiled grimly. She still could be. A fallen angel. There were innocents and there were those who had given in to temptation. Most women fell into the latter category anyway. The ones he'd painted in the past had been tempted by earthly rewards, not thinking of the consequences. He'd saved them before it was too late, helping them rise before they'd sold or soiled their souls.

He wasn't happy about the possibility of not saving his Angel of Earth in time. She was on the brink, making choices that would lead her down the wrong path—thinking she could avenge Natalee's death. But she was mistaken. He had to stop her soon, before she put her soul in danger, trusting the wrong men.

He just needed to move faster than he'd thought, before she connected too many dots and a picture came into focus. She'd probably figured out that the painting had been donated from the Springfield estate, and the detectives who hounded her would be hot on the trail. Especially after Cromby's murder.

He looked to his right at his *Angel of Water* and a thrill ran through him. He'd reclaimed the painting. Just as he'd reclaimed the *Angel of Air* weeks ago. She now sat next to her sister, soon to be joined by *Angel of Fire.* If they couldn't be with Nigel, they should be with him. Nobody else comprehended the power or appreciated the meaning of his work. Not even Arthur Cromby, who'd paid several pretty pennies to own one of his works. It was regrettable that someone who admired his art had to pay such a high price, but there'd been no other way. He hadn't been able to retrieve it before the auction.

Cromby's death would be on Lawrence Springfield's head. If the idiot hadn't donated *his* work to the charity auction, it would never have been necessary to take it back.

It had been so easy, really. Cromby had been surprised when he'd called him after the auction, claiming to be the artist. But when he'd told him he could prove it to him, the man had immediately let him come over.

The only drawback was that the police now knew the

painting was important. They had a few crumbs of a trail to follow—back to the Springfield estate. But they'd get no farther.

He smiled. Nigel's son wouldn't be able to help. He'd have no clue.

But Vanessa Knight. Now, there was a woman who appreciated the finer things in life. She understood the depth of one's soul that went into creating a painting. She might even appreciate being a chosen one. One of his angels, forever immortalized in vibrant oils.

He was surprised to find tears pricking at his eyes. Before, whenever he'd felt the emotional pull of his work sucking him under, he'd called Nigel. But of course he couldn't do that anymore. Nigel had been his savior. His own personal angel.

And now there was nobody in this world who understood him.

He squeezed his fists tighter, his nails biting into his palms, then forced himself to relax. It would never do to hurt his painting hand. He'd need that to finish his collection.

Besides, maybe there *was* one person on this earth who could understand him. One who had an appreciation for the fine arts and an eye for talent. Vanessa, despite the earthly temptation of Noah Crandall, might just *get* it. *Maybe I can save her yet.*

A plan formed in his mind. As if his spirit had been reborn, his painting came to life as excitement grew within him. He'd soon have someone to share this with again. And who better than someone who knew Natalee personally? Vanessa would share his dream as Nigel had. *And* she would become a part of it as one of the angels. The ultimate honor.

TWELVE

AFTER A ROCKY NIGHT's sleep filled with dreams of Natalee, Noah and Kenneth—all angry at her for various reasons—Vanessa rose early and headed to the warehouse studio. Having expected to spend her Sunday morning returning from the Hamptons, she was blessed with the rare gift of time to do whatever she wished. And what she wished was to get all her conflicting emotions out of her body and onto the canvas.

Letting herself into the warehouse, she promptly locked the door behind her. With the auction artwork no longer in the back of the building, she felt more confident working here. There was no reason for Natalee's killer to return. He'd gotten what he wanted. But she didn't want to tempt fate. She hoped Holt's profile would soon reveal *why* the killer wanted that painting.

Turning her cell phone to vibrate and cranking up the radio, she put an apron over her favorite work outfit—a gray cotton tank top and tattered blue jeans, both softened from repeated wear. She closed her eyes a moment, letting her thoughts and emotions flow over her, feeling the vibe of the rock music she preferred when she was in this kind of mood. As inspiration struck, her paintbrush moved and she lost herself in a blur of color that became shape.

Some time later, a pounding on the door, barely heard over the Foo Fighters CD, crashed into her alternate reality, bringing her back to earth with a bang. She glanced at the clock and blinked, surprised it was nearly lunch-time. She'd been painting for three hours without a break.

The pounding at the door resumed. Her muscles pro-tested as she unfolded herself from the stool and turned down the music. "I'm coming." Impatience rang in her tone. "Who is it?"

"Noah," came the equally terse reply.

Embarrassment flared in her cheeks, but she knew she couldn't avoid him forever. He was on an important mis-sion to help the Sandoval family, but then he'd be gone, back to Chicago. In the meantime, she supposed she'd have to face him sometime. She unlocked the door and swung it open, then blocked the entryway. "What do you want?"

He glared at her, and still his sweeping glance heated her to her core. She turned away in self-disgust. Her body reacted to him no matter what her brain told it about his callousness, his shallowness, his...

She heard him shut the door as she moved farther into the studio. He was still glaring at her when she spun back around. She knew she must look like a wreck. She'd pulled her hair into a short, spiky ponytail, and paint dotted her apron and her bare arms. "Might as well make yourself comfortable." She yanked the apron off and started clean-ing her supplies. She'd have to take a lunch break, any-way, or she'd get another headache. When he didn't say anything, she looked up to find he'd followed her to the sink. "Cat got your tongue?"

"I've been trying to reach you all morning."

"I've been here. Turned off my phone to avoid inter-ruptions." *He* was exactly the kind of interruption she'd hoped to avoid.

"It didn't occur to you that someone might be worried?"

That *someone* being him? She nearly laughed. "No. Frankly, it didn't."

"We're supposed to have an interview with Springfield."

"That's not until this afternoon."

"After how we left things last night, I thought you might back out."

It was her turn to be irritated. She'd do anything for Natalee, come hell or Noah Crandall. Still, she wanted him to squirm a bit, maybe feel a little guilty. "Why? Because you rejected me? Or accused me of offering a pity fuck? No, that's not humiliating at all. Especially after I crawled into your lap and practically begged you to make love to me and you said, 'Gee, thanks but no thanks, I'm not that desperate.'"

The line of his jaw grew hard. "It's not like I didn't want to…"

She raised her hand to stop him. "Whatever. It's over. Won't happen again. You had your shot at quick, hot, meaningless sex."

"You would have regretted it."

She forced a gruff laugh past the tightness in her chest. "Of course I would have. As you said, I don't really know you. For all I know, you coming to my rescue last night could have been about ensuring I help with Natalee's case."

He looked as if she'd slapped him. "It wasn't." He drew something out of his shirt pocket. "But that brings me to the reason I needed to talk to you last night…"

Ah yes, she'd forgotten until after he'd left. He'd wanted to talk to her about something. Her jumping his bones hadn't been on his agenda. *Stupid.*

Reaching for the photograph he held, she forced herself to think about Natalee. "What is it?"

Before she could grab it, he jerked it just out of reach. "It's Natalee. It's difficult to look at. It may even give you nightmares."

She ignored a sudden chill and held her hand out, palm up. "Show me."

He'd been right. It was a horrendous picture, even though, as an art major, she'd seen many depictions of human life wasted. Of course, those were usually battle scenes or famous works of fiction, and the work was on canvas or a sculpture, not a photograph in vivid color showing an event that she knew to be real.

She pressed the fingertips of one hand to her lips as she gazed at Natalee in death. Charred flesh extended from her naked abdomen up her neck, almost to her cheekbone on one side. Her head was tilted back, her arms thrown over her head.

Vanessa's gaze flew to Noah.

He smiled grimly. "So you recognize the similarities, too."

She studied it again. Natalee's body, posed so much like the woman in the painting that had been stolen. The woman by the water. But this time it was trial by fire.

Bile rose in her throat. "Dear God, there are more."

NOAH INSISTED on accompanying Vanessa home so she could change. He wandered around her living room, picking up a piece of pottery here, a small sculpture there. Her apartment was a mix of textures and colors that he found fascinating. Besides, he couldn't sit still, and he found moving about her personal space, touching her things, helped soothe him. The adrenaline still hadn't completely faded after his morning dash to find her when she hadn't answered her phone or her door. He'd imagined Kenneth stopping by for Round Two of their argument. Or worse—

her assailant, Natalee's killer, coming after her again. He couldn't help worrying over such scenarios. It came with carrying a badge.

But she was okay, he reminded himself, though he indulged in another long glance beneath hooded lids. From where he stood near the doorway that separated her living room and kitchen area, he could watch her making a quick lunch. Seeing her again, especially in her house, where they'd almost...was almost unbearable. If he'd only let his conscience take a vacation last night, he would have woken up with her here this morning. The thought tortured him.

She made two sandwiches, sliced them in half and set them on plates on the small kitchen table before gesturing to him to take a seat. She'd barely spoken a word since absorbing the impact of the picture he'd shown her.

They sat at the table and she kept her gaze averted. *Damn.* This tension between them would inhibit the investigation. Part of that was his fault, and he'd have to rectify it if they were to work together.

He lifted half his sandwich. "Is this a peace offering?" He gave her his most charming smile. Apparently, he'd lost his superpowers because she didn't return the gesture.

"Necessity. Can't have either of us fainting at Springfield's house. Talk about a social *faux pas.*"

He bit into his sandwich with a grunt of appreciation. She'd added extra slices of meat just for him. Diego had a serious shortage of edible food in his apartment, and since the pastries were long gone, Noah had settled for a mug of black coffee for breakfast.

"So we're meeting up with the SSAM team there?" Vanessa licked a crumb from her lips. His gaze hovered there a second.

"Actually, just Becca. We're using the cover you created—

that a magazine reporter wants to interview him—and we thought she'd fit the ticket. We don't want to overwhelm him with too many people." Noah had left early this morning, both to track down Becca and to avoid Diego, who'd still been asleep. Noah wasn't sure how Diego would fit into the investigation at this point, and he certainly didn't want to risk blowing things with Springfield.

She toyed with a crust for a moment. The memory of those deft, delicate hands slipping down his chest to his belt buckle almost had him choking. He forced himself to chew and swallow.

She dusted her fingers on a napkin and her brown eyes met his gaze. "Are *we* okay? I mean, working together. I want to help Natalee's family find justice. If I've messed that up in any way, I would never forgive myself."

He gave a wry grin. "We'll work together fine." As long as he could forget the feel of her mouth on his.

An HOUR LATER, Noah and Vanessa announced their arrival at the security desk in the lobby that connected several grand maisonettes in Beekman Place, a coveted area of Manhattan. A butler led them to a front room, obviously meant as a living room but with a combination of scents that wasn't all that inviting. The view, however, was of stunning private gardens and the East River beyond.

She took quick inventory and frowned. "He didn't waste any time redecorating. Nigel's only been dead and gone a couple of months."

That was the mixture he'd detected—paint, new leather and the chemical smell of newly treated fabrics. "You said you didn't know the Springfields well."

"I saw Nigel a couple of times at art functions and stopped by here to appraise one of his paintings, so I've been in this room before. I've met Lawrence but haven't talked to him much. I could tell father and son weren't on the same plane. Natalee's notation about his interest in money confirms my brief impression of the man."

As if on cue, Lawrence Springfield entered the sitting room with a slumping gait, his red bowtie claiming Noah's attention before his gaze traveled upward to the man's round face. His glasses were too large, his nose too small. And his blond hair was thinning, but had been carefully combed into place across his forehead.

"You must be Detective Crandall?" Springfield's head craned around him to locate Vanessa. "And Miss Knight. Where is this reporter you mentioned? I only agreed to talk with you in exchange for having my story publicized."

"Becca Haney will be here soon, I'm sure." Noah smiled in reassurance.

"Actually, I just got here." Becca rushed into the room and took Springfield's hand in a firm handshake. Her windblown pixie good looks and bright smile were meant to disarm him. "Your butler let me in earlier but said you had a phone call. I was just taking a quick look around the gardens while you finished up. I hope that's okay."

Noah translated her message. She'd been scouting for security threats, a good idea when two people associated with the painting had been murdered. And, of course, there was Vanessa's attack to consider. It was very possible she was in more danger simply by agreeing to come with him today.

"As a writer, I'm fascinated by settings." Becca's tone was admiring. She practically gushed, still holding Springfield's hand between hers, capturing his gaze with her bright brown eyes. "This one would be a *primo* backdrop for a family saga."

Springfield beamed but then pulled his hand away with a puzzled look. "I was told this would be an interview for a serious article that would mention the rest of the art collection going up for sale. What's this about a family saga?"

Becca placed her hand on the man's forearm, reestablishing contact. "Of course. The article is all about the collection. Forgive me, but my brain always jumps ahead to other possibilities when such a worthy family is involved. Biographies, film rights. But *you* have my *entire* attention." She leaned into him. "Are you ready to answer some questions?"

Springfield's bowtie quivered as he gulped. Obviously, Becca's superpowers were in full force. "Certainly. Fire away."

"Glad to hear you're the cooperative type. That should be a nice change of pace." The voice coming from the entryway had Noah muttering a curse. He should have known he wouldn't be able to keep Diego away from this investigation for much longer.

Noah introduced Diego to Springfield. "I didn't realize my *partner* was going to make it here today, Mr. Springfield. I apologize for the interruption." Diego shook the man's hand, nodded at Vanessa and quirked an eyebrow at Becca. "This is Becca Haney, the reporter here to do the story I mentioned." Noah gave Diego a look he hoped his friend would interpret correctly. *Don't fuck with our cover.* "She was just about to ask a few questions about the missing painting and Mr. Springfield has graciously allowed me to be here in case it could help the investigation. He was reluctant to allow strangers into his home."

"Sounds like I'm right on time." Diego's look dared Noah to object, but doing so might ruin their chances of finding out important information from Springfield, who was already frowning at the undercurrent of tension. The eagerness Becca had brought about in the man was quickly dissipating. He could easily cease cooperating and order them out of his house.

"What can you tell us about the painting you so generously donated, Mr. Springfield? I heard it brought in tens of thousands of dollars for charity." Becca took a pen and notepad out of her shoulder bag while hustling him to a chair.

Springfield scratched his head as he sat and the others took seats on the nearby couch and matching chair. "Not much. Don't know why anyone would want to bid on it, let alone steal it, to tell you the truth."

"It wasn't signed," Vanessa said. "Do you know who the artist is?"

"No. That was one of the reasons I'd chosen to donate it. I didn't think it was worth much on the market, being from an unknown artist."

"What about your father? Did he ever say anything about it?"

"The old man loved art more than his family." Springfield sniffed. "My mother left him decades ago. Smart woman. Unfortunately, *I* was stuck here. Not that he noticed."

"Was the stolen painting one of his favorites? Were there others like it?" Vanessa's eyes were bright. Noah recalled her words after he'd shown her the picture of Natalee. *Dear God, there are more.* Could she be right? Could there be more?

"One other that I know of, very similar to the stolen one. I told the police about it already." He frowned at Noah and Diego, who obviously represented the cops he thought he'd spoken to.

"May I see it?"

When Springfield seemed to hesitate, Becca leaned into him again. "It could be very important to the article,

Mr. Springfield." She lowered her voice conspiratorially. "In fact, if I mention its connection to the painting stolen during Mr. Cromby's murder, it could very likely bring in the highest amount when you auction off your father's collection. Collectors love their pieces to have stories attached to them."

A moment later, Springfield was leading them all up a grand staircase to the upper level of the elegant townhouse. He went down a long hall, then stopped outside a door. "This was my father's bedroom. I don't go in here. But once, when he was still alive, I was walking by and happened to see into the room. Thinking about the stolen one brought it to mind again."

Their host pushed open the door to the master bedroom. Inside, the five of them stopped in front of the four-poster bed, and Springfield stared at the opposite wall. "It's gone!"

"The painting's gone?" Diego looked at the blank wall. "You didn't move it? Would anybody else have had access to it?"

Springfield shook his head. "Only the staff, but they never come in here anymore. Not since Father died."

"And you don't know when it went missing?"

Again, Springfield shook his head, going pale as he realized what this meant. "It was on the list of estate items, so it was here a few weeks ago. Somebody stole it."

Vanessa stepped forward. "Do you have any photographs of the work?"

He seemed to come back to himself. "Yes, of course. It was part of the extensive inventory I had done before I decided what would go up for sale, and what could be donated. I'll be right back." He made a hasty departure, leaving the rest of them standing in shocked silence.

"How does this guy do it?" Becca shook her head in

wonder. "This place has a twenty-four-hour security desk in the lobby, in addition to a beauty of a security system. I saw it myself when I checked out the garden. Springfield strikes me as the type who has it on most of the time. Probably only turned it off because he was expecting us."

"And whoever stole this one had to know exactly where to look," Noah said, watching Diego as he moved about the bedroom, opening drawers and closets. "This painting was in a very specific place, right where Nigel Springfield must have seen it upon waking every morning."

Vanessa nodded. "One might say it held a place of honor. I would guess Nigel knew the artist."

Diego grunted. "Wish *we* did. We need a name, people." He pulled open a bedside drawer and scanned the contents. "Well, hello." He lifted an orange plastic pharmacy bottle and held it up. "Looks like the elder Mr. Springfield was taking the same sedatives that were found in Natalee's system."

Noah stepped forward to take a look for himself. "Doesn't mean anything."

"Could be another link between Springfield and the murders."

"Which Springfield? I seriously doubt Lawrence Springfield would care enough about art to murder someone in order to get his painting back. And as for Nigel, he's been dead for a couple months. There's no way he could be involved in Natalee's murder, or Cromby's."

"Well, whoever painted these pictures for him could have had access to these drugs, too. We can process the bottles for prints."

"Put them away. We don't have a warrant. Besides, it could take weeks to match prints."

Diego threw the bottle back into the drawer and slammed it shut.

Springfield came hurrying into the room, oblivious to the sudden tension. "Here's a photo taken last month, when I had everything appraised."

Vanessa took the photo, her eyes widening. Everyone else crowded in to get a look.

"Same artist?" Noah asked.

The image was so similar to Cromby's stolen one that the resemblance could not be denied. Only this time, the subject was not emerging from water, but was floating through the sky. Wind seemed to flow and move about her, lifting long blond strands of hair. Her white gown billowed around some parts of her, clinging to other parts, emphasizing her womanly curves. Her arms were lifted and outstretched, as were the woman's in the painting from the auction.

As in the photograph of Natalee at the scene of her murder.

Noah looked to Diego and caught the narrowing of his eyes. He obviously saw the similarities, too, and had to be thinking about his niece.

"Yes." Vanessa's reply seemed to echo in the quiet room, her gaze locked on the photograph as if memorizing every detail. "Same artist. It must be part of a series with the other one." She paled, no doubt realizing what the rest of them were already thinking. The woman in this painting could very well have been a victim like Natalee. As could the woman in Cromby's painting. That would make three victims, four including Cromby. She turned to Springfield. "Did your appraiser note a name for the painting, or for the artist?"

He shook his head. "No. Just a description. It was like the other one, the one I donated to the auction. No signature. I never heard Father call it anything."

"How long had he had it?" Noah asked.

"A year, maybe longer. Like I said, I didn't come in here." Springfield tensed, his bowtie quivering with the movement.

"And it always hung here?"

"As far as I know."

"In going through your father's financial accounts, have you come across any unexplained payments, particularly anything related to art?"

"There were several donations to charities and organizations that promote the arts, but nothing that stood out. I could ask my accountant." Springfield turned to Becca, his eyes bright. "This'll make one hell of a story, won't it? A regular mystery. And when I get my paintings back, they'll sell for hundreds of thousands."

If he ever got his paintings back. They had to find the killer first.

AN HOUR LATER, Vanessa rode in the back of the rental car, heading toward the studio at the Chelsea warehouse. She had hoped to relieve her heavy heart through some cathartic painting but that wasn't likely until she could be alone. Noah had insisted on driving her, for her safety. Diego was there, too, determined to be involved in every aspect of the investigation from now on. After listening in on Springfield's conversations with the NYPD, Becca was on her way to talk with Damian and Holt. They'd be probing their FBI contacts for victims whose descriptions matched the women depicted in the paintings. It was looking more and more likely that Natalee's wasn't the only life this sadistic artist had claimed.

"I want to see the warehouse where you were attacked," Diego said from the passenger seat.

"No problem." Vanessa rubbed at a temple.

Noah's gaze met hers in the rearview mirror. "Head-ache again?"

"It'll be fine. I've got aspirin at the studio."

Noah pulled into a small public parking lot and they all got out. Though Noah walked beside her as they headed for the warehouse, she felt miles apart. They'd treated each other as acquaintances during the visit to the Springfield estate, but she felt the undercurrent of heat and tension that connected them.

She rubbed at her forehead again.

Noah glanced down at her. "How often have you been getting the headaches?" The worry in his voice had her throat tightening. He might be concerned, but he wouldn't be the one to comfort her. As much as she wanted him to wrap his arms around her, she couldn't deal with another disappointment or she might snap in two.

"Don't worry. It's not from the concussion. Just stress overload." She pulled her key from her purse as they stepped up to the door. Opening it, she instantly sensed something was wrong.

Noah's body tensed as if preparing for action. Or an attack. "What?"

"I don't know. Just a feeling." As if someone had been there. Someone who shouldn't have been there.

Noah's brow knit. "Atherton already dismissed the se-curity guard?"

"We didn't need him anymore. All of the auction mer-chandise is gone. The warehouse is empty."

"He should have kept the guy on, at least until we fig-ure out how the murders are connected to the gallery."

The seriousness in his gaze sent a chill through her. Right. They still needed a big, bad guard. And since they didn't have one, the boogey-man could be hiding in the warehouse again. Great.

Noah signaled to Diego to stay with her and then entered the building. He returned a few moments later, tucking his phone into a pocket and looking tense. "I just called the SSAM team. They'll be meeting us here ASAP."

Diego's eyes narrowed. "What's wrong?"

"The paintings are here."

She pushed past Diego, feeling nauseated. The monster had invaded her space yet again.

"Vanessa, don't—" Noah cursed as she ducked under the arm he put out to stop her.

She gasped. Four easels were set up around the studio area. Her own art, the piece she'd been working on just that morning, had been carefully moved to a corner. On the spotlighted easels sat four twenty-four-by-thirty-six-inch canvases. The first was the one that had gone missing from Nigel Springfield's bedroom wall. The second was the one that had been stolen from Cromby after being auctioned off.

"Oh, no," Vanessa said as she spied the third painting. She heard a sharp intake of breath and Diego came to a stop beside her.

"Everyone out." But Noah's words were too late to protect his friend.

There, sitting before Diego's wide eyes as his face grew stiff with rage, was a painting of his niece. Red-orange flames licked Natalee from below, stretching up toward her face and charring exposed flesh black in its wake. Like the women in the other two paintings, she appeared to be rising above her surroundings, her face and arms outstretched to the purple-orange sky as she begged for something. Mercy? Redemption?

On the fourth easel rested a blank canvas. Taped to the lip of each easel was a note card with neatly stenciled writing. Vanessa stepped forward to look at the card attached to the first painting, the one with the woman who appeared to be floating through the sky.

"Don't touch it," Noah said sharply. She glanced up at him, adrenaline kicking her heartbeat into overdrive, then crouched to read the small writing without touching it.

"Well, what does it say?" Diego's words were impatient.

"Ascending Angel: Angel of Air."

Noah sucked in a breath. "So the second one is what? An angel of…"

Vanessa nodded, moving to the next painting and, without touching it, finding a similar notation on the card. "Water. And Natalee…*Ascending Angel: Angel of Fire.*"

"And the fourth?" Diego asked. "Why send a blank canvas?"

"Probably a message," Noah said.

"For who?" Vanessa swallowed the sour fear that rose up into her throat as Noah stared hard at her. His look was unmistakable. Whatever the message was, it was for her.

THIRTEEN

WITHIN THE HOUR, Damian, Holt and Becca arrived at the studio. They'd notified the NYPD, and Detective Hollister, who'd been assigned to Natalee's case, had arrived at almost the same time. He'd nodded a terse hello to Diego, been introduced to the SSAM group, and immediately joined Holt in examining the paintings. It was obvious to Noah and everyone present that this was a collection that needed a fourth angel to be complete. It didn't take an art expert to figure that out, though the reasons for putting the artwork on display for Vanessa were murky.

"I think he intends Miss Knight to be the Angel of Earth." Holt's words raised gooseflesh on Noah's skin.

"Me?" Vanessa's voice was pitched higher than normal, as was the laugh that followed. "That's ridiculous."

Noah feared that Holt was right. It had been his gut instinct, too. Four elements. Three angels. The guy needed a fourth. And for some ungodly reason, he'd stolen the paintings and brought them here, to *Vanessa's* studio. What else could it mean?

"No." Vanessa shook her head in denial. "He probably wants me to put them on display in the gallery. Artists crave recognition. He just wanted someone who would realize that the collection should be kept together."

He touched her shoulder, squeezing gently. "I won't let anything happen to you."

"Nothing like *that* is going to happen to me." She swung to Diego, whose attention had been glued to his niece's image. Her face softened. "I'm so sorry, Diego." His only response was to press his lips together.

"She was already dead when he painted it," Noah said. "And according to the ME's report, she was heavily sedated, remember? She wouldn't have felt anything." But Vanessa and Diego didn't appear to be listening to him at the moment.

Three paintings. Three victims—no, four, counting Arthur Cromby. Maybe more. Maybe Vanessa was next. His gut clenched at the thought.

"The paint's still tacky. It's not completely dry," Vanessa said, as Holt bent forward for a closer look at the *Angel of Fire*.

"I guess it's now safe to assume the killer and the artist are one and the same," Damian said.

"Either that or they're working closely together," Noah said.

Holt continued to examine the paintings. "I think Damian's right. These killings have the mark of a one-person job."

Detective Hollister looked up from a pad of paper on which he was jotting down notes. He'd already compiled a list of everyone present and their roles in the investigation or relationship to Natalee. "Dr. Patterson, do you know anything about who these other victims could be?"

"We're looking into that with the FBI."

"While you follow up there, I've got a team coming in here to dust for prints. I'll talk to Mr. Atherton about who else may have had keys to the studio, as it doesn't appear to be a break-in this time. We'll canvass the neighborhood for anybody who saw anything this afternoon between the time Miss Knight left and the time she returned. I'll do this the *right* way."

Diego stiffened as Hollister's gaze landed on him.

Holt seemed to sense the tension. "Let's take a closer look at these *Angels* before the fingerprint team arrives, shall we? Vanessa, anything you can add?" His face was set in grim lines as he studied the paintings. Vanessa was right on his heels, pointing out the characteristics—brushstrokes, depth of color, perspective and positioning—that indicated the paintings were done by the same man.

"You okay?" Noah asked Diego. He could feel the frustration rolling off him in waves.

"No," Diego said. "The killer is playing with us. This is *his* game. And I have to play by the rules." His gaze was on Hollister. "We're getting nowhere."

Damian overheard and moved closer. "The NYPD will have the results from analysis of Arthur Cromby's body. Any evidence found at the crime scene should be processed within a couple days. They'll be dusting for prints here, as the detective said. We'll have those in a few days, too, I'm sure."

"So we wait." Diego waved a hand at the paintings. "And in the meantime, this monster is looking for his next victim, so he can create another goddamn work of art out of her? Fuck that." Diego spun on his heel and stalked away. The front door of the studio slammed behind him, leaving an uncomfortable silence in his wake.

Noah heaved a sigh and was about to go after him when Becca stopped him with a hand on his arm. "Let me try."

"He doesn't know you."

"Sometimes that's better."

"Hey! Wait up."

Diego stopped at the corner and turned. Becca Haney hurried toward him, the breeze lifting a short blond lock from the top of her head. The SSAM agent seemed too slim and pretty to take down the bad guys, but he knew from experience with the female officers in his department to never underestimate the power of a woman. Her tailored pantsuit could hide a sidearm as well as her just-as-dangerous feminine curves.

A light citrus scent reached his nostrils as she stepped up into his personal space, the top of her head at his chin, even with her modest black heels. He refused to step back, even when she jabbed him in the chest with a finger. He found himself intrigued by her fingernails. They were short but manicured and painted hot pink.

"If you think you're the only one who cares about this case, you're wrong, buddy."

"In case you missed it, the name's Diego. And what business is it of yours?"

"I've worked with Noah before. He's working his ass off to help you. He called in the big guns, took time off from his job, and you repay him by insulting his friends and stalking off in some kind of tantrum? That's an asshole thing to do to a best friend, someone who's stood by you no matter how you treat him."

He ran a hand through his hair and blew out a breath. "He's a good friend. But it isn't enough. Nothing is going to be enough."

Becca pursed her lips as she contemplated him. "Let's get something to eat."

"Huh?"

"Down the street. We passed a deli on the way here. Looked like the good stuff, and I haven't had a New York City pastrami sandwich in years."

One second she was verbally flaying his hide, and the next she wanted to have dinner? It was the type of stormy contradiction that appealed to his dark mood. "I don't understand you."

"You don't have to." Grinning impishly, she grabbed

his hand and pulled him across the street. Her fingers were cool and sure in his. "But you do have to get away from all of this, just for a little while. And you have to eat. You certainly won't be much of a team player if you faint, big guy. Not that you're much of a team player right now."

He ignored her jibe as his stomach tightened. He hadn't eaten since…Christ, when had it been? Last night? No, Noah hadn't been there to force him to eat, and he hadn't had any appetite after the funeral, so he hadn't eaten at his mother's house, either.

Becca's hand was warm in his as she pulled him toward the deli. He gave in, taking an extra step so they were side-by-side. The feel of her calluses, placed exactly where they should be for someone used to practicing at a firing range, brought a smile to his lips. She wasn't as small and innocent as she looked. In fact, he'd bet she was a force to be reckoned with, and that he'd only caught a glimpse of her true power. He wondered what kind of force she'd be in bed. If the sparkle in Miss Haney's eyes was any-thing to judge by, she'd be a wildcat.

He pushed such thoughts aside as they entered the deli. The delicious aroma of roasted meat, freshly baked bread, frying onions and spicy mustard met his nose. His mouth watered like a Pavlovian dog's.

Becca still hadn't pulled her hand from his and she tugged him to the counter. "Large pastrami on rye." She turned to him with a questioning look.

"The same." Only after he gave the guy at the counter his order did she let go of his hand. "With sauerkraut," he added.

Becca rewarded him with a smile. "On mine, too, please."

"Hey," he said to the man at the register, "anybody sus-picious hang out in the neighborhood this afternoon? Did you see any deliveries at that warehouse down the street between noon and three?" The deli was several buildings away, but there was a small chance…

"Nah, didn't see anything." The man put their sand-wiches on the counter.

Diego paid, noting that Becca didn't object. The minx probably thought he owed her for dragging him away from what could have been an embarrassing scene. He'd wanted to wipe the superior look off Hollister's face. Diego felt guilty every second of every day for touching Natalee's body, but he'd have done a damn good job investigating if they'd let him stay involved in the case.

Claiming a table near the window, they ate in com-panionable silence for several minutes. But Becca was thinking about something. Hard. He could see it in the little line that formed between her eyes. He polished off his sandwich as he waited for her to speak.

Wiping at her lips with a napkin, she erased an intrigu-ing dot of mustard that had captured his attention. She cleared her throat, yet she still didn't speak.

He arched an eyebrow in question. "You have some-thing to say?"

"I'm not sure how to bring it up."

Did she feel the sexual pull between them, too? Would she address it? She certainly wasn't the type to shy away from confrontation. Diego liked that in a woman. Just as he liked the confident way she held herself. Not to men-tion the feisty way she dealt with him.

"Maybe you should just spit it out," he said. "We're probably thinking the same thing." He hoped. God, how he hoped. It had been a while since he'd had a warm woman to lie beside him. And he could really use that now. Maybe it would soothe the ache that was with him day and night, even if the comfort was just temporary.

"Had Natalee talked about any boyfriends?"

The question threw him so off guard he had to rewind it in his head. "Boyfriends?"

"Well, I was just thinking that she may not have gone willingly with this guy, since her purse was found in the alley, but that doesn't mean she didn't know him. Or that he didn't know her. Maybe she was having a secret affair?"

"I highly doubt it. As far as I know, Natalee didn't date much. Probably not at all. And she was a very open, easygoing girl. The idea of a secret affair would be a long shot. She was an honor student who focused on her schoolwork."

His niece had never really talked about it, but he got the impression she was trying to make a better life for herself. Make better choices than her mother had. Olivia had picked an asshole for a husband and he'd abandoned them. And if Diego ever saw the man again... His fingers tightened around his cup of soda.

"She didn't mention anybody creepy hanging around, either?"

"Not that Olivia—her mother, my sister—mentioned."

"Still, was Natalee the type of girl who would have discussed that kind of thing with her mother?"

"Absolutely," he replied without a doubt, scowling at the implications. Noah had asked him similar questions a few days ago, and Diego had gone through Natalee's room and had found nothing. Becca's response was a husky laugh that deepened his scowl.

"I'm not accusing your niece of anything. I remember what that age was like, that's all." The twinkle in her eyes confirmed that she had some interesting stories in her past. "It just seems that the paintings this guy's made are so personal. You can feel the emotion in them, the desperate plea for salvation. Like Vanessa said, it makes me think he's been very selective in choosing his subjects. Wouldn't that mean that he'd at least seen Natalee from afar, probably several times?"

Diego nodded, intrigued by the idea. "It's a reasonable deduction. Or it could just be that he's a lunatic who thinks he knows his victims on some deeper level."

"But going with the first theory, it would be likely that he had more up-close contact with her than we assumed."

"Maybe," he conceded. "Or maybe she caused a blip on his radar because his *Angel of Water* painting was given to the auction and Natalee just happened to be the one collecting donations."

Becca popped the last bite of her sandwich into her mouth and wiped her fingers with a napkin. "We should get back, discuss this with the others. On the way, we can stop in the shops that were open today, see if anyone saw anything in the last few hours. We should also interview the security guard and the guys who loaded and drove the truck that transported the items to the hotel. Maybe they saw someone hanging around."

The reminder that they had concrete things to focus on had him feeling more positive. He eyed Becca with respect and a touch of awe that she had been able to turn a crappy day into a ray of hope. She had an innate enthusiasm and hopefulness that he was seriously lacking right now.

"THE *ANGEL OF FIRE* was hastily put together," Vanessa said to Holt and Detective Hollister as they watched an NYPD crime scene technician gently dust the paintings' frames for prints. "But the artist's work is all the more amazing because of it. He still took time for the details."

"If he's rushed, maybe he thinks we're close to catching him," Hollister said hopefully.

"Something triggered this rush," Holt agreed. The mindhunter had been alternately gazing at the paintings and jotting down notes for the past hour, creating his own kind of portrait—this one of a serial killer. The faraway look behind his glasses cleared as he focused. "I think he'll act again soon. He'll want to complete his collection."

Vanessa shivered at the thought of another murder like Natalee's. She felt a reassuring presence at her side and didn't have to turn to know who was there.

"Come with me," Noah whispered, taking her arm and pulling her into the warehouse area where they could have some privacy.

"What?" She removed her arm from his grasp.

"Let me take you home."

"I can't. I want to help. I have to. Would you rather I sit at home and wait for this guy to contact me again?"

His lips pressed together. "I'd rather you not be involved at all."

"May I point out that *you're* the one who got me involved in all of this."

"You were already involved, you just didn't know how much. The killer's after you now, too. And the more you help, the more danger you're in." He rubbed a hand over his mouth, as if he could stifle the words.

Her gaze unconsciously went to the spot where she'd awoken in his arms after she'd been attacked. She shivered.

He pulled her close. "I'm sorry. I'm worried," he said against her hair. "A guy's allowed to worry, right?"

She pulled away. "We'd better get back in there." Her eyes scanned him in confusion. His actions were incongruous with how they'd left things, or with their tenuous truce. And now, here he was being as tender and caring with her as a lover. "I'll be okay. If you want to worry about something, worry about the investigation."

Back in the studio, she noted that Becca and Diego had returned. They were in quiet conversation with Holt and Hollister. Damian was speaking on the phone.

"Thanks. I owe you." Damian hung up and turned to the group. "Good. We're all here. Let's get organized." The group gathered closer. "Under the guise of an impromptu sixtieth birthday party, my ex-wife Priscilla has agreed to set up a gathering of various artists and collectors in the New York City area. And though the NYPD will want to finish examining this evidence, I'm sure we can get the paintings out of their custody in time for the party." He glanced at Hollister, who nodded.

"That can be arranged," the detective said, jotting something down on his notepad.

"What do we need the paintings for?" Becca asked.

"The plan is to lure the killer with an exhibit of his collection and a hint that they're to be auctioned again. I'll let Holt explain."

"I've been working on a profile," Holt said. He smiled at Vanessa. "I've had a lot of help, and I think we can make some assumptions about the killer based on these paintings and his crimes. Given that he stole the paintings, only to send them to Vanessa, I believe he intended her to watch over them. He'd see putting them on display at a party in order to build interest in another auction as a breach of his trust. A betrayal. The fact that she's handing them off so callously, and that they'll likely be separated again in an auction, added to the fact that Springfield would make a bundle off the set, might be enough to push him out of hiding. He'll be angry."

"At the very least," Damian added, "someone might recognize the work and be able to identify the artist."

"That's generous of his ex-wife to offer her home for a party," Vanessa murmured to Noah. She gasped as realization hit. "Wait…Damian Manchester. He was married to *Priscilla Manchester?*"

"You know her?" Noah asked.

"Not personally. But everyone in the New York art world knows *of* her." And any artist would be honored to be the focus of attention at one of her parties. Would that draw the killer out? The need for recognition?

"I'll need all of you there," Damian continued, "working the room, learning what you can to find out who this artist is. Be cautious. He's probably killed at least four people and is looking to make it five."

"When is this party, sir?" Becca asked.

"A couple of days. Vanessa, I know it's a risk, but I'm hoping you can help make this a reality in such a short time. Your experience and connections will be invaluable."

Vanessa nodded. "Of course. I'd be happy to help make up a guest list, if Mrs. Manchester needs help."

"That's a good start, especially if you can include people from the auction. I'll put you in touch with her."

"What else can I do?"

"You've been helping Holt with the profile. And served as a contact point at the gallery. That's all we can ask."

Becca's forehead wrinkled. "Will the killer strike again, even with Nigel gone? It seems Nigel was his biggest supporter, maybe even his financier."

"Nigel was already dead when the killer did this—" Holt gestured to the *Angel of Fire,* "—to Natalee Ortega. He'll feel compelled to complete the series."

"And the final piece will involve the element of earth," Noah said.

"Yes. Traditionally, there are four earthly elements. Air, or wind. Water. Fire. Earth."

"Do you think Vanessa's his target?"

"I wouldn't rule it out. The killer seems to have made a connection with her. But does he see her as one of his angels?" He shook his head. "It depends on his definition of *angel,* I suppose. And whether she represents *earth* to him. The idea of melding earthly elements and heavenly representations is, in itself, confusing. If we can identify these other victims, assuming they were real people, and find out more about their lives, then we'll know more about what he looks for in an angel, and why each represents that element."

Diego shook his head. "I don't understand. How could Natalee represent fire?"

"Her passion, maybe?" Vanessa suggested. "She lit up inside when she talked about art."

"Can you think of any link to fire on a more concrete level?" Holt asked.

"She was taking a pottery class at the community college. They use a kiln—could that be the connection?"

Holt rubbed his jaw. "Possibly."

Noah's brow crinkled. "And why angels? Is he religious?"

Holt looked at the paintings, then at Vanessa. "What do you think? What's your interpretation of his imagery?"

Vanessa felt everyone's eyes on her. "There's no depiction of the typical religious icons or holy symbols such as crosses. I told you yesterday at the Cromby estate that I felt something from the *Angel of Water* painting. I get the same impression from the other two. A feeling of release, of seeking forgiveness, and of receiving divine mercy. A type of salvation."

"I get the same impression. I believe the murderer

sees himself as a powerful person. One who can pick and choose who he paints, and by doing so, pick and choose who receives divine intervention. But following organized religion? No."

"Yeah, he kind of missed the whole 'thou shalt not kill' message in Sunday school," Becca said.

"He's cocky enough to see himself as his own religion," Holt continued. "Probably even thinks he's a direct agent of God. He may have the delusion that he *is* God. The four elements—earth, wind or air, water, and fire—probably represent earthly bonds. And when he kills the women, they become angels, released from their physical constraints." Holt took off his glasses and rubbed them with the edge of his T-shirt—a souvenir from the Bronx Zoo. Vanessa wondered if he'd taken his son there, and how he kept the family stuff separate from the criminals he thought about day and night. "At least, those are my impressions thus far, with the information I have." He replaced the glasses on the bridge of his nose and looked around expectantly.

"Where does Nigel Springfield fit into the picture?" Hollister asked. "Why would two of the paintings end up at his estate?"

"Nigel is known for supporting the arts. My guess is he was supporting this particular artist."

Diego shifted his weight. "We found a bottle of pills in his nightstand. The sedative was the same one found in Natalee's system."

Hollister turned his sharp gaze on Diego. "You were in Nigel's bedroom? When?"

Diego held his gaze. "You really want to know?"

After a moment, the detective shook his head. "By the book from now on, Diego."

Holt rubbed his chin. "If the killer broke in to get the painting back—"

"—which couldn't have been easy unless he knew Nigel and knew exactly what he was looking for—" Becca inserted.

"—he could have stolen some pills then."

"And the fact that he used a sedative with Natalee," Damian said, "does it indicate that he knew her and respected her, and wanted to reduce her suffering?"

"Maybe. But it also may be that he's exact in how he positions his subjects. He wanted her flesh to burn only in certain places, as evidenced by the cream he applied beforehand to retard the spread of fire. If she'd been awake to struggle, it would have changed his painting dramatically."

"He's meticulous. A planner. Organized."

Becca nodded. "He was careful enough that nobody saw him when he delivered the paintings here today. Diego and I stopped at the stores in the area, the ones that were open today, anyway. He probably used the alley, but it was still broad daylight. The paintings aren't large, so the task wouldn't have required a delivery truck. He could even have stacked them in the trunk of a car, if it was large enough."

"And we still don't know how he got in," Noah added.

"I'll be questioning Atherton about who had keys next," Hollister said. "I checked in with the detective in charge of Cromby's murder and they found nothing useful on the surveillance tapes from the hotel lobby. Apparently, they're aimed at the main doors and the check-in desk. The lobby phone is practically under the cameras."

"Damn." Another possible lead slipped through his fingertips.

"Still, he may start acting more erratically," Holt suggested. "He's cautious now, but Cromby's murder indicates he had to move fast. I believe we're pushing him to make quicker decisions than he'd like. The paint on the *Angel of Fire* is still wet. He was rushed, as if he knows we're on his trail. He may have given Vanessa the paintings knowing that he doesn't have much longer, trusting that as an art aficionado she'd take care of them."

Damian's gaze traveled around the group. "Which is why this party will be important. If he sees his paintings unappreciated again, maybe he'll step forward."

"Or he'll go into hiding," Becca suggested.

"Or he may start making mistakes if he becomes more desperate," Damian said. "Especially if we push harder. All we need is one mistake."

FOURTEEN

"WHAT'S WRONG, *mijo?*" Estella's gentle endearment lifted the corners of Noah's mouth.

Twenty-four hours after the group had dispersed from Vanessa's studio, he sat across from Diego at the table tucked into the corner of Estella's tiny kitchen. Only two days before, the place had been overflowing with platters of food after Natalee's funeral. Estella had invited—no, ordered—them to come over and consume the leftovers. Noah, thinking Diego could use some time with his family as well as a good meal, had readily agreed.

"Nothing."

She put a fist to her hip. "Don't lie to me. I know you better than that."

"He's got a crush," Diego said, smirking in a way that took Noah straight back to grade school.

Estella nodded. "Miss Knight."

Noah scowled. "No. I mean, it's not anything."

Estella simply laughed. "I don't blame you. She's pretty. And smart."

"And out of his league," Diego said.

"There's nothing there," Noah insisted.

Estella placed a hand on his shoulder, leaning close so he couldn't look away from her steady gaze. "Don't let your past determine your future. What happened to you wasn't your fault, and it's time you realize that and choose to be happy."

A shiver ran through him, quickly followed by the hot

flash of anger that hit him whenever the past came up. He shrugged. "That isn't important anymore."

She threw her hands up. "*Ay, Dios mío.* Of course it is. Our pasts make us who we are. You've got a loving heart but it was ground under the heels of those...*parents* of yours." Her brown eyes brimmed with pity and Noah looked away. "They chose the path that led to their destruction, God rest their tortured souls." She made the sign of the cross over her chest. "But they're gone now. And by denying yourself the joy of trusting someone, you're robbing some deserving woman of your love."

"It's no use, Mama," Diego said. "He's a bachelor to the end."

Noah's gaze pinned Diego. "Can we change the subject?"

Estella sat a plate of bread, fresh from the oven, on the table. "What did you two do today?"

"A little of this, a little of that." Diego dodged the question with expertise. They'd actually walked the streets of Chelsea, showing Natalee's picture and searching for anybody who saw anything of interest. It hadn't been productive. Diego had checked with Hollister, and the detective had actually agreed to speak with him. But he didn't have much to share yet. The fingerprints were still being processed. His talk with Atherton had revealed that a set of spare keys to the gallery and warehouse had gone missing that weekend. Given that Saturday had been so busy following the auction, and only Jesse and Fiona had been at work, anybody could have snuck in to snag the keys from Atherton's desk.

"What's that delicious smell?" Becca asked, her nose leading her into the kitchen.

Noah heaved a breath in relief at the much-needed interruption. Until he saw who followed in her wake.

Vanessa greeted Estella with a smile. "Thank you for inviting us over. My cupboards are bare, I'm afraid." She introduced Estella to Becca.

Noah ignored the tightness in his belly as he feasted his eyes on Vanessa. He'd wondered how she'd fared after the profile yesterday—when Holt had basically said she was the killer's next target. Noah had asked if SSAM could protect her, and Damian had assigned Becca to be Vanessa's shadow, which alleviated some of Noah's concerns and let him off the hook. But damn if he hadn't missed her smile. He was pretty sure it wasn't the leftover lasagna that was making his mouth water.

"Well, this is turning into a regular SSAM meeting, isn't it?" Diego said, his gaze on Becca. He'd told Estella about the team helping with the investigation, though he hadn't mentioned the possibility of a serial killer's involvement, not wanting to upset her further.

"Anything new?" Noah directed his question to Becca. She took the seat next to Diego, leaving the last remaining one to Vanessa. Right next to Noah. No, it was definitely her making his mouth water. He found himself leaning toward her slightly, inhaling her unique scent.

"Damian chatted with his contact at the NYPD. A couple extra officers are interviewing guests from the auction attendee list. He's talking to Springfield, trying to get a better idea of who Nigel might have supported. Nothing significant or out of the ordinary so far. You?"

Noah and Diego had been beating the bushes all day too. "Nobody on our lists raises any red flags."

"Have you had any other ideas about who the artist might be?" Diego asked Vanessa as Estella set full plates in front of the newcomers.

A furrow formed along Vanessa's brow. "I keep thinking it has to be someone who frequents the gallery often.

Fiona, Jesse and I spent today going over our customer and artist records." Her gaze flicked to Noah. "Without Lance knowing, of course. It helped me come up with the guest list for Mrs. Manchester's party, anyway. We invited anyone who seems suspicious or is particularly interested in oil paintings."

"She's been amazing," Becca said around a bite of garlic toast. She swallowed and dabbed at her mouth. "I've been watching the three of them at work all day and they've been working their tails off to personally call everyone on the guest list to invite them to Priscilla's party. When Damian said we'd be having a party on *Wednesday,* I thought it could never be done in time. But it looks like it'll work."

Estella patted Vanessa on the shoulder before shuffling away to put a tray of chocolate chip cookies into the oven. "I appreciate what you're doing." She turned to the group and Noah's heart twisted. There was a sheen of tears in her eyes. "You all will find justice for our Natalee. I know you will."

"THIS IS YOUR SOLUTION?" Jesse looked at the mannequin with raised eyebrows.

It was Tuesday evening, and Vanessa had needed some semblance of the human form for her class to draw. It wasn't Noah's sculpted body, but it would have to do. "It's just as good as the real thing."

Jesse adjusted another spotlight onto the male form. "Without all those pesky emotional entanglements."

Vanessa grunted in agreement. "And Rico Suave doesn't talk back."

Jesse chuckled. "He's got a name, huh? Well, nice to meet you, Rico." He glanced at Vanessa. "Anything else you need here?"

She looked around. The chairs and easels were ready and waiting for the students. Jesse had arranged the lighting and easels the way she'd asked. "Looks good to me. Thanks for your help."

"No problem. I'm just glad you didn't wrangle me into posing."

Becca came from the warehouse, where she'd stepped out to take a phone call. She gave Jesse a friendly slap on the back. "You would have been a natural, you know. The ladies would have been drooling over you."

He shook his head with a self-deprecating smile. "I sacrifice enough of myself for the arts."

"When do I get to see your latest?" Vanessa asked.

He busied himself with arranging a couple of stools in front of easels. "When it's time. I've been dabbling in clay lately."

"Sounds like fun."

He glanced at the corner. "And your piece? I see you've started another."

She grimaced. "Started, but far from finishing." Though she'd had more inspiration lately. "I'm still hoping to have enough pieces for a show next year."

"Maybe Atherton will host," Jesse said. She shrugged. Lance's mood changed on a whim. Someday she'd have her own gallery. Somewhere she called the shots. "Why didn't you ask him to hang the *Angels* in the gallery? You could have avoided this whole party."

"We couldn't have monitored them closely," Becca said. "The team will be all over Priscilla Manchester's penthouse on Wednesday night. By revealing them at the party, we've narrowed the window of opportunity for the killer to strike. And the only way into her home is through the private elevator that leads to her front door. We control the circumstances."

Jesse looked doubtful. "And you're sure he'll come?"

"We've included a teaser in the invitations," Vanessa said. "He'll know the *Angels* will be on display, and that they'll be up for sale soon."

"He won't be able to resist," Becca added.

"He's got to be pretty upset," Jesse said. "You're not worried he'll come after you?"

"That's the idea," Vanessa said, her throat going dry at the thought.

The first of her students arrived and Jesse said a quick goodbye. Becca faded into the background. Over the past two days, Vanessa had gotten used to her shadow. And she had been relieved when Damian had called to tell her the class rosters hadn't raised any concerns. Her current students had been cleared as potential suspects in Natalee's murder.

Soon, the twelve seats were filled and she began her brief lecture on muscle groups and techniques for sketching and painting them. The students shuffled about, setting up their blank canvases on the easels and removing charcoal pencils from their bags as they prepared to create their outlines. She turned on the CD player, letting classical music fill the room.

The turning of students' heads toward the front door drew her attention there, as well. Noah stood just inside the studio, rubbing the back of his neck with one hand. She quietly moved over to him so as not to distract the group further.

His eyes narrowed on the mannequin and she could have sworn she saw a blush creep up his neck in the dim light. "I've never done this."

Was he really considering...? She laughed. "You don't have to. I didn't really expect..."

"That I'd follow through," he finished. "I know. But here I am, all yours."

Her students' curiosity remained focused on them and, after a nod from Becca acknowledging that she knew her personal safety was covered, Vanessa motioned for Noah to follow her outside. Once on the quiet sidewalk, within the privacy of a lighted circle from a streetlamp, she turned to face him. "I appreciate the gesture. I really do—"

His gaze moved from their surroundings to her face. "It's not a gesture. I made a promise." He stood so close she could smell the tang of male sweat. Had he been out in the summer heat again today, trying to find Natalee's killer? Of course he had. Probably pounding the pavement, researching the people she'd put on Priscilla's guest list so they'd be prepared for the party tomorrow evening. "As a general rule, I try to avoid commitments, but when I make one, I keep it."

"At least you're honest, though you made that commitment under false pretenses."

His eyes darkened. "It was still a commitment. And I intend to follow through."

"Not like the other night, when you left me high and dry." Shocked at herself, she resisted the urge to slap a hand over her mouth. Had she really just admitted to him that she'd been crushed by his refusal of her advances?

A strangled groan escaped his throat. "You don't think I regret that?"

"Maybe it was for the best."

His gaze dropped to her lips. "I've been dreaming about the taste of you ever since."

The air froze in her lungs. His eyes reflected the low lighting as he leaned forward, slowly, giving her time to object as his mouth came closer to hers. She stood immobile, the physical and mental command centers of her body battling it out. She fought the desire to stand on her tiptoes and capture his lips for herself. Doing so would be tantamount to waving a white flag. She wasn't sure she was ready for that. Surrendering herself to this man would put her heart at risk, and risk another rejection.

"I can't." Her protest was a whisper of breath as he moved from the corner of her mouth down her jaw line. His lips barely brushed her neck just below her ear, one of her most sensitive areas. She couldn't control a shiver.

"Just one taste." His low murmur was hot against moist skin. Her breath caught. His hands moved to her waist, then skimmed her hips, pulling her closer to him, fitting them together. "Then I'll stop."

She tipped her face up to his. He immediately closed the distance and captured her mouth, his lips moving over hers in fierce possession. She tasted a hint of the coffee he must have had at some point that afternoon.

Noah was offering himself to her—for a moment, at least. It was a heady feeling. She was certain that he didn't open himself up to others often. It was a rare gift, but it was also temporary. A shimmery mirage that could turn to sand in an instant.

Pulling away, she took several steps backward to stay out of reach. "I have to go. Class."

"Right. Where do I change?"

Her eyes widened as he reached for the edge of the T-shirt he wore, showing a strip of hard abdomen just above the waistline of his jeans. Did he mean to strip right in the middle of a public sidewalk? Deserted at this time of night, but still public. "N-no." She held up a hand, palm out. "I mean, you don't have to."

"I told you I'm committed to this." He was serious.

God, letting this man walk around her studio naked would give the females in the class heart palpitations and turn the men green with envy. Not to mention what it would do to her.

"They've already started with the mannequin." She jerked her eyes away from the still-exposed two-inch band of skin. "Changing over now would mean starting a whole new project. I'll spare you your commitment. This time."

She quickly turned and went back into the building, willing her body back under control. How much longer would Noah be around to stir her body? A few more days and surely they'd have a concrete lead on the killer. Two weeks, tops, and he'd have to return to his job in Chicago. She only had to keep her head until then.

It seemed like an eternity.

THE NEXT AFTERNOON, at her desk at the gallery, Vanessa kicked off her heels and massaged one foot. She'd been on her feet all day again, but it was a good thing. Business had definitely picked up since the auction, and Lance was pleased. He still scowled at her regularly, though, and she guessed he suspected she was working with the authorities—even if Diego, Noah and SSAM weren't technically *on* the case—to find Natalee's killer. After all, Becca had walked her to and from work for the past couple days.

Still, the success of the auction was the only Atherton Gallery news lately, so he was content to keep his suspicions to himself. For the moment. It could also simply be the calm before the storm.

She looked up to find Lance making his way to her desk. She hastily dropped her foot and slipped her shoes back on, rising to meet him halfway.

"I've been meaning to talk to you." He cleared his throat. "About a promotion."

Her heart knocked against her ribcage. "Promotion?"

"In addition to your usual work with customers here, I'd like you to be in charge of special functions, such as the auction last week. But not always charitable affairs. Atherton's can be known for charity *and* for making money for clients who will give us a chunk of change to find wealthy buyers for their merchandise."

"Of course."

"You'll receive a raise, but it will involve more work. More hours."

"I understand." There would be nothing else to fill her hours after the investigation was over, anyway. And with any luck, Natalee's family would have their justice soon. "Thank you."

"We'll discuss terms on Monday. I hope you'll remember this generosity when you're at your gala this evening. If Priscilla Manchester were to become a benefactor of our gallery, it would be a huge boon."

So he did know about the party. She wondered if he knew that Fiona and Jesse planned to attend and help find a killer, too. They hadn't mentioned Lance pressuring them.

"Of course," she murmured as he moved away.

The sneak. Timing an announcement like that with a request to use her resources to better his business. But could she really blame him? After all, she was a hot commodity in the art world now.

She sat and spun around in her chair, her sore feet forgotten. She snatched up her phone as it rang. "Vanessa Knight."

"Angel of Earth," said the voice, the same deep rasp she recognized from her attacker and from the call she'd received a week ago. "Only you're no angel."

Her pulse pounded in her ears. "Excuse me? Who is this?"

"I am deliverance. I'll save you from yourself, from your unwise choices, and from earthly temptations, before it's too late."

FIFTEEN

BECCA STOOD in the living room of Diego's apartment. "Did you find out from your sister if Natalee received any trinkets or messages before her death?"

Diego shook his head, thinking back over his conversation with Olivia. "Nothing. And we had already checked her cell phone. There were no strange numbers on it." She had let him look through Natalee's things again, in case his niece *had* actually planned to run away with a boyfriend-slash-killer. This time, she'd found the strength to help him without breaking down. But their search had yielded nothing but the memories of a vibrant, social, well-adjusted teenager. Yet Holt had profiled a killer who knew his victims. Who chose them because of who they were, and what they represented to him. If the profile was correct, Natalee had to have known her killer to some degree. At the very least, she'd run across his path before the night she'd disappeared.

The thought of his loving niece having her trust turned against her burned like acid in his gut. Olivia had promised to talk to Natalee's friends to see if they knew anything more.

Becca's brown eyes were soft with compassion. She reached out and ran her fingers along his forearm, as if petting a beast who needed soothing. "We're getting closer. I can feel it. He contacted Vanessa today."

"What?"

"We've rattled him." She frowned. "But he also told

Vanessa she's the missing angel. Looks like, unfortunately, we were right in that assumption. He told her she's making improper choices."

"So he probably knows about the party tonight," Diego guessed, feeling a punch of adrenaline.

Becca nodded. "And if all goes well, we'll have the guy in custody by morning."

God, he hoped so. He just wanted this to be over, to feel like himself again—whole, without this ache in his gut. Becca went a long way toward filling that hole with her understanding looks and soothing touches, but he knew it wasn't real life. How could it be when he wasn't feeling like himself?

She stood. "Speaking of the party, I've got to go pick up Vanessa so we can get ready." Smiling, she did a pretty little twirl in front of him. "Can't wait to see you in your tuxedo." With a saucy wink, she opened the apartment door, then paused. Sober again, she turned. "I don't think Damian's told Noah about this latest development with Vanessa yet, so…"

"I'll tell him." His friend was currently in the other room, getting ready for the night's festivities. "He'll be pissed," he muttered as Becca closed the apartment door behind her.

He sat down heavily at the breakfast bar, flipping through the ME's file on Natalee once more. Through SSAM's resources they'd obtained a similar file on Arthur Cromby days ago, but it wasn't much help. The killer knew how to be careful. He'd been prepared. No DNA, no fingerprints. They were still waiting for a hit on the few partial fingerprints they'd lifted from the *Angels'* frames at the studio. At the moment, there was nothing new, nothing to go on.

Nothing except a mindhunter's profile and the theory

that the artist of the *Angel* paintings was the killer. Weren't artists supposed to be free spirits who appreciated and created beauty instead of destroying it?

"Did I hear a woman's voice out here?" Noah emerged from Diego's bedroom, fastening the cufflinks on his tuxedo shirt. His face was smooth from shaving, his hair a darker blond than usual, still damp from the shower.

"Becca was here."

Noah arched a brow in question. "And?"

"Looks like your lady got a call from our guy today."

Noah's body tensed, and Diego wondered for the hundredth time how deep his friend's feelings went for the woman who'd brought Natalee into this mess. "A threat?"

Diego nodded. "In a roundabout way. Told her she was the Angel of Earth and he was going to save her, or something like that. The good news is, our guy's still around. And he's pissed."

"I'm also guessing that he didn't leave a trail."

"Damian works fast. His contact was able to trace the call to a payphone in the Chelsea area. The NYPD dusted for prints on that phone, but it was wiped clean. And there weren't any surveillance cameras in the area. Nothing there to go on."

"Of course not. I'm beginning to think this guy is a ghost." Noah sent a hand through his neatly styled hair, sending it askew in his frustration. "Why wouldn't she call me?"

Diego smirked. "My turn to guess. I'm thinking she told you to keep your distance."

"I was trying to give her space, but it looks like that's going to have to come to an end."

"She's got the SSAM team to rely on for protection. It doesn't have to be you. In fact, Becca is escorting Vanessa to the party, and she's more than capable of keeping her safe. Just leave it to the security expert."

"I know it doesn't *have* to be me," Noah growled, clearly unhappy with Diego's suggestion.

Diego hid a wry smile. Logic and emotion were often at odds when it came to matters of the heart. Looked like his friend was finally figuring that out.

VANESSA PAUSED in the entryway of Priscilla Manchester's penthouse, her nerves tied into a great big knot that sat in her stomach, swelling until she almost couldn't breathe. Or maybe it was her dress squeezing the air out of her. The sleeveless indigo bodice clung, emphasizing and lifting her breasts while the long skirt flowed out from her waistline, swirling about her silver-sandaled feet. She felt like a princess. A princess stalked by a beast.

Priscilla Manchester came forward with both arms outstretched, taking Vanessa's hands in her own. "It's so good to meet you in person."

"I feel the same," Vanessa said, immediately warming to the woman she'd spoken to half a dozen times over the past three days. "Happy birthday, Mrs. Manchester."

"Thank you. And please, call me Priscilla." Her voice dropped conspiratorially. "Between you and me, I could use a friendly face. These men have been prowling the place for an hour now, scouting out every possible hiding place or escape route."

Vanessa looked toward the men Priscilla indicated. One of them was her hostess's ex-husband Damian Manchester. He, Holt, Noah and Diego formed a formidable male wall as they stood in a circle at one end of the large living room, discussing something. Something important, no doubt, and probably of great interest to Vanessa, since her safety seemed to be on the line. The knot in her gut expanded, pushing on her lungs.

"Don't get me wrong," Priscilla continued. "I'm grateful they're here. But they've got me on edge with their grim expressions."

"I know what you mean." Though Vanessa would feel on edge with or without their help. The memory of the call she'd received earlier still gave her goose bumps. The gritty voice echoed in her head. Exactly which of her choices had he referred to that had been so wrong?

Becca came in through a glass door and joined the women. "It's getting dark. I made a quick sweep of the wraparound balcony, as well as the rooftop garden. Detective Hollister and I surveyed the lobby and briefed the security guards on duty there."

Fiona and Jesse arrived as Becca gave her report.

Fiona's gaze went to the gold strappy stilettos Becca was wearing to match her gold sheath. "You did all that walking in *those?*"

Becca laughed. "You do what you have to in this business."

Jesse shifted his weight. "If you ladies will excuse me, I think I'll join the guys."

As he left, Fiona rolled her eyes. "He must think there's a more interesting discussion going on over there. Definitely a testosterone imbalance in this room. I don't know how you work for an organization like SSAM, Becca, taking down the bad guys and working around that solid male flesh all the time." Fiona tapped a French-tipped finger to her lips. "On second thought, that doesn't sound so bad. They clean up well, anyway."

Vanessa resisted the urge to look toward the other side of the room and admire Noah in his formal party attire.

She'd caught a glimpse of him as she'd entered and it had been enough to make her break out in a sweat.

Becca smiled. "It took me a long time to be treated as one of the guys. I'm proud that I achieved that. And I'm an asset to the team when it comes to dealing with men, especially the bad guys. They let down their guards. Nobody would expect me to have excellent marksmanship and a black belt in Tai Kwon Do."

No, they wouldn't. Becca's short blond hair was done in the style of old Hollywood glamour. The woman was like a beautiful golden trophy. Not some kick-ass security specialist.

"Well, I suppose it's good news that nobody has tried to break in before the party," Priscilla said, returning to their earlier topic.

Becca frowned. "It's more likely our guy will be a guest tonight. Someone who knows the art community here in town, and is probably very involved in it in some way. Like Holt says, you probably know him." Seeing Priscilla pale, she hastened on. "Of course, he could be wrong."

Vanessa doubted it. The man had extensive knowledge of and experience with serial killers. The profile of the killer he'd sculpted over the past few days had been detailed. He'd revealed more tidbits just that afternoon when she'd reported the threatening phone call, including the fact the killer would be fairly young—in his mid-twenties or early thirties—and that he'd be handsome and charming. Which was just great. That included half of the artists she knew, several of them good friends.

Holt had also reported his suspicion that the guy was gay but in the closet. That had shocked the heck out of the team. But it also made sense, considering he had an unusually secret and close relationship with Nigel Springfield. After all, there had to be some way the killer had known how to move about the Springfield home without detection, where to find Nigel's pills, and that the *Angel of Air* hung in his bedroom, as well as a reason why that painting had held a place of honor.

Priscilla checked the slim diamond-encrusted watch at her wrist. "The guests should be arriving shortly." She nodded to a servant waiting out of earshot in the wings, who presumably went to notify the caterers. She moved toward the group of morose-looking men. Becca, Fiona and Vanessa followed in her wake.

Vanessa wanted to sink into the floor when Noah's attention fell on her. Her skin heated under his direct gaze as it swept down and back up her body, caressing her face and body without a touch. But when his eyes narrowed, she knew part of the heat she sensed from him was anger. It sparked her own temper. What the hell did he have to be so angry about? *She* was the one a killer was targeting.

"Can I have a word with you?" Noah asked, taking her by the elbow and pulling her into another room before she could answer.

"Well, hello to you too, Noah." A tactile person, she longed to run her hands down the smooth lines of his ebony coat, maybe grip the lapels and tug him closer. She wanted to press her lips to the warm smoothness of his cheek while sucking in a deep breath of the musky aftershave he used.

Instead, she kept at least two feet between them and clutched her traitorous hands together.

"You okay?" he finally asked, seeming to bring some dark emotion under control. "I heard about what happened today."

No, I'm scared to death. "Yes, I'm okay."

"Why didn't you call me?" Noah asked. "I'd have dropped everything and been there in no time at all."

"Really?" Given the way they'd been trying to dance around each other, except for that kiss outside the studio, she hadn't wanted to rely on him.

"Yes, really."

"It wasn't necessary. There were plenty of people around until Becca came to escort me home. I was safe."

Music swelled as Priscilla cued the string quartet that had set up in one corner of the living room to begin playing. Guests mingled in there, and in a dining area with a full spread of fabulous food, as well as in the large conservatory where they stood now. The *Angels* were hung on the wall in the front sitting room, under spotlights. It was everyone's hope that someone would recognize one of the three paintings or the artist and say something. One member of the team would be in that room at all times to engage people in conversation, hoping for a lead. The floor-to-ceiling windows revealed the lights of New York as dusk became dark.

Noah's frown remained, so she reached out to rest her hand on his forearm. "It's okay. *I'm* okay."

"For now." He shook his head as if shaking off dark thoughts. "We've got to find this guy tonight so you'll be safe once and for all."

"Then let's do it. Show time." Pasting a bright smile on her face, she moved away to mingle with the other guests, trying to forget that one of them wanted to kill her.

"YOU KNOW YOU have an amazing opportunity here." Priscilla's whisper tickled Damian's ear. The feel of her breath against his skin sent his mind spiraling back in time. Memories of many such parties, many years ago. A different lifetime.

Damian turned his head slightly, inhaling the subtle perfume she imported from Europe once a year. The same flowery scent he had bought for her for their anniversary every year for nineteen years. He tried to ignore how close her mouth was to his. She was a beautiful woman, and she wore her sixty years well.

"What opportunity?" He turned his gaze back to the people around them, moving his mouth away from the temptation of hers.

They were in the corner of the sitting room, watching guests who stopped to admire the paintings. But the crowd seemed more interested in their cocktails and hors d'oeuvres, oblivious to the depictions of women in their last moments of life that hung on the wall. Of course, few people knew the women had been real, flesh-and-blood people.

"For fundraising."

He used the excuse of taking a sip of his soda to force his mind to focus. "Fundraising?"

She gave an exasperated sigh. "For SSAM. I know you already rely on the deep pockets of several of our old friends in Chicago to hunt those vicious criminals. And you've obviously built a rich and loyal fan base—resourceful people willing to help any way they can. I think a lot of my guests would be intrigued by your organization. They're always looking for a good cause to throw their money at, especially when it's something worthy of delicious gossip at parties."

The thought had crossed his mind, but he hadn't wanted to use Priscilla. As it was, he was lugging around a truckload of guilt that weighed down his conscience when it came to her. He'd failed her after their daughter had died. Talk about baggage. And this was, after all, her birthday party. He'd turned it into a hunt for a killer and she hadn't batted an eye. Maybe he'd underestimated her strength all these years. After all, she hadn't been the only one to quietly fall apart after Samantha's death.

"You're a remarkable woman, Cilla. I don't think I've wished you a happy birthday yet."

A spark lit her blue eyes. "No, you haven't."

"Happy birthday."

"Thank you. It's been the most interesting birthday I've had in years." She sauntered away and struck up a conversation with an elderly man standing nearby.

Admiration curved Damian's lips. Priscilla Manchester had landed on both feet.

And he hadn't.

Nightmares of Sam's abduction still haunted him. Not that his ex-wife wasn't still in pain over the loss of their daughter. He'd sensed the shadows of pain lurking beneath the teasing. Part of her easy banter was an act. He well understood the need to hide your hurt from society. To try to pretend life was black-or-white normal when it was all kinds of shades of messed-up instead.

Grabbing two flutes of champagne from a passing tray, he moved toward where she was laughing at something the other man said. He couldn't drink much. He was on duty. But he could still toast her birthday. After all, they'd made it through hell and back—maybe not together, but they'd each found their ways back to the land of the living—and each year they survived was a milestone worth celebrating.

HE MINGLED. He laughed. He acted normal.

But he didn't feel normal. He missed Nigel so much his heart ached. Nigel would have loved a party such as this—all the glamorous dresses and fancy people. The sparkling conversation and constant flow of alcohol. The food wasn't bad either, he thought as he snagged a canapé from a passing tray.

And she was here. Their angel.

Oh, Nigel, you would have loved her.

Her dress swirled around her calves like a caress when she walked. He held his breath as she made her way across the room to where he stood admiring the paintings. His work. His angels.

Anger flared before he tamped it down again. He couldn't show his emotions here. It wasn't safe. He'd entrusted his collection to Vanessa, expecting her to appreciate them for the art they were. But she'd made a mockery of them by setting them up for everyone to see, tempting people to bid on them with the stories of murder that lay behind each one.

Murder? It was salvation.

And she thought she could *use* them to lure him out. Use *his* angels. Did they think he was stupid?

She would have to pay for that. His angel had fallen, but he'd lift her up again. He'd help her fly despite her broken wings.

"They really are breathtaking, aren't they?" she said. A smile curved her red lips. He would put a smattering of dirt there. A smear of mud across one cheek, perhaps. Some in her hair. Smudges down her pristine white arms.

"Yes." He turned back to the paintings. "Especially when they're all together like this. Any idea yet who the artist is?"

"No," she said, looking around. "It's still a mystery." She had no idea that the artist stood right beside her.

He glanced at his unknowing subject, taking in her profile, the little point of her chin and elegant line of her nose. Her skin had a delicious creaminess to it that he couldn't wait to touch. He knew just how he'd mix his paints. A touch of yellow ochre with the flesh tint. Perhaps just a tiny bit of crimson to add rosiness.

She moved out of the sitting room and back into the more crowded living room. He allowed his gaze to follow her, memorizing the gentle sway of her hips, the soft flow of satin around her as she seemed to drift.

His angel.

"WHOEVER HE IS, he certainly blends in," Diego muttered.

"Didn't expect him to walk in with a big red *K* for *Killer* painted on his forehead, did you?" Noah's own frustration added sharpness to his words. He breathed a sigh of relief as Vanessa moved back into the room. He was uneasy whenever she left his sight, but he had to give the man an opportunity to approach her. And one of SSAM's team members was always watching, no matter which room she moved to.

His eyes skimmed over her body and a different type of frustration took hold. God, she was beautiful. And he wanted her to be his. A twinge of jealousy had him turning away from the lovely vision. He was like a kid with empty pockets looking in a toy store window.

Or a neglected young boy trying to feel like part of a family. Unworthy. Wanting what he couldn't have.

"You're sunk, buddy," Diego said with a grim laugh.

"What?"

Diego jerked his head toward Vanessa, who had joined a small group at the other end of the room. "Her. You've got it bad for her."

"It's just lust. I'll get over it," Noah muttered. "She already has."

Diego's contemplative gaze found Vanessa. "You sure about that? She's looking this way right now. Perhaps I should wave her over."

Noah resisted the urge to slug his friend. "We're here as backup, remember. And she's doing her job."

"Working the room. Doesn't look too difficult for her. She seems like a classy woman."

"She is."

"And smart."

"Your point?"

Diego smirked. "I think it's already been made. I hope you know what you want. Because with a woman like that, you may be out of your league."

Didn't he know it.

"HIDING?"

Vanessa looked up from the tray of food she'd been inspecting to find Diego observing her. She gave a guilty smile. "Needed a break." And the kitchen had been as good a place as any, still near enough to other people to be safe, but away from people she had a duty to make conversation with. Though she loved the topic, how many times in one week could she discuss the future of contemporary art? The staff hustled and bustled about her as they loaded trays with food and drinks.

Diego nodded. "Me too."

"Besides, Becca's standing right outside the door."

"Yeah, I saw her."

"No luck finding the killer?" She tried not to show disappointment, but she knew Diego had to be just as disappointed anyway. And she sensed part of his anger and frustration this past week had been directed at her. Did he blame her for Natalee's death? "I'm sorry about what happened to Natalee. I truly cared about her."

His black-brown eyes met hers. He huffed out a breath. "I know. I've needed…I don't know. A scapegoat, I guess. And you were handy."

She snagged two appetizers off the tray in front of her and offered one to Diego. He accepted, his hands looking big as they gripped the toothpick that held the tiny morsel. She nibbled at hers. "If it helps, I blame myself, too."

He looked up sharply. "A lot of that going around. It doesn't help, either. Doesn't bring her back."

No, it didn't. Nothing could. She felt the sadness rolling off the man before her. Natalee had touched so many people in her short life. "Noah's close with your family. Did he know Natalee well?"

Diego snorted. "He was gone before Natalee was out of elementary school. Any memories he has would be of a young girl."

"Gone?"

"He left New York about ten years ago. Purposely sought a new life far away from us." There was hurt in Diego's tone.

"But why? I thought he was part of the Sandoval family." She'd admired that closeness. They were such a loving family. For someone to turn his back on that without good reason...

"He was. But no matter what we told him, he always felt like an outsider." Diego looked around as if unsure he should say more.

"That's hard to believe. Estella is so welcoming. She thinks of him as a son."

Diego winced. "I know. It hurt her when Noah moved away, checking in about once a year. He sends cards and gifts to her, but it's not enough. She's forever hopeful he'll come around." His gaze met hers and she knew he'd made a decision. Some of the tension went out of his shoulders as he turned toward her. "His family life wasn't the best, growing up. When they bothered to be sober, his parents stomped all over what confidence he might have developed when we were young. I'm not sure he ever got past it. Not fully, anyway. It's still hard for him to believe he's…" He paused, looking for the right word. "Loveable."

She frowned, remembering what Kenneth had said about Noah's past. *He's the offspring of a coke-addicted whore and an alcoholic.*

Seeing the consternation on her face, Diego gave a rough laugh. "And see, that's why he covers it with a rough exterior. Because he doesn't want anybody's pity."

Vanessa recalled Noah's words the night she'd tried to seduce him. He'd accused her of offering him her body out of pity. She grimaced at the memory.

"It's one of the reasons he went into the academy. I followed because…well, because we were brothers." He paused before continuing, as if deciding how far to go. "We had been with the NYPD for a few years when his parents were involved in a big drug bust. They chose death-by-cop rather than go to jail again. But the guys in the department…well, there was some razzing involved. Noah couldn't stand the constant reminder of where he'd come from, the smirks of his coworkers. He wanted a clean start, so he left. His pride was more important than his ties here." Diego shrugged as if it didn't matter, but it had to have hurt. "I've probably said too much."

She touched his hand. "I'm glad you did." So much about Noah's character, and his reluctance to share himself, was clear now. "And the juvie record?"

Diego looked at her in shock. "Hell, you know about that?"

"Kenneth's private investigator must have been thorough."

"It wasn't anything serious, but I'll save that story for later. It would be better if he told you. As for the rest of this, you didn't hear it from me." That he'd taken her into his confidence at all told Vanessa that all was forgiven between them.

Diego snagged another morsel as a waitress arrived to take the tray. The woman smiled warmly, with definite invitation in her eyes, but Diego seemed not to notice. He returned her smile absently.

"Here you guys are," Becca said, as she pushed through the door to the kitchen. Diego's return smile for *her* was much warmer. "You okay?" she asked Vanessa.

Vanessa nodded. "I just needed a moment." She jerked her head toward the door. "So many people in there."

"I know what you mean. But I have to get back. It's your shift to watch the Angel Room," Becca told Diego.

The Angel Room. It was what they'd labeled the sitting room that displayed the collection. Vanessa shivered. If the killer had his way, her image would be hanging there next.

"I'll be back in there soon," Vanessa told Becca in answer to her concerned look. "I might step outside—just a couple feet from the door—for a quick breath of fresh air."

The other woman glanced at the bustle of activity and then out the window to the well-lit balcony. She nodded and linked arms with Diego. "No farther though."

"Promise."

The pair left to rejoin the party.

The kitchen was suddenly too warm. Vanessa stepped outside, noting that a few partygoers were already on the stone patio that lined the entire side of the penthouse, enjoying the breathtaking view of the city. Potted plants and cheery flowers were clustered in several places along the railing. A dozen or so guests were scattered in small groups, enjoying the cool summer evening air or a cigarette. As promised, she didn't go more than a few steps, making sure to stay within the circle of light just outside the kitchen window. Rolling her head along her shoulders, she willed her tense muscles to relax.

Noah had been an unwanted child. The thought tore at her chest. He was a strong, dedicated man. He deserved love as much as anyone else did. Someone should show him that. *She* should. And not out of pity, but because she wanted to. She wanted him. And she was tired of letting him push her away.

Tonight. Tonight she would make a move. And maybe find some of that *frivolous fun* Fiona had lectured her about.

Her tension was turning to liquid heat at the thought of a night of abandon in Noah's arms when the sound of a footstep came from the shadows to her left. She turned quickly and took a step back toward the door.

"I was hoping you'd come out here."

"Kenneth?" She hadn't seen or heard from him since Saturday night. Now, he seemed to emerge from the darkness.

As he stepped forward, the light glinted in his narrowed eyes. He swayed a little, saluting her with his empty champagne glass. "Give that lady a cigar. She certainly doesn't want a ring." His laugh was harsh.

A glance showed that people were within shouting distance if she needed help, but guilt kept her quiet. Surely Kenneth didn't deserve the cold shoulder at such a high-profile party. The gossips would rip them both apart. Besides, she'd rather the SSAM team focus on finding a killer, not breaking up a domestic dispute.

"What are you doing here?"

"What, you're the only one who can have rich friends? I am an invited guest of my client. You know, the artist accused of ripping off other people's work? He's got connections in the art world, too…and therefore, I've got connections. I don't need you." He tipped his glass to take a gulp of champagne, frowning when he realized it was empty. He threw it into a nearby potted palm.

"I'm sure you don't. Good night." She turned to go back inside, but he gripped her arm tight and swung her back to face him. Trying to pull her arm away only made him grip harder.

"You're a cold bitch, you know that? I didn't do anything to deserve how you treated me."

"We weren't good together," she hissed. "You must have thought the same thing at some point, or our relationship would have moved further along. Instead, you waited until I was a more suitable trophy."

"Well you're certainly a trophy now—you even come with reward money."

"What are you talking about?"

Kenneth sneered. "Your mother offered me money to get you to the altar. Fast. I guess she's worried you'll let some blue-collar loser like Crandall ruin you in your current state of mind. And after this weekend, she thought I might need an incentive to look past the trouble you're causing."

"She wouldn't—" Vanessa stopped. Sylvia Knight would do whatever she had to in order to control her world and the people who populated it.

"I'll share the money with you."

"I don't need the money. I'm happy where I am."

"Like that job of yours is going to get you anywhere. It can't give you the family you want. *I* can. Or is someone else warming your bed at night? One look from that smooth talker was all it took to get you to spread your legs, wasn't it?"

"You're a bastard." She tried to pull away. The grip he'd maintained on her arm was cutting off the circulation, and she could smell the sourness of alcohol on his breath as he leaned closer. He'd definitely had more than the one glass of champagne. "Let go or I'll scream."

"You heard the lady," a voice said from the doorway.

Noah. Oh, thank God.

Kenneth's sneer widened. He leaned down, tugging her closer so he could talk in her ear. "You could have had everything. Instead, you're settling for—" he paused and looked at Noah, "—nothing." He planted a hard kiss on her lips that had no tenderness, no love in it. Suddenly, he was ripped away from her and shoved to the ground. Noah shielded her with his body.

"How about I call you a cab, Kenny-boy?" Noah was already pulling out his phone.

"Don't bother. I have a car and driver waiting." Kenneth pulled himself back to a standing position, dusting himself off and shooting them a look of contempt. "Remember what I said," he told Vanessa before stalking off toward the party.

Noah eyed her with concern. "What did he say?" His fingers skimmed over the red marks on her arm. There would be a bruise there by morning.

"Nothing important." But everything she was wondering about. Would a brief affair with Noah be *settling?* In a way, yes, since she wanted so much more from him. But as his light, probing touch brought shivers to her skin, she couldn't help but think of the rewards for settling. When he was gone, it would hurt, but she had the feeling only he could open her up to a whole other world that was out there.

"Let's get some ice for that arm."

Noah moved toward the door, but she took his hand and stopped him. "Do we have to stay any longer? The party's winding down, and I've got ice at home."

"I don't want you to go home alone," he said. "There's still a killer out there."

"I didn't say I wanted to go alone." Her gaze held his, trying to convey the decision her heart had made. She wanted him. He wanted her. She was willing to risk everything for a brief glimpse of happiness. "I want you to come with me."

SIXTEEN

FROM HIS VANTAGE point near the string quartet, Diego could observe the entire writhing room of guests.

"Anything?" Becca asked.

He shook his head, trying not to let disappointment weigh him down. He'd set his hopes on this evening. "Not a thing in here, or in the Angel Room. Where did Noah disappear to?"

"I sent him to check on Vanessa."

He smiled. "Good."

"Do you think they'll figure out that they care about each other?"

"He hasn't made one intelligent move where that woman's concerned."

"Then we'd better find them and show them how it's done." Linking her arm with his, she tugged him from the larger room through the Angel Room. His eyes avoided the *Angel of Fire* and Natalee's image. Looking at it earlier had made his gut ache to the point he'd worried he'd toss up the fancy little snacks he'd consumed.

He felt Becca shiver and placed a hand over hers. "Cold?"

"They give me the creeps." Still, she looked over the small group gathered in front of the paintings with a security expert's eyes and a siren's smile. She was a vision tonight in shimmery gold, all movie-star glamour and sex appeal. She sighed. "Too bad the guy we're looking for probably fits in here better than we do. He'll be harder to find than we thought."

"Unless he makes a move on Vanessa."

"Let's go check on them."

In the kitchen the process of cleaning up had begun as the eleven o'clock hour approached. And they still weren't any closer to finding Natalee's killer. Frustration tore at his insides like tiny knives.

At that moment, Vanessa came in from a door to the outside, accompanied by a welcome breeze of cooler air. And Noah, looking bewildered and flustered and determined all at once.

"Problem?" Diego asked.

He shook his head. "Nothing I couldn't handle."

"Kenneth was out there." Vanessa jerked her head toward the back door.

Diego's eyes narrowed. "You think he could be the killer?"

"No. I mean…I never thought…no." She seemed stunned at the suggestion.

"You're sure?" His eyes met Noah's.

"He's more the overt asshole type than artistic crazy person," Noah said. "He just wanted to give Vanessa a hard time. I think she's ready to call it a night."

"I'll get my purse," Becca said, turning to go.

"Don't bother," Noah said. "I'm taking her home tonight."

And wasn't there an onion's-worth of layers in *that* statement? Diego picked the layer that meant the most to him. "You're giving up on finding the killer?" He'd had too many hopes pinned on this night to give up now.

"The guy's either not here, or he's not going to make a move in this crowd. We'll compare notes tomorrow. Besides," Noah added with a sidelong glance at Vanessa, who looked pretty damn flustered herself, "I think Vanessa's had enough confrontation for one night."

"Wait. About Kenneth…" Becca looked around to see if anyone was listening. The staff continued to clean, but their group was attracting some curious looks. She lowered her voice to a whisper. "Should I tell Damian to put him on the suspect list?"

"No," Vanessa said at the same time Noah said, "Maybe."

Vanessa stared at him. "You really think he could be a killer? There's no way he painted those paintings." She scoffed. "When it comes to art, he only knows what I've told him. As you so eloquently put it, we're looking for *artistic crazy*."

Noah shrugged. "He certainly seemed agitated enough to kill tonight."

"For good reason." Vanessa and Noah shared a long look. She broke the contact first. "But I *would* have Damian or Holt look into Kenneth's current case. He says he's representing an accused art thief. Something about a stolen Van Gogh."

Becca nodded. "I'll pass that along. And if you're taking Vanessa home, I suppose it wouldn't hurt if I followed Kenneth when he leaves. I guess we can talk to Damian about closing down shop here for the night."

"Call me when you have anything set up for tomorrow." Noah grabbed Vanessa's hand and practically dragged her out of the kitchen.

Becca watched them with a thoughtful look on her face. "Guess he doesn't need me to play Vanessa's bodyguard tonight."

And Diego guessed he wouldn't see much of his roommate until morning, at the earliest.

DAMIAN WATCHED in admiration as, despite her fatigue, his ex-wife made small talk with a departing couple with her usual grace and poise. She'd made sure to introduce him around tonight, mentioning SSAM without making the organization a focus. He only hoped it hadn't scared their prey away. If the killer knew the head of an elite private crime-fighting organization was in attendance, would he run or get cocky? Holt seemed to think it might actually lure the sick bastard into a false sense of confidence, which was the only reason Damian had allowed Priscilla to say anything about it.

"I hope your birthday wasn't a total bust," he said as Priscilla watched the elevator doors close behind the last of her guests and came over to his side.

She gave a tired smile. "Not at all. This party was more than I was going to do, anyway. I haven't really celebrated milestones like this since…" She shrugged and avoided his gaze.

"Since Samantha died. I've been the same way." Worse, actually. He'd become a hermit. At least she still had ties to society. Obligations that pulled her forth from her cave. Everyone had his or her coping mechanisms. He would respect hers.

His was SSAM, which he made sure consumed all his free time and energy.

Her blue eyes glazed with tears that she quickly blinked away. But to his surprise, she didn't avoid the subject of their daughter. "You can let go, you know."

"Let go?"

"Of the guilt. I know you blame yourself for what happened to Sam. And I admire what you're doing. But it won't bring her back."

His chest tightened, as it always did when he imagined his thirteen-year-old daughter as he'd last seen her, so beautiful and innocent. He often wondered what she would have been like today. A wife? A mother? Would he have been a grandfather by now? It hurt too much to contemplate. "I haven't caught her killer yet. I made a promise."

"And you think I didn't?" She choked back a sob. "I made a vow on the day I held our precious baby girl in my arms for the first time that I would protect her from the evil in the world. Isn't that a mother's job? I had to live with that failure for years. Until I found help. A support group. Friends who understood. I've learned to forgive myself."

A bark of harsh laughter escaped him. "Forgiveness. I don't even know what that is." Maybe that was why he worked so hard at what he did. He couldn't forgive himself, and he damn well couldn't forget. But he could work day and night to keep some other man, some father who didn't appreciate the priceless gift he had, from going through the same pain.

"It won't bring her back." Priscilla laid a hand on his arm. "You've got to find a way to live again. A life outside of work." She swiped away a tear from her cheek with her free hand. A crack in the dam had let a trickle of emotion through her usually composed façade, but she wouldn't let the dam break entirely. "You owe it to yourself. You owe it to her."

He didn't want to talk about this. Not here. Not now. Probably not ever. So he went on the attack. "And you? Is that what you're doing?" He waved a hand at the fancy furniture and big rooms. It all seemed like some silly fairy tale, but he knew it was important to Priscilla. Still, did anyone who had been there tonight really know her, even a fraction of how he'd known her long ago? "Is this the life you wanted to live?"

She glanced around her, a faint upturn to the corners of her trembling lips. "No. But that dream was taken from us." She drew herself up. "That's enough sharing for one evening, I think."

"It's more than we've done in decades," he muttered. He happily changed the subject. "I appreciate all you've done tonight."

"Did it help?"

That was the million-dollar question. "We won't know until the team compares notes on the guests tomorrow morning. I'll take the paintings with me tonight and I'll let you know if we learn anything. In the meantime, stay safe, Cilla." Her eyes teared again at the fond nickname and he couldn't resist reaching out to touch her soft cheek with the back of one hand. Her eyes fluttered shut, then opened again, her tears gone. He let his hand fall away.

"You, too." She moved away.

Within moments, she was the consummate hostess again, addressing a member of the remaining catering staff. Maybe she *had* moved on. Maybe he was stuck in a hell of his own creation, doomed to take down other people's monsters but never his own.

"Noah's taking Vanessa home," Becca said, having appeared at his elbow from somewhere. The woman moved with the stealthy sleekness of a cat.

"Good. At least we know she'll get home safely." He turned to her, one of his newest and brightest security experts. She and the rest of his SSAM team were why he still had hope he would find his daughter's killer. And prevent other deaths. Despite Priscilla's advice, he could never let go of the fire inside him that helped him make that difference. "Make sure he and everyone else gets the message that we're meeting at eight in the morning in the warehouse studio, assuming Vanessa can arrange it."

"I'm sure she can." She looked as if she would say something more, and he waited for the pert questions he'd come to expect from his forthright employee. "She's a real class act, sir."

He followed her gaze and saw that she was speaking of Priscilla. "Yes, she is." He waited for more impertinence, but it never came.

"Good night, sir."

Had it been a good night? He sensed he and Priscilla had reached a new understanding of each other. That was good.

Vanessa was safe. That was good, as well.

But his ex-wife had stirred longings and emotions within him that had been long buried. The long-term impact of that remained to be seen.

THE MOMENT NOAH closed Vanessa's apartment door behind them, he tugged her to his chest, pressing his hands against her back to mold her hot, tight body to him. His lips found hers and locked on for dear life.

He wouldn't overthink it. Not this time. He wasn't sure how she'd forgiven him for being a total dick last time. For some reason, heaven had smiled on him and granted him his one fervent wish.

Vanessa would be in his bed.

Well, he'd be in hers. But first…

He reluctantly pulled himself away, sucking in a much-needed breath. "Let me check the place out first." In the fastest security check ever, he looked in every possible hiding place, relieved to find her home empty.

"Noah?" Vanessa's worried voice called from the entryway.

"I'm here," he said, coming from the bedroom to rejoin her. "All clear." He pulled her back into his arms.

He drank in long sips of her as he reached behind to lock the front door. His fingers quickly launched a new quest, fumbling for the enclosure of her dress.

She huffed a laugh against his lips. "Side zipper," she said, barely breaking contact. His hands skimmed her sides, located the hidden zipper and quickly went to work. The soft swish of fabric met his ears as the garment slid to the floor.

Vanessa's breath came in hot, delicious pants against his mouth. Her hands worked in a flurry of frustration to tug his bowtie from his neck and undo his cufflinks, swiftly moving to the belt at his waist. It was as if she didn't know where to work first, so she tried to be everywhere at once.

They laughed into each other's mouths while peeling articles of clothing away. The pieces were left in a trail of debris as he backed her toward the hallway.

"Bed. Now," he mumbled against her mouth, adding a nip of her lips to punctuate his need. They half walked, half stumbled their way down the hall.

Not moving fast enough. He hiked her body up against his, relishing the smooth feel of her naked legs wrapping around his waist. The only things between them now were his boxers and her black silk panties and strapless bra. Barriers to success, though he did like the lace trim. Well, he was sure he'd like it if he'd take the time to look at it. What he could feel of it evoked such sinful images that he staggered. He focused on tactile sensations to reorient himself, and one hand slid down over the side of her breast and back to her hip, then gripped her buttocks to lift her closer against him, rubbing her hot center against his arousal. He'd make her put the silk-and-lace confections back on later—much later—so that he could properly appreciate them before they went for Round Two.

Round One was going to have to be hard and fast. The way Vanessa was shoving her hands through his hair and devouring his mouth left him no doubt that was what she wanted too. After all, the inferno had been building between them for days, and they had unfinished business from last Saturday night. He was starting to think up against the wall to his left would be as good a place as any to slake their thirst for each other.

His fingers pressed into her thighs, hoisting her high enough so he could reach around and find the sweet spot that he knew would bring her pleasure. He found her through the moist, thin silk, and pressed down. She moaned her approval and bit his lip.

"Hurry." Her ankles locked against the small of his back. He pushed through her bedroom doorway and tumbled them onto the bed, immediately shifting his weight so as not to crush her. She lifted her hips and ground them against his groin. He groaned. If that was how she was going to play it, hard and fast it would be.

"Damn." He leaned his forehead against hers and tried to catch his breath. He had a condom with him. Or he had, before he'd left his pants on the floor near her front door.

"Nightstand drawer," she murmured, reading his mind. She unlocked her ankles long enough for him to remove his underwear, find a condom and slip it on. Her gaze swept over him and she licked her lips, a wicked light in her eyes. A light he'd put there. Whatever he'd done to deserve this night, he'd do it over and over again if it meant more looks like that from her. *Thank you, Jesus.*

Slowly, she undid her bra—it was black as sin and just as lovely—and slipped it off, tossing it away before scooting out of her panties. He prowled like a jungle cat across her body, admiring her soft beauty. The window blinds were open slits that allowed moonlight to spill over her,

her creamy body contrasting with the deep brown of her eyes and hair. She was glorious.

He bent to lick the pebbled nipple of a generous breast, and reveled in her purr of contentment. He bent to the other breast, and she arched against him. His hand found the damp curls between her legs as she spread them wide, welcoming him and wrapping her arms around his neck to pull him to her.

But he wasn't done with the rest of her yet. He wanted her to moan and writhe. To beg for him. Just for him. Within moments of his pleasurable assault, she was doing just that, his name a groan on her lips.

"Now," she begged, tugging him to her. "I need you *now*." He obliged, slowly inserting himself into her moist heat. He ached to reach his release, but wanted her right there with him when he found it. He wanted her with him all the way.

They found a slow rhythm together and quickly built it into the inferno again. He locked gazes with her, watching the flames dance. Each time he sank into her, it felt like coming home.

Home? He froze. He'd never had a home. How the hell would he know what it felt like?

He slid out and into her again, harder, struggling to push aside all thought. He flicked his thumb across her sensitive nub. A gasp of pleasure escaped her lips.

Home to him had been filled alternately with shouts of anger or empty space, depending on whether his parents were around or not. Mostly, it had been *not*. Sometimes for several days at a time.

Home, for him, had been loneliness and pain. Feelings of inadequacy. Neglect.

But with Vanessa, something was different. He'd found what home should be.

And it scared the shit out of him.

He almost pulled away, rocked to his core by the fear of something nameless. But Vanessa chose that moment to lock her legs around him and pull him deeper. Her tight muscles clenched around his erection as an orgasm shook her, and he threw his head back and found his release along with hers.

They lay still for several moments afterward, his forehead pressed into the pillow next to hers as their breathing returned to normal. One of her delicate hands stroked absently up and down his back. Comforting. But his thoughts would not be calmed.

He shifted off her, rolling to his back. She followed, sprawling halfway across his chest.

Vanessa wasn't *home,* he told himself. Nobody and nowhere was home for him.

Chicago. The world of violent crime he moved through every day. Those were what he knew. What he was comfortable with.

THE WARM BUBBLE of happiness Vanessa woke up in, encircled in Noah's arms, couldn't last. The real world would intrude soon enough. Still, she clung to the dream as long as she could, waking her lover by kissing her way across his bare chest. His hand came up to stroke her hip.

"Mornin'," he mumbled, kissing her forehead sleepily. And they should be sleepy, she thought with a lazy smile. They'd spent most of the night waking each other up. It was only seven-thirty. She had another half hour before she had to get up if she wanted to be at work by nine. She'd have to rush, but it would be worth it.

She inhaled the warm male scent of Noah, closing her eyes as she pictured waking up this way every morning for the rest of their lives. Forcing her eyes open, she quickly discarded the dreams, determined to settle for whatever time they had together. After all, he was supposed to be her rebound guy. A temporary fascination. Frivolous fun.

But as her body awakened again under Noah's increasingly ardent strokes, nibbles and kisses, she knew she was deluding herself. He could never be a rebound guy. She'd experienced a level of passion and intimacy last night that told her she was already in too deep.

As he kissed his way down her body, a knock at the front door made them both freeze.

"Damn," he said with a wry grin. "They found us."

"Wouldn't whoever it is have called first?" she asked.

His sigh was a whoosh of hot breath against her bare stomach. "They probably tried. But I left my phone in the other room."

"In your pants." Her eyes widened as she realized what the living room must look like, their garments strewn about. She must have forgotten to put her own phone on the charger again. She shoved him off her and jumped out of bed, racing to her closet to throw on some clothing. When she looked back she found him grinning, his hands tucked behind his head, elbows out to either side as he watched her. "Don't just lie there, get up. Someone obviously needs one of us."

"I'm enjoying the view. And I'm keeping a promise to myself. I didn't have a chance to properly appreciate those spectacular undergarments of yours last night."

With a groan of frustration, she turned away to tug on some jeans and heard the bed creak as he rose. He placed a kiss on her bare shoulder and then grabbed his boxer shorts off the floor. The knocking came again.

"I'll handle it." Noah's long strides took him quickly out of the bedroom. Vanessa checked her face and hair in the mirror, smoothing down the errant strands, and rushed after him. She hoped he'd think to pick up their clothing before answering the door.

"We're on our way there now," Diego was saying as she came out of the bedroom. He coughed to cover his embarrassment as he caught sight of her. Becca grinned at her from beside him.

"On your way where?" Vanessa asked, relieved to see that Noah had pulled on his tuxedo pants and his dress shirt, though he'd left it hanging open, exposing a stretch of bare chest. She blushed at the memory of kissing her way down that chest. And back up again.

Diego tossed a duffel bag to Noah, who caught it and peeked inside. "Thanks, man."

"Thought you might want a change of clothes before we head to the meeting. Damian wants to get an early start." He glanced at his watch. "You've got ten minutes before we have to leave if we want to be on time. I tried your phone, but…"

"We'll hurry."

Her blush deepened. She knew exactly why Diego hadn't been able to get in touch with them. And Diego knew, too. Noah spun, duffel bag in hand, stopping to place a hard kiss on Vanessa's mouth before disappearing down the hall.

Her lips tingled with the brief, intense contact. "Um, coffee anyone?" She turned toward the kitchen to hide the flush that had crept up her neck and spread to her cheeks.

"No time," Becca said. "Go ahead and get ready. We'll keep ourselves occupied for a few minutes."

"Help yourself to anything you want." She gladly escaped, trying to ignore the sounds of the shower—*her* shower—running on the other side of her bathroom door. Where Noah was naked. She glanced at the bed, where the sheets lay in a tangled heap. How she wished she could rewind the morning and wake up a few minutes earlier. She'd give herself enough time to take that shower with Noah. The water shut off even as she had the thought, and she reluctantly turned to gather more appropriate clothing before taking her own quick shower.

Alone.

SEVENTEEN

VANESSA LED the SSAM team into the warehouse studio where they'd decided to meet. She was surprised to find Priscilla Manchester among their number.

"Holt received some news from his FBI contact this morning," Damian said after they'd all grabbed stools and folding chairs and set up in the studio area.

"He's been searching through unsolved cases for women victims who drowned," Holt said. "In particular, cases near a beach. We may have found a match for the *Angel of Water*. Since we had a pretty good image of what she looked like, courtesy of our killer, my contact was able to narrow the possibilities down to a woman's body found on a private stretch of beach near Miami in March of this year. Her name was Lisa Roma."

Vanessa saw the picture as it was passed around the group. Lisa was similar in build, facial structure, and hair length and color to the depiction of *Angel of Water*. The body was posed with its face tipped upward, eyes closed, arms outstretched.

A muscle in Diego's jaw jumped as he looked at the photo. "Just like Natalee."

Holt nodded. "I think the killer would see it as his duty to represent them as true to life as possible. He'd pose them as he intended to paint them."

"Miami is a prime area for artists." Priscilla looked surprised that she'd spoken the thought aloud, then glanced around at the group as if she wasn't sure she had the right to speak. Damian's raised eyebrows indicated he was interested in what she had to say.

Vanessa nodded. "Miami is one of the centers of art in this country. This artist could live there."

"And came to New York City in time to kill my niece." Diego's voice was filled with disgust. "How convenient." In quiet sympathy, Becca touched his hand.

"He has connections here," Holt said. "After all, his paintings surfaced in the Springfield home. Mrs. Manchester, did you know Nigel Springfield?"

She nodded. "A little. We served on a board together, an organization that funded the arts. Other than that, we bumped into each other occasionally, but he'd been so sick this year that he dropped out of society. Then, a couple months ago, I saw the obituary in the paper."

"What is your impression of his son Lawrence?"

Priscilla's tinkling laugh filled the room. "Lawrence couldn't give two figs for art."

"He's as different from Nigel as night from day," Vanessa said.

"Then how was Nigel attached to this artist, this killer?" Damian asked. "Could he have been involved in the murders? He sounds like he was sick."

"Sick, but not frail," Priscilla explained. "In fact, before the cancer took hold, he prided himself on keeping fit. And he was a patron of the arts. He traveled the world looking for interesting works of art and promising artists. According to rumor, he became personally attached to a few budding artists and supported them financially. While I can't picture Nigel killing anyone, I suppose he could have become involved with a murderer."

Damian turned to Becca. "Get in touch with Lawrence Springfield. See if he's heard from his accountant yet, or if

he can shed light on artists Nigel may have been supporting. And find out if any of them are in the Miami area."

Vanessa absorbed the flow of dialogue around her, all
the while studying the photograph of Lisa Roma. She was
likely the *Angel of Water.* A victim, just as Natalee and
the *Angel of Air* were.

Noah voiced her next question. "What about victims
who could have been the *Angel of Air?* Any leads?"

Holt shook his head. "So far, my contact hasn't found
anything. Besides, there's little background in that painting to indicate where it was. With the *Angel of Water,* we
theorized that she was near or on a beach because of the
granules of sand in the painting. The size of the waves
he'd painted even indicated an ocean rather than a lake.
We had a bit more information."

"What about the guy Kenneth Barnes is representing?"
Diego asked. "Could he be the killer? Or Kenneth? They
were both at the party last night."

Holt nodded. "I had a chance to chat with the defen-
dant at Priscilla's. Cocky guy, and he thinks he'll beat the
rap, especially with Kenneth as his lawyer."

"He must have contacts or deep pockets to afford Kenneth," Vanessa said.

"And bail. He claims he was set up with the Van Gogh
he's accused of stealing. Was holding it for a friend or
something like that. He's an artist from a wealthy family, so there's no need to steal."

"So he's innocent?"

Holt huffed. "Not if I'm any judge of character. He
strikes me as the type who was raised with a silver spoon
and likes to test society's limits, thinking he can get away
with anything. And I'd bet good money he'll get away
with this, too. But murder?" He shook his head. "I don't

think so. And Kenneth? He was with Vanessa the night
Cromby was murdered."

Vanessa's phone buzzed in her purse and she discreetly
moved outside to take the call. She glanced at her watch.
She still had fifteen minutes until her shift started at
Atherton's, but she'd have to leave soon. "Hello?"

"Vanessa! Oh, thank goodness," Fiona said, sounding
breathless. "You need to get to the gallery right away.
Atherton's lost his ever-lovin' mind."

"What's he done?"

"You'd have to see it to believe it."

"I'll be there soon." Hanging up, she moved back inside, noting that Noah had moved to watch her from the
door while she was away from their safe circle.

He ducked his head down as she entered. "What's
wrong?" he said in a low voice, not wanting to disturb
the discussion going on among the others.

"Fiona says I have to get to work now."

He looked from his team to her. "I'm coming with you."

"Is HE A complete idiot, or what?" Fiona asked as she stood
beside a gaping Vanessa. The *Angels* hung in a neat row
in a position of prominence in the gallery. They had their
own wall, claiming one's attention the minute one walked
through the glass doors.

The question didn't warrant an answer. Of course
Lance was an insensitive idiot of the highest magnitude,
but he was also a savvy businessman. "How did he get
them?" Vanessa's eyes moved over the three paintings.

Noah hung up his phone and joined their conversation.
"I just spoke with Springfield. Apparently, while the party
was in full swing last night and we were all occupied, his
lawyer moved quickly to get a judge to release custody of
the artwork from the police. So when Damian turned the

Angels over to the NYPD after the party, the paintings were then released to the Springfield estate. Springfield gave Atherton permission to display them for a limited time at the gallery before they go up for auction as a collection at Sotheby's."

Jesse came over to them with a newspaper in hand. He frowned. "Springfield stands to make a fortune. And I'll bet he's the one who leaked the story behind the paintings, and how they're linked to murder. It's all over the internet, and in this morning's *New York Times*."

Vanessa felt ill. Had her idea to pretend they were writing a story about Springfield and the paintings gained them an interview but created a worse problem? The man now seemed to have delusions of grandeur.

Lance came from the back, frowning at Noah before turning to the rest of them. He rubbed his hands together. "Okay, people. Be ready for big numbers today."

Hand curled into a fist, Vanessa took a step forward, but stopped when Noah touched her arm. Oblivious to his employees' dark expressions, Lance went to unlock the front doors, where several people were already waiting. One was a reporter.

In disgust, Vanessa turned on her heel and walked to her office. "How could he do this?" she asked, sensing Noah was behind her.

He closed the door and leaned against it. "Is it any surprise? He's doing what any business owner would do."

"Doesn't make it okay." She paced her office, trying to let off some extra energy. She threw an arm toward the front room where a low hum indicated several conversations were going on. The crowd of spectators was growing. "People are going to think I'm a part of this. That I support exploiting the victims depicted in those works. For God's sake, one of those paintings is Natalee."

"And yet you work for him. Why don't you quit?" Noah pushed away from the door. "Stand up for what you believe."

Like *he* did. Whether he was aware of it or not, he probably believed that working as a detective made up for his past, made up for feeling like he was nothing. He'd made himself into something, choosing a career that gave him a status with which nobody could argue.

She crossed her arms. "I do. I stand up for what I believe."

He gave her a half smile that made her bristle. "Not really. Not when it causes waves. Not when it really matters."

"Like *you* do?"

"When it involves finding justice for someone, hell, yes. I make waves. I do what it takes."

"I need this job." Because when the investigation was complete, and he left, there would be nothing else to fill her time. He shook his head and she felt disappointment radiating off him. Her face flushed hot. "What I don't need is grief from you. I know what's right without your help. That pulpit you're preaching from is built on a pretty shaky foundation, don't you think?" She regretted the words the moment they were out of her mouth.

His eyes narrowed as he stalked forward. "If you're referring to the way I was brought up, my so-called parents weren't the only ones who shaped my past."

"No? Well you certainly act like it. Estella and the Sandovals were always there for you. They had more influence on the man you are today than your parents, and yet you turn your back on them."

"Which is why I'm here today," he retorted sarcastically. *"Helping them."*

Because this was the one area he felt he could help

them. Finding justice was something he felt confident in. Family matters, not so much. Her heart twisted for him. "Maybe you should remember who's in your corner, instead of who isn't, the next time you feel sorry for yourself."

He flinched, then seemed to harden all over. She'd pushed him too far. "Becca will be here soon," he said. "Damian wants her to monitor the crowd today. I've got other things to follow up on."

She kept her hands fisted at her sides rather than reach for him as she wanted to. She shouldn't have gone down this road with him. After all, he was supposed to be her fling, and here she was forcing him to face down a past he refused to acknowledge.

"How is she?"

Becca stepped aside and allowed Noah to enter Vanessa's apartment. "She's still asleep. Had a hard night." Judging by Becca's face, she blamed *him* for that. She turned and began gathering up the blankets from the couch that she'd slept on.

Almost twenty-four hours after their argument, Noah still hadn't been able to get Vanessa out of his head. And then he'd received a call from Fiona early this morning that had his heart in his throat. Overnight, the *Angels* had been stolen from the gallery. He'd rushed to dress and get across town, needing to see Vanessa with his own eyes and make sure she was safe. "I owe her an apology."

She stacked the blankets on a chair. "Looks that way. She's a good woman. She'd be worth fighting for, if you want a long-term thing."

And didn't that sum it all up nicely? "I don't know what I want."

"Then don't fuck with her."

He was afraid it was too late for that. He heard the sound of a shower turning on from the direction of Vanessa's bathroom. "I got a call from Fiona at the gallery. The paintings went missing again. The place is in a panic."

"I would imagine so."

"Damian and Holt are following up now. They'd like you to talk to Springfield and see if you can get more information about who Nigel supported. He connected with you at the interview the other day."

"And Vanessa?"

"I can take Vanessa to the gallery today. I'd like the opportunity to apologize," he added when Becca didn't budge.

"Okay, then." She gathered her overnight bag from the table. "I'll see you soon."

Becca hadn't been gone long enough for Noah to sit down when a knock came at the door. He swung it open to find Sylvia Knight on the threshold, holding a bag. Despite the windy morning, not a hair was out of place.

Her mouth set in a firm line when she spied Noah. "I guess I shouldn't be surprised to find you here."

"Vanessa's busy. Can I help you?" He seriously doubted it. She looked like a woman with purpose as she breezed past him. She stopped in the middle of the living room and plunked the bag down on the coffee table. It tipped over and magazines slid out across the surface.

"Yes, as a matter of fact." Her smile brightened. "I brought some bridal magazines for Vanessa." She glanced toward the closed bedroom door.

"She's in the shower." He enjoyed the spark of irritation that lit the woman's eyes.

"You shouldn't be here."

"I'm here to protect her."

"If you want to protect her, you'll stay out of her life. She's made for other, *greater* things."

"I agree."

Her eyes widened. "You do?"

"I don't want to hurt her." But he couldn't stay away. And he couldn't leave things the way he had yesterday. She'd been trying to help him and he'd snapped at her. Thrown off by the sudden, comfortable connection with Vanessa and her ability to see right through him to his core, his self-preservation instinct had made him act like a jerk. "I'm here because she's in danger."

"Kenneth can take care of her."

"Not this time." He doubted Kenny-boy had what it took to protect her in any situation, but he bit his tongue.

Sylvia's face softened. "You showing up has given her a nice distraction. In fact, I'm grateful, because having a little competition seems to have pushed Kenneth into finally making a commitment. But it's time for you to leave. Staying—getting more involved—won't help Vanessa."

"That's the *only* reason I'm here. To help Vanessa."

"In the long run, you'll hurt her. Did she tell you about her dream to open her own gallery? And to have a family?" She gave him a sympathetic look. "No, I can see she didn't. Can you honestly say you can give her what she really wants? I'm asking you not to ruin her chances at long-term happiness just so you can get your kicks for a few days."

THE WATER HAD lost its near-scalding temperature but had served its purpose. The shower had invigorated her after a difficult night, and helped her come to a decision. She'd find Noah this morning and make things right. She couldn't go through another night without settling things.

She scrambled into some work-appropriate clothes and

left the bedroom, still fastening an earring. She came to an abrupt halt as she saw two unexpected guests. An unlikely pair, at that. Her mother and Noah stood in her living room. Becca was nowhere to be found. Sylvia Knight was giving Noah a wary look and Noah looked like he wanted to bolt.

"Mother." Vanessa felt adrenaline flood her system as if preparing for war. Her protective instincts leaped to life. She moved over to stand near Noah. Tension radiated off him in waves. "I wasn't expecting either of you."

"I came to relieve Becca," Noah said. "Got a call from Fiona. The paintings went missing again this morning."

"Stolen? Again?" She snatched her cell phone from the table where it had been charging and saw that she had turned the ringer off. She'd missed several calls from Fiona.

"So Becca's off to talk to Springfield and see if she can shake loose any other information. Seems he won't talk to anyone but her."

Her mother's brittle smile turned to her. "I had no idea you needed a guard day and night."

Vanessa didn't really want to get into it. "It's just temporary. They think I can help with figuring out why Natalee was murdered. What brings you here?" Her mother rarely ventured to her apartment, especially at this early hour on a weekday.

Her mother gestured to the coffee table. Dozens of magazines were spread across its surface. "I brought these. Thought you could use them to plan your wedding." Her gaze slid over Noah. "Your friend was kind enough to let me in."

Vanessa's stomach turned over. "What wedding?"

"To Kenneth, of course." She waved a hand. "Oh, he told me you're being difficult, but I explained to him that you're just making him work for it. It'll all be fine. After all, you have been together for two years." She looked at Noah. Her words were for both of them. "It would be ridiculous to throw that away for some *phase* you're going through."

"I think maybe I should step outside and let the two of you talk." Noah was avoiding eye contact and Vanessa couldn't read his body language. "I'll wait outside the door until you're ready to leave."

"But—" Vanessa's objection died on her lips as he quickly let himself out without a backward glance.

Her mother's speculative gaze swung from the door to Vanessa. "It's the best thing, really. You're a smart girl. I know you know that Kenneth has so many more possibilities than a solitary detective from Chicago with no future and no past to speak of. It can be frightening to finally get everything you ever wanted, but you're about to."

"How would you know what I want? I already told you Kenneth and I aren't good together."

Not like her and Noah. They were *amazing* together.

The thought rose in her mind, unbidden, then lodged there. The passion they'd shared and the connection they'd developed in such a short time was so natural. So right. And yet he was pulling away from her. Had she misinterpreted their connection?

Weariness weighed on her. She rubbed her forehead and bit back a sigh. "I have to get to work. We can have this conversation later."

Her mother surprised her by laying a gentle hand on Vanessa's cheek. Her eyes turned sad for a moment. "There's no such thing as a happy ending. But you and Kenneth *can* have a good life together. The money we're offering when you get married—you could use it to start your own gallery. You could have all your dreams—marriage, family, career—it's up to you."

Stomach twisting with frustration, Vanessa watched her mother leave. Kenneth wasn't for her. She was more certain than ever about that. But Noah...he was a whole new bundle of uncertainty. What could she say to change beliefs ingrained within him since birth? Somehow, she'd break through. She'd make Noah understand that *he* was what she desired, that she didn't care about his past. She admired the man he was now.

And she was willing to take him on his terms. As an artist, she opened her heart to emotion on a regular basis, and had always been rewarded with something beautiful. She wanted to take the risk with Noah. Some temporary, frivolous fun, if that was all he wanted.

Even if, ultimately, it broke her heart.

THE MOMENT THEY entered the gallery, Noah excused himself to talk to the SSAM team huddled in the corner. He hadn't spoken a word during their drive, despite Vanessa's attempts to draw him into conversation. She'd finally given up, deciding she'd wait until his black mood was gone and he was open to listening to her side. She had no idea what her mother had said to him, but it couldn't have been good.

Spying her, Jesse rushed over and grabbed her hands. "Oh, thank God you're here. Please tell me you ordered the delivery service to come pick up the *Angels* last night. Lance's name was on the pickup invoice. It was a legit shipping company—they came in and boxed it all up. The order had Lance's signature, so I assumed...I thought he'd had a change of heart, but he says he didn't order it." His mouth was pinched and he squeezed her hands so tightly that they began to go numb.

Vanessa wished she could give him better news. "I'm sorry, but no. Is that what happened? Someone arranged for a real delivery service using a forged signature?" What a clever way for a thief to keep his hands clean.

Jesse shoved a hand through his short dreadlocks. "Shit. Lance is going to kill me. I should have double-checked with him."

Vanessa couldn't argue that. Nobody at Atherton's Art would have ordered such a move. The paintings had attracted new customers. They were a boon to Lance, who was headed in their direction, his face set in stone. Jesse abruptly let go of her hands. They tingled as normal blood flow resumed.

"So you had nothing to do with this, either?" Lance asked Vanessa without preamble.

"No. Do you have a copy of the work invoice?" she asked Jesse.

Jesse nodded. "Yes. Yes, of course. I gave it to them." He gestured toward Noah, Diego, Damian, Holt and Becca. Detective Hollister was there, too.

Lance looked toward the group. For once, he didn't seem annoyed by the presence of the SSAM team. "The paintings are long gone. Jesse packed them up last night. No clue where their final destination was. Why the hell would he think I would ship the paintings away?"

Jesse looked from Lance to Vanessa, and back again, as if someone would save him from further embarrassment. "I thought maybe you were putting them into storage. Or maybe you had an attack of conscience and decided using those girls was wrong."

Lance's gaze turned steely. "Get back to work."

Jesse hurried to the back just as Fiona was coming out of their office.

"What was that all about?" Fiona asked.

"He chewed Jesse out," Vanessa explained.

"We have a gallery to open for the day," Lance said. "I suggest you get those other paintings hung so we don't have a bare wall."

Fiona glanced at the blank space where the *Angels* had hung yesterday. "The pieces we took down are still in our office. Didn't even have time to get them to the warehouse. I'll go get them."

"I'll help."

As they hung the paintings, Vanessa could feel Noah's gaze on her. When she looked back at him, he didn't look away, but he didn't smile either. In fact, there was no sign of warmth or welcome. No flash of remembrance of shared passion. His lack of emotion cut her up inside.

Deciding to push the envelope, Vanessa went to join the gathering. "Any new leads?"

Becca showed Vanessa the invoice. "The shipping company confirmed delivery of the paintings to Miami, Florida. And now our hypothesis of where the *Angel of Water* came from appears accurate."

Damian's eyes held a glint of triumph. "We were just making plans. The NYPD will be contacting the Miami Police Department and notifying them of the investigation." Hollister nodded in acknowledgement. "Noah and Diego will follow up with the delivery company and track the exact destination. Becca will stay here with you."

"What can I do?" Vanessa asked. The idea of sitting around all day, waiting for information, was unappetizing.

"Business as usual. We need you here, working in the gallery as if nothing is amiss. The killer might be watching."

"Or he might be in Miami." Vanessa's protest went unheeded. In reality, there wasn't much she could do to help right now.

Noah and the others left, leaving Becca to watch Vanessa go through the motions of a normal day at the office. Focusing on art sales would be difficult when she longed to talk to Noah and to help with the investigation.

It only got worse when, at six o'clock that evening, Vanessa looked up from her desk to see Becca in the doorway, ready to escort her home. Becca again, not Noah. Noah hadn't even called. She'd been hoping to meet up with him on her lunch break to apologize, but he hadn't responded to the invitation she'd left on his voice mail.

Becca raised an eyebrow. "Not happy to see me?"

Vanessa summoned a smile. "Sorry. Long day. Any developments?"

"The good news is Damian was able to confirm that the deliverymen took the paintings to Florida." She frowned. "The bad news is they were already delivered."

"Someone had to sign for them on the other end, didn't they?"

"The orders were to deliver the paintings to an art commune named New View. Someone signed for them there."

"Who?"

"Name on the receipt is Nigel Springfield. Of course, we know it wasn't him."

"Well, the police should be able to check on them there, then, right?"

"Apparently it's not that easy. They're waiting on a warrant. The commune is very secluded, very protective of their residents."

"Sounds like a possible lead on where to find the murderer, though, doesn't it?" Vanessa felt her heart rate kick into gear. At least something would make Noah happy today.

"Yeah." Becca dropped her gaze to the desk. "Some of the team's already headed to Florida."

Her stomach dropped. "Noah?"

Becca nodded, meeting her gaze again. Sympathy shone in her eyes. "He and Diego caught a flight earlier this afternoon."

Without a word of goodbye. A fist squeezed around Vanessa's heart. Looked like her frivolous fun wasn't so much fun anymore. And she was becoming increasingly aware that it wasn't as frivolous as she'd like to believe, either. Somewhere along the way she'd allowed her heart to become involved. She'd fallen in love.

EIGHTEEN

AFTER A RESTLESS NIGHT, on Saturday morning Vanessa came to a decision over her second cup of coffee.

"We're going to Florida," she told a surprised Becca. Rumpled from another night on Vanessa's couch, the other woman simply smiled.

Vanessa ran to the bedroom and threw enough necessities to last a few days into a small suitcase. With one hand, she dialed her phone. *Damn. Voice mail.* At the beep, she left a message. "Hey, Fiona. I'm sorry to do this to you, but I have to leave town for a few days. Can you cover at work? I don't know when I'll be back. Yes, it has to do with Natalee, and yes, there will be a certain handsome hunk there." She smiled as she thought what Fiona's reaction to that would be. "I'm taking your advice."

She needed Noah. Needed to see him, needed to explain. Needed to show him that she loved him. She wouldn't risk scaring him by telling him with words how she felt, but he deserved to at least *see* that someone cared enough to follow him, to watch out for him. He hadn't had enough of that in his life, and she suspected he wouldn't believe that love was possible for him. She'd show him different. Whether he'd want to be in her life or not, for better or worse, she couldn't let him walk away like this.

She made the dreaded second call.

Her employer answered on the first ring. "I hope you're not calling in sick. I need you at the gallery today."

"I know, but it's important. Something's come up. I have to leave town."

The silence on the other end was deafening.

"I'll only be gone a few days," she hurried on, wanting to get through the phone call and get back to the preparations for the trip. Spying a pair of flip-flops in the back of her closet, she tucked the phone against her shoulder and dropped to all fours to dig them out. "At the most, a week."

"Is this about Natalee's case?" His words could cut diamonds. "About the *Angels?*"

Damn. She froze where she was on her closet floor. "What? No. Well, yes." Why lie about it? It was none of his business, anyway. She had some vacation time coming.

"The *appropriate* authorities in Florida are looking into it. I made it clear how I feel about employees becoming involved in the investigation."

"Yes, well…"

"I don't want the gallery involved *in any way.* And you certainly don't need to be so involved that you leave work for several days. We've been swamped."

"Fiona and Jesse can handle it for a couple days. Besides, the auction and excitement of the last week wore me out. I could use a break."

"Then perhaps you're not ready for that promotion."

He was going to rescind his offer? "That's not necessary, Lance. I haven't taken a vacation in years. I have time saved."

"And this is the peak of the summer tourist season. Now is the time to capitalize on the success of the auction and the increased flow of customers at the gallery. You can take a nice, long vacation in a month or two."

"Fiona and Jesse are more than capable…"

"A few customers have specifically asked for you. They

assumed you'll be handling our next auction, and have some pieces they'd like to sell."

"And I'll be there," she said, a bit giddy that people were asking for her by name. This was what she'd wanted, the success she'd been reaching for. Her blossoming reputation would help her establish her own gallery someday. "I'll be gone a week at most. I promise." The lengthy pause had Vanessa's momentary euphoria fizzling out. Her palms sweated as she waited.

"Unless you're at work on Monday morning, don't bother coming back at all."

He was *firing* her? Vanessa tried to suck in air as the room swirled. She crawled to her bed, leaned against it and stared in disbelief at the open suitcase strewn with clothes.

"The ball's in your court now," he continued when she didn't speak. "I'll have your answer Monday morning."

The dial tone hummed in her ear, and she threw the phone on the bed. She'd simply have to help the SSAM team wrap things up by tomorrow night. She could do that. They were closing in on the killer. She could feel it. Of course, the other edge of that sword was that Noah would then be free to return to Chicago.

"So HERE'S THE PLAN." Becca handed her a keycard to the room they'd be sharing. She'd managed to snag the one next to Diego and Noah. "Diego says they have dinner plans in half an hour. That'll give us a chance to settle in, and I can check with Damian and Holt and see if they've learned anything else while we were in the air."

And it would give Vanessa an opportunity to down some aspirin to combat the headache that was stomping through her brain like a herd of buffalo. She couldn't blame her concussion anymore. The bump had gone down several days ago. It was definitely tension that was getting to her now, even surrounded by the gently swaying palm trees and brilliant sunshine of coastal Florida. It had taken all day to catch a flight to Miami, but they'd finally arrived. Of course, the summer heat could be affecting her head, too. It was well into the nineties and humid enough to make her think she'd just stepped out of the shower.

Once in their room, Becca set her bag down on the bed closest to the door. The bedspread, along with the curtains and general décor, were done in pleasant shades of cream, light blue and tan that evoked images of a sandy beach and gentle surf. But that reminded her of the *Angel of Water* painting, and why they were here.

"By the way, Diego hasn't told Noah we're here. According to him, Noah's been a bear today. And you haven't been so cute and cuddly yourself. What's up between you two?"

"Don't you have to call Damian or something?" Vanessa searched through her purse for her pill bottle. She liked the other woman but didn't want to deal with anyone right now. Scratch that. She didn't want to deal with anyone but Noah, who wouldn't be in the mood to listen. She was still trying to figure out what she was going to say to him to break through his walls of steel.

"I can take a hint." There was a smile in Becca's voice that told her the other woman wasn't offended. She pulled out her cell phone and moved to the balcony. "I'll just make that call."

Vanessa made quick work of unpacking, shaking her head at the emerald-green bikini she'd impulsively tossed into her case—this was Miami, after all. When she'd grabbed the suit, she'd imagined taking a quick dip in the Atlantic with Noah in the moonlight—if they managed some downtime after solving the case, of course. She shoved it back into her suitcase with a stab of regret.

In the bathroom, she swallowed some aspirin, splashed water on her face and felt almost human again. But strong enough to confront an iron-willed Noah? She wasn't sure anything would be enough to convince him that she wanted him, and only him, even if only for a brief time.

But she wouldn't know unless she tried. The waters of seduction were murky and treacherous territory in which she could barely stay afloat.

Should she knock on the door that separated their adjoining rooms? She chewed on her bottom lip as she paced to the door, then back to the bed.

The balcony door slid open and Becca stepped back into the room, a grim look on her face.

Vanessa's concern was immediately redirected to the investigation. "Maybe it's my turn to ask if *you're* okay. I'm sorry if I was gruff earlier."

"It's to be expected when your man is being a butt-head." Becca's frank response surprised a laugh out of Vanessa. "He was supposed to apologize yesterday morning. Guess he mucked that up, too. I could tell by the way he ran off to Miami without a word. Don't worry. He'll come around."

"Apologize?" Vanessa snorted. "Far from it. Of course, my mother was there, and who knows what she said that changed his mind."

"I know Noah. He's conflicted because he's an honorable guy, and he's afraid he'll hurt you. He'll realize you two are good together. He just needs a little push."

NOAH SAT IN A CORNER booth at the bar, scowling down at his menu because…hell, he didn't know why. He just felt lousy. In contrast, Diego sat across from him, a grin on his face, not even glancing at the list of entrees the hotel had to offer.

Noah narrowed his eyes on him. "Something amusing you?"

"Yeah. Your pissy mood." He leaned forward as if dropping a secret on him. "Even a fool could see that you miss Vanessa. Guess you're no ordinary fool."

"Guess not." Noah glared in the hopes it would stop him from commenting further. His relationship with Vanessa, or lack of one, was none of Diego's damn business. He didn't know the woman, or her deepest desires. Not like Noah knew them.

On the heels of that thought came a memory of her body coming alive beneath his. He crushed the image mercilessly. He'd always known that his affair with Vanessa would be unbearably short. Short and sweet. He just hadn't thought it would only last one night. Heck, he'd had another week of so-called vacation to indulge himself in her.

But then he'd had a wakeup call in the form of Sylvia Knight. She could have saved her breath. Vanessa wasn't a woman to play with and leave. Besides, the more he played with her, the harder it was going to be to leave. He recognized that now. The realization had hit him like a kidney punch when he'd equated her with *home*.

His own mother hadn't given a shit about what happened to him. Wouldn't have fought to make sure his dreams came true. Which reminded him why he'd avoided family. Getting your hopes up led to pain, and he'd rather spare Vanessa that kind of heartache. It would be better for both of them if he backed off.

Diego's attention went to something across the room and his smile broadened. Apprehension shimmied up Noah's spine as he turned to see the reason for the idiotic grin. He froze. Becca and Vanessa were making their way through the bar area, headed directly for his table.

What the hell?

"Gentlemen." Becca greeted them, sliding in next to Diego so that Noah had no choice but to move over to make room for Vanessa.

Too late, he realized he should have insisted they grab one of the four-sided tables with chairs instead of the cozy booth that suddenly felt like a cage. Vanessa's light scent hit him like a battering ram, reminding him of how he'd immersed his senses in her, burying himself inside her sweet heat. *Home.* His heart jackhammered at the thought of the word. She was getting to him, into his head, into his soul.

"What are you doing here?" His question was more of a bark than a query and she winced.

She opened her mouth to reply but Diego jumped in. "They're here to help, of course."

Noah scowled at his so-called best friend. "You knew they were here?"

"Been in the loop the whole time. Doesn't feel so good to be left out, does it?"

So this was some kind of payback for not including him at the Cromby crime scene and the Springfield interview? Diego was going to put Vanessa at risk to prove some stupid point? He had to restrain himself from jumping across the table and grabbing him by the collar. He turned his attention to Becca. "How could you bring her here? You're supposed to be keeping her safe."

She shrugged and snatched up the menu Diego hadn't even looked at. "We don't know that the killer is here. He could just as likely still be in New York City. Damian approved the decision. I figure, between the two of us, we can keep her safe, right?" Her eyes twinkled as they met Noah's. The minx was up to no good.

The waitress came by to take their orders and Noah resigned himself to spending the next hour sitting next to Vanessa.

"I talked to Damian," Becca said after the waitress left. "He and Holt think they should stay behind in New York in case the killer's there, but Holt's wondering if shipping the paintings to Florida was a ruse."

"To throw us off?"

"Or to lead us here." At Becca's statement, Vanessa shivered beside him.

"Either way, we've got the bases covered now and Damian can do his job from there. What have you guys been up to?"

Diego draped an arm along the booth behind her. "Oh, you know, soaking up some sun, working on our tans and chatting up the local beach babes." Becca slugged him in the stomach lightly. He grunted and smiled. Noah felt a tug of jealousy at their easy way with each other. "We got in contact with Manchester's local connections with law enforcement about the Jane Doe we believe to be the Angel of Water."

"What about the commune where the paintings were delivered?" Vanessa asked. "Have they cooperated yet?"

"New View." Noah frowned. "Even when someone answered the phone, they resisted answering questions. It's private property. The local judge doesn't think there's enough evidence that the commune is connected to the murders to issue a warrant. In fact, he says there's only proof of one murder so far—Natalee's—and that was in New York."

"So what are we doing here? Let's go to New View and get some answers."

Noah put a hand on Vanessa's arm as if she was going to jump up and leave right then. "Diego and I were there today. Couldn't get past the front gate."

Becca toyed with her straw. "I talked with Springfield early this morning, before we caught our flight. His accountant found some interesting information. Four years ago, Nigel had a sizeable amount of money sent to New View Artist Commune. He's sent a hefty amount to them every year since."

Noah's skin prickled. "So there *is* a definite connection." Damn, they were close. "We just need a way in. Only invited guests are allowed on the premises."

"And they're not friendly with law enforcement," Diego added. "We learned that today when we waited at the gate for someone to drive out. Eventually, someone did. With a shotgun and a warning. They see any outsiders as an invasion of privacy, any type of government agency as trying to control them, and they promise their artists solitude."

Becca looked at Vanessa, and Noah felt a twinge of apprehension. "Which is why Damian approved us coming to Miami. He suspected we'd need Vanessa's influence to get us an invitation onto that property."

"But that's no guarantee the artist we're looking for is even at the commune," Diego said. "According to Priscilla, Nigel funded a number of artists and projects. We could be wasting our time. Maybe the killer knew someone there and sent the paintings to them for safekeeping."

"One of us can head back out there tomorrow and try poking around again," Noah said. "But the other needs to go to Greenmont, Florida."

Becca leaned forward. "That's the other reason Damian wanted us here. We can break up into groups."

Vanessa held up a hand. "Wait, I think I missed something. What's in Greenmont?"

Noah was reluctant to get her any more involved in the investigation, but she was determined. She might as well know everything and be able to better protect herself. "After our visit to the Miami P.D. earlier, we got a call. They think they found a victim who might be the Angel of Air. A young woman named Melody Rappaport was killed in Greenmont four years ago. The murderer was never found."

"Where's Greenmont?"

"Small town a couple hours' drive inland from here."

"What makes Holt think this woman is the Angel of Air?"

"Long blond hair, willowy build, blue eyes. And her body was found hanging in a barn, her arms strung up in the same position as Natalee's and Lisa's. The only odd thing is her murder was years ago."

"Holt thinks she was the first," Becca added, "and that the killer recently sped up his timeline because of Nigel's illness. He thinks that was the trigger for the escalation."

"That would confirm his theory that the killer and Nigel Springfield had a special relationship," Vanessa said.

Forced to sit so close to her, Noah felt her quiver of excitement at finding a possible piece of the puzzle. He understood that emotion, that surge of adrenaline that meant justice was close. It was a heady feeling.

"In my talk with Springfield this morning, I learned that he, too, suspected Nigel might have been gay," Becca said. "He'd heard rumors that his father had been having affairs with artists he supported. His mother died a decade ago in a car accident, so we can't get her view on this theory."

Noah had also received a phone call from Holt with his analysis. "And with Nigel ill, our killer wanted to complete their collection and was suddenly faced with a deadline. Nigel's death may have pushed him to come to New York City. Where he found Natalee by tracking the donation of his other painting."

Becca nodded. "Sounds logical." She grimaced. "As logical as crazy can be. I propose Diego and I go fish around in the Angel of Air's hometown and see what we can find. In the meantime, you and Vanessa could visit the artist commune, with police backup."

Vanessa nodded in immediate agreement. Noah scowled. No matter how much he wanted to protect her, it seemed he only succeeded in dragging her deeper into the investigation.

Still, he needed her. They needed her, he corrected. *They. He* would be just fine without her. And he'd keep telling himself that until he damn well believed it.

THE WARM, SALTY TANG of the ocean air flowed over him like a balm. The clouds darkened in the twilight, and Miami's colorful neon blinked to life as darkness encroached. Standing on the beach at sunset reminded him of special times. Nigel's visits had been the highlights of the past four years. And despite the age difference, they'd enjoyed the vibrant nightlife of the city almost as much as they'd enjoyed exploring its culture together.

Nigel had found him—no, he would have said he *discovered* him—at a contemporary art museum in downtown Miami. They'd been sitting on adjacent benches, admiring the same painting, for nearly half an hour before they'd noticed each other. Nigel had offered to take him to lunch, where he'd gently chided him for ditching high school to go to a museum. What Nigel hadn't known was that he'd hitched rides, traveling several hours to get there to see that exhibit.

It was divine intervention.

But, Nigel confessed later, he'd been secretly intrigued by him. A kindred spirit, he'd called him. And in each other, they'd found common interest, delight and passion.

Now, at twenty-two, he felt used, the life squeezed out of him until he was empty like an old tube of paint. Twisted and dried up without his partner. Though they'd only seen each other every couple months, he had made the most of those times. They'd shared so much. Long walks. Long talks. Nobody had understood him until Nigel. And Nigel's words and dreams had become his creed.

Angels. Women are angels, Nigel had said. *But so misguided. Easily corrupted.*

It had explained all his confusion about his mother—who had looked like an angel but had been led into drugs and prostitution time after time by the wrong kind of man.

Women should be kept pure. Frozen at that stage of their lives, in their beautiful innocence.

And then he'd known what he had to do. He'd known what Nigel had been telling him.

When he sent Nigel the first portrait, after Melody had ascended to be with the angels, his mentor had surprised him with a vacation cruise to the Bahamas.

His first angel had been obsessed with the spiritual, with the unseen and ethereal, and therefore had become his *Angel of Air.* Nigel had loved the painting at first sight. He hadn't asked any questions about the subject of the artwork, or what had happened to her, but he suspected that Nigel knew the truth. And approved. And Nigel's approval meant everything. He'd known he'd done the right thing when Nigel had rewarded him with a cabin at New View, where he could indulge his passions.

He had always intended to make a complete set. Then

Nigel had become sick. He'd rushed to create another angel, part sacrifice to the gods to cure the cancer and part need to impress his lover. The latter mission had succeeded. Nigel had appreciated that Lisa—a young woman who'd run away from her family, who'd offered to prostitute herself to him because she wanted to live a bohemian life on the beach and needed money—had been saved before she'd taken that ultimate step. He couldn't let her do that. She was going to taint all that was pure inside her.

But in the end, the gods hadn't appreciated his sacrifice. A tumor the size of a baseball had ultimately taken down his lover. Though Nigel had been brought to tears by the *Angel of Water,* emotional over the love and work he had put into it, the cancer had continued eating him from the inside. Nigel had died a few weeks later.

But then, Nigel's death and the donation of his painting to Atherton's auction had led him to Natalee. He'd known it as soon as he'd seen her fiery passion, a need to prove herself that would become her downfall, if not stopped. She would become the *Angel of Fire*. Had Nigel led him to her from beyond? He liked to think so.

And now, completing the series had become his mission. Only one remained.

Turning from the darkening evening sky, he made his way back to his car. If their mission was to be successful, he had work to do and not much time in which to do it. His next angel awaited salvation.

NINETEEN

VANESSA PICKED at her food, aware of every movement Noah made beside her. He seemed determined to put on a nothing-significant-happened-between-us attitude and participated minimally unless talk turned to the investigation. Occasionally, the heat from his thigh would singe her as it touched her leg. But he would quickly break the contact.

Finally, Noah moved to sign the check, his warm shoulder brushing hers as it had so many times during the last hour.

Vanessa summoned a yawn. "I think I'll head up to bed. It's been a long day and I haven't slept much lately." She reddened, her gaze flying to Noah. The corners of his mouth turned up in a grim semi-smile as she quickly looked away again.

Too late. They were both remembering the night they'd spent in each other's arms.

Becca covered the awkward moment. "Actually, I don't think bed is in the cards for you just yet. You told me the nightlife was too hot to miss around here."

"Um, yeah." Vanessa wondered where her new friend was going with this. "But aren't you supposed to be heading out to that town where the Angel of Air is from?"

"Greenmont. Well, yes, but that doesn't mean *you* can't go out. In fact, that's the perfect start to your assignment. It's Saturday night. The clubs will be packed. There's got to be one or two places where artists like to hang out in. You could finagle that invite to the commune."

"Is that true?" Noah directed the question at her.

"Yes." Vanessa could think of at least one place she should definitely check out, and one person who could get them into that commune. And she doubted Noah would let her do it alone. Despite his silent treatment, she knew he would protect her with his life. Besides, he'd want to be a part of the investigation at all levels.

"Then let's get to it." He nudged her to slide out of the booth ahead of him. Opposite them, Becca and Diego moved to leave too. "The sooner we take a look around, the sooner we can get to bed. Since you need your rest and all."

Her cheeks reddened. She wanted to smack some sense into the man. As if she wouldn't rather spend the night in his arms. Lucky for him, he strode ahead to summon an elevator, putting him out of her reach.

Back in her room with Becca, Vanessa shot her a look. "You know very well that you and I could have scoped out those clubs together. I don't have to do it with Noah."

"He's the only one who can go with you. It's more than a two-hour drive to Greenmont, where this victim was from, and Diego and I want to be ready to ask questions first thing in the morning. We'll take my rental car and leave tonight." Becca turned her back on Vanessa to repack the few things she'd removed from her suitcase. Still, Vanessa heard the smile and the hint in her voice. With their chaperones gone, it would be the perfect time to reconcile with Noah.

"Are you trying to drive me crazy?" Vanessa selected a slinky red midthigh-length dress she'd brought in case she had time to go out dancing to celebrate after finding Natalee's murderer. What she really wanted was to dance on the monster's grave. She'd chided herself when she'd slipped it into her suitcase, but now she was glad she'd brought it. Despite her reservations about going out with Noah tonight, she was looking forward to it. She'd always loved the nightlife of Miami. Here, the air vibrated with an energy like no other.

And being by Noah's side would give her a chance to start showing him how she felt, to show him the future they could have if he would just open up to her.

Although, considering the way he'd glared all evening, being by Noah's side would also be pure misery.

Becca's lips curved into a smile as she eyed the red dress. She whistled. "He doesn't stand a chance."

DIEGO STEPPED UP to Noah, purposely getting into his space. He'd damn near chewed his tongue off trying to keep his opinions to himself during dinner and afterward, while enduring the elevator ride with the women. But now that they were in their room behind closed doors, Diego let his disbelief show. "*What* is your problem, man?"

"Currently? You're in my way." Noah gestured to the closet Diego blocked, his voice and face carefully devoid of all emotion. But Diego could see that maintaining a mask of indifference was difficult for him. Noah wasn't indifferent, he was just being a dickhead. And it was Diego's duty, as his brother-from-another-mother, to point it out to him—as often as possible until he came to his senses.

"You've got a gorgeous, intelligent, and God-knows-why *willing* woman trying to get your attention, and you're acting like you've got something better to do."

Noah aimed his indifference at Diego. "I *do* have something better to do. Find Natalee's killer. Find justice for your family, remember?"

Diego's mood dipped. "Yeah, I do. Every damn second of every damn day. But that doesn't mean you have to become obsessed with Natalee too. You're doing everything you can to help me, man. And I appreciate it. But you don't have to screw up your life." *Like I have.*

Noah's jaw relaxed. "You're not screwed up."

Diego gave a harsh laugh. "Yeah, I am. And I may be out of a job when this is all over. But that's not the point. We're talking about you now."

"You'll get back on track," Noah continued, apparently more willing to dwell on Diego's difficulties than his own. "Becca helps, doesn't she?"

"She's a Band-Aid." And didn't that make *him* feel like the dickhead? He'd always enjoyed women, and made sure they enjoyed their time with him, too, but this was the first situation where he'd found himself using a woman for comfort. The fact that Becca didn't seem to mind their unspoken arrangement didn't ease his guilt. They would be going their separate ways once the investigation was over and Natalee was at peace.

"Becca Haney is a friend of mine." Noah's voice was heavy with warning. "And you are too. This is heading for a bad place."

"Like the place you're in," Diego tossed back at him, trying to get the topic back to Noah's love life. The guy couldn't see how far he'd already fallen for Vanessa Knight. "You don't *have* to be alone. You *choose* it. It's just plain stupid."

He'd never understood Noah's decision to isolate himself. Sure, Noah's birth family had been the pits, but he was by no means alone. He had the Sandoval clan to turn to whenever he needed them. They were his real family.

Diego had tried hard for those first few years after Noah had moved away not to feel bitter and angry. Not to take it personally that his best friend in the whole world hadn't felt the same way about him. That he could let his past interfere with his happiness, walk away and make a whole new life. He'd never looked back, other than a phone call every few months. This, between friends who'd had each other's backs every freakin' day of their child-hoods—when they'd been bullied, when Noah had been teased for not having lunch money or clothes that fit right.

"I am not talking about this with you. And especially not now, when I have work to do." Noah nudged Diego aside and yanked clothes out of the closet, then tossed them on the bed with more force than was necessary. "We *both* have work to do."

"All work and no play…" Diego pulled out his suitcase. He was still packed, so he had nothing to do but wait for Becca—and bug Noah mercilessly.

"Yeah, I've had enough of that attitude to last my life-time," Noah muttered, tugging off his shirt and pulling on another, a tropical print in muted colors he'd picked up at the Miami airport so that he could blend in with the tourist crowd.

"Ah, so now we're getting to it." Diego rubbed his hands. "I wondered when your parents would pop up." He sat in the room's sole chair, planted his elbows on his knees and waited. Noah simply gave him a dark look and went back to pulling on a pair of beige slacks. "Look, you aren't your parents. I could no more picture you *playing* like they did—partying instead of watching their kid, squandering what little money they had on their next high—than I could picture Vanessa being that irrespon-sible. Neither of you is the type to abandon your duties, or to think so little of yourselves as to throw a chance at real love away."

Noah sat on the bed, stretching his long legs out before

him and crossing them at the ankles, just as he crossed his arms to show that he still wasn't happy with their conversation. But he was listening now. That was something, at least.

"I like not having any responsibilities to abandon," Noah said.

Diego snorted. "Sure. That's why you took on a job in law enforcement. So you wouldn't have responsibilities." He met Noah's eyes, suddenly all seriousness. "And that's why you felt you had to come back to help me and my family. Help Natalee. Because you didn't have any of those pesky family ties. Face it, you're not the loner type. You try to be, but everybody needs someone." Christ, now he sounded like some sappy love song. Was he getting through or was he mucking this up? "What I mean to say is, you don't have to do this *life* thing on your own. There is no way in hell you'll end up like your parents. And I seriously doubt, after what you grew up with, that you'd pick a woman to share your life with who would live like that either."

Noah seemed to take a few moments to absorb this. His scowl remained, but he didn't object, didn't leave. Whether he was digesting what had been said or blocking it all out, he kept his thoughts to himself.

Diego gave it one last try. "You grew up an outsider in your own family, and now you can't see yourself ever being an insider. Maybe it's time to change that way of thinking. On that note, I think it's time I hit the road with Becca." Diego stood and lifted his suitcase, pausing to arch a brow at his friend. "And in the time I have left with her, I don't plan to be an outsider."

TWENTY MINUTES LATER, Noah paced the hall outside Vanessa's door, trying to forget Diego's words. What did he know about love anyway? Diego hadn't been an outsider looking in all his life. He'd always been a part of it all, surrounded by caring and support. He'd never known what it was like to go for days without seeing your mother and father, wondering if you had enough food in the cupboard to get through the weekend, until you got to school and a friend or a teacher took pity on you, donating half a sandwich or an apple.

Diego had never known what it was like to wear clothes that were worn through at the knees or a size too small. Or how to negotiate with the landlord who came to kick the family out when the rent didn't get paid.

Noah knocked on Vanessa's door. It was time to focus on the evening ahead. It would be hard enough to find Natalee's killer with his thoughts distracting him. But to do it with Vanessa, the ultimate distraction, beside him...

The door opened and suddenly he was face-to-face with the woman who filled his dreams. His breath caught. A short, tight-fitting red dress clung to every curve. Strappy red heels became natural extensions of her legs, making them appear longer than he knew, from intimate experience, they were. Her dark hair brushed against her bare shoulders, its sheen matching the warm glow in her eyes. Her tongue flicked out to nervously lick her lips—lips painted in a deep red that had him thinking of the sweet juicy burst of cherries. He swallowed hard.

"I'm ready." She sounded slightly breathless herself. Could she be nervous? He sure as hell was, and felt the need to wipe his sweating palms on his pants.

Instead, he cleared his throat. "The cab's waiting downstairs."

"Cab? Didn't Diego leave your rental car here?"

"A cab will be safer tonight. No dark parking lots in strange neighborhoods. It'll drop us right at the door."

And he wouldn't have to be alone with her. "Let's go." He gestured for her to go in front of him. A mistake, since now he was mesmerized by the way her dress hugged the curve of her ass.

In the lobby, a couple of tired businessmen caught sight of Vanessa and immediately perked up, sending smiles she easily returned. The spark of jealousy that flared further soured Noah's mood. He had no right to feel possessive of Vanessa. No right at all. He'd given up all of that voluntarily.

Diego was wrong. The Sandovals might have found that miracle, the mythical family life that only existed in the television shows he'd watched as a latchkey kid, but Noah knew it was a rare phenomenon. He'd lived the other side of it. He saw it every day in his job.

Vanessa shivered as they stepped outside.

"Cold?" he asked, part of him hoping she'd say yes and he'd have an excuse to pull her closer. The other, realistic part of him knew that would be the absolute worst thing he could do.

She shook her head. "No. Just one of those weird shivers. Like someone was walking over my grave."

He frowned at the reference, looking up and down the street for anybody who might be watching them. The roads were clogged with cars, including the cab waiting at the curb. Weekend traffic and summer tourists probably compounded the problem. "There's a killer out there, but we'll be fine tonight. Chances are we won't find anything anyway and will come home disappointed."

"Well, aren't you a ray of sunshine?"

"It's called being realistic. You should try it sometime." Noah knew he'd not only put his foot in his mouth with that comment, he'd shoved it so far down his throat there would be no digging it out. Which was all for the best anyway. Let her think he was a jerk. It would keep her from getting the wrong idea.

Except, *shit,* she was looking pretty damn hurt. And, *Christ,* she was blinking back tears.

Crandall, do not apologize. Do not put your arms around her.

He shoved his hands into his pockets. "Look, nothing's going to happen to you. We're just looking for a way into New View."

Vanessa simply nodded.

Noah exhaled in relief as they slid in. "Where to?"

"Tabula Rasa," she told the driver.

"Isn't that Latin? Blank slate?" Noah asked.

"It's a night club," she explained as they sped away from the hotel, their faces alternately cast in shadow and lit by neon as they passed through the city. She was quiet for several minutes. "You think there's a chance this guy could be at the club tonight?"

Noah didn't want to worry her, but she needed to be on guard. "We don't know for sure he's even in Miami. But yes, there's a chance. However, I doubt he'd be at this particular club on this particular night." *Or he could have followed her here.* In which case Noah was practically handing Vanessa to him on a silver platter. Even though being close to her was driving him insane with need, Noah wouldn't be able to leave her side. It would be sweet torture. It didn't help that her dress left little to his imagination, or that he remembered what her soft skin felt like beneath his fingertips.

His thoughts turned another direction as they pulled up to the club. A line of people waited to get past the dark-skinned, beefy bouncer at the door. Women were in everything from sundresses to slinky skirts and halter-tops. Men wore slacks and open-necked shirts or colorful silk.

Noah wondered if he should flash his badge to get in, or wait in line for what looked like over an hour for their turn. But as they got out of the cab, Vanessa looped her arm through his and pulled him toward the bouncer. The purple neon sign that hung over the door reflected off the man's shiny, bald head and the diamond stud in his ear.

"Pretend you're with me." Hurt laced her words.

Pretend? She was obviously still angry and trying to hide it.

With no fear, she walked right up to the thick-armed tree trunk of a man. Pumping dance music, loud conversations and the clanking of glasses escaped from the open door behind him. "Hey, Little John."

The bouncer's face lit up with surprise, a wide grin transforming his fierce features. He brought her free hand to his lips as if he were some charming duke. "Hey, sweet thing. Haven't seen you here in a while."

"Six months, I think."

"Looking good, as always, sugar."

"Thanks. Busy tonight," she said, gesturing with her hand toward the group in line.

Little John nodded. "Pierre's back with a new act. Might want to wear your raincoat." His straight white teeth disappeared as he assessed Noah. "Or maybe your guy would *like* to see you splashed in paint."

She shot John a mischievous grin. "He doesn't know what he's in for."

"Really?" He gave Noah a second look as he chuckled, then gestured to the door. "Go on in. Charlie will want to say hi."

"Thanks," she said, giving him a peck on his cheek before tugging Noah along behind her like some kind of accessory.

"You're a regular here?" Noah shouted to be heard

over the music that thumped against his eardrums. He'd never been the dance-club type, and he wouldn't have placed Vanessa in that group either, but her hips swayed to the beat and her toe tapped as they squeezed into a small space at the bar and waited for the bartender to notice them.

She nodded. "Whenever I'm in town, which is a couple times a year. A lot of artists hang out here. Charlie likes to display art of various types—everything from new musicians to modern sculptures, to Gallagher-types who'll splash the crowd with paint or fruit or whatever. The line grows week after week because people are curious who and what he'll have next."

"Ah. I guess that explains why Little John thought I might get hosed tonight." He looked to the opposite side of the large room where a DJ spun music from behind a plexiglass window while a man in what was once white overalls used fancy tea cups to splash neon orange, yellow and green paint up on to a canvas, not caring that drops of it hit the crowd. A black light made the canvases seem ultra-bright while the paint glowed as if alive. On either side of him, two women in black barely-there bikinis, their skin glossy with wet color, writhed to the music against tall white backdrops. Noah supposed it was all part of Pierre's vision, whatever that might be.

"A hosing can be arranged," she shouted over the climaxing tempo of the music. The glint in her eye and the smile on her lips drew his attention.

He wanted to kiss her. Hell, he wanted to lock his lips to hers and taste her for several long hours. He wanted it with a fierceness that ached in his gut. And then he wanted...

He turned away to look over the crowd. It didn't matter what he wanted. He couldn't have it. He couldn't let himself even think it was a possibility. But Diego's words kept coming back to him. Did he need to change the way he was thinking, to believe that he belonged? Was it as simple as that?

Vanessa reached up and turned him to face her. She tilted her head back in invitation, putting a hand behind his neck to pull his face down to hers so he could hear her over the noise. "Just for the record, I *am* realistic. And *you're* not being realistic if you think my desire for you will just go away." She pressed her lips to his before he could respond. Her tongue traced the seam where he tried to keep her out—for about all of three seconds.

Losing control, he opened his mouth to her. At first, it was a sip of her. Then it was a gulp. Then he was drinking from her lips as if he was dying of thirst and she was an oasis. The music became a dull throb in the background as she aligned her body with his.

"You two want to put in an order or what?" a male voice shouted over the noise. Humor lit the bartender's eyes.

Noah immediately pulled away from Vanessa. He was shaking, damn it, and he would have taken several steps back if he could have without bumping into another person. Instead, he followed Vanessa's drink order with his own and tried to control the need taking over his body. The last thing he needed was to lose focus when a killer could be after her.

She smiled at him, running the palm of her hand across his shoulder to his neck, intending to tug him close and pick up where they'd left off.

"Don't do that again." He captured her hand in his.

TWENTY

VANESSA BLINKED back her surprise. Noah had almost given in, accepting what they both wanted. She'd felt his surrender. But somehow he'd reined it in again.

What more could she do to make it clear she was happy to go home with him—other than throw herself on top of him in the middle of the dance floor? If she'd learned nothing else from her recent experiences—losing Natalee, seeing what the other women in the paintings had gone through because of the monsters in the world, and becoming the target of a serial killer herself—it was that she had to seize an opportunity for happiness when she had one. She wasn't some delicate seashell fresh from the ocean that he had to protect.

She wanted him. Hard edges, dark past, shifting moods and all.

And he clearly wanted her. A smile of satisfaction curved her lips. He'd pressed hard against her and more than kissed her. He'd wanted to devour her. She was sure of it. Perhaps, later, when they weren't working on the investigation, she'd push him until he lost that stronghold on his control and gave in.

She spotted an artist she knew standing at the bar and struck up a conversation. Over the next half hour, she made her way through the crowd, stopping to talk several times along the way, dropping subtle hints that she and her fiancé—Noah had scowled at her improvisation, but she was in the mood to torment him—were interested in seeing some new artwork to decorate their New York penthouse. In particular, they'd heard good things about the work coming out of the New View Artist Commune.

Really, she was biding her time until she could speak to Charlie Morton, owner of Tabula Rasa and local supporter of the arts, whom she'd spied across the room. He was always surrounded by people, but she knew eventually she'd have an opportunity to talk with him.

Charlie's face lit up with pleasure as, twenty minutes later, she came over to the group of people who'd gathered around him. He broke away from them to embrace her, kissing each of her cheeks.

"What a wonderful surprise." Charlie smiled broadly. His hair was as dark as the black-painted ceiling above them, his teeth flashing white against tanned skin. The open collar of his pink shirt showed a sprinkling of dark hair. "What brings you to town?"

"The usual," she said.

"Looking for the next hottest thing in art? You're a difficult woman to satisfy, Vanessa Knight, but I enjoy the challenge." He glanced over her shoulder and winked at Noah. She introduced the two men, keeping with her story that Noah was her fiancé. She figured it was better than introducing him as a cop, as that would make it more difficult to secure an invitation to the commune.

A cheer went up from the crowd as someone sat behind a set of bongos on stage and began to play. Pierre had finished his canvas with a last splash of neon glow paint and an assistant was moving it to the side to set up a fresh one. The writhing women had completed their canvases as well, but seemed reluctant to relinquish the spotlight and were gyrating to the drumbeat.

Charlie followed her gaze. "I'm guessing Pierre's not

the type of artist you're looking for, though he's been a very popular draw lately."

"I'll bet." Flamboyant hedonism and sensuality came across in every splash of paint, in every uninhibited movement of the women's bodies. The color and freedom echoed Miami nightlife perfectly. "Actually, I'm looking for something specific this time, a new artist."

"Got a name in mind?"

"Unfortunately, no, but we've seen his work in New York. He's got a rather annoying habit of leaving his paintings unsigned. I've heard he may be connected to New View Commune, but that's about all I know."

"Ah, New View. Lots of great talent coming from there. They're rather private about their artists. And they won't let just anybody in."

"That's what we heard." Vanessa put an arm around Noah's waist, tugging him closer. "Didn't we, honey?"

She felt him stiffen. She was well aware she'd gone against his edict—not to kiss him or touch him—not to *affect* him—again, but she was done with doing what he wanted. What about what *she* wanted? She wanted to push him until he lost control again.

"That's right." Noah shocked her by wrapping his arm around her. His thumb brushed against the side swell of her breast and she bit back a gasp. "What can you tell us about New View?"

Charlie looked thoughtful. "They're about an hour out of town and have almost a hundred members, from what I've heard. The artists there like to keep to themselves. It was created when a local artist opened up an old campground property he'd inherited. Some of the members of the commune live in cabins there and some just commute when they can. Kind of like a vacation spot for them.

Though what anyone wants with a rustic cabin in the middle of humid swampland is beyond me." He shuddered.

"But you can get us an invite? Maybe as an advance wedding gift?" Vanessa gave Charlie her most charming grin.

"You've done so much for my artists over the years, how can I resist? Let me make some calls. You two stay and enjoy the music while I see what I can do."

"Perfect." She rose on tiptoe to plant a smacking kiss on his cheek.

"I assume you got all of that," she shouted over her shoulder to Noah, who was close on her heels as she walked away. Not that he could have moved farther away, since her hand held his captive.

"Yeah. Good work." It was a compliment, but Noah issued it through gritted teeth. The hold on his control was tenuous indeed. She smiled.

The music took a slower turn and couples came together in the dance area. Taking advantage of the situation, she pulled him toward the dance floor.

"What are you doing?" he asked, digging in his heels.

She tugged until he moved his feet again. "You heard Charlie. We're supposed to hang out and enjoy the music."

She pulled him into the throng, his heat like the bright Florida sunshine as they were forced into an intimate embrace in order to keep from bumping other couples. Wrapping her arms around his neck, she pressed her body to his. She purred deep in her throat, stretching against him like a cat.

NOAH STIFLED a groan as Vanessa's body slid along his. The vixen. Increasingly brazen as he continued to push her away, she was now attempting a seduction right in the middle of a public dance floor. Unfortunately, his body seemed under her control, responding to her touch, her smile, the look in her eyes. As if she were the key to unlocking him.

He indulged in the overwhelming sensation of belonging to someone for a moment, losing himself in her hooded gaze. *Just one more night,* her bedroom eyes beckoned. They were supposed to be looking for a murderer—one who intended to make her his next victim—and yet she seemed oblivious to everyone and everything but him. It was a heady feeling, no doubt heightened by the element of danger. And he loved it. Loved being wanted by someone to the point she had no thought for herself, only for him. As if she were totally his.

When she gently pressed her fingers to the back of his neck, rising on tiptoe to meet his lips with hers, he couldn't resist. Didn't want to. Maybe he was at fault for surrendering to her kiss at the bar earlier and giving her the wrong idea. Maybe he was weak for not sticking to his principles, but hadn't he made it clear to her already what she was getting into? Proceeding in this way after his repeated warnings was her decision.

His rationalization process complete, he captured her mouth in a deep, hard kiss that was half pent-up frustration and half warning. But one taste had his senses spiraling with longing. Her scent filled his nostrils, and he wanted more. He wanted to immerse himself in her deepest places and inhale her warm scent.

Vanessa opened to him as if reading his mind, subtly rubbing her body against him as her mouth welcomed his. The heavy dance beat thrummed through his body as she sucked his tongue deeper into her mouth. His arms locked around her waist, raising her higher against him and she wriggled yet closer.

As the music ended and an up-tempo beat began, he

tore his mouth away from hers. "You're downright dangerous."

Her wicked smile only made him want her more, which irritated the hell out of him. Perhaps he should just take what he wanted and teach her a lesson. He set her on her feet and, grabbing her hand, pulled her behind him to the bar.

He ordered them a couple of drinks and stared at her, hard. "Have you forgotten why we're here?"

"No." Her chin, the delicate point on her heart-shaped face, tipped upward. "I can leave my number with Charlie and we could head back to the hotel."

Her breasts brushed his arm and he forced himself to lean away. She was sending him an open invitation, but he wasn't sure accepting it was in his best interest, let alone hers.

And why did he care what was in her best interest, some devil of a voice asked. Could it be he cared too much for her already? That wasn't possible. He'd erected defenses long ago against that kind of thing.

But they hadn't really been tested until now. Until Vanessa.

He breathed a sigh of relief as he caught sight of Charlie Morton making his way through the crowd toward them. The man stopped at Vanessa's side and smiled at her. "Got you an invite. Someone will meet you at the gate at ten tomorrow morning to let you in."

She threw her arms around Charlie. "Thank you so much."

"My pleasure." She let go and he handed her a folded paper. "Directions to the compound. It's off the beaten path and can be hard to get to. Better pray that storm that's supposed to hit tomorrow goes off course. Some of those back roads aren't paved."

Vanessa took the map and gave him a kiss on the cheek. "You're fabulous."

"Yes, well, make sure you tell everyone that." With a laugh, Charlie waved a goodbye and was quickly swallowed up by a group of people waiting to talk to him.

"Isn't this great?" Her enthusiasm was palpable. He'd miss that when he left. "Somebody at New View has to know who painted the *Angels*. Now we can find the paintings, track the killer and get back to New York."

And he'd go back to Chicago and probably never see her again. They'd soon forget about each other.

Noah tossed back the last of his drink and tried to drown the tiny doubt that niggled at him, saying that he would never completely move on from the earthshaking experience he'd had with Vanessa.

SLIDING INTO THE backseat of the cab, she made room for Noah, both amused and annoyed when he stayed as close to his door as possible, thus avoiding physical contact with her. She affected him, all right. No matter how hard he tried to resist.

For a moment, on the dance floor, she'd seen the passion in his eyes flare just before he'd kissed her with a heat that scorched her to her toes. She'd felt his arousal time and again tonight. And still he fought it. He fought letting her get too close in any way.

"Why were you in juvie?" The question popped out, but she was glad she asked it. He acted as if he had things to hide, and was ashamed of what Kenneth had uncovered, but she doubted whatever he had done was as bad as he thought. If he was an officer of the law now, whatever he'd done had to have been forgiven.

Noah acted as if he hadn't heard her. "It's smart to keep sex out of this. We wouldn't have worked out in the long run." He frowned at the back of the cab driver's head. "One of us would have ended up hurt."

Her nails bit into her palms. The silence following his practical analysis stretched into a growing chasm between them. It was two in the morning and she was exhausted. She let her head tip back against the seat of the cab, wishing Noah had his arm around her. The desire was a constant ache inside her.

The sight of their hotel was a relief and she practically launched herself from the car the moment they arrived. Stumbling, she cursed as she removed the ridiculous cherry-red heels and walked barefoot into the hotel.

She jabbed at the elevator button and waited for the doors to open so she could escape inside. Finding her keycard in her purse, she practically jumped when a hand touched her bare shoulder.

"Next time, wait for me." Noah's tone was gruff. "I had to pay the driver. Keep your head on. There could be danger anywhere, even in the hotel."

She swallowed the curse that rose to her lips. He was right, but she wasn't the only one who wasn't safe right now—she wanted to hit him with her high heels. She wanted to scream. Frustration ate her up inside.

Instead, she bit her lip. Hard. And endured the silent elevator ride with him. The quiet gave her time to regroup. Noah wanted her and she wanted him. She just had to remember that. She'd show him that it was okay for him to give in to that desire. That his feelings were safe with her.

At the door to her room, he held out his hand to stop her. "I have to check it out first, make sure nobody's in there." She slapped the keycard into his open palm and remained in the hallway. He emerged a few seconds later. "All clear."

He handed back her card, his fingertips brushing hers briefly as he held her gaze. "I'm sorry."

Oh, Noah, if only you could see the truth.

She'd help him see it, see that they were good together. And if emotions were too powerful for him to address, she'd find a physical way to show him. She tossed her heels into the closet and began unzipping her dress even as he stood behind her in the open doorway.

"What are you doing?" His words sounded as if he'd choked them out.

"I'm going for a swim. Thought you might like to join me."

"It's the middle of the night. Pool's closed."

"That's why I'm going down to the beach." She pushed her dress down over her hips and bent to scoop it off the floor. She heard a hiss, like a sharp intake of breath, but forced herself not to look back at him.

"Definitely not. You wouldn't be safe."

"I would if you came with me. I won't be long."

"Go to bed, Vanessa."

"I'm too keyed up. A swim will help me sleep."

She walked to her dresser and pulled her bikini out of the drawer. Finally, she turned to face him. "Are you just going to stand there in the open doorway, letting the whole world see?" She reached behind her to unhook her bra.

NOAH STEPPED into the room and closed the door. He couldn't take his eyes from Vanessa as her bra fell to the floor. Her ripe round breasts were bare to his gaze. She wriggled her hips, scooting her underwear off until it fell to her ankles. Noah gulped. She was trying to seduce him again. What was worse, he could feel it working. A man could only withstand so much, after all, and he was sorely tempted to give in to her, especially when she promised it would only be a short-term relationship. That was what he wanted, right?

Then why did the thought of seeing Vanessa for a short time, then letting her go, piss him off? He ached for her, and the thought that she was perfectly willing and accessible didn't help.

Inwardly, he panicked. "Forget the beach. Go to bed. You're not being rational."

Her eyes sparked with inner fire and he knew he wasn't going to win this argument. She spun on her heel and marched into the bathroom. He heard the soft click of the door behind him.

And still his body insisted on wanting her. Parts of his brain were beginning to rebel, too.

Maybe it could work between us. Maybe if I actually tried to stand and fight for what I want rather than turn tail and run, things would work out.

He wouldn't know until he tried, right?

Shit. He was in deep.

The bathroom door opened. Vanessa, clad in a butter-yellow sundress that brushed the back of her knees, headed to the door to the hallway without a backward glance. She knew he'd follow her like a puppy. The elevator doors slid closed in front of them. Not a word was spoken, as if he wasn't even there.

At the lobby level, the doors opened and she squared her shoulders. Her flip-flops made a soft thump-thump noise as she led the way into the warm night air and down a stone pathway. A breeze lifted the edge of her dress, exposing more of one creamy thigh and sending her hair swirling around her shoulders. The sound of the Atlantic surf swelled and receded in the distance. His practiced glance took in the shrubbery that lined the path and rustled with the wind. But he searched for a threat that wasn't there.

Still, they were taking a chance coming out into the dark like this. Out where it was deserted. *Reckless*. But he couldn't resist seeing where this was headed. He had a feeling what happened next could make or break him.

She didn't look back again. Not one time. Didn't give one goddamn thought to her own safety or his plans for sleep. She simply trusted that he would be there to protect her. She trusted *him*.

A hundred yards from the hotel, the path ended at a gate in a waist-high stone wall. As Vanessa opened it, the creak of hinges rusted by the continuous assault of salty air squealed into the quiet night. Only the moonlight and a few vacant cabana tents, emblazoned with the logo of the hotel, inhabited the beach beyond.

Rather than give her the satisfaction of joining her in the ocean, Noah stopped amid the shadows of the palm trees near the gate, watching Vanessa move toward the water's edge. She paused to kick off her sandals. Her arms crossed in front of her as she grabbed handfuls of her sundress and lifted, pulling the garment over her head.

Noah sucked in a breath, his gaze pinned on her as she ran into the water and performed a shallow dive. Mesmerized, he watched the ripple in the waves where she'd disappeared. Moving into the shadows of one of the cabanas along the hedges that separated sand from the green lawn of the hotel property, he found a lounge chair from which he had a clear view.

Vanessa's head poked above water farther out from shore. He surveyed the beach. They were still alone. Nobody had followed except him.

And nobody was there to watch if he stripped off his clothing and followed her into the surf. His imagination taunted him with images of what sins he and Vanessa could commit, their bodies hidden by the dark ocean. Oh, the pleasures he could bring her. And vice versa.

His body tightened in response to the remembered feel of her body arching against his, her gorgeous legs wrapping around his waist as she demanded more. He knew it would be good again...if he let it happen. She'd been anything but subtle about what she wanted from him.

Realizing he was locked in a tense forward-leaning position, as if he were about to launch himself onto the beach at any second and plunge into the water after her, he forced himself to be vigilant. He scanned the area once more before allowing himself to lie back in the chair and enjoy the view. It wasn't long before she was walking from the water, limiting her excursion to a quick dip. Her body glistened in the sliver of moonlight that filtered through the low clouds, making her skin appear to glow like the neon paint they'd seen at the bar earlier. But this was so much more sensuous than the anonymous female bodies who'd writhed to the beat at Tabula Rasa. They weren't Vanessa. They didn't have her spirit, her inner beauty or her kind heart.

Her dark hair was plastered to her head and neck, accentuating the natural beauty of her cheekbones, her heart-shaped face, her skin. She was a nymph emerging from the sea, sent by Triton just for him.

She crossed the beach, coming nearer, her gaze meeting his, daring him. He rose and moved a step toward her, but stopped while he was still within the shadows of the overhang. "What are we doing?"

"Swimming?" She still hadn't donned the sundress, and he tried to ignore the punch to his chest that stole his air at the sight of all that slick, wet skin. Water dripped off her, and sand clung to her feet like makeshift slippers. Gooseflesh sprang up on her bare abdomen and arms. Her nipples, hardened to pebbles beneath her bikini top, begged for his touch, for the warmth of his mouth. He nearly groaned aloud as his body answered the call of hers.

He gritted his teeth against a surge of desire. "You know what I mean. You're trying to seduce me again."

"I didn't want to return to New York without at least dipping my toes in the ocean. And now I'll head back to the room so you can sleep. You won't have to deal with me ever again after tomorrow." She moved closer, intending to pass him on her way to the path that led to the hotel.

The thought of her returning to New York—without him—sent a surge of panic through him. "Don't leave." Whether he meant the beach, the state of Florida, or *him,* he didn't know.

Her eyes sparked and her lips parted on some retort that was never spoken. He didn't want to talk anymore. He reached for her and pulled her against his body. His hands sank into her slick hair, tilting her face as his lips claimed hers. His tongue pushed into her mouth when she opened it on a gasp. He took what he wanted without apology. Without excuse. And certainly without thought.

He was tired of thinking, anyway. He'd made his decision.

Her hand slid up his chest. Her body shivered against his, reminding him how she must be chilled, even in the seventy-degree night air, by the breeze and dampness of her skin. His fingers looped beneath the straps of her top and tugged them down her arms. He led her deeper into the shadows of the cabana, reaching out and pulling the string that held the flaps of material open as he passed them. They fell shut, enclosing them in their own private world. The distant lights of the hotel made the white material of the cabana seem to glow.

"Noah?" Her confusion made his name sound like a plea. "You're sure?"

Was he sure? He was sure if he didn't have her, right here, right now, he would hate himself in the morning. He couldn't let her leave. Not like this. Damned if he did, damned if he didn't. He needed Vanessa Knight to make the yearning stop.

Too choked with emotion to respond with words, he dipped his head to hers, this time delivering a tender kiss that had her rising on her tiptoes to deepen it. With a growl, he swept an arm under her legs, lifting her against him. He carried her the few steps to the reclining lounge chair he'd had fantasies about only minutes before. Depositing her there, he swiftly lost his clothes to gravity, leaving them in a pile on the sand. The heat of her gaze swept over him, arousing him further, the proof of it already reaching for her.

She reached behind her to finish untying the bikini top that hung from her breasts, already loose since he'd undone the shoulder straps. Tossing it aside, she reached for the bottoms, lifting and wriggling her hips as she removed the piece and it joined the discarded top.

He stood admiring her for a long moment, taking in her simple beauty. Her gentle curves begged to be cupped and stroked by his palms. Other curves begged for the lick of his tongue. He knelt between her legs.

"You're beautiful," he breathed, kissing his way up her abdomen to her breasts. She arched when he suckled one taut nipple. This time, he didn't need a second invitation. His hand came up to cup her most sensitive area, and he dipped a finger into her wet heat. She cried out. He increased the rhythm, mimicking the act his body longed to perform with hers. He couldn't wait any longer. He slid his body along hers, and she welcomed him with open arms. A merging of the deepest, most profound kind.

This is right. This is home.

Their combined climax hit him hard, an explosion of light and passion. He heard his name ring in his ears when she shouted her release. And though her name remained unspoken on his lips, it echoed in his mind.

Vanessa.

He held her close, recovering from the intensity of the moment.

Only Vanessa.

He shifted until he was beside her and held her to him. The night was calm around them. Inside, he was anything but calm. Something had broken. She'd crashed through the armor that had coated his heart. And yet he'd survived.

He loved her.

His heart thumped harder as the words echoed in his head. *Love?* What did he know of it? The idea was so new he didn't want to analyze it. He just wanted to enjoy it, and the surprising contentment that accompanied it.

"Noah?" Her breath fanned his chest. She sounded concerned.

He ran a hand down her arm, trying to decide how he could show her he loved her without having to admit it. He wasn't quite ready for that. "Destruction of property."

"What?"

"Earlier you asked what I was in juvie for."

"You destroyed property?" The disbelief in her voice made him smile.

"I was twelve, and I was trying to get the dealer my parents were scoring from to stay away from our neighborhood. I took a baseball bat to his car. He pressed charges."

"A dealer called the cops against a little boy?"

"Guess he was more afraid of the story getting around that a kid had bested him than of the cops finding anything against him."

Her arm tightened around him. "I'm sorry your childhood sucked."

"Yeah. But I'm not that scared, lonely kid anymore." He was starting to wonder if he ever had been. There had been rough times, but he'd made it through. He'd stood up to people he'd needed to stand up to. The brief stint in juvie notwithstanding, he'd always remembered what was right and what was wrong. And he'd had the Sandovals to love and guide him. He hadn't been the best son and brother in recent years. In wanting to escape the bad parts of his past, he'd forsaken the good ones. He'd make it up to them.

"You should be proud of who you've become," Vanessa said.

"I'm starting to get that." It had only taken thirty-six years.

TWENTY-ONE

VANESSA PRIED one eye open and came face-to-face with the hotel's bedside clock. Seven in the morning, and she'd been sleeping like the dead. The vibration of her cell phone against the bedside table permeated her brain.

The other eye opened as she realized she was still entangled with a warm body. Noah was in her bed. He'd asked her not to leave, but in the end, it was he who'd made the choice to stay. She'd sensed she'd finally broken through some barrier. Though they hadn't spoken of their new connection, she felt it. The way he'd looked at her in the cabana, before he'd made love to her, as if she were something precious and rare, had made her breath seize in her chest. He'd looked at her like that, and loved her in an unspoken way, when they'd returned to her room. A smile curved her lips.

Her phone continued to jostle on the table. She slowly pulled her legs from underneath one of Noah's. He moaned and shifted onto his back, but didn't wake. She moved into the bathroom to answer the call.

A glance at the caller ID had her brow furrowing as she answered. "Jesse?" She kept her voice low.

"Morning, sleepyhead. Can you meet me?"

Vanessa blinked back confusion. "I'm in Florida."

"I am, too."

"What? Why?"

"I insisted on coming with Fiona, who *insisted* on coming to help support you."

She searched the bathroom for something to wear. "But—"

"We're in the lobby. Fiona was looking back over the guest list from the auction and thinks she has a lead. Thought maybe you'd like to join us for coffee first."

"Um, okay." She was still trying to wrap her brain around the idea that her friends were in Florida. Coffee would help clear the cobwebs.

"I've already ordered your favorite, so don't waste time. See you in a few."

Vanessa hung up. Jesse's call had been unexpected, but was also perfect timing. There was something she wanted to discuss with Fiona and him without Noah around. Vanessa had been thinking about how to resolve the issue of distance. Now that the emotional gap had been bridged, she'd tackle the problem of physical distance. She didn't want to go on living in different cities. But for the plan she had in mind to succeed, she needed the help of her friends.

Her phone's power indicator showed it had little juice left. She crept from the bathroom, plugged the phone into its charger and left it on the bedside table.

A glance at Noah revealed he was sleeping soundly, his face relaxed. She didn't see any need to wake him. She didn't intend to go anywhere other than the cluster of tables at the coffee kiosk in the hotel lobby, where she wouldn't be alone.

Using the complimentary pen and pad of paper, she jotted a quick note to Noah. She pulled a pair of shorts and a tank top from her suitcase and shoved her feet into her flip-flops. What the hell were Fiona and Jesse thinking, getting involved in this mess? Lance was going to fire them all. This was crazy, but then, Fiona did have a tendency to be impulsive.

There was no sign of them in the lobby, but she saw

Jesse outside. He waved at her through the glass door and jogged out of sight. Vanessa pushed open the door and ran toward him. He came to a stop as a cab sped away.

"What's going on?" she asked, panting as she stopped beside Jesse.

He gestured to the cab, which was stopped at a light a couple blocks down. "Fiona just took off."

"She's in the cab? Why?"

"She got a call as soon as I hung up with you. Remember that lead I mentioned? A contact of hers was able to get her into New View if she meets him right away. She wants us to catch up. I tried to stop her, told her it was dangerous, but…" His gaze was full of concern as it met hers. "You know how Fiona is when she gets something in her head. Come on, she left me the rental. We'll catch her before she does something stupid." He grabbed her hand and started toward the parking lot.

"I should get Noah." She tried not to stumble in her flip-flops as she kept pace with his long strides.

"There's no time. We'll lose sight of her." He glanced down the street where the cab was waiting at a light. "You can call him from the car."

"And Fiona, too. I'm going to chew her out for this." She tried to stop but his momentum was too great. "Wait. I don't have my phone."

"You can use mine. Come on." He tugged her through the parking lot to a car. "We have to hurry."

Feeling uneasy about leaving Noah but even more worried about losing Fiona, she buckled herself into the passenger seat. "Phone?" She held out her hand.

"In a minute. Let's get on the road first. I don't want to lose her."

But on the street, there was no sign of the yellow cab.

Jesse took a couple turns that got them onto a highway. "Do you know where you're going?" she asked.

"Absolutely." The change in his voice from worried to calm certainty sent a chill across her skin. "And that cab is long gone by now. I paid him well to disappear."

"Jesse? What's going on?"

He grinned. "This is your lucky day, angel. You're about to be saved."

DIEGO STRETCHED LANGUIDLY, then propped his head up on one hand, his elbow on the pillow as he enjoyed the show.

Becca, loosely wrapped in a towel, her wet hair smelling of ripe berries, bent over to dig clothes out of her suitcase. Catching his look, she smiled and let the towel slip a little lower, revealing the side of a small, perky breast. He'd enjoyed that breast thoroughly late last night after the long drive to Greenmont, a small town that didn't even warrant a dot on the map. It was more of a gas stop than a town, really.

But being with Becca had made up for the rundown motel that had been the only available shelter.

"Come here." His voice was still rough from sleep.

She smiled and shook a finger at him. "Uh-uh. No time for that now. You've been lazy enough as it is, and we have work to do."

Like he needed a reminder.

Rising from the bed, he swatted Becca's cute little behind before turning the shower to hot and climbing in. Through the opaque shower curtain, he saw her standing at the sink, brushing her teeth and going through the normal morning ablutions. Briefly, he let himself wonder what it would be like to have her with him like this every morning.

He quickly shoved such thoughts aside. His obligation

was to his family, and to Natalee first and foremost. Becca had provided a pleasant diversion to help temper the pain and anger, but he knew she was just that.

And she knew that was all this affair was. A diversion.

"I found a map of the area in the front of the phone book in the drawer." Becca raised her voice to be heard over the shower. As she applied lip balm, Diego had a flash of memory—her hot mouth on his ribcage, then across his belly, slowly inching lower. "Only about two hundred names in that thing. More like a pamphlet than a book. The sheriff's office is only a couple blocks away. I'm hoping someone will be behind the desk this early on a Sunday."

Diego shut the water off and stepped out from behind the curtain. Her gaze caressed him appreciatively, but her demeanor was all business. He grabbed a flimsy off-white towel from the rack and slung it around his waist. If the way the light showed through it was any indication, it had seen years of use.

"If he's not there, we'll call 911." Hell, he'd rob the gas station if he had to. Whatever it took to get face time with someone who could finally give them answers.

She stepped up to him and wrapped her arms around his waist. The top of her head barely came to his shoulders and he controlled a shudder as she leaned against his chest. "No need to do that. I'm sure we'll find someone. We're close. I can feel it."

He could, too, and it scared him. His gut had rarely been wrong before, but if it was wrong now, if they were on the wrong trail, he didn't know if he could stand the disappointment. He'd been kicked in the teeth so many times the past couple weeks that he'd lost count. And if it hadn't been for Becca, he'd be lost.

He placed a kiss on the top of her damp blond head and moved out of the circle of her arms. "Then let's get going."

Shortly after seven, they entered the sheriff's department and Diego was surprised to find a young man in uniform doing paperwork behind a beat-up metal desk. He looked up as they entered. The tag above his shirt pocket said Deputy Warring. "Can I help you?"

Becca turned her dazzling smile on him and flashed her credentials—the ones Damian Manchester provided all his SSAM employees. She introduced Diego as an NYPD detective and he showed his badge.

The deputy eyed them, probably running down the list of reasons a security specialist from Chicago and an NYPD detective would end up in Shitsville, Florida, and coming up empty. "And what brings you to our town on this fine day?"

"We're working on a case that may be related to an unsolved murder here—a woman named Melody Rappaport."

There wasn't even a flicker of surprise in the deputy's face, though the case was four years old. Deputy Warring leaned back in his chair and motioned for them to sit in the two chairs facing his desk. "What makes you think your case and Melody's are linked?"

"May I?" Becca gestured to the file she'd brought with them. When Warring nodded, she laid out pictures of the three *Angel* paintings.

His gaze remained on the picture of the *Angel of Air*. "That looks like Melody."

"It's called *Angel of Air*."

Emotion flashed across Warring's face but was quickly controlled. "She was found hanged, and held in this position by ropes. Did you catch the murderer?"

Becca shook her head. "That's why we're here. We're still trying to put a name to this killer."

"Try Reggie Pierson."

Finally. Diego sat forward so suddenly that he drew Warring's attention. "What makes you so certain Pierson is the killer? Nobody was arrested for Melody's murder."

"He was a suspect, but there wasn't any evidence to bring him to court." Warring looked unsettled about that. Maybe they'd find an ally here after all. "Not just that." He swiveled in his chair and removed a file from a nearby filing cabinet. He set it on the desk but didn't offer it to them. Diego's fingers itched to reach for it. "I went to high school with Reggie. Seemed likeable at first glance. Very smooth. But I always thought he was playing us, you know?" He shook his head. "Things started happening around here our senior year. Town had a series of animal mutilations, all pets that had been strung up in the owners' yards."

"And Reggie Pierson was a suspect?"

"Not right away. He was still the golden boy at our school. Track star. Quarterback. But one of the pets, the coach's Doberman, was found gutted and strung across Coach's fence for all to see. The night before, Pierson had failed to get first place in some meet and Coach chewed him out publicly about not coming to practice the day before."

"So he was questioned?" Becca asked.

"The way I heard it, Reggie acted as if Coach had been right about giving him hell, and that he'd been fine with doing his penance. Claimed he'd been home in his bed all night the night Melody was killed and couldn't have done it."

"But you obviously have your suspicions."

Warring nodded. "Always have. Ever since Melody

was killed." He slid the manila file folder across the desk toward them. "Prettiest girl in our senior class. And the most unattainable. Her parents were strict, and she wasn't allowed to date. That didn't stop her from trying, though. Reggie was one of her friends. She always claimed he had an artist's soul, which we didn't understand. Apparently, painting was one of his hobbies, but he didn't tell people at school about it. It came out after the murder, and he was teased mercilessly."

"Any idea why he'd target Melody?"

"One day at school, she and Reggie had an argument. Something about her trying to sneak out to see a boy. She finally asked him to stop lecturing her, explaining that he didn't have any say in what she did or who she saw. She said they couldn't be friends anymore." Warring paused a moment, his eyes narrowing. "That day I saw what pure rage looked like. For a split second, his face said it all. He covered it pretty quick, laughing off her objections in front of our classmates until they were laughing with him—he could be charming that way—but I'd seen his true feelings.

"She was found hanging from a rafter in an abandoned barn two days later, her arms strung up as if she were on a cross or something. But nobody suspected Reggie Pierson, local all-star. Everyone assumed it must have been some crazy drifter. She was a sweet girl, and well liked around here."

"No evidence connecting Pierson to it?"

"Other than that look only I saw and a gut feeling?" Warring shook his head. "None. It's one of the things that drove me so hard to join the sheriff's office after graduation. Melody deserves justice." He nodded his head at the folder. "Still an unsolved homicide, four years later.

I sure would like to close it, so I'm going to let you look through that."

Becca opened the folder and began reading through the contents. "What happened to Reggie after Melody's murder?"

"Left town not long after, and I lost track of him. There was nothing to hold him here. His mother was on drugs, so he was a product of a foster-care system that shuffled him around almost yearly. He tried to make up for that by being the all-star athlete. But when someone hinted that he might be attracted to his fellow teammates—as a homosexual...well, he didn't stick around long. He left the day after high school graduation."

"And Miss Rappaport's family? Do they still live in town?"

He shook his head. "Moved away a few months after her funeral."

"Was Reggie Pierson religious?"

"Not that I know of. Why?"

"We're looking for a man who seems obsessed by the difference between earthly bonds and heavenly ones."

"People frequently referred to Melody as an angel, what with her blond hair and religious family and all. Her father was pastor at the Protestant church down the road."

Diego and Becca shared a look. Was that where the monster's obsession had started? With Melody Rappaport?

"Do you happen to have a photograph of Reggie?" Becca asked.

"Actually, I do. Keep all the high school yearbooks here." Warring dug out a yearbook from a full bookshelf and flipped through it. "Here you go."

Becca examined the picture, then looked up sharply, her gaze colliding with Diego's. He glanced at the picture and gritted his teeth. There, before them, was a picture of Natalee's coworker. Vanessa's coworker. The killer had been under their nose the whole time.

"Jesse," Diego said.

"Reggie Pierson," Becca corrected, dialing her cell phone.

NOAH CAME AWAKE with a sudden feeling of alarm. The chill of the sheet next to him told him that Vanessa was gone, and had been gone for some time. She wouldn't have left him. They'd had a beautiful night together. Each time he'd touched her, he'd become more aware of his feelings for her.

Love. Jesus, who'd have thought Noah Crandall was capable of it?

Though he hadn't spoken the words, Vanessa had returned his tender touches in a way that told him she loved him too. He'd opened himself up to discussing his past and she'd rewarded him.

But now she was gone. Her cell phone was on the bedside table, charging. Next to it was a note. *Gone downstairs for coffee with Jesse and Fiona. Be back soon.*

He was still puzzling over the sudden appearance of Jesse and Fiona in Florida when his cell phone rang. Diego's number showed on the screen. "Did you find anything?" he asked the moment he connected.

"The identity of our killer." Excitement hummed beneath Diego's words.

"Please tell me I heard you correctly."

"The name's Reggie Pierson. But we know him as Jesse."

Noah's head came up sharply, and he stared hard at the empty place on the bed where Vanessa had slept, curled against him. "What?"

"Yes, *that* Jesse. You may want to warn Vanessa in case he shows up."

"No." Blood roared in his ears. Vanessa had no reason to distrust Jesse. He was a friend.

"What's wrong?" Diego's voice mirrored Noah's concern.

Noah began pulling on his clothes. "I haven't seen Vanessa this morning. I just found a note that she was meeting Jesse and Fiona for coffee." He grabbed Vanessa's cell phone from the nightstand and quickly selected the menu and found the most recent calls. The last call received had been thirty minutes ago, and it was identified as Jesse's number.

The bastard had a head start.

"Noah, are you there?" Diego's words startled him. He'd forgotten he was still on his own cell phone with him.

"Jesse's got her. I've got to go." He hung up and pulled the rest of his clothing and shoes on. He raced to the elevator, detouring at the last second, choosing to take the six flights of stairs rather than wait.

The coffee kiosk was busy with morning customers, but no sign of Vanessa, Jesse or Fiona. He stopped at the front desk and flashed his badge at the customer standing there. "Police emergency." That gained him the desk clerk's full attention and the customer stepped aside. "Have you seen Vanessa Knight this morning? She's a guest in room 622. She was supposed to meet some friends in the lobby for coffee. Kind of on the short side, shoulder-length brown hair, brown eyes." Hair that felt like silk sliding between his fingers. Eyes that melted like chocolate when he made love to her.

Her fingers flew across her keyboard for a moment. "She's still checked in. I haven't seen her."

"What about a man, about six foot two, brown skin, short dreadlocks?"

"No, I'm sorry. I don't remember anyone like that. It's been a busy morning."

"Thanks." He went through the lobby and out the front entrance, looking in either direction on the sidewalk. There was no sign of them.

Perhaps she hadn't gone with Jesse. Maybe she'd gone back to the beach where they'd... He took off at a trot down the path to the sand. If he found her there, thinking about what had happened between them, what would he do? Admit that he loved her and offer her forever? His off-and-on behavior had just been a mechanism to avoid the truth. He loved Vanessa Knight, and it had scared the shit out of him. But that particular fear was now gone. Amazing what one night could do.

Diego had been right. Noah was the one keeping himself from having a happy life—and his asshole parents had succeeded in making him nothing, after all. They'd convinced him he was unworthy of love.

Vanessa had shown him different.

The beach was empty at seven-thirty on a cloudy Sunday morning. Charlie Morton had mentioned something about expecting storms today.

Vanessa wasn't on the beach. Or emerging from the frothy surf like a sea nymph. Or in the cabana where they'd made love in the shadows.

Noah had a horrible feeling he knew exactly where she was. Did she know yet that she was in danger? Or was she even still alive?

Ignoring his shaking hands, he punched a series of numbers on his phone. His long strides ate up the distance between the beach and the hotel as he waited for someone to pick up. He didn't have to wait long.

Holt answered on the first ring. "I just spoke with Diego. He says you think Jesse has Vanessa."

"He does," Noah said. "Please tell me she's still alive."

Holt hesitated, probably reading Noah's emotions loud and clear. "My *expert* guess is she's still alive. He's got plans for her. There's not much time, though."

"It'll be enough."

"He's got to know we're close on his heels. But he'll be compelled to finish his paintings first. She's the *Angel of Earth*. He'd go where he feels comfortable. Where nobody would find him, at least for a few hours while he poses and paints her. It would likely be somewhere he's been before, and knows the territory."

That definitely sounded like the commune. "I'm heading to New View." Noah raced to the parking lot.

"I'll have Damian get the local police to send some units out there ASAP. Diego and Becca are already on their way. New View's about halfway between Miami and Greenmont, so you should be there at about the same time. Wait for them at the gate."

They wouldn't get there before him. And he wouldn't wait. He'd be damned if he'd sit around and wait for help when Vanessa could be fighting for her life at that very moment. He was determined to make up the thirty-minute difference. He'd do everything he could to find her first. And if he found her...no, *when* he found her, he wouldn't let her go.

Noah jumped into his car. "Find out if Jesse—or Reggie Pierson—rented a car. Get an APB out."

"Already working on that with the Miami P.D. We're also tracing cell signals to get a location."

"You won't find anything." Jesse was clever. He had managed to lure Vanessa out from under his nose. He'd bet that Jesse had destroyed or left behind his own phone to avoid detection. But it didn't matter. Jesse knew where he was going, and had laid out his plans for Vanessa. Fear slammed into Noah's chest like a wrecking ball as he swung the car out of the lot. "How did this guy slip under our radar?"

"We got in touch with Fiona. She said Jesse went home by noon yesterday, saying he was sick. Hollister found out Jesse was on an afternoon flight to Miami." Holt sounded tired and disappointed. "I can't believe I missed Jesse as a potential suspect."

"He didn't fit the usual serial killer mold. For one, he's part African American. He crossed racial lines when he killed, which is atypical. And they weren't sexual crimes, as they seemed to be at first."

"Doesn't make me feel any better when another woman's life is at risk."

"Then I'll just have to stop him before he takes another life." Thankfully, early Sunday morning traffic was light. He'd be able to make up some time.

"Be careful. Jesse is a big guy, and I get the impression he's ready to die. His lover is already dead, and he knows he's not coming out of this situation unless it's to go to jail."

"Or to hell." Noah didn't care which, as long as Vanessa came home safe.

THOUGH FEAR had her wanting to claw her way out of the car, Vanessa tried not to lurch for the door handle the moment the vehicle came to a stop. Running was out of the question. Jesse would catch her within moments. He kept himself in shape, she was in flip-flops, and he obviously knew his way around this remote area. They'd passed a sign for the New View Artist Commune, he'd stopped to open a gate to which he had a key, and then he'd turned onto a narrow dirt road. About a half mile and a couple turns later, they'd stopped at the small, moss-covered, sagging cabin that now sat before them.

Still, knowing he had horrible plans for her, it crossed her mind that running would be preferable to this waiting game.

Jesse turned to her and flashed a grin. "Welcome to my humble abode."

As he got out of the car and made his way around the back to the passenger side, Vanessa tried to make a plan of escape. For the last hour, they'd gone from highway to back roads to sun-baked, tire-rutted dirt trails that had rattled her teeth. She'd waited for a chance to jump from the car, but Jesse had obviously known where he was going—and that there'd be no stops where she could escape. Her mind grabbed at the hope that was quickly slipping away.

The morning sun warmed the shabby cabin, but slate-colored clouds were building rapidly on the horizon. All around, large trees provided some relief in the form of shade, but humidity clogged the air. Cicadas sang and frogs chirruped. Were they near a swamp or lake? Remembering her quick glance at the map Charlie had given them that detailed the route to New View, the commune was located quite a ways inland, and then north a bit, but there had been several turns and she'd lost track.

But knowing where she was didn't really matter. Wherever she was, it was the middle of hell.

And even if she ran, the dangers lurking out there seemed insurmountable. Unless she could find one of the other artists on the commune's property.

She tried to jerk away as Jesse opened her door and reached for her. He grabbed her arms and hauled her from the car like a sack of groceries. She bit back a cry of pain as his thumbs dug into her arms.

"Detective Crandall and the others will be looking for me," she said, hoping to make him see reason. *Please. Please let Noah be looking, and please let him know where to look.*

"He won't find you. Not in time." He half dragged her to the cabin door as she dug her heels into the ground. But the damp dirt was loose. Inside, the one-room cabin was only slightly cooler, and definitely without air conditioning. It had a sink, hotplate and small refrigerator that hummed in one corner, a sagging single bed in another, and a toilet and sink were curtained off in a third. A rickety table and two chairs completed the décor. The artists at New View apparently had a rustic interpretation of life's necessities.

Her heart stopped. Along the wall beside the door were the missing paintings. The *Angels*. He'd shipped them to himself and had someone here sign Nigel's name to claim them. And he had to have known they'd track the shipment. He'd meant to lead them here the whole time.

"Beautiful, aren't they?" His voice held a breathless quality that showed his pride in his work.

"Not as beautiful as the flesh-and-blood people they represent were."

"They're what brought me to Atherton's. After Nigel's death, I heard Lawrence was making arrangements to donate one of the paintings to the auction. It was fate. Learning of the auction led me to Natalee, Atherton's and you."

She spun to face him rather than look at the angels… at what she was to become. "By now, the authorities have got to know I'm gone."

He nodded. "And they know I took you. Which means they also have an idea where to find you. But they won't."

His matter-of-fact tone jolted through her like ice water sluicing through her veins. Jesse was a man who knew he was hunted. He knew he didn't have much time. And still he'd taken her and planned to end her life, making her into some two-dimensional depiction of whatever his reality was.

To hell with that. Vanessa felt anger surge and found the strength to tear herself from his grip.

Jesse laughed. "You can have a bit of freedom, angel, as long as you stay in the cabin and well away from the door. I have to get my stuff together anyway. Besides, if you try to run, the alligators will get you. The swamp isn't far." He moved about the room, gathering paint supplies and putting them into a duffel bag. He grabbed a clean white canvas from the corner. With his back turned to her, she edged toward the table of instruments, eyeing a palette knife that lay there. It wasn't very sharp, but it was something. She grabbed it and lunged for him, jumping on his back and aiming the knife for his neck. She heard him cry out as she felt the resistance that meant the knife had connected with flesh.

Jesse tried to shake her off but she held on to his neck tighter, trying to wrap her legs around his waist. He was too strong, and her grip was slippery from the blood at his neck. He bent over at the waist and shifted his weight suddenly, throwing her off balance so that she lost her grip and hit the ground on her back. Stars exploded behind her eyelids and the air whooshed from her lungs. Pain shot up and down her spine.

"Nice try." Jesse grabbed a towel from the kitchen and held it to the wound in his neck. She sagged against the floor with a moan. She hadn't jabbed the knife deep enough. The blood flow was already decreasing. "This was meant to be. I was meant to save you. You can fight, but it won't change anything, because we were predestined to do this. I chose you."

He hefted his bag of painting supplies and the canvas and set them by the door. If he had to carry that much stuff, surely there would be another opportunity to get away. He wouldn't be able to hold on to her.

But then, he could simply drop everything and chase her down. What was better, a quick death or a slow one?

Don't think that way. Think of what you can do instead of what you can't.

Jesse must have sensed her thoughts. He lifted a roll of duct tape. "In case you're dreaming up any other ridiculous notions of escape, I'll be binding your wrists before we leave."

"Leave?"

"We're going on a nature hike. I have the perfect spot in mind." His smile indicated she should appreciate his forethought. "And don't worry—you won't feel a thing. I'll drug you when the time is right." He grabbed her wrists and taped them together in front of her, then used them to haul her to her feet. The room spun for a moment but she gritted her teeth until the world righted itself.

Keep him talking. Delay him. Noah's voice was in her head, giving her strength as if he were actually there, his arms around her, reassuring and protecting her.

"Is this what Nigel would have wanted, killing innocent women?"

Anger flared in Jesse's eyes. "You have no right to ask me about him."

"I have every right if I'm one of your so-called angels. I can't believe he'd condone murder. He was a pillar of the community, particularly the art community."

"He understood me. He *got* me." Jesse's eyes misted and he shook his head violently. "He was my friend, my mentor."

"Your lover. But he wouldn't have understood *this*." A

flash of lightning lit the windows, immediately followed by a clap of thunder that shook the thin walls. A storm was brewing fast. Surely he wouldn't try to drag her outside and paint in bad weather. The thought nourished a grain of hope inside her.

Jesse laughed. "Who do you think funded my work here? Nigel knew about the angels. Knew the truth."

Good God. Nigel Springfield had been an accessory to murder? He'd fed this man's madness. "But why? Why kill these women?" *Why me?*

"I freed them. Nigel and I, together, freed them. He understood, explained that what I did…that I didn't have any choice but to kill Melody. I gave her wings to fly before she corrupted herself. Corrupted the boys who wanted her."

Melody? She must have been one of the victims.

"She's with her Savior now, like she always wanted to be," Jesse continued. "I kept her pure before she could give in to temptation. She was a good girl."

"What about the others?"

"My *Angel of Water* was an artist I knew. Lisa was about to ruin her life for a sailor. Was going to sell her body to live on the beach. Stupid bitch. And Natalee… well, she had so much fiery passion, I knew it was only a matter of time before ambition burned her from the inside." Another rumble of thunder had them both looking out the bare window. "We have to get a move on. It's a bit of a walk, and mud will only make it harder." He smiled. "But then, mud is essential to my work. Surely, as the Angel of Earth, you can appreciate that."

He meant to hike through a storm? "I don't understand. You know you'll be caught, especially if you hang around here. What do you hope to accomplish?"

"Salvation. All I need to finish this is you. Our last angel.

You'll save us both." His eyes glistened with purpose. Come hell or high water—or torrential downpour—he wouldn't be stopped. Despite the heat, a chill ran through her.

TWENTY-TWO

"When it rains out there, it'll become one big sucking swamp," Damian warned Noah through the phone. "And I'm not just talking about the mosquitoes."

Damian had called him to provide support—even if only by phone—while Noah raced to the commune. Unfortunately, the local police were at least twenty minutes behind him. But having a phone connection helped. Noah had a feeling the other man knew just how much he needed someone else's voice running through his head right now, to combat the images of what the killer could be doing to Vanessa at that very moment.

Another flash lit up the sky, followed by a crack of thunder that brought his gaze from the road to the thickening black clouds. "Sounds like it's about to get wet."

"You see the sign for the turnoff yet?"

He peered through the raindrops that splattered against the windshield as his hand searched for the knob that turned on the wiper blades. Desperate, he was driving as fast as he could on the dirt roads. Assuming he'd made up some time by breaking land-speed records, it still left Jesse with a significant head start. He prayed that Jesse had obeyed traffic laws and speed limits to avoid getting pulled over. And he was counting on his assumption that the monster had complicated plans that required some preparation.

"Noah?" Damian's concerned tone brought him back to his question about the turnoff.

"Should see it anytime now. And I may lose signal again." Their conversation had been intermittent the last several minutes as he'd headed farther off the beaten path. He needed to pay attention. Diego had driven when they'd come out here yesterday, and there had been some tricky turns.

"The Miami police should be catching up to you within the next twenty minutes."

Noah saw the next turn coming up through the curtain of rain that suddenly poured from the sky. He didn't tell Damian that he had no intention of waiting for backup. He had a sense of urgency he couldn't explain. He had to find Vanessa *now*.

The hairs on the back of his neck stood at attention as lightning rent the sky, followed by a crack of thunder so loud his teeth rattled. The beeping in his ear told him his call had dropped, and he stuffed his phone into his shirt pocket as he caught sight of the metal signpost that announced he'd arrived at New View. Below, it indicated that it was a private artist community and no trespassing was allowed. It wasn't just any metal signpost, but some elaborate melding of reclaimed junk metal, twisted, partially rusted, and reaching for the sky. A manmade lightning rod, Noah thought as he turned into the drive. He and Diego had spent a good chunk of time near that signpost yesterday, trying to find a way in. He'd had to warn Diego not to scale the fence and risk legal action, but today was a new day. With Vanessa involved, Noah wouldn't hesitate to crash through the gate if that was what was required. The gate was open, however, probably left that way by Jesse. Which meant the man either didn't care that people were after him or he wasn't worried. Another chill ran through him.

The tires skidded in the mud that was quickly mucking up the road, and Noah gripped the wheel harder to hold the shuddering car steady. The single lane went for nearly a mile with several turnoffs into dark, wet woods. Noah stuck to the bigger road that ended in a makeshift parking lot. Parking lot, hell—it resembled little more than a mud pit.

A sprawling ranch-type compound sat beyond it. The architecture expressed so many different styles that Noah guessed the original cabin had been added onto as needed. The land surrounding it was lush and green from daily rains, the muggy air so thick and wet Noah could swear he tasted the mud pie Diego had once dared him to eat when they were too young to know better.

Like the house, the half-dozen cars that lined the front were an eclectic mix. Everything from a beat-up rusty VW bug at least three decades old to a Jeep better suited to the muddy environment to a newer model BMW. The collection of license plates was just as varied, but none were from New York. And none looked like a rental, though he had no idea what Jesse might be driving. He suppressed his frustration as he ran through the downpour toward the front door, sliding in the mud and righting himself before falling.

He stopped under the covered shelter of a small porch, staring with disbelief at the front door. Someone had decided an old walk-in freezer door would make a great entryway. Apparently, the people at New View had jumped on the "recycle, reduce, reuse" bandwagon. He lifted the old-fashioned metal knocker, shaped like a gator with a ring in its mouth, and rapped it against the door. The noise rang in his ears.

A woman who appeared to be in her early sixties, her pure white hair pulled back into a smooth waist-length ponytail, answered the door. Thankfully, she wasn't in possession of the shotgun that one of her cohorts had threatened them with yesterday. With narrowed eyes, she looked him over. "How did you get through the gate? We don't have any approved visitors on the schedule until ten today."

Noah bit back his impatience. *Flies and honey.* Nice would yield quicker answers. He resisted the urge to flash his badge, thinking it would only put the woman off. "The gate was open. I just need a moment of your time."

Her hand came to rest on a thin hip. "You selling something?"

"No." He caught her suspicious look. "I swear. I just need some help."

She eyed him a moment longer. Another rumble of thunder echoed through the cypress trees. "Well, you must want my help pretty darn bad to come all the way out here in this mess. Either that or you don't have a lick of sense. Come in." She moved aside for him to enter.

"This is fine," he said, stopping in the entryway. "I just wanted to ask you a question."

"Shoot."

He drew his cell phone out of his shirt pocket, thanking God it was still mostly dry after his hunched-run through the parking lot. He loaded the photo that Holt had texted him—a picture of Jesse taken at the auction a week before. "Do you recognize this man?"

She narrowed her eyes. "Looks like Reggie. His hair's much shorter, but it's him all right."

Noah's heart pounded in his ears. "Is he here? At the compound? Have you seen him lately?"

At the alarm in his voice, she looked up sharply. "What's he done?"

"Look. I need answers. Where is he? Does he rent a cabin or a room here?"

The woman shook her head. "I can't tell you that. The artists here pay for privacy. Hell, half of them are hermits and recluses. Seeing you barging in, looking crazed, soaking wet and mud-splattered, would set them back years. And I'd lose income."

Noah shoved a hand through his hair in frustration, scattering droplets of water. "A woman's life is in danger." He drew in a shaky breath to calm himself. "He paints women. The women he paints are murder victims."

The woman put a hand to her mouth. "Are you saying Reggie's a murderer? What proof do you have?"

"I don't have time to tell you everything. Just trust me, please. He's abducted a woman, and if there's any chance he's got a private cabin here, he's probably taken her there. He's got her there now. I have to find them."

The urgency and desperation in his voice finally seeped through the woman's layers of defense. "I signed for his paintings a couple days ago, like he asked me to. He picked them up here yesterday."

"Is he still around?"

"Don't know, but he's got a cabin Nigel rented for him. I'll get you a map of the property."

Ten minutes later, Noah peered through the windshield as his wiper blades swept aside fat raindrops. They could barely keep up as the downpour increased. A dilapidated cabin stood hunched beyond a towering cypress. He claimed his gun from under his seat and ran for the cabin, using the trees as cover. He found a window and looked inside, but other than some rudimentary furniture, it was empty. Abandoned.

He moved as slowly as he dared, trying to quell the sense of urgency as he forced himself to search the grounds for clues. He circled the building, finding a smudging of mud near the edge of the porch, where the dirt met a lush bed of green. He was no Boy Scout, but it seemed there had been a shuffling of feet here. A few yards farther, in the carpet of grass and moss, he spied the broken stems of flowers. Someone had walked here.

He dared to move more quickly now that he had a direction. A few minutes later, he stopped cold as the eerie sound of a bellow reached him. It wasn't human, and as a native New Yorker, it definitely wasn't something he'd heard before. But given his surroundings, he was afraid he knew exactly what it was.

The alligator sat a few yards to Noah's right, half in and half out of a lake, the rain pounding against his thick hide. Noah aimed his gun, not wanting to shoot. The creature's eyes seemed to examine him. Noah sidestepped along his path. The alligator bellowed again, but didn't charge.

I'm not after you, fella. Just let me be on my way.

His gaze and his aim never leaving the gator, he sidestepped a few more times until he was farther away. When he heard a female cry of pain from the direction he'd been heading, he tossed all caution to the wind and ran.

VANESSA SAW an opportunity and seized it. Jesse stopped and bent to put his supplies under the shelter of a broad tree, and she realized they'd reached their final destination. It was now or never. So she turned and ran. Branches grabbed at her and she pushed past them. Ferns crumpled under her feet. With her wrists bound, her balance was impaired, further complicated by the slippery, sucking mud. She cried out in pain as one flip-flop slid too far, twisting her ankle. Still, she stumbled forward. The pounding of heavy footfalls sounded directly behind her just before Jesse tackled her and she went sprawling on her stomach. He landed on top of her.

"I told you trying to escape is pointless." His hot breath fanned her ear. He rose and hauled her up against his chest.

She cried out as her weight landed on her hurt ankle. He bent to hoist her over his shoulder in a fireman carry. With little difficulty, he got her back to the grove where he'd left his materials and dumped her at the base of an old cypress. Her elbow struck one of the large roots that bundled with others to form the tree's trunk and she let out a cry of pain. With her hands unavailable, she hadn't been able to catch herself. Soft moss did little to cushion her fall. Her bound hands immediately went to her hurt ankle, where pain shot up her calf in knifelike pulses.

Jesse looked around with satisfaction as the rain lessened to light sprinkles. His art supplies and canvas were protected from the wetness by a garbage bag and a heavy-duty toolbox.

She didn't have much time left. Good God, what was coming next? He'd hung a woman, drowned another and burned the last. She was the Angel of Earth. And she had a sickening idea how he intended to kill her.

"Promise me you won't bury me alive." She heard the pathetic plea in her voice but didn't care.

Jesse laughed. "It would be hard to paint you then. No, I figure I'll have to do you like I did Natalee. Don't worry," he continued, kneeling in the mud at her side to wipe wet strands of hair away. He scooped some mud with two fingers and smudged it across one of her cheeks. "You'll feel the prick of a needle. Your heart will simply stop. You won't feel any pain—just like Nigel and Natalee."

Vanessa gasped. "You killed Nigel?" The man had

killed his own lover. What hope was there for her? How could she have worked beside Jesse for months and not seen this side of him? His charm had covered a sickness that nobody had suspected. Grief for his lover had driven him farther down the path of madness.

"The cancer was eating him up. He asked me for relief. Asked me to save him like the others. His pills were perfect for the job. Since then, though, I've found an injectable sedative that works faster. It won't take long." Another scoop of mud was gently, almost reverently, smeared down her neck and across her upper chest. Then, he touched a finger to her lips. "Just a touch here, I think."

Vanessa leaned forward to bite his hand in a desperate hope that maybe if he was hurt he wouldn't be able to paint and he'd call the whole thing off. He jerked his hand away before her teeth could connect with his skin. "There's no point in resisting the inevitable. Embrace it. It's time." He raised his face to the sky. "Nigel, it's time for the last angel."

"He's not up there. In fact, as your co-conspirator, I'm pretty sure there's a special room in hell for him. And there's another one for you. You'll *never* be together again."

Jesse punched her in the jaw so hard and fast that her head snapped back against the base of the tree. Black dots danced before her eyes and she wondered if she'd reinjured the bump on her head that had caused her concussion.

A hysterical giggle bubbled from her bloodied lip. What did it matter if she was injured? She was about to die.

"Damn it! Look what you made me do." Jesse leaped away from her. "Now you'll have a mark. And you're bleeding." He pulled at his short dreadlocks, looking truly upset that he had hurt her. She laughed harder. "You're trying to corrupt me. Trying to ruin everything."

She looked up at him standing over her. The rain had stopped and the clouds were starting to break up like an ice floe in the sky behind his head. Greenish light filtered through the trees, and the sound of gentle drips of rain from the foliage combined with Jesse's heavy breathing.

"And the light's perfect now," he said, his fists clenching as he tried to control his anger. "It *has* to be *now*. Maybe if I cover it with dirt…" He shook his head then raked his fingers down his face. "No! Damn it, that won't be right. The balance will be off."

"Your balance is off." Vanessa's laughs subsided to hiccups. Her vision blurred.

Get it together. Noah will be here any minute. He'll save me. Jesse's not the one who can dish out salvation—Noah is. I am. It's my life.

"Shut up!" Jesse screamed, hauling her suddenly to her feet. She swayed, but his grip held her, digging into her arms. She'd spoken her thoughts aloud. "I'm your savior, Vanessa Knight. Don't forget it."

Despite the duct tape, she reached for his face, raking her nails down his cheek and taking satisfaction in his howl of pain. She would not go quietly. If they hadn't already figured out that Jesse was Natalee's killer, Vanessa's dead body would provide the DNA evidence to identify him.

Jesse threw her down to the ground again and she rolled to her side, feeling the mud suck at her skin and clothes. She lay there, biting back pain and drawing in breaths of air. The sound of the garbage bag rustling had her turning her head slightly toward him, smearing mud across her cheek and hair. The sight of the hypodermic needle he withdrew sent her pulse racing harder.

Time had run out. "No."

Jesse grinned as he dropped to his knees beside her. "I am your salvation. I chose you. You should feel honored."

"Drop the needle and step away from her," Noah shouted.

She let out a sob of relief as her gaze found him standing at the edge of the cypress grove. Feet planted in a shooter's stance, he aimed his revolver at Jesse. Noah was smeared with mud too, as if he'd wrestled with Mother Nature herself to catch up to them in time.

The moment hung, suspended in the thick humid air, as the two men faced off. Then Jesse grinned and drove the needle toward her neck with sudden speed and force.

The report of a gunshot echoed as she tried to roll away. She braced herself for the prick of the needle, but it never came. Jesse's body hit the ground next to her, the thud softened by the wet dirt. He didn't move again.

"Is he dead?" She was sure she'd shouted the question over the ringing in her ears.

Noah moved forward, his gun still on Jesse. He felt for a pulse. "Yes." He snatched up a boxcutter from Jesse's toolbox and sliced neatly at her bonds, releasing her wrists.

Vanessa launched herself into his arms, not caring that her ankle throbbed or her head ached or that she was covered in mud. As she clung, shaking, he held her close.

"You're okay now. You're okay. I promise I'll keep you safe." She felt his warm breath against her neck as he exhaled a shaky breath. He pulled away suddenly as he heard rustling and voices nearby. "Over here!" A moment later, a half-dozen people broke into the grove.

Diego picked his way through the mud, a gleam of satisfaction in his eyes as he spied Jesse facedown on the ground. He squatted down next to his body, checking the pulse for himself.

Becca arrived right behind him with several police officers. Seeing that Jesse was well taken care of, she went immediately to Vanessa. "Are you okay?"

"She will be." Noah's words sounded like a vow. Vanessa met his gaze, wanting him to see how much he meant to her and hoping he didn't need too much more time to realize they were meant for each other.

Diego rose. His hands were shaking. "He's dead. I can't thank you enough."

"You and your family already have," Noah assured him. The two men embraced. "It's over. I hope Natalee can find peace now."

"Me, too."

"We'll have to give a statement to the police, but I want to get Vanessa checked out at the hospital. And of course, get back to the hotel and get cleaned up."

"Go. I'll stay here and make sure things are taken care of." His gaze again went to Jesse as if the monster would rise from the dead and kill again.

"I'll stay with you," Becca offered. "Go ahead," she told Noah and Vanessa. "I'll have an officer meet you at the hospital for that statement."

"You know how to reach us," Noah said, rising and pulling Vanessa up beside him. Despite the soreness at her ankle, she was determined to make her way out of the grove and away from the horrid scene. They were almost back to the car when she couldn't bite back a groan.

Noah immediately took her in his arms and carried her the rest of the way. He tucked her head against his chest and she felt his quick but steady pulse. "Rest on me, sweetheart. I promise I'll always be here to lean on."

She looked up suddenly at the serious tone of his voice. He set her down next to his car, leaning her against the passenger side as his eyes met hers. "That's two promises you've made today, Noah. You promised you'd keep me safe from here out, too."

He nodded. "You remember what I said about commitments?"

"You don't take them lightly." Her heart was pounding, and not just from the strenuous hike. She bit her lip, afraid to hope. "I thought you wanted time."

"I did. I think I lived a lifetime in the hours you were missing. I don't want to miss another lifetime without you." Setting his hands on the roof of the car on either side of her, he leaned forward until his lips met hers. The kiss turned fierce, full of the frustration and fear, the hope and relief, of the morning's events.

When she finally pulled back for breath, she shook her head, afraid to believe it was true. "You're sure?"

He nodded. "Absolutely. You are amazing, and I can't wait to see what's next in our adventures in New York."

"I'm not going back."

His forehead crinkled. "What? You have to. Everything's waiting for you there."

"Not everything." *Not you.* She could pursue her other loves elsewhere, but one love—the one that mattered most—was in Chicago. "You weren't the only one who lived a lifetime in the past two hours. I promised myself, if I made it through…" She stopped to swallow and he tipped her chin up to look at him.

"What?" he encouraged.

"I'm starting over. New city, new life."

He stiffened. "Where?"

"Chicago—"

He interrupted her announcement with a kiss meant

to brand her. It was several delicious moments before she got back on track.

"I'm going to make the Ortega-Knight Gallery a reality. A tribute to Natalee's dreams as well as my own. I'll ask if Fiona wants to go into a partnership with me. She'd be great. I think I have enough saved to make a start." She shrugged. "Either way, I'll figure out a way to make it happen."

"I'm sure you will. *We* will."

"Really?" She looked at her hands, absently running them over his chest. The drying, crusty mud on his shirt testified to what they'd been through together. What they'd survived. "I didn't want you to think I expect anything long-term to happen with…us."

When she looked up again, he was smiling the smile she'd been sorely missing the past few days. "There'd better be things *happening* with us. I've got plans for you, sweet Vanessa, and it'll take a lifetime to see them through. I should have told you last night, the moment I realized. I'm not wasting any more time." He blew out a breath that fanned the hair at her brow. "Look, I don't want to beat around the bush anymore. I'm an idiot." She laughed and he smiled wryly. "I finally realized I deserve a happy ending, too. And if I don't deserve you now, I will fight like hell every day to make myself a man worthy of you."

She sought his lips. When they pulled apart, she smiled. "You were always worthy of me. And of the Sandovals. We wouldn't have fallen in love with you otherwise."

Slowly, his grin widened. "Love?"

"Yeah, I said it. The L-word. You got a problem with that?"

"No, ma'am." His gaze held hers. "I'm getting used to

it. I love you, too. And I love the Sandoval clan. I have a lot to make up for with them, as well."

"Then let's get the hospital out of the way so we can get to work on that happily-ever-after."

Life was short, after all.

* * * * *

REQUEST YOUR FREE BOOKS!

2 FREE NOVELS
PLUS 2 FREE GIFTS!

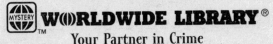

WORLDWIDE LIBRARY®
Your Partner in Crime

YES! Please send me 2 FREE novels from the Worldwide Library® series and my 2 FREE gifts (gifts are worth about $10). After receiving them, if I don't wish to receive any more books, I can return the shipping statement marked "cancel." If I don't cancel, I will receive 4 brand-new novels every month and be billed just $5.49 per book in the U.S. or $6.24 per book in Canada. That's a savings of at least 31% off the cover price. It's quite a bargain! Shipping and handling is just 50¢ per book in the U.S. and 75¢ per book in Canada.* I understand that accepting the 2 free books and gifts places me under no obligation to buy anything. I can always return a shipment and cancel at any time. Even if I never buy another book, the two free books and gifts are mine to keep forever.

414/424 WDN F4WY

Name _____ (PLEASE PRINT)

Address _____ Apt. #

City _____ State/Prov. _____ Zip/Postal Code

Signature (if under 18, a parent or guardian must sign)

Mail to the Harlequin® Reader Service:
IN U.S.A.: P.O. Box 1867, Buffalo, NY 14240-1867
IN CANADA: P.O. Box 609, Fort Erie, Ontario L2A 5X3

Want to try two free books from another line?
Call 1-800-873-8635 or visit www.ReaderService.com.

* Terms and prices subject to change without notice. Prices do not include applicable taxes. Sales tax applicable in N.Y. Canadian residents will be charged applicable taxes. Offer not valid in Quebec. This offer is limited to one order per household. Not valid for current subscribers to the Worldwide Library series. All orders subject to credit approval. Credit or debit balances in a customer's account(s) may be offset by any other outstanding balance owed by or to the customer. Please allow 4 to 6 weeks for delivery. Offer available while quantities last.

Your Privacy—The Harlequin® Reader Service is committed to protecting your privacy. Our Privacy Policy is available online at www.ReaderService.com or upon request from the Harlequin Reader Service.

We make a portion of our mailing list available to reputable third parties that offer products we believe may interest you. If you prefer that we not exchange your name with third parties, or if you wish to clarify or modify your communication preferences, please visit us at www.ReaderService.com/consumerschoice or write to us at Harlequin Reader Service Preference Service, P.O. Box 9062, Buffalo, NY 14269. Include your complete name and address.

WWL13R

ReaderService.com

Manage your account online!

- Review your order history
- Manage your payments
- Update your address

---

*We've designed
the Harlequin® Reader Service
website just for you.*

Enjoy all the features!

- Reader excerpts from any series
- Respond to mailings and special monthly offers
- Discover new series available to you
- Browse the Bonus Bucks catalog
- Share your feedback

Visit us at:

ReaderService.com